FRAGILE

REMEDY

MARIA INGRANDE MORA

FRAGILE REMEDY

MARIA INGRANDE MORA

Mendota Heights, Minnesota

First Edition
First Printing, 2021

Book design by Sophie Geister-Jones
Cover design by Jake Nordby
Cover images by Nithid/Shutterstock, vareyko toma/Shutterstock, Dmitrıch/Shutterstock

Flux, an imprint of North Star Editions, Inc.

Library of Congress Cataloging-in-Publication Data
Names: Ingrande Mora, Maria, 1980- author.
Title: Fragile remedy / Maria Ingrande Mora.
Description: First edition. | Mendota Heights, Minnesota: Flux, 2021. |
    Audience: Grades 10-12. | Summary: The only way sixteen-year-old Nate, a Genetically Engineered Metatissue, can get life-saving medication is to work for a shadowy terrorist organization, which would mean leaving the boy he loves.
Identifiers: LCCN 2020008089 (print) | LCCN 2020008090 (ebook) | ISBN
    9781635830569 (paperback) | ISBN 9781635830576 (ebook)
Subjects: CYAC: Genetic engineering—Fiction. | Terrorism—Fiction. |
    Gays—Fiction. | Science fiction.
Classification: LCC PZ7.1.I58 Fr 2021 (print) | LCC PZ7.1.I58 (ebook) |
    DDC [Fic]—dc23
LC record available at https://lccn.loc.gov/2020008089
LC ebook record available at https://lccn.loc.gov/2020008090

Flux
North Star Editions, Inc.
2297 Waters Drive
Mendota Heights, MN 55120
www.fluxnow.com

Printed in Canada

To every one of my teachers.
Even the math ones.

CHAPTER
ONE

N ate knew better than to slow down on the elevated rail, but he dropped to a crouch anyway. His stomach growled at the sound of fluttering wings. Picking up a sharp piece of broken pavement, he scanned the air to take aim.

A hoarse laugh escaped him. "Those aren't gulls."

Ribbons of fabric snapped in the smog-choked wind from laundry lines strung between corroded water towers. Staring at the frayed edge of a sheet stained with exhaust, he dropped the rock and absently rubbed the callus on his pointer finger. It's not like he would have managed to hit the bird.

His hands ached.

So did his feet from keeping a brisk pace to dodge Gathos City commuter trains that never slowed down as they passed over the Withers.

Below, someone was shouting about spoiled sludge-rat broth. The ugly thuds and cries of a scuffle broke out. Nate spared a glance over the edge of the rail before a swoop of vertigo struck him. He pushed gritty hair behind his ears. High up or not, running the rails beat dealing with streets crowded with hunger and hurt.

The tracks shuddered.

Nate's body went cold. A train growled at his back.

Fear jolted through him as he sprinted to the next support beam and swung down onto its rusty rungs. A pale girl scrambled down alongside him, narrowly avoiding getting flattened. They exchanged tight nods as the train blasted by, raining hot gravel down on them.

Shielding his eyes with one shaking hand, he dared a look at the blur of the commuter train, hungry for a glimpse of the beautiful gearwork. It was too fast to make anything out. And maybe that was how the Withers looked to the commuters—just a smear of faded color and decay.

Nate coughed against his arm. His chest ached sharply, and a thread of worry wound through him, bigger than the bitterness that struck him every time a train passed, carrying people who weren't tired or scared.

It hasn't even been a week.

He didn't have time to go to Alden's for help. If he reconciled himself to the mercy of Alden's pace, he'd never get to the port before dark. And before he sold the tech-guts weighing his pockets, he had to sell the precious fishing line he'd bartered an afternoon of tinkering for. If he struck a good bargain, he could get enough credits to buy fresh greens. A month of dried meat and watery broth wasn't doing the gang any good.

Another cough rattled his chest, and he grimaced.

"Lunger?" The girl covered her mouth with the back of her grubby hand and ducked away like she smelled something bad. She gestured to the faded, torn lung-rot quarantine poster on the support beam above them. Someone had drawn a dog peeing on the swirling Gathos City logo.

"Very funny." Nate rolled his eyes. No one had lung-rot anymore.

As one of Gathos City's experiments, he knew that better than anyone. His kind had been developed by scientists to fight the lung-rot outbreak, and later—when the lung-rot was gone—to be used up. Harvested by the wealthy. Kept endlessly asleep or left awake to participate in the horror of it. At least that's what people said when they whispered about GEMs.

Even that word was nicer than the truth. *Genetically Engineered Medi-tissue.*

He wasn't supposed to be here.

She arched a bushy eyebrow. "What then?"

The stray thought of this girl somehow discovering what he was made him itchy to keep moving. He climbed back onto the rail with a groan, wishing he had the strength to rip the poster down, ball it up, and throw it at her face. "It's nothing. Just the dust."

She swung her wiry body up onto the concrete rail platform and tugged at the blue bandana around her neck. "You should wrap something around your face when you run the rails, kid."

"I'm not a kid." Nate wasn't tall by any measure, and this girl only came up to his ears. Irritation—and fear he didn't have time for—sharpened his tongue. "I'm older than you."

"Wanna bet?"

"Only if you're betting with sausage."

She laughed. "I'd rather bet with my life than a piece of good meat."

"I'm nineteen." He was sixteen, but nineteen sounded more distinguished.

"Nineteen? That's a funny name. I'm Val." She took off with a limber jog.

Nate didn't bother to catch up. The ease of her pace prickled at him. His boots felt like they were full of stones. "My name isn't Nineteen, little brat!" he called out. "It's Nate."

"I *am* older than you." Val flashed gray teeth at him. "Watch yourself."

"*You* watch yourself," he shot back, sore. He didn't care if she was twelve or twenty. His odds of actually living to nineteen were slim.

He'd only been awake for a few hours, but he felt like his clothes were made of lead. He wasn't supposed to be this tired. Not this soon.

"Sure you're not poorly?" Val slowed her pace until Nate caught up.

A headache began to bloom, blood pounding between his ears. Her prying was making it worse. "It's not catching."

Val grunted. A couple of kids sprinted by them as the rails began to rumble again. The ache thrummed behind Nate's eyes.

When had he had his last dose of Remedy? Four days? Maybe five? He could usually go two weeks before the hurting started.

"Move, you fool!" Val grabbed his arm and pulled him into a run. They collapsed onto the next support beam. The train roared by, wheels hissing against the steel track. Silver and black whooshed overhead, too fast to focus on. Too fast to comprehend. "You'll be nothing but a stain if you keep courting trains like that!"

Hot embers stung Nate's knuckles.

The train was gone. He could feel his heartbeat in the thick silence.

He pressed his forehead against a cool rung and willed his body to stop trembling. He'd never come that close to getting struck before. If Val hadn't been there, the train would have eaten him up.

I should have gone straight to Alden's.

He wouldn't do Reed and the gang any good smeared across the concrete.

Val flicked his ear and offered her bruised hand. "Come on. Where you headed?"

"The port." He let her drag him to his feet.

She shook dust out of her short, choppy hair. "Funny. You don't smell like fish."

Nate's arm still stung from the force of her grip—a reminder that she'd saved his life. He offered the truth in exchange. "I've got a spool of fishing line to sell."

"That's hard to come by," Val said, gaze keen.

Nate shrugged. He didn't have to tell her where it came from. Once people knew you were a Tinkerer, they started thinking about all the things that needed mending. He didn't have time for that.

"You look like a dead sludge-fish." Val brushed pale specks of gravel from her shoulders. "I don't want to step in your guts next time I'm on the rails."

Embarrassment flared at Nate's cheeks. She was right. He never should have walked the rails in this state, and he was too sick to finish his errands before nightfall. In the darkness, the only trade to come by was chem and flesh. No one would want the scraps of tech-guts that weighed down his pockets. He was too small to defend himself when night drew bleary-eyed fiends from their dens. He needed to go to Alden's.

Now.

Bitterness dried his mouth. "I'll take care to avoid the trains."

"You talk awful high-class for a thieving tech peddler."

He trailed her steps, wishing she'd hurry up and run off so he wouldn't have to talk to her. "You're awful nosy for a stranger."

"No such thing as a stranger in Gathos, Nine—"

"It's *Nate*," he interrupted, losing his patience.

"I like Nine better." Val took on the disinterested tone of the tinny loudspeakers at the city gates. "*Everyone is encouraged to help each other through these unforeseen circumstances,*" she intoned, reciting the recording.

Nate couldn't help a small smile. Her impression was spot-on. "Right. '*We're all in it together.*'"

"'*Stay tuned for further announcements regarding the quarantine.*'" She hitched up her sagging, stained pants and finished with a rude gesture aimed toward the gleaming skyline of Gathos City across the wide sludge-channel.

Lung-rot might not kill people anymore, but decades of quarantine killed plenty. Violence boiled over in the hot months, and exposure and fires ravaged the dwindling population in the cold. Chem killed, making dull-eyed fiends out of anyone who tried to numb the pain of starvation.

A flutter ran through Nate's belly—fear or excitement or hunger. These days, it was hard to tell the difference.

The weight of his errand nagged at him. His gang was hungry.

And they were waiting.

Though she outpaced him, Val lingered. Her gaze darted to his trembling hands. "Haven't I seen you around Victory Park?"

A prickle ran down Nate's spine. He'd lived in that neighborhood once. Years before. She had no way of knowing that.

"No, I live by the market on 53rd." Unsettled by her interest in where he lived, he forced himself to smile through the lie. "Always have."

"My cousin's family lives in the library over there. You know the place?"

Folks had converted the huge library into family housing decades ago, after the books had gotten torn up for bedding and kindling. It was one of the safer places to live—full of people raising little kids.

"Yeah, I see it every day." Nate hadn't seen it in months. The gang stayed away from that side of town. They didn't steal from families.

"Maybe I'll see you around." A crooked tooth caught against her lip when she gave him a sly smile.

"Walk well, old lady." Nate swung down a ladder, knowing Val wouldn't follow if she really had somewhere to be. And if she did tail him, he'd lead her in circles until he passed out or she died of boredom.

"Gods watch you, Nine," she replied easily. The roar of a passing train drowned out her laughter as she braced herself for the next blast of exhaust. The scorching air stung Nate's skin. When the cloud of dust and smoke faded, she was gone.

Nate skirted a tent city crowded in the bombed-out shell of a building. Some days, the people who lived there got fired up and strung out on chem and hurled rocks at the passing trains.

It was quiet today, colorful tarps sighing in the breeze. A handful of Servants in drab robes walked from tent to tent, murmuring prayers in hushed tones and asking after those frail with age and sickness. Nate had always been fascinated by them. They believed in the Old Gods, a mythology that, for most, had long been overtaken by science—by the things people did to each other with no help from the makers of the world. He longed for the simplicity of believing in something good.

He'd seen too much of the bad to have faith.

Still, the Servants intrigued him. They alone gave aid to the sick and suffering in the Withers. Those who were chosen by the Servants to join their ranks left behind their families and vowed to care for those who could not care for themselves. They lived together in sick-dens, helping anyone they could.

Feeling one of their gazes, Nate ducked his head automatically. Attention was rarely a good thing in the Withers, and he'd learned a long time ago to stay small and quiet. A short Servant with white hands and a face hidden by her hood stopped to watch him stumble along. She continued to study him too closely, and he let his hair fall into his face and hurried off—wary of questions. When he glanced over his shoulder, she was still watching him, her face shadowed by her hood.

Whatever she thought she had to offer, it didn't matter. Servants' prayers and salves couldn't help him.

Two scrawny children chased a chewed-up plastic ball around in the mud and paused, watching Nate closely as he shuffled by. He offered a wave and earned a pair of scowls. A grin tugged at his dry lips. They were smart to be suspicious. It would keep them alive longer.

Nate approached the bustling heart of the Withers. The quarantined island had once been known as Winter Heights—the largest of the chain of islands that dotted the wide sludge-channel that ran through Gathos City.

Here, in the oldest neighborhood on the decaying island, the musical sound of voices echoed between crooked buildings. Nate crammed into a narrow alley, avoiding the crowded main street, his boots squelching through muck and filth on the pavement. It wasn't easygoing, but at least he wouldn't get flattened by a train or trampled.

He shook with exhaustion and braced himself against a rough brick wall to catch his breath.

The smell of rendered fat overtook the alley's musty stench. His stomach rumbled, but he knew better than to fall for the oily scent of grease. Most street meat in the Withers was a mixture of guts and gravel.

And he couldn't eat until he'd sold the gang's haul and picked up enough food for all of them to share.

He might have enough time. The sun winked down at him

between the slats of rusted fire escapes. As long as he kept this pace, he could make it to Alden's for Remedy and over to the market before sundown. He wouldn't be able to sell the fishing line there, but he could sell the rest.

Val's words itched at him. He'd never liked the common prayer: *Gods watch you.*

Nate wanted to believe in the Old Gods—ancient makers of thunder and dirt and blood, according to Servants and old folks. But he knew where he came from.

Not from the deep jewel sea or the tall trees that had once stood against the storms that battered the islands of Gathos in the summer. Not from the gray sky or the green shadows of dusk. Not dropped from the beak of a fat gull, the way children sang when they pointed at the birds that rode the smog-breezes high overhead. In the Withers, babies were plenty—and died plenty too.

Nate tripped on a pothole, stumbling to his hands and knees. Pain flared at his joints. Sighing, he scrambled back up and wiped his stinging hands against his coat.

Hurt made him maudlin and clumsy.

The horizon tilted, and his elbow scraped along the grime-smeared brick as he righted himself. His feet dragged, heavy. Uncoordinated. He couldn't have jogged if he'd tried.

So much for keeping this pace.

At least he was close to where he needed to be.

On the stoop of Alden's shop, he doubled over with dry heaves, suddenly grateful for his empty stomach.

"My," a voice said at his ear. "A lost little boy."

Nate jerked away, struck by the urge to lean in—and the revulsion that followed. "Alden, you rat."

Alden caught his wrist and tugged him into his curio shop. "You should keep a better lookout when you're wandering about."

He scanned the street behind Nate and slammed the door, setting the chimes off so loudly it made Nate's eyeballs hurt. Broken-glass suncatchers in the front window cast tiny rainbows all over the shop. Nate's breath hitched softly, and he ached with more than sickness. Despite everything, the shop still felt like home. Having a real place to stay had been so much easier than scrambling to find safe hideouts with the gang.

"You look vile," Alden said impassively.

He stood a head taller than Nate, willowy and graceful, black hair spilling down his back like ink. He'd been beautiful once, before he'd ravaged his body with chem. Alden wasn't much older than Nate, but he carried himself like a man three times his age, as if the air around him weighed too much.

"I realize that," Nate bit out. "I almost got smashed by a train. A girl pushed me out of the way, or I would have been a stain on the tracks."

"Thrilling," Alden murmured.

Alden's grandmother came out from behind a woven curtain. "GEMs don't grow up," she announced, laughing like a gull and pointing a knotted finger at Nate. Fran's face was so wrinkled the folds drooped over her jewel-black eyes. She wore her hair in a neat silvery bun at the top of her head.

"I'm not grown," Nate said, unbothered by the sound of his

secret. Fran's mind had gone long before Nate had met her. No one would believe her if she claimed to know a fugitive GEM.

She poked his ribs and belly as if examining an exotic fruit before turning her attention to a bowl full of faded sequins on the counter. Embroidered robes swayed from her shoulders, hiding the frail angles of her body. Unlike Alden, she had always treated Nate like family—at least when she could remember who he was. His skin stayed warm where she'd touched him.

Alden locked the shop door. He swept his thin arm out like he was putting on a street-corner play, sizing Nate up with an elegant wave. The movement faltered, and he frowned. "You really do look dreadful."

"I need Remedy." Nate crossed his arms and sagged against the counter. "I'm tired."

The weight of his understatement hung between them. This wasn't normal exhaustion. He stared Alden down, daring him to acknowledge it. Wondering, for a sickening heartbeat, if he had a part in it.

"But I have guests arriving soon." Alden curled his long fingers around Nate's shoulders, his touch icy. "Impatient guests."

"They can wait." Nate didn't want to think about the stuffy basement or Alden's guests. Alden didn't sell the moldy herbs in gleaming canisters or glass jewelry glittering around his shop. He sold high-quality chem to anyone with enough credits to buy a few minutes of peace.

Most of the time, Alden's guests were sweaty and thin and haunted by their hunger. The worst were curiously well-dressed and lingered in the shop, touching everything within reach and sneaking glances at every dusty nook and cranny.

When those people came around, Alden made Nate hide in Fran's bedroom, surrounded by her silky robes and mildewed books and baskets full of colorful yarn.

Nate squirmed, tugging his shoulders out of Alden's grip, already feeling like he'd been here far too long.

"And what if I'm impatient?" Alden understood the needs of the fiends who stumbled wild-eyed into his shop—he looked the same way every morning.

His hungry gaze was the perfect cure for nostalgia. Nate fought the urge to storm off. If he did, he'd be dead in days. Maybe hours.

"You can't make me," he said instead.

"I can be persuasive, darling."

"Not as persuasive as you think."

Nate only had the upper hand in one way: he'd already left once. Alden's need, laid bare and tormented, hadn't been enough to keep Nate around, and he'd finally left him. Nate hadn't even known if Alden would survive or if his heart would give like the fiends on the street who fell asleep on doorsteps and never woke up.

He'd leave again before he allowed Alden to sink into the suffocating grip of his own desire.

"You haven't even asked what I'm offering." Alden kissed the top of Nate's head and sputtered, gagging like he'd tasted something awful. Which was probably true. Nate hadn't bathed in days.

The ache behind Nate's eyes rattled around in his skull

with each word. It sapped his anger. All he wanted to do was curl up on the floor and close his eyes before the pain blossomed. He didn't care how much he sounded like a demanding child. "Just help me, Alden."

"How do you explain all these visits to your darling Reed?" Alden asked.

Nate bristled, but couldn't work up the energy to stomp across the room away from Alden's knowing gaze. Couldn't do anything except tremble. The thought of Reed waiting for him made shame and desire collide in his blood, a hot-and-cold feeling that didn't do anything for his headache.

Reed didn't know what Nate was hiding. Couldn't know.

"It doesn't matter what I tell him."

When they'd first met, Alden had seemed like the wisest, most sophisticated person in the Withers. He flirted with Nate relentlessly, but it was just Alden's nature. He'd flirt with a lamppost if he thought he could get something from it.

Now they both knew Nate had something to give.

"I think I have a right to know what stories you're telling about me." Alden clasped an arm around Nate's chest and held him still while Fran came close again, sniffing the air and cackling softly.

"He's sick, my boy." Her voice rustled like dry paper. "Sick, sick."

"Please, Alden. It's not lasting as long."

"He's dying!" Fran crowed.

"Enough, Grandmother!" Alden snapped, releasing Nate to shoo Fran through the curtain to her bedroom. He stood in the folds of the blood-red fabric as if wearing a cloak, turning his black eyes on Nate.

"You're not dying," he said. It sounded like a question.

"If you won't let me have Remedy, I'll go to someone else." Nate's voice thinned. "I have to."

"Do you really think others will go to the great lengths I've gone through to keep you safe?" Alden enunciated each word tightly. "Do I need to remind you just how many people would happily snatch you off the street?"

"You don't care about keeping me safe. You just want to keep me." Nate pressed his fingers to the ridge of bone at his cheeks. Even his teeth hurt.

"One and the same, sweet thing."

"Alden."

"Anyone who has Remedy will hand you over to the Breakers the moment you ask for it. They'll never let you go. You'll go to the highest bidder before you can beg the Old Gods to end it all."

"Stop."

"You'll spend the rest of your life strung up in a basement far less hospitable than mine." Alden's steely expression faltered. "They'll take everything, Natey."

The echoes of what had passed between them left no doubt in Nate's mind. If Alden had nearly killed him, a stranger would do far worse.

Nate grabbed Alden's cold hand. "Then don't make me wait. I'll let you feed next week," he said, knowing he wouldn't. Never again. Not when he couldn't go a solid week before stumbling around half dead. Not when it put Alden at risk of relapsing. "You know my word is good. I can't be sick like this. I've got to move this tech and bring food home for—"

"For the gang," Alden spat, shaking off Nate's hand. His gaze went cold. "Reed's merry band of orphans and whores."

Nate bit back a reply. There was no use talking to Alden once he shut off like a snapped wire. It was all business now.

Alden led him into the small side room with a locked curio cabinet. "Don't make bargains you can't keep," he said quietly. "It's not a good look."

Nate shied away from Alden's ornate, rusted mirror and smoothed back the stringy dark hair that had fallen from his ponytail. He hated seeing his reflection—the deep circles under his gray eyes and streaks of soot mottling his golden-brown skin like bruises.

He knew he looked sick.

He knew that's all that Reed saw. Weakness. Illness.

Secrets.

Someone quickly becoming a liability to the gang.

A cramp twisted his body. He sank into the cushions in the corner as the last of his strength gave out, exhaustion snipping the tendons holding him upright. It wasn't supposed to happen this fast.

Alden glanced over his shoulder and frowned, his icy gaze softening. "Nate."

"Please." Nate's teeth chattered. "Hurry."

"So pushy," Alden said tightly as he unlocked the cabinet and shifted aside delicate bottles full of street-meds and chem-laced tinctures. He exposed an antique safe and pressed a code into the switchpad that Nate had installed two years ago. The door creaked open to reveal thin glass vials of pale-blue liquid—Remedy. "If you're in such a hurry, go back to the city for it."

Nate choked on a grunt of laughter. "I'll pass."

In Gathos City, he'd be kept in a chilled box, hooked up to a machine cycling air and waste. He'd sleep forever, fed upon until his body finally decayed. GEMs kept the wealthiest people healthy and happy in the city. But even the poorest in the city had unimaginable luxuries. Soft, clean beds. Climate control. Fast cars and motorized bicycles. Bright lights that gleamed night after night across the sludge-channel. Beautiful music that drifted toward the Withers when the wind shifted on a quiet day.

I can't remember.

Nate hugged his middle, trying to banish the memory of what his aunt Bernice had always told him about the fate of GEMs in Gathos City. He didn't want to think about the horror, only the short time he'd felt safe in the city's skyscrapers—the snatches of patchy memories. Ivy greener than anything in the Withers, clear water that tasted sweet and clean, and playing in the sun-warmed dirt of his mother's greenhouse, lungs full of damp air thick with the rich scent of growing things. Her voice, sweet and babbling like running water, filling every silence with words he couldn't recall.

"Don't vomit on my upholstery." Alden decanted the Remedy into a smaller vial. The liquid gleamed vivid blue, as if lit from within.

"Where do you get it?" Nate asked, not for the first time.

Alden prided himself on carrying the rarest, most expensive

chem, but Remedy was something else altogether—medicine that wasn't supposed to exist outside of Gathos City. The med clinics didn't have it. The Servants didn't have it.

"That's not for you to worry about." Alden locked the safe and hid the entrance with dusty bottles. He quieted. "You can't tell anyone you're getting it from me. You can't let anyone find out."

Like Bernice with her spotted hands and her gaze as sharp as a live wire. *Never tell them what you are. Never let them know.*

Nate was so tired of keeping secrets. He had to sleep so he wouldn't feel the sick coming on, like his lungs were filling with cold sludge. He needed to rest. He didn't want to think about the haunted sound of Alden's words. He didn't want to think at all.

He closed his eyes.

"Natey." Alden pushed Nate's hair behind his ears with trembling fingers. "You have to wake up, honey. I didn't know it was that bad. You know that, don't you? Open your eyes and drink this up. Be sweet for me and take your medicine."

"I know what you're really worried about." Nate groaned and welcomed the clink of glass against his teeth. He didn't want to be awake, but he didn't want it to hurt anymore either.

Alden tipped the vial onto Nate's tongue and made soft, clucking sounds. "Don't fuss, Nate. Drink it all."

Nate didn't need encouragement. He swallowed the acrid liquid, Remedy burning down his throat, and licked his lips to catch every drop. A cool, pleasant sensation seeped through his chest. Whatever it was made of, Remedy chased the sick out of him like the chem people took to heal rotting wounds and ward off fevers.

"Alden, you're a prick." Nate opened his eyes. "You could have killed me."

"Me? If I hadn't spotted you wandering like a lost kitten, you would have died on my doorstep. What did you think you were doing, waiting to see me when you felt that bad?"

"I lost track," Nate said, cross. He didn't want to admit the truth.

It's getting worse.

Alden's voice was close. "Your life isn't something you should lose track of."

With the pain gone, Nate's senses returned to him gradually. The dry, musty scent of old cushions flooded his nose. Alden clutched Nate to his narrow frame, sharp elbows stabbing him with each breath and long hair tickling his nose. Nate batted at the blue-black strands, and a rush of fondness chased away the last of the hurt. Though he knew he should hold on to anger, his falling-out with Alden still gnawed at his heart.

Before Alden's relentless hunger had spoiled everything, he'd been Nate's only friend.

"I'm sorry I can't feed you."

Alden's eyes widened a fraction before he recovered with a bony shrug.

"I mean it," Nate said. Normally, he wouldn't feel bad about denying Alden the chance. Alden's habit made him feel used at best and disgusted at worst. But woozy with relief, Nate wanted to share the peace he felt. He wanted to smooth away the tension that never left Alden's face.

Feeding on Nate used to give Alden the flushed glow of health he normally lacked. It had been over a year now. And it showed in the shadows beneath Alden's dark eyes. Nothing on the street came close to the properties of a GEM's blood.

"We can't have you starving your orphans, I suppose." Alden's voice was poison, but concern pinched his brow.

"I'm happy with Reed and the gang, you know. They're . . . it's a family."

"A family you lie to."

"I—"

"You know they only want you for your tinkering," Alden said.

Nate tried to tell himself that Alden was only being cruel, but it was probably true. Why else would they want him around? "That's no better than what you want me for."

A muscle at Alden's throat twitched like a plucked string. "That doesn't make it untrue, dear."

"I'm the best Tinkerer around." He wasn't too sure about that, but it felt good to say. Felt good to show Alden that he was needed, even if it was only for what he could do. "Of course they want me for that."

"You're as modest as ever." Alden slipped away from Nate and pulled his hair into a quick, twisted braid. He gave a delicate shrug. "Go sell your tech and bring the bread home for the *family*. Does that make Reed your brother, then? How titillating."

"Stuff it, Alden. It's not like that." Ducking his chin to hide a blush, Nate stood slowly. His legs didn't wobble. "I'll be back next week, when I have time to stay. Not a market day, all right?"

"And stay you will, my love," said Alden with a toothy, sharp smile.

For now, they could both pretend it would be for more than tinkering around the shop and keeping Fran company.

The front door chimes rang out, and Alden blanched, taking Nate by the sleeve with a wrenching grip. "Go out the back, Natey. Get moving. You're not the only busy one around here."

Ushered into the dank alley, Nate jumped at the sound of the door slamming behind him. The smell of sun-ripe piss flooded his nostrils. Unease settled in his bones like sludge, but he didn't look back.

CHAPTER
TWO

N ate dug into his deep pockets and drew out handfuls of
tech-guts. He turned over bolts and uncoiled wires until
they glittered like treasure on Judy's table, where she sold odds
and ends under a patchwork awning. She held a bundle of red
wires to her magnifying glass and squinted. When sunlight
caught the polished handle, hazy memories crowded the edge
of his awareness. Cold glass. Smooth metal.

Pain.

"Gods watch you!" someone called out—the cheerful close
to a transaction.

His gods had an ugly name.

"Your mice have been at play, I see." She tapped the glass
against the table and eyed him impatiently.

He blinked, inhaling the stench of the market to clear
his head. Every layer of rot and grease rooted him here in the
Withers, far from the hurt. "I came by this honest, ma'am."

They both knew better, but it didn't hurt to follow the
script. He didn't want to find another buyer. Judy didn't pay
as well as others, but she didn't sell to the Breakers. Nate was

willing to sacrifice credits to keep the gang's tech out of their violent hands.

The Breakers had come into power three years before, after the two most influential street gangs decimated their own ranks in an ugly turf war. Life in the Withers didn't change much when regimes changed. People stayed hungry. Food continued to make its way into the markets—diverted from the rations given to those who registered as workers.

They'd started out harmless enough, doing all their business by Courier and paying off A-Vols. They cleaned up the worst of the pleasure houses and pulled aggressive trappers off the streets. But then they started driving families out of perfectly good housing to set up shop behind locked doors and shuttered windows. They rerouted the power lines and made entire neighborhoods pay for electricity with food rations. When small-time gang leaders stood up to them, those leaders ended up dead—with their bloated bodies on display in their own territories.

And then they'd put the word out: They wanted GEMs, and they'd pay in Gathos City credits for them. While Nate didn't want his tech to end up in their hands, he wasn't much interested in catching their attention either.

Judy arched a silver brow as she adjusted her glasses. "I'm sure you're honest as the dawn. I can give you fourteen credits for the lot. Not a half-credit more."

"All right," Nate said.

"All right?" Judy snorted. "You've never taken my first price before. You in a hurry?"

Nate tried to offer her a reassuring smile. "It's been a long day."

"No trouble, I hope." She passed him a crust of bread.

He took it and ate with quick bites, his stomach twisting gladly, despite the mold that stuck to his tongue. "I'd never bring trouble to you, Miss Judy."

How bad do I look that Judy's feeding me?

"I'm not worried about trouble," Judy said. "Go on home to your mice and get some rest."

Nate shook her strong hand over the table covered in tech-guts and broken toys and dodged around tables to the center of the market. Food stalls carried fruits and vegetables ripe with an oversweet, half-rotten smell and street meat simmering in enough spice to blast away the taste of decay. Gathos City sent food onto the island through the tunnel gates twice a week for registered workers with vouchers. Most of it ended up in the market, trading hands a dozen times.

With the credits he'd made selling tech, Nate filled a bag with stale bread, mottled red apples, and a musty rope of dried meat. A small table covered with fragrant fruit caught his eye as he left the market.

"How much are these?" he asked the produce seller as he skimmed his fingers over the fuzzy pale-orange skin of a fruit he dimly recognized. He couldn't recall what it tasted like or the name of it.

"Peaches? Half-price. They ain't wormy." The man spat a dark stream of gunk into a chipped bowl of frothy liquid at his feet.

Nate wrinkled his nose. "What will one credit get me?"

"Three."

"How about four?" Nate asked, regretting not haggling with Judy.

The man snorted and palmed four of the peaches with his fat hands. "Fair enough."

Nate dropped his last credit into the shopkeeper's change bowl. The fruit smelled like wet sugar. Reed would love it.

By the time Nate left the herbalist's shop, the sky had thickened with dusk. He jogged along the cracked sidewalk, wary of the thinning crowds and creeping shadows. He'd lingered too long tinkering in exchange for healing salves.

A hollow-cheeked girl stumbled out of an alley, tugging a scrawny child who fought her clawed grip on his hand. The boy's gaze flew to Nate, wide—beseeching. "I don't wanna," he said, and it was little more than a rasp. As if he'd screamed his voice away long ago.

Nate froze, and the girl turned wild eyes on him. Her lips curled to reveal gray teeth and bleeding gums. A chem fiend, deep in hunger. Furrows of raw skin striped her bare arms. She looked him up and down, no doubt sizing up the heavy bag at his back. He sank his hands into his pockets automatically, covering the clanging tins of valuable salve.

He knew he should run. In a fight, he wouldn't stand a chance against a fiend gone mad with want. Instead, he asked, "Where are you taking him?"

Her laughter was the sound of rusted hinges. "The trappers. What's it to you? Got a better offer?"

The boy began to croak, eyes dry and sunken. Too thirsty for tears. "Mama . . ."

Nate shuffled back, sick. She couldn't be more than seventeen. And at best, selling her son to the trappers would offer her a few days of solace. At worst, she'd gorge herself on chem and her heart would stop before she had a chance to mourn him.

"Wait!" She reached with a clawed hand, dried blood beneath her nails. "What will you give me for him?"

Even if Nate had chem to offer, they couldn't take another child. Pixel was already one little one too many.

He ran from the boy's fevered cries and her scraped-bone shouting. His bag thumped against his back, an echo to his thundering heartbeat, and he only slowed when he reached a crowded intersection and his frantic pace would draw too much attention.

Gasping to catch his breath, he scrubbed his eyes, his face hot with shame. By morning, the boy would be in the trappers' hands.

There's nothing I could have done.

But that was a hollow comfort.

He knew what it meant to be a commodity. Traded and shifted from hand to hand.

Disposable.

Nate left the main street and dodged between rain barrels in a space too narrow to be called an alley. His head ached like it did every time he let himself consider his origins. Despite his talent with tech, he couldn't wrap his mind around Gathos City science. Creating life and changing living bodies didn't make sense, but here he was. Living, more or less—and free of Gathos City.

Freer than that boy would be come morning. He couldn't shake the lingering grip of regret. He'd had a chance, in that moment, to do something—and he'd run away. More evidence that he was a coward.

He couldn't—wouldn't—tell the gang what he was or where he'd come from. None of it. He was stolen goods, and the Breakers loved nothing more than hoarding contraband. The price for a child sold to the trappers was nothing compared to what the Breakers offered to anyone willing to turn in a GEM.

Nate couldn't force his friends to choose between loyalty to another street kid and the opportunity to rake in a huge bounty.

Guilt formed a knot in Nate's throat. His gang was sitting on a fortune. And they had no idea.

Because he wasn't brave enough to tell them the truth.

What if they turned me in?

No one knew what happened to escaped GEMs who took up with the Breakers, but no one ever saw them again once they did.

Chased by his thoughts, Nate squeezed between one last set of rain barrels into Heights Square. Here, the skeletons of long-burned benches rose from the ground, and a mangled playground tilted against the pavement. Broken streetlights hunched over the packed-dirt lot. He fought the urge to linger beside a crackling bin-fire, but he wasn't the only one drawn to the soothing heat. A lively crowd gathered—a marketplace of transactions Nate wanted no part in. He kept his head down and hurried.

As he weaved his way across the square, a honeyed scent stopped him short. Only one thing smelled like that to Nate—other GEMs. He whirled, bumping into the person walking behind him and mumbling an apology as the man pushed him away with a muttered curse. He was flotsam on the sludge-channel—too short to see where he was going and small enough to be jostled around.

When he gained his balance, the scent was gone. A hollow thud of loneliness took his breath away. Or maybe that was hunger. Maybe the achingly familiar scent had been the peaches in his bag, overripe and sweet.

He wasn't far from the hideout now, and he broke into a shuffling run for the last block. Darkness deepened the alley he turned into. His skin crawled as he left the bustle of the street for the darkness between two buildings. He felt his way along trash bins and moth-filled air-conditioning units.

Nate left the bag at the bottom of the secret entrance to the hideout and crawled up the duct slowly, fingers sweaty against the creaking ladder. He needed to shake off the mess of his thoughts and focus on what he'd accomplished: the Remedy had soothed away the tremors, and he had a good haul.

Reed won't suspect anything.

If he told himself that enough times, maybe he'd stop going hollow with dread every time he got back to the hideout.

Nate banged out the day's entrance code.

The hatch opened immediately, and Reed's hand jutted out, catching onto Nate's coat with a clawing grip. "You're late."

Nate had never seen anyone quite like Reed—with dark-brown skin, coppery freckles, and bright-green eyes. Reed was beautiful, even with his face lined with worry. His concerned expression made Nate's belly do a little flip.

"It isn't night yet." Nate gestured down the duct with a nod. "Brick better get the bag. I'm done climbing for the day." He crawled out of the hatch and lost his balance.

Reed caught him with both arms and went still, eyes darting to the press of their bodies. The warmth of his hands seeped through the rough fabric of Nate's coat. He searched Nate's face, lips parted gently like he couldn't remember what he wanted to say. Nate shivered and stared at his mouth.

Brick bumped them on her way down for the bag of food. Her red hair stood on end around her freckled face like a halo of fire, and her cold blue eyes honed in on Nate. "You look like a starved cat."

Flushing, Nate pulled away from Reed's grip and let Brick pass. He wobbled toward his bed, trying to shake off the wooziness Reed's touch had given him—or Reed would think he was chem-struck on top of being late.

Fiends weren't welcome in the gang. No exceptions. None of them were immune to Reed's keen observations, the sweeping gaze that seemed to notice every bruise and scratch.

Reed always paid especially close attention to Nate. "No trouble?"

The words lingered between them, heavy with something between suspicion and concern.

"All smooth." Nate sank into his nest of blankets and unlaced his filthy boots. He forced himself to meet Reed's gaze, wondering what Reed saw when he studied him. "Really."

Softening, Reed crouched and nudged Nate's hands away, taking over with the knots. "I believe you."

Nate watched Reed's nimble fingers make quick work of his fraying laces. "Miss Judy gave me bread. I think she wants to take me in."

"Tell her she can't poach my Tinkerer."

His.

A hoarse, strange laugh bubbled out of Nate's mouth. He tried to cover it with a cough.

That got Reed sharp all over again. "Did you find medicine?"

Panic flared in Nate before he remembered telling Reed he had a headache the day before. He nodded, throat dry from the thought that Reed knew how sick he really was—and why.

"You look better now." The tips of Reed's fingers skimmed Nate's bare ankles. He smiled, but concern tightened his mouth. "I guess."

"You *guess*? I better wash up." Nate pulled his hair free of its tie. It swept forward in a greasy curtain, and he wrinkled his nose at the smell of sweat and street.

"I think that'd be best for all of us," Reed said, blowing Nate's hair out of his face.

They were too close in that moment. Too much. Nate wanted to crack himself open and tell Reed everything—that he wasn't a chem fiend, that it was worse.

The hatch slammed shut with a clang that made Nate jump right out of his thoughts. Brick emerged with the bag of food. She let it dangle from one finger, her wide bicep flexed. "Too heavy for you?"

"I got it that far, didn't I?"

Before Brick could answer, Pixel leapt up and swung from Brick's arm alongside the bag, her bright grin tugging a reluctant smile onto Brick's stern face. Pixel dropped to her feet and grabbed the bag. She was small and wiry, with deep-brown skin and hair pulled tight into three ponytails that blossomed into tight curls. Her dark eyes lit with joy. "Apples!"

"Apples?" Reed asked, brow raised. His fingers still rested on Nate's ankles, and Nate shivered. The weight of the day eased, as if Reed had plucked it from him, and for the first time in hours, he drew a full breath.

"They're probably wormy," he said.

"Are you trying to distract me?"

Nate laughed as Reed took off to investigate the fruit. "That's what the peaches are for."

Ducking behind a makeshift sheet-metal wall, Nate washed up in sour rainwater. He scrubbed the grime from his hands and fingernails. The water chilled him, and he focused on the iciness to ward off the heat Reed had left coursing through his body. By the time he returned, wrapped in a rag quilt, Sparks was finishing putting the food away under weighted lids that kept the rats out. Mostly.

Her hands moved swiftly, glossy brown curls in ringlets that brushed her shoulders. Without sparing Nate a glance, she asked, "How are you?"

His breath sucked in. At that, she looked up, one delicately plucked eyebrow arching. She had black eyes and a full mouth and a way of using silence as a weapon.

It's a normal question. She's not that suspicious.

But Sparks knew better than anyone else what sickness and lies usually meant. She'd kicked chem before she joined the gang.

He steeled his voice. "Tired. Had to take the long way back around a fight in the street."

She hummed, the sound too low for him to know what to make of it, and climbed into her bunk. She pulled a blanket over her shoulders, dismissing him.

"You can't distract me forever," Reed said, startling him. He sat on the stained concrete floor beside Nate's blankets and tossed a rag at Nate's face with a thin smile.

Nate caught it and dried his hair. "A girl on the rails asked me where I lived."

Reed frowned. "A girl on the rails ought to know better than that."

His response confirmed Nate's suspicions. It had been strange of her to press. "I didn't tell her anything."

"Of course you didn't. What kind of medicine did you find to make your head feel better?"

"The herbalist on 57th gave me a tincture." The lie slipped out smooth as a breath as he sat beside Reed. "There's some tins of salve in my pockets for that scratch on Pixel's ankle too."

Reed's smile faded. "Did the herbalist say what's the matter with you? Why you've been feeling bad?"

"I told you it's not catching, Reed. I won't get any of you sick."

"That's not what I'm worried about." Reed cupped the back of Nate's neck and pulled him close to examine his face.

"The herbalist said I'm not getting enough greens." With

Reed's face so close and his hand so warm, the controlled tone of Nate's lie slipped. All he had on was a thin bath sheet that wasn't going to hide a thing if Reed got him riled up. "I bought some. And the tincture helped. It's fine, Reed."

"None of us eat enough of anything," Reed said. "But you're the only one around here who looks half dead half the time."

Embarrassment swelled in Nate's chest. No matter what Nate did, Reed was only going to see him as a liability. A lie waiting to get found out. And he wasn't even wrong about that.

Nate swept Reed's hand away, drawing on a flare of anger. It felt better than hurt and a lot better than longing. "If I'm not doing my job well enough, find another Tinkerer."

Pain flashed in Reed's eyes before he went still. "I like my Tinkerer fine." He stood and closed the makeshift curtain around Nate's bed. "Get some sleep."

Hot with shame, Nate pulled his clothes back on, fabric sticking to his damp skin. He curled into a tight ball that didn't make him feel any better about snapping at Reed for no good reason. As the others chatted, Nate struggled to get comfortable and shed the weight of guilt on his chest. Reed was the only person he wanted to impress, but all he did was disappoint him.

The day lingered like grease on his skin, unease mingling with the reek of sweat still clinging to him. He rolled over and bunched up the blanket under his head, one ugly thought turning to another, until a little knot of fear in his belly made itself known.

He'd gotten through today. But what would happen tomorrow? He'd never gotten so sick so soon after taking Remedy.

Pixel pushed the curtain open and crawled into his bed. He drew her close and sighed out a breath that became a yawn.

She couldn't have been much more than five when Reed found her crammed in a duct while scavenging. According to Reed, it had taken an hour and several bite wounds to get her out. She'd only known her name—and couldn't tell them how she'd gotten there or anything that had happened to her before. They'd had no use for a child in the gang, but she'd fallen asleep in Reed's arms, and he hadn't been able to bring himself to put her down anywhere but the shelter of their hideout. Brick said that for a few weeks, they'd talked about finding a family for her, somewhere she could grow up safely without having to run and starve and scavenge.

But no one in the Withers wanted another mouth to feed.

She was still small and fit neatly in Nate's arms. "You're shivering," she said.

"No, I'm not." When she didn't argue with him, he squeezed her gratefully. "Did you practice today?"

"I got the crank-light to glow, but it stung me."

Nate chuckled. It felt good, a tiny release in his chest. "If it stung you, you're definitely doing something right. I'll show you how to make it stop doing that later. How's your ankle?"

"Better. Sparks put your salve on it. It stinks."

"I think you mean *thank you*. You should be more careful climbing in here."

"Reed won't let me scavenge until I get good."

Reed will never let you scavenge, if he can help it. "Then get good without hurting yourself."

She huffed, elbowing him, and he smiled.

"Will you tell me more about Bernice?" Pixel asked, her whisper barely audible.

Nate pushed up one elbow. Her eyes were glittering jewels, watching him closely—excited for a story. She was always listening more than anyone gave her credit for, paying attention—and learning. He liked telling Pixel about his life before joining Reed's gang. His elderly aunt had been dead for years, but he could remember the feel of her thin skin and the smell of her heady perfume like it had only been days.

"Bernice lived in Gathos City before she lived in the Withers."

"You told me that part already."

"Hush and let me tell my story," Nate said fondly. "Bernice made the trains fast."

And then they passed her by.

"How?" Pixel asked.

"Because Bernice was a Tinkerer, like you'll be someday. And she wasn't only a Tinkerer—she was one of the first. She made me learn the name of every tool in her dusty old apartment. I got stung plenty of times too, touching live wires. I had blisters all over my fingers, and every night she'd rub salve on them to make them feel better."

"Like for my ankle."

"Exactly." Nate pushed his hand into hers. "Feel the rough places?"

His fingers were gnarled, with thick calluses from his tools and adjusting thin, sharp wires.

Pixel scratched her nail at a callus. "Will I get them too?"

"You will. And they'll protect your hands."

"They'll make me stronger," she said, fierce.

"Exactly," Nate said. "Now rest, Pix."

The others prepared to scavenge in the night. Reed's voice rumbled like soft music. Nate longed to go to him and apologize for pushing him away, but it was better like this. The closer they got, the harder it was to hide.

And the more he'd hurt Reed in the end.

The hatch opened with a creak and closed with a rattle. Nate untangled himself from Pixel.

"Walk well," he whispered, locking the hatch behind them.

A dream shook Nate out of sleep. He'd been in the car with his parents, speeding across Grand Cosmos Bridge from Gathos City to Winter Heights. The memory struck him often when he talked to Pixel about Bernice. His mother planting kisses on his cheek while he wiped each away, grimacing and confused. His father murmuring her nickname. *Ivy, it's time.*

Except this time, instead of telling him to be very quiet and pushing him into a plastic box between stinking pallets of rotting food, his parents had pulled him back into the car. Instead, the car had crashed and rolled off the edge of the bridge into the dark sludge below.

The swooping sense of falling took Nate's breath away as he shook off the fog of the bad dream.

He scrubbed his hand through his sweaty hair and reminded himself that his parents hadn't given him away—they'd saved him. Smuggled him from the shadowy people who never let him stay with his parents for long, who always brought him back to the laboratory, to the cold and the hurt. His parents had taken him from Gathos City and given him to a kind, old aunt in the Withers. They couldn't have known that Bernice would die before he was old enough to know what to do with the rest of his life.

He wondered—forcing himself not to be hopeful—if they were still alive. All three of them had supposedly died in a car crash, but he certainly wasn't dead.

Yet.

If they still lived, where were they?

Did they wonder where he was?

The question raked across his insides. He shook it off. He'd never know one way or another.

He rolled over and bumped into Pixel, who slept with her mouth open wide and her arms stretched above her head. Nate smiled. He drew his blanket over her legs, smoothing the folds until his hands stopped shaking.

He crawled out of bed. The skylight above was a dark, gaping mouth.

Under the glow of a crank-light, he set out the pieces of an old stun gun Reed had found while scavenging the week before. It wasn't in good shape—the circuit board had rusted over. But Nate'd already managed to rewire half of it. His mind quieted as he worked, hunched over the delicate web of tech.

Sweat beaded up at his hairline by the time he ran out of the thin wire he needed. He flexed his cramped hand and carefully put his tools away, wiping each clean with the edge of his shirt. It hadn't taken as long as he'd hoped, and sadness from the dream still clung to him like the grime from the street.

Bernice had known everything there was to know about tinkering. And so many things about Nate himself. She hadn't been a scientist like his parents, but she'd lived in Gathos City long enough to know all about the GEMs kept locked away.

She would have been able to tell him why he was getting sick so fast between doses of Remedy.

Remedy kept GEMs alive when their bodies began to falter at an unnaturally early age. It was one more awful way for Gathos City to control their property. Bernice hadn't understood the mechanics of it. She'd rasped out a low sound and said, "Your *mother* tinkered with flesh, not me. I stick to guts that don't bleed."

Even Alden didn't have an explanation that made a smudge of sense. Not that Nate really needed to know anything but how much better he felt when he had Remedy—as if it bathed him in light from the inside out.

So why isn't it working the same anymore?

Nate searched for something else to occupy his mind. Dirty sheets and old rags hung like faded pennants from the scaffolding along the wall. He straightened the bunks, climbing from one to the next, folding blankets and shooing away pests. The others would return home exhausted and ready to sleep—and they'd appreciate not getting bit to pieces in their beds.

He woke Pixel up before dawn. Holding her small hand, he helped her climb up the scaffolding. They squeezed out the small skylight to the flat roof of the utility building where Reed had discovered the perfect abandoned space for a hideout a few months before.

As he gently massaged her scalp, she fell asleep again in

his lap. Nate listened to her even breathing and stared out at the smudge of a horizon, waiting for the sun to rise over the endless sea and the towers of Gathos City.

It no longer felt real that he'd grown up in those towers, shuffled back and forth between cold, sterile laboratories and a warm place where his parents held him like he might disappear if they let him go.

As the sun drowned the stars out, he caught himself holding his breath, eager for the dazzle of its glow. He couldn't remember his mother's voice, but in that moment he recalled her laugh—the way she'd scruffed his messy hair when he beat her at a card game she'd only just taught him. The memory sharpened like the blade of light at the horizon. He fought the urge to wake Pixel and tell her about the illustrated playing cards, each gilded with a depiction of one of the Old Gods. Tidal waves and thunderheads and craggy mountains and rolling fields ripe with wildflowers.

He closed his eyes, reaching for more, but all he could see was his mother putting on a gray coat and a silver name tag, her gaze shuttering as she reached for his hand and told him it was time to go to work and study his special blood. Getting on an elevator that took them so high his ears popped. Never crying, because it made her cry too. And he hated that more than he hated what they did to him.

"Ow." Pixel winced, twisting to look up at him with sleepy, owlish eyes. He'd clutched her arm.

"Sorry, Pix," he whispered. "Let's go downstairs and wait for Reed."

Later that morning, all that was left of the memory was

the feeling of crisp playing cards in his hands. Sharp, waxy edges and heavy card stock. He grabbed a rusty crank that left a ruddy stain on his skin.

Nothing was clean here.

"Why can't we have a name?" Pixel asked. "We could be the Alley Cats."

The crank gave a wretched creak as Nate drew the skylight closed against the piercing morning sun. Sunrise became something hot and ugly so quickly.

Reed clung to the exposed rafters like a spider, tugging at one finicky shutter that never closed all the way. "Because we don't want people to know who we are."

They didn't scuffle over turf or fight on the streets. They didn't take over whole blocks like the Breakers did. The gang was safest with no reputation at all—just a handful of kids in the shadows.

"And cats work alone," Nate said.

"You sure?"

Nate shot her a warning look. "They eat their kittens too."

She stuck her tongue out, and Nate grinned, warmed by a rush of fondness. She had a way of getting underfoot, but it wouldn't be the same without her around. For that, they overlooked the fact that she didn't pull her weight.

If they were only scavenging abandoned buildings, Reed would probably let her run with him and Sparks and Brick, but the pickings were better—and the work riskier—in workhouses. It was too dangerous. A-Vols might overlook a kid snipping wires from an exposed circuit board, but they wouldn't turn a blind eye to a gang breaking into a workhouse.

Authority Volunteers—criminals from Gathos City who chose life in the Withers over incarceration—got extra food rations for acting as a police force. But they didn't keep the peace. They hunted street kids, collecting a small bounty of credits for turning them in to the workhouses. It was a death sentence. Every day, workers collapsed or got mangled by machinery. A-Vols dragged the bodies out of the workhouses to the sludge-channel where families were lucky if they managed to pay their respects before the tide came.

Nate hated A-Vols as much as he hated trappers. Pleasure houses and street chem weren't legal, but A-Vols did nothing to stop any of that. They were useless.

Reed reached out and banged the gearbox when the shutter got jammed.

"Gentle with that!" Nate cringed. The last time the skylight shutters broke, it took him a week to repair them. Nate turned the crank again cautiously and held his breath. The shutters snapped shut, blocking most of the daylight from the narrow room.

Reed shot Nate a bright smile, and it was like their fight had never happened. Like the morning sun had burned off the soreness between them. "It worked, didn't it?"

When Reed smiled like that, it tickled Nate's ribs. He struggled to find his voice. "Next, you'll be calling yourself a Tinkerer."

"I've already got a Tinkerer." Reed climbed down the scaffolding and grabbed a plastic bucket hanging from a tack, plunking it down in the middle of the room. "Show and tell!"

Sparks emerged from her bunk, tucking her straight razor

into the small leather kit she kept hanging from a nail. Her jaw was freshly shaved, and she'd stained her full lips blood-red. When she ran with Reed at night, climbing through small spaces and poaching tech-guts, she wore her curly black hair in a tight ponytail. Now it fell loose around her face in glossy ringlets.

When Nate had seen Sparks fight off two trappers with nothing but a piece of rebar and one of her shoes, he'd understood exactly how she'd shaken off chem and clawed her way out of the sick. She was tougher than any of them.

"These looked useful." Sparks shrugged and dropped a set of shiny, numbered buttons into the bucket. "If you can't sell them, give 'em back."

When Sparks couldn't sleep, she sewed clothes from scraps and embellished them with sparkly bits and trinkets from the leftovers no one wanted to buy from Nate at the market. Whenever she managed to finish something, she pressed it under her mattress. Someday, she'd say, she was going to have her own booth, make money, quit stealing.

"They'll sell." Nate tested the weight of the buttons. "Quick too."

"You better keep one if you want it." Reed tipped the bucket back to Sparks, who took one of the buttons with a nod and climbed back up to her bunk. She tucked it into the metal box that held the shears she kept as sharp as Reed's knife.

Brick shuffled over with a wide yawn. She dropped a coil of bright-yellow wire on top of the pile of buttons. "I didn't get much," she said, giving Nate a look that dared him to complain about it.

Reed slapped her back. "That's because you carried a stovepipe clear across the Withers."

"Think it'll work?" Brick pointed at the dented pipe in the corner.

"I hope so. Looks like it, anyway," Nate said. The rusted-out stovepipe in their hideout leaked, and every time they tried to cook, it made everyone cough for an hour. They'd been in this place longer than any of the others Nate had known in the year since he'd joined up with Reed's gang. It was finally feeling worth it to make serious repairs.

"Good." Brick tugged one of Pixel's ponytails as she crawled into her bunk. Pixel glanced up from fussing with her rag doll's hair and gave Brick a crooked grin.

"Brick's been rescuing Reed from fights since they were knee-high," Sparks had told him the first month Nate had run with Reed's gang. She'd stayed up late, helping him organize a box of sewing needles the gang had found in a rotting attic the night before. "They grew up under their mamas' beds in a pleasure house. No place for little ones."

Brick wasn't tall, but she was big—with arms the size of Reed's thighs. A bruise or scratch always mottled the pale skin at her stubborn, boxy jaw. According to Reed, she'd never been bested in a fight.

"Don't ever kill somebody 'cause you're mad," Brick had told Nate once after showing up at the hideout with her knuckles split and bloody. "The stillness is forever. You gotta mean it."

Nate wasn't sure if he could kill someone, even if he meant it.

Reed emptied his haul into the bucket, his backpack like a dirty animal vomiting up wires and scrap metal. "Ah, wait," he said, mumbling to himself. Nate suppressed a laugh as he dug through the bucket, wincing at the sharp wires. "Almost forgot."

Nate squinted at the flash of polished metal in Reed's hand. "What is it?"

A hesitant smile dimpled Reed's cheeks. He wrinkled his nose like it itched and shrugged. "Found it wedged between some pipes in a wall. Must have gone down a sink ages ago."

Reed unfurled his fingers one at a time, his grin softening to something proud and secretive. A silver pendant rested in his palm. He turned it over to reveal a polished stone or shell—pearlescent gray, tinged with blues and pinks and vivid greens. "I thought she'd like it."

A woozy heat crept through Nate. He smiled so wide his dry lips stung. "It's perfect."

Pixel strung necklaces of greasy bolts and buttons. She'd treasure a real piece of jewelry. Nate forced himself to stop grinning like a flying fiend before Reed thought he'd gone addled, but the warmth lingered. Reed was kind when it didn't make sense to be.

Reed tucked the necklace into his pocket and dragged the bucket across the floor to Nate's workstation. The handle sagged with the weight of all they'd scavenged in the night. "So how'd we do, Tinkerer?" he asked, voice deeper—as if putting the little treasure away had snapped him back to practicality.

Pretty things wouldn't feed them.

"Not bad." Nate reached in to fidget with the yellow wires from Brick's haul. He held them to the bright crank-light attached to the pallet he used for a table. Colored wire would fetch the highest price. The fishermen who lined the dangerous, unstable shoreline used it for lures to angle for sludge-fish.

To sell it, he'd have to try his aborted trip to the port again. He still needed to sell the fishing line, so it would be a rewarding trip. But this time, the strange girl called Val wouldn't be there to save him if he passed out in front of a train. He told himself he'd wait until he felt well enough to walk that far. What was one more lie?

Reed crowded close, pale-green eyes narrowed in a careful squint that made him look like he actually knew a rotting thing about tech—which he didn't. Reed had grown up mending his mother's lacy things. He was nimble-fingered, but didn't know a switchpad from a sandwich. Until Nate had come along, Reed's gang had barely gotten by scavenging tech.

It was Nate's one source of pride. He'd helped them. They were better fed now, and they scavenged faster now that they knew what to look for.

"Is it enough to stock the pantry?" Reed asked, tweaking the springy end of the wire in Nate's fingers.

"I said it's not bad." Nate's breath stuttered as Reed bumped against him. Reed was strong and lean, muscles filling out his clothes.

Nate's clothes hung off his angular body. And he wasn't pretty like Reed. He hated the way his gray eyes bugged out a little too much and how often people asked him if he was ill—especially when the sun stayed behind the smog-clouds for too many days. Those were the weeks he avoided the mirrors in the marketplace, dreading a glimpse of his bronze skin gone sickly gray.

He couldn't imagine Reed wanting to be with someone who looked half dead, someone troublesome and secretive.

But sometimes, Nate woke up disoriented and hot, skin prickling with half-remembered dreams. He'd never touched anyone the way he touched Reed in those dreams—darting his tongue out to taste the soft skin at Reed's throat, Reed rumbling deep in his chest and clutching him closer, hot and sweet at Nate's mouth.

Nate knocked over a stack of gutted switchpads and crouched to pick them up, focusing on the task until the warm buzz of Reed's touch passed. He fumbled the haul out across the pallet table and glanced aside to see Reed watching him with a silent question furrowing his brow.

"I can sell most of this." Nate cleared his throat to cover the strain. "Some I can melt down. We can eat off this for a week."

"What about the headaches? Will you be able to get something for that?"

All the warmth slipped away.

"I'll take care of it." Nate shrugged, forcing his voice to remain even. "Alden will have something, and he owes me credits."

Reed's fingers tightened around a shiny metal pin on Nate's worktable. "You don't need to go to him. He's mixed up with the Breakers."

Frustration spiked through Nate. Reed wouldn't understand. "He's not—"

"Even if he's not, he's still pushing the worst kind of chem." Reed's breath hitched, the sound sharp and irritated. "You know that."

Not the very worst.

Alden liked to call his chem "artisanal," which was a rot-filled way of saying he was too stubborn and proud to work with the Breakers. He worked with cooks who had been in business since before Alden was born. He didn't rely on chem runners working the street. He let the fiends come to him.

"I did a lot of tinkering for him," Nate said. "Might as well cash in on that for a few tinctures." It wasn't that much of a stretch. Nate often bartered his tinkering when scavenging got slow. He was young for a Tinkerer, but his work spoke for itself once he was given a chance.

"They say Alden owes half the Withers credits for one thing or another," Reed said.

The opposite was true. Alden detested being in debt and loved cashing in on owed favors. "He's not as bad as you think," Nate said.

Alden was probably ten times worse than Reed thought.

Reed let go of the pin, and it rolled in a semicircle, rustling a whisper-soft sound like music. "Right," he said, tapping his fingertips against the table. "And I'm the king of Winter Heights."

"It'll be fine." Nate reached for Reed's fidgeting hand, realizing too late that the comforting gesture might be mistaken for something else. His calloused fingertips dragged over the back of Reed's hand in an awkward, slow caress.

He knew better than to touch a live wire with his fingertips. It was the first thing Bernice had taught him: check with your knuckles, so that the current doesn't close your fingers into a fist and burn you to bits from the inside out.

"You don't . . ." Reed sighed and studied their hands.

They never talked about what they were. Reed needed a Tinkerer, and Nate needed shelter. But Reed didn't pull away.

Holding his breath, Nate let himself wonder if this was what Reed wanted—if he wanted to know what would happen if they got closer. How it would feel.

All Nate had to do was lean over the little table. He'd never kissed anyone before, but he was pretty sure he could work out the mechanics of it.

Reed abruptly turned his palm up and caught Nate's fingers. "You don't have to keep secrets from me."

Nate drew away from Reed's grip.

"I know." Nate busied himself with the tech and kept his gaze low, afraid his eyes would spill over with tears if he looked up. He wanted a friend. He wanted Reed. But Reed wanted to dig up the truth—and that was more than Nate could give him.

Reed lingered a moment, as if waiting for Nate to say something. Then he sighed and walked away.

THREE

Nate shrugged on his bulky coat. His skin prickled with sweat and itched from the musty fabric, but it was worth it to keep his belongings to himself. A coat was better than a backpack that anyone could grab and run off with. He filled his pockets with colorful wire and shiny buttons and, after a moment's debate, left his tool belt. The walk to the port would take all day. He wouldn't have time to barter his tinkering.

"I'm off," he said, hushed. The girls were already asleep.

Reed came close, damp from scrubbing off the night's grime. He smelled like skin and sweat, and Nate could barely make sense of his words. "You remember the password?"

Nate closed his hand into a fist around small metal brackets in his pocket. The pinch sharpened his focus, helped him stop thinking about how he wanted to press his mouth to the gleaming places on Reed's neck.

"I always do."

Reed used a code of taps and knocks to spell words out. When Nate had asked him where he'd learned it, he'd gone quiet for a long time before answering. "I made it up. So me and Brick could talk when . . . when it was busy."

Nate had imagined Reed huddled under a creaking bed, hidden from customers who didn't care if a whore was grown. That day, he'd worked with Reed for hours until he'd memorized the rhythm.

Tonight, when Nate returned to the hideout at sundown, he'd tap out the password in Reed's code—the code only the gang knew.

Reed fussed with Nate's coat, patting down the wrinkles and brushing dust and dirt off. Nate endured it without reaching for him, but he ached to still his jittery hands. To draw him close and see what it felt like to hold him.

Once, warmed with a tangle of admiration and need, Nate had thrown his arms around Reed before leaving for the day, and Reed had stiffened and stared like Nate had a bad case of mouth sores. Nate had gone to Brick that night, asking what he'd done wrong.

"He hasn't had enough practice being loved on," Brick had said, shrugging. "He doesn't know what to make of it, s'all."

When Reed finished checking Nate over this morning, Nate gave a playful shimmy, imagining his pockets weighed down with small, heavy credits.

"It'll be a good day. I know it."

Reed made a dubious sound. "Keep your eyes open. And try to find more fruit at the market. I think it's good for all of us."

"I will." Nate would find fruit, not because people said it warded off rashes and sores, but because it made Reed smile. Nate turned to climb through the hatch, and Reed gripped his arm. He glanced back.

Reed's mouth opened and shut. And then he swallowed

and lowered his eyes, his hold softening and not quite letting go. "Every time you leave, I wonder if you'll come back."

Nate's breath caught against his ribs. He knew that Reed suspected him of using chem, but Nate never thought he'd figure him the type to run off with the gang's haul and never return. "I'm not a thief," he said in a harsh, hurt whisper.

Reed made an exasperated sound and let go of Nate's arm. "That's not what I meant. I mean I'm afraid you'll ..."

"Afraid I'll what?" Nate let out a tight, confused sigh. "I don't know what to make of you sometimes."

Reed's soft laugh broke the remainder of the tension. "I can tell."

Nate *definitely* didn't know what to make of that.

"Just be safe, Nate."

"I will." Nate avoided Reed's gaze as he slipped through the hatch and climbed down the duct. A blast of rancid air from the street below stung his throat. On a good day, the Withers smelled like steaming shit and gasolex.

There were rarely good days.

The duct emptied into a hollowed-out air-conditioning unit hidden behind a pair of rusted trash bins. Gagging on the thick stench of rot, Nate slid down and landed in the stuffy cylinder. He crouched there long after he'd caught his breath. His head ached, but maybe it wasn't anything. Just a normal headache.

Or Reed twisting my guts inside out.

On this block, no one paid much attention to anyone else. Foot traffic moved steadily, as if everyone had somewhere better to be as soon as possible. Nate couldn't afford to stand around, trying to untangle his feelings. He took a deep breath and squeezed out onto the crowded street.

Three small children—around Pixel's age—played on the front stoop of a building that leaned slightly to the left. Barefoot and shirtless, they grappled and dragged the biggest toward a sloped basement door.

"Why do *I* always have to be the GEM?" the biggest kid whined out, half-heartedly fighting the little ones off. They ignored the protest, shouting and scrappy.

"The Breakers have you now!"

"We're rich!"

A skeletal woman with thinning hair like old straw leaned out the open window behind them and smacked the closest child with a broom handle. "Quit that now," she said, pale gaze darting out into the street as if she was worried someone had overheard the children. Her eyes met Nate's, and he turned away, dodging deeper into the crowd.

He pulled his coat tighter.

Of course the Breakers would want GEMs. He'd seen the rapture on Alden's face enough times to know how valuable he was. Even in the decay of the Withers, people would find a way to pay handsomely for what the elite of Gathos City experienced. A wave of revulsion chilled him.

Everyone knew someone who knew someone else who swore they'd seen a GEM taken into one of the Breakers' hide-outs. Brick had told them her version one night as they huddled around the stove, rags tied around their faces to keep the worst of the smoke out.

"Three went in, two came out—two and enough credits

to buy meat for a year. Fresh meat. Meat still bleeding," she'd said. "We could find a GEM instead of all this rotting tech, and we could buy housing papers. Stay in one place forever."

"That sounds boring," Pixel had said, biting her lip.

"And I don't want to stay here forever." Sparks had spoken with raw conviction. "I'm going to the city to make a real living when they open the gates."

"You could make a real living as a Courier right now. Secrets don't weigh much." Brick had barked out a laugh when Sparks punched her arm. "But I'd rather sell a GEM."

Nate had watched the fire that night, unable to look at Reed—too scared he'd see Brick's bloodthirsty want mirrored in his eyes.

A barking voice announced fresh steamed buns, and Nate's attention rapidly shifted to the thought of a greasy, hot break-fast. A man bumped into Nate while eating one, oily juice dripping into his beard when he mumbled an apology with his mouth full. The tech in Nate's coat could buy dozens of those pillow-soft buns full of spiced gull.

At least the sickness wasn't affecting his appetite.

Nate ambled toward the rails with his hands stuffed in his pockets to keep stock of the wire and rattling buttons. An approaching train hummed in the distance—the first of the morning. The trains passed at a regular enough cadence that as long as he got up on the track soon after one had gone by, it was a safe bet that he could get to the next ladder before the following train arrived. Once in a while, people miscalculated and jumped to avoid being struck.

It never ended well.

There was no sense in climbing halfway up the ladder to wait for a train to go by, so he paused in the breeze below the rails. It whipped between the buildings, cooling the sweat at his neck and stirring his hair. He brushed away the tickle, and something lifted him from his feet and tackled him into the gravel.

He didn't have time to scream.

Dirt and dust filled his open mouth, his nose. His teeth rattled, and his bones shook, and he lay there, helpless and terrified, as pain rammed him like blows from a hammer.

A hollow crack sounded, and another, each reverberating through his body, shaking him apart. Heat and light flared behind his eyelids and seared his skin. He managed to roll and cover his head, dimly aware that he was still alive and nothing was really hitting him at all.

It's an explosion.

When the sounds stopped, he registered the wheezing of his own breath and the high-pitched ringing in his ears. And the heat. *Gods, it burns.* He crawled away from it, coughing on dust and spittle, his eyes watering and each blink gritty.

Everyone around him was white with dust. Someone stumbled by bleeding, the red on her face vivid against the chalkiness. Nearby, a body lay in the dirt, unmoving. And above them, a half a block away, the tall railway was just . . . gone. Obliterated.

Rubble smoked and steamed below. Half of the station remained, flame creeping along the beams, the overhang. Anyone who had been on or below the rails must have died in an instant. The few windows that had remained on the buildings to either side of the rail were gone now. Glass glittered in the street, reflecting the flames.

Nate gathered himself up, wiping the dust out of his eyes. He felt along his body, but nothing seemed to be broken. He'd narrowly escaped the worst of the explosion and the falling rubble.

His hands trembled.

He'd only been near an explosion once before, when an accident had rocked one of the workhouses a few blocks from Bernice's apartment. That night, Nate ran to check on her, forgetting in his panic that she'd died days before. The fire outside shone through the open window and flickered on her empty bed. Unable to get back to sleep, Nate had picked the lock on Bernice's safebox and found a faded ticker-paper clipping. According to the ticker, he'd died in the same fiery car wreck that had claimed the lives of his parents—Vivian and Tariq Land. The bodies had never been recovered.

Overcome by the memory now, Nate narrowly avoided getting trampled by the crowd swarming away from the fire. He ducked behind a low wall and gulped wet breaths, trying to calm the sickening race of his heartbeat.

A high-pitched wail pierced through him. He jammed his palms against his sore ears, but it didn't muffle the frantic sound.

What is that?

And then it sparked.

A train whistle and brakes shrieking in tandem.

The oncoming train was crashing.

Curiosity took over, despite the screaming instinct to stay hidden.

Nate peeked over the low wall and gasped, his dirty hands covering his mouth. The train approached too quickly, barreling toward the flaming gap in the railway where the explosion had demolished it. He watched, frozen in place, as the train careened over the edge and crumpled like foil in the rubble.

The sound of it was awful—he felt it in his jaw and clamped his teeth against the pain. Screeching and tearing. Metal against metal. The lead car lit up with a scarlet fireball and thick black smoke, and only then did the rest of the train groan to a horrible stop.

Gathos City trains had a dozen cars. Only two were lost, and one more dangled from the jagged edge of the ruined track. Flames licked toward the rest, climbing the twisted wreck of the lead cars.

Nate drew himself to stand, his knees shaking. *The cars are full. They're full of people.*

Heat blasted his face. A crowd began to gather at a safe distance on each side of the elevated rail. People were shouting about the Breakers, cheering for them.

The train whistle gurgled and died, and Nate's stomach turned when he recognized the muffled sound that replaced it.

The surviving passengers were burning.

Ragged howls ripped from burning throats, hands clawing against unbreakable windows, and the roar of flames flickering with the stomach-turning greens and blues of melting tech shook the air. The mangled cars groaned and vanished behind the smoke.

Nothing to be done for them but hope it ended quickly.

Nate wiped his nose. The dangling car wasn't on fire yet. Fists pounded against the windows, and faces distorted with terror pressed against the glass.

"Burn!" a Witherson yelled from a balcony nearby. "Burn, bastards! You left us to die!"

The people on the train were citizens of Gathos City. By any Witherson's definition, they were enemies for abandoning Winter Heights to disease decades before. But screaming and desperate, they didn't look like enemies. They looked helpless. Hundreds and hundreds of people who would die in agony if no one helped them.

Nate knew better than anyone else what people in Gathos City were capable of. But Bernice had always told him that it was the ones in charge, the ones at the top of the tallest towers, who established the systems that let them shit on everyone else.

Not everyone could be bad.

Pushing his fingers into his pockets, Nate squeezed the thin wires and sharp edges of buttons until his palms stung. He could leave now—run in the opposite direction. He wouldn't have to watch them burn.

He thought of the little boy dragged to the trappers by his mother. Reed's gang, unaware of the danger they were in by crossing the Breakers and hiding a GEM. Nate spent so much time convincing himself that there was nothing he could do— no way to make things better. But this time, that wasn't true.

I can help them.

Biting his lip, he tore out of his coat and crammed it into

an empty fire bin, brushing soot onto it to make it look like trash. A dirty coat beat having the entire haul stolen.

He'd never forgive himself for that.

Nate ran toward the flames.

Thick, oppressive heat pushed him back. It smoldered in his throat, sucking the breath from his lungs. He stumbled to a stop beside an older man and a girl skirting the edge of the violent flames. The man wore a tool belt. Another Tinkerer.

"We're not gonna get to it this way!" he called out to the Tinkerer, shouting over the roar of the fire. "What about the next ladder?"

The man nodded, and they took off running and climbed the rusting rungs along the next support piling. Here, the cars remained upright on the track.

Nate tried not to look down. The wind whipped smoke in curling tendrils around his body.

The fire in the distance wasn't as loud, but it gurgled—an eerie sound like metal brought to a boil. Nate climbed onto the narrow ledge beside the car and startled when the emergency exit hatch opened. He braced himself, not sure what to expect from a Gathos City commuter.

A man with blood on his hands helped a younger woman from the hatch. Both were dressed in monotone form-fitting clothing. Blood ran down her face from a split at her forehead. She looked at Nate like she could see right through him and limped onto the narrow ledge beside the train.

The man hesitated. Others climbed out behind him, each as dazed and bloodied.

"Come on!" Nate shouted, gesturing to the ladder he'd

climbed up. The man and woman flinched. "You have to get down there, before the fire spreads. Get down to the ground!"

They began to move, and relief softened the edge of Nate's frustration. The passengers could get out on their own. As long as they moved their rotting feet, they'd be all right. But he still needed to get to the cars where the exit doors were jammed against the guardrail and light posts, trapping the passengers inside.

"Nate! Nate!"

Reed and Sparks pushed through the growing crowd below, waving him down frantically. Reed's skin shone with sweat, and the whites of his eyes were big. He had on one of Brick's shirts. Backward.

Nate pictured him grabbing whatever was nearby to get out of the hideout as fast as he could. Goose bumps rose up on his bare forearms despite the heat.

"Nate!" Reed shouted. "Get back from there!"

It felt good that Reed was worried about him—until Reed got close enough for him to see the terror in his eyes. He was afraid of fire. And here Nate was, trying to walk into it.

"Do you have tools on you?" Nate yelled back. No sense in apologizing. He couldn't stop now.

Reed's eyes widened more, and he opened his mouth, looking like he wanted to pluck Nate off the railway and shake him silly. But Sparks took off up the ladder, pulling off her backpack. She reached Nate quickly and handed him a wrench she used as a weapon and a rusted set of wire cutters she used to cut findings for the clothes and jewelry she made.

"That's all I have," Sparks said, breathless. "You're crazy. Let the rats burn, Nate."

"They're people. I can do something."

Sparks grabbed Nate's sleeve. "Do something smart and get out of here. Do you want to burn up with them?"

The other Tinkerer and the girl with him had already climbed atop the nearest car and walked along it carefully, toward the fire. Tinkerers weren't Servants. They didn't have a code of conduct or a mission. But knowing how to fix things when no one else did still meant something. It *had* to mean something.

"I'll be careful."

Sparks sucked in a breath and took Nate by the back of the neck to pull him close. "Don't get killed."

"I said I'll be fine! Get these people down the ladder, okay? Maybe they'll listen to you and Reed if you don't snarl so much."

Sparks's lips twisted into a small grin. "That's a tall order."

"Try to get them to stay together. It's gonna get ugly."

The crowd of onlookers below wasn't scared—they were angry and hungry and likely to pluck every last trinket and scrap of clothes off the survivors. Nate couldn't do anything about that.

Sparks watched him for another moment, shaking her head. "You're crazed," she said. But it didn't sound like an insult, and when she let him go, she began waving down the survivors from the train.

Nate swung over to a set of thin rungs and climbed to the top of the car. Wind whipped smoke against him, and he ducked, coughing at the bitter, stinging taste of chemicals—and the unmistakable smell of charred meat.

This was a terrible idea.

The train car shook under his boots. He shuffled along the top, pitching back and forth to keep his balance. If he slipped and fell off, he'd be lucky to land on the tracks and not far below on the unforgiving concrete.

"I'm Nate!" He shouted through the smoke to the other Tinkerer. "Think anyone else will come up?"

"Reckon not. I'm Dres. That's my daughter, Sandy. She tinkers fine, but I won't let her too close to the fire."

Sandy picked her way ahead with nimble steps, two blonde braids bouncing against her back. She wasn't much older than Pixel.

"Maybe you should send her back down. No telling what's gonna blow next," Nate said.

The man smiled a blackened, half-toothless grin. Sun-blisters covered his pale nose. "That's what makes it fun."

Nate's heart raced. The roof of the railcar rattled beneath his feet with the pounding blows of the people trying to get out. Nothing about this was *fun*.

"Sandy!" Nate called. "You try the window back here, okay?"

Dres met his eye and nodded, allowing his daughter to move past and work on the window farthest from the blazing fire a few cars ahead of them. Nate went to work on the emergency hatch jammed against the guardrail. No amount of force would pry it open. But if he could take the hinges apart, it would slide down and in, and the people inside would be able to climb out. He tried to ignore the screams and blistering heat, hands shaking despite the simple work. Sweat dripped into his eyes.

Nate had heard plenty of rumors about the Breakers cooking explosives, but they'd never done anything like this.

No one had ever interfered with the speeding trains that led from Gathos City over the Withers to the smaller residential islands on the far side. Once in a while, people tried to run along the rails over the sludge-channels, but the trains came too frequently. They crushed anyone foolish enough to make a run for it.

What if Gathos City punished everyone in the Withers for this? They had the means. They could stop sending food rations over. They could cut off electricity and water.

Focus.

Nate spared a glance over his shoulder at the darkly dressed Gathos City commuters gathering in tight herds in the growing mob. Servants crept out into the crowd like ghosts in their gravel-colored robes and crouched beside people who writhed on the ground, burned and broken from the wreck. Nate exhaled heavily with a fleeting moment of relief. Servants took a vow to protect and care for anyone in need, whether they were old and dying or from Gathos City.

He scanned until he spotted the yellow scarf in Sparks's hair and Reed beside her, running his hands through his short hair with frantic jabs. When their eyes met, Nate looked away. The year before, he'd toppled off an electrical pole after getting distracted by Reed's dazzling green eyes and the caged-bird flutters they caused in Nate's chest. He couldn't afford to slip now.

The first hinge came apart with a quick pull, but the second was jammed. Nate took the pieces he'd already removed and fastened them back together to make a lever. He wasn't strong—so he'd learned other ways to find strength. Bracing his boots against the hot metal, Nate threw his weight into it and loosened the stubborn bolt. It clanked to the ground, and the seal on the hatch popped open with a gasp of smoky air. Nate used his legs to pry it open all the way.

"This way is safe!" Nate yelled. "You need to hurry." He tucked the borrowed tools into his belt and grabbed on to the edge of the hatch to vault inside.

For a moment, all he could do was stare at the white seats and gleaming walls. Piercing lights strobed, and a low, chiming alarm sounded over and over. The sweet, sharp smell of *clean* brought on a memory as clear as a windy day. His mother's hand in his in the back seat of a car while his father drove, quiet and distant as ever.

The people inside rushed to the hatch, startling Nate out of his thoughts. He backed up against the window, grabbing on to the plush seats for balance. They clawed for a way out the narrow exit, fighting like street dogs. Ignoring the fray, Nate vaulted over the backs of the tall seats to make it to the other end of the car. He had more work to do. The steel door from this railcar to the next was locked.

The handle was warm to the touch, but people stumbled and flailed in the smoke and heat behind the thick glass. They weren't burned up yet.

"I'm going to get this door open!" he shouted. He could rewire the lock, but it would take more time than the people in the smoky car had. The pressure hinges would have to do. But the cables holding them together were too thick for Nate to cut on his own.

A handful of commuters hung back, allowing the rest to exit first. Nate whirled on them and coughed until his throat cleared. "I need another hand on this. Please. It'll open the door!"

"You're one of the sick ones." A tall man with white hair and dark-brown skin approached with halting steps. He wore a suit finer than any cloth Nate had ever seen and a narrow tie with an elaborate pattern gleaming with little bits of metallic thread.

"No one here is sick anymore." Nate struggled with the wire cutters. "And I don't have time to talk."

The man pushed up beside him and pressed his full weight into the cutters. For a long moment, their efforts were futile. Then the cutters snapped shut, and the wire gave. Nate wound it out of the hinges.

"Nothing's happening," the man said.

"Give the door a good push. Hard, with your shoulder."

When the man pushed, it gave a little. Nate joined in, straining and digging his boots against the carpeted floor. The door gave way, falling into the car with a jarring thud, and they collapsed onto the floor with its momentum. The people inside stampeded toward the exit hatch.

The white-haired man rolled toward Nate and cast an arm out, bracing him from the feet trampling them, but it was no use. Passengers billowed from the flaming car like the smoke that chased them. They stomped and climbed over Nate, sharp heels biting. When the thudding blows finally stopped, Nate touched a painful, hot spot at his hairline, and his fingers came away bloody.

Nate scrubbed his hand against his pants, anger twisting his face into a grimace. Even after saving them, he meant nothing to the commuters of Gathos City.

"I'm so sorry," the man said, pushing up onto his hands and knees as gingerly as Nate did and looking as bad as Nate felt. Blood ran down his chin from a nasty split lip. "They're afraid."

Smoke poured in from the other car. Nate's anger dampened. They'd almost cooked to death in a metal prison. He'd walk over someone too, if it meant catching a breath of air after choking on poison.

Nate wondered what he'd do for Remedy if he had to. "I know."

"My name is Ben. Thank you for doing that."

Ben helped Nate up, and they approached the hatch shakily. The last few passengers in the car worked together, offering the wounded help up through the hatch. One of them gave Nate a suspicious look.

"This boy freed us." Ben stepped between them and Nate. "Help him up."

One of Nate's tools fell. He reached with numb fingers, but wasn't able to grasp it before the men lifted him up and pushed him through the hatch, out into the open air. Nate spun, trying to gain his bearings. Dres put an arm around his back, and Sandy ducked under his arm.

"I feared that might happen," Dres muttered, wiping Nate's forehead with a greasy rag.

"It's not that bad." Nate drew in gulping breaths. He was crying a little, but mostly from the smoke.

Gathos City passengers poured from the emergency exits of each car. At least they were smart enough to fear burning up more than they feared the Withers. They climbed down the ladders at each support beam like ants.

Sandy made a face. "Your head is bleeding."

Dres reached down and helped Ben out of the hatch. Ben made a low, whistling sound. "It looks different . . . like this."

"When you're not speeding by?" Nate glanced back through the hatch at his wrench on the floor in the railcar but didn't have the energy to go back for it.

"Yes," Ben said absently. "There's so much space."

A robed woman in the crowd beckoned him, and he made his way down the ladder to the ground below and took her hand. She led him away to the crush of robed Servants, and Nate squinted. Something about the curl of her fingers was familiar, but the blood in his eyes blurred his vision. When he wiped his face, Ben and the woman were gone.

Nate hadn't thanked Ben properly for trying to protect him in the train car. Crowds swarmed around the survivors from the city. They were swallowed up, part of the Withers now whether they liked it or not. Chest sore and head throbbing, Nate wondered if all he'd done was lead them to a different violent end.

"Careful there," Dres said, taking Nate by the elbow. "You're wobbling."

Dres and Sandy helped Nate down the ladder. The moment

Nate's feet reached the ground, Reed's arms wrapped around him like a vise.

Reed was slick with sweat and cool to the touch, and his heart beat so hard it vibrated in his chest. Nate wrapped his arms around Reed in a clumsy hug, shaking too much to do anything but get close. "It's okay," he tried to say. It came out like a sob.

Dres scruffed his big hand into Nate's hair. He dropped the other onto Sandy's shoulder, directing her into the crowd. Reed led Nate away from the railway, but Nate stumbled with each step, unwilling to let go of Reed and walk properly. If he let go, he was going to fall. His legs were finally catching on to the terror he'd ignored in the train.

Twisted metal creaked, and the flames made a hungry rattling sound. The crowd was loud too, shouting at the survivors. Nate pressed his face against Reed's arm to block it out. He'd helped them get free of the fire, but they weren't much safer down here.

Sparks took his hand and tugged him along.

"I lost your wrench," he told her hoarsely before darkness swamped his vision.

CHAPTER
FOUR

The thick sting of smoke and flaming gasolex burned in Nate's nostrils. He opened his eyes and caught a bleary look at Reed and Sparks arguing a few steps away. Several blocks down the street behind them, the railway billowed fire and smoke. He turned his head slowly, fighting dizziness. A rough brick wall poked at his back through his thin shirt.

"You shouldn't have come out here!" Sparks was saying.

"He could have burned up there." Reed rubbed his palms against his short hair as he paced. "He could have died."

"And now we got seen helping those sludgestains out of the wreck because you stuck your neck out. To what? Watch him try to kill himself?" Sparks gestured toward the black smoke in the sky. "It's not like you did anything."

"What if we hadn't come? He's out cold. Anyone could take him."

"Take him where? You're not thinking straight, Reed."

"Look at him! Of course I'm not thinking straight!"

"Hey," Nate said after three aborted attempts to speak around the sticky soreness in his throat.

They both turned. Sparks blew out a heaving breath.

Reed balled his hands into fists, coiled up like he was about to snap in two.

"I told you," Sparks said, slapping Reed's shoulder. "The smoke made him pass out. He's fine."

"His head's gashed open." Reed scowled. "He's not *fine*."

"I'm okay." Nate mapped out the swollen, sticky spot with his fingers. His pulse throbbed through his head, hot beats of pain. "Ow."

"That was great, you know." Sparks offered Nate her yellow scarf. "You got everyone out. I mean, not the ones in the first car—they're charred up—but the rest."

"How are the people who got out?" Nate licked his dry lips. He took the scarf and pressed it to his head. His blood left a vivid red stain when he checked, but it wasn't a lot. Head wounds always made a mess.

Reed glanced at Sparks and gave a quick shake of his head.

"What?" Nate asked.

"It doesn't matter." Reed crouched, focusing on Nate. He drummed his fingers against his thighs. "Don't think about that right now."

"I'm not a kid. Tell me." Nate glanced at the smoke. "Did they kill everyone who made it out?"

"They didn't kill *everyone*," Sparks said. "Just some of them. The rest ran off. A few went with the Breakers."

"The Breakers? They were really there?" Nate wiped grit out of his eye and stared at her. Everyone knew about the Breakers, but hardly anyone knew someone who ran with them. Knew what they looked like. They were shadowed, buzzing messages on tickers and the offer of work to anyone willing to run chem. Powerful people who sent Couriers out to carry their messages and the A-Vols to do their dirty work.

"Three of them, anyway. You should have seen them. Dressed fine as can be." Sparks pretended to adjust the collar of her shirt and threw her shoulders back.

"How do you know it wasn't people from the wreck?" He looked at Reed.

"I wasn't watching all that." Reed rubbed the back of his head. "I was watching you."

The air felt thinner for a moment.

"I'm telling you, I saw," Sparks said. "They didn't come from the wreck. They had fancy stun guns and handed out food and medicine to the crowd. Asked the ones from the wreck if they had GEMs with them. They didn't seem that bad. And they said they did it for us. For all of us."

"They're terrorists." Nate thrust the bloody scarf at her, wondering if she'd forgotten the part where his head had almost been kicked clean off, thanks to what they'd done. "They just killed loads of people!"

"I didn't say I was signing up to blow up trains with them. They didn't need to do that." Sparks quieted as if she expected one of those fine-dressed people to be right behind her. "Just saying they had nice clothes. And maybe they were only trying to help us."

Reed shook his head, frowning. "I don't like it. They were too bold today. Going after the city trains. Walking around in the sun like they didn't care who saw them. Sparks said the A-Vols didn't go near them, like they were scared to."

"And trappers?" Nate asked. It wasn't like trappers to be

out in the daytime, but the explosion would have shaken just about anyone out onto the street.

"I don't know. It was so crowded."

Nate recognized the frustration that tightened the skin around Reed's eyes. Just because they didn't see trappers didn't mean trappers didn't see them.

He hated that hollow sensation of not knowing, especially when not knowing could mean somebody getting hurt. Reed was the same—always trying to stay one step ahead of anything that could harm his gang. And he couldn't stay ahead if the unknown darkened the path and tripped him up.

Blowing out a noisy breath, Reed crouched in front of Nate. His skin gleamed, the freckles on his nose bright as flecks of polished metal.

Nate ducked his head. "Sorry I made you come out here."

"You didn't make me do anything." Reed brushed Nate's hair behind his ears and stayed close—closer than he needed to be. "How are you?"

"I'm okay, Reed."

Reed's expression went pinched. "Are you?"

A wave of sharp sadness gripped Nate. No matter what he did, Reed was still going to try to pry secrets out of him. They could never have a moment of just being close. "My head hurts, but I guess that's nothing new."

"You look pretty bad." Reed stroked Nate's jaw with his thumb and tilted his face up to study the cut at his hairline.

Nate didn't know what to do with his hands, so he pressed them against the dirty pavement. "Do you remember when the water main broke and we all went to see?"

That day, Reed had stripped down to his tattered boxers in the spray. Drops of water caught the sunlight, casting rainbows that shimmered in the air, and everyone laughed and played like little children. Nate hung back, and Reed dragged him into the spray in his clothes, soaking Nate until the water glued his shirt to his back. Reed drew him close and spun him into a whirling dance. Nate pulled back—scared—ducking out of the water and away from how bad he wanted Reed.

He wanted him just the same now, even smoke-stained and ripe with the scent of fear.

"I remember." Reed walked his fingers along Nate's temple, carefully feeling for bumps. "Why?"

If Nate could climb up onto a burning train, he could show Reed what he really wanted. At least once, anyway.

Even if it was selfish.

"No reason." He took Reed by the back of the neck and pulled him closer. Reed tilted his head, as if expecting a whisper at his ear, so when Nate leaned in, the kiss pressed against the side of Reed's mouth.

Sparks let out a low laugh. She probably thought Nate was delirious from the smoke and the trampling.

Maybe I am.

Reed's lips parted with a surprised sound, and Nate fumbled for an angle that made it feel like a real kiss. He scrabbled closer, his fingers catching in Reed's loose shirt, and bumped Reed's mouth with his tongue. Reed pushed him away.

"Nate." He shook his head, eyes big and startled. "No."

Nate shrugged out of Reed's grip and wiped his mouth—

wiped away what he'd done. Shame seared through him, hot as a fever. What was he thinking?

"Nate," Reed said, softer this time.

The gentleness was worse.

"It's fine." He took a choppy breath. "Sorry. It's my head." Maybe Reed would forgive him if he blamed it on getting his brain rattled.

Sparks made a big show of turning back to look at them now that the kissing had stopped. She started to say something and stopped short when a young boy and girl ran by, their shoes slapping hard against the pavement. They ran like they'd stolen something or were trying not to get stolen themselves.

Nate recalled the children playing outside—how they'd played at Breakers and GEMs.

Something shuttered inside of him. Nothing was ever going to change what he was. Now that the Breakers were bold enough to walk around in the day, it would be easier than ever for Reed to turn him in and take whatever reward the Breakers had to offer. Reed had a perfect way to keep Brick and Sparks and Pixel fed and sheltered.

And Nate was keeping that from him. From all of them.

"We need to go," he said, gripping the wall to stand. His head went sludge-filled, and he tried not to retch.

Reed steadied him. "You need help."

Nate fought the urge to shove him away. Embarrassment stung like a torn blister. But Reed wasn't the one who deserved getting shoved and snapped at. "I'm fine."

"I know a sick-den nearby." Sparks fidgeted with her sleeve where it covered the silvery scars that mottled the inside of her arms. "Bunch of Servant weirdos, but the lady in charge let me stay as long as I needed to. I saw her helping out at the wreck. Maybe she's got room for one more. And you're small."

"I'll use the salve I got for Pix. It's fine." Nate sucked a breath in, teeth clenched. He'd forgotten the most important thing. "My coat! It's in a fire bin up the street. It has all the buttons and wires in it still."

"Don't worry." Reed's hand brushed against Nate's, and he gave him a quick, strange glance before taking him by the elbow. "We'll find it."

Walking amplified the sharp pulse of Nate's headache, but it wasn't half as bad as thinking about how stupid he'd been to kiss Reed.

"The explosion woke you up?" he asked, hoping that talking would make them look more like friends on a stroll than tired scavengers looking for stolen tech in a bin.

"It knocked me on the ground. I thought my bones were cracking open."

"Everyone in the Withers must have heard it," Sparks said.

"Any closer, and I would have got burned up. Hold on—it's this one." Nate retrieved his coat from the fire bin. A cloud of ashes rose from the wrinkled fabric. He sneezed. "How do you think the Breakers did it?"

"You ought to know, Tinkerer," Sparks said. She walked in front of them, waving her arms and elbowing people to clear the way for Nate's uncoordinated steps. "Isn't that what you do?"

"That's a different kind of tinkering." Nate pulled his coat on and patted as much of the dirt and ash off as he could. It stuck to his palms and crusted around his fingernails. "I've never worked with explosives."

"Think they'll send more A-Vols to break up the crowd?" Sparks watched the distant Gathos City skyline like she wasn't listening to a thing he said.

Nate stumbled with a wave of nausea. The smell of burning flesh clung to his hair. People had died, roasting in the twisted metal. He didn't want anyone else to die today. "I hope not."

"Wish I could have got some fancy things from that train," she said, wistful.

"We don't scavenge by day," Reed said. "It's reckless. And this was reckless enough." When he made his voice like that— sharp and sure—he didn't sound like another kid at all.

Sparks gave a shrug, but she lowered her chin. Even in a small gang, the order of things mattered. And Reed was in charge.

It had been reckless for Reed and Sparks to come out looking for him. Both of them had had narrow misses with trappers. Reed's green eyes and Sparks's silvery scars made them easy to spot. Especially in the clear light of day.

Trappers didn't take well to being outrun.

Guilt gnawed at Nate. They'd always worked so hard to stay in the shadows.

"Wishes?" he asked. During the coldest days and nights of the last winter, Pixel had made up a game of wishes. She'd known exactly how to bring them comfort. Nate needed it now. If he didn't stop gnawing on his own guilt, he was going to collapse in a useless heap.

"It's not a good day for wishes," Reed said shortly.

Nate kept up as best he could, clumsy with pain and lingering sickness from the acrid smoke. He had plenty of wishes—but right now all he wanted was a way to go back and fix the rift deepening between him and Reed.

Maybe it was already too late.

Talking had always sealed up the cracks that let fear and doubt in. He and Reed had volleyed quiet conversations through the frigid winter, through all the times when someone didn't show up when they were supposed to and life had to carry on with a great big hole full of wondering what had happened.

They passed the dentist's shop. She sat on the porch, waiting for someone to come by needing a tooth yanked out of their gums. A tool older than she was gleamed in her broad hands.

"We're near Alden's," Nate said, realizing Reed had wisely led them on a wide, wandering path back to the hideout. "He can stitch up my head if it needs it." Better Alden than asking the dentist to give it a go. She had kind eyes, but no one ever walked away from her store smiling.

Sparks made a face and snatched her bloody scarf out of Nate's hand. She examined it with a frown. "What's that sludge-puddle know about mending?"

"I've seen him do it." Which wasn't exactly the truth. But at least Alden had clean, sharp tools.

Alden had gotten chem-spooked and tried to pick up a broken glass with his bare hand. He'd stared at it, watching the blood run down his forearm. Nate had shouted at him for being foolish and sewn up his bloody flesh in thin rows. Once

Alden had passed out and quit flinching, it hadn't been much different than working with a delicate circuit board.

Reed took Nate by the chin to squint at his hairline. He sighed, his breath warm on Nate's face. "You can't do it with what you have?" he asked Sparks.

"Not unless you want him to look like a patchwork quilt." She leaned in close and grimaced at Nate's wound. "Might be an improvement."

Nate shrugged Reed off and scowled at Sparks. "It's up to me, you know." He didn't need a festering head wound further complicating his life.

"Yeah, I know." Pain crossed Reed's face. "I can't stop you."

"Can't stop me from fixing my head up?" Frustration made Nate's words ugly and sarcastic. Not everything was a secret. Not everything needed to be picked apart and unraveled. For once, he just needed help. Not Remedy. Not anything but a clean needle and strong thread. "Thanks."

He stomped ahead of them, his coat spitting puffs of ash with every angry footstep. He didn't have to turn back to know that he'd hurt Reed. Reed followed silently, close enough to catch him if he stumbled. Close enough to make Nate feel like a worm.

Near the shop, a column of black smoke from the wreck loomed over the skyline. People hovered in windows and doorways, watching it curl into dense clouds of smog.

"Is the city attacking us?" a child asked.

"They're gonna burn us all away," a creaking voice said.

It was Fran standing at the curb a block away from Alden's.

She wore a fine embroidered shawl and a string of black beads, like she was going to a party.

"Fran, you should come inside." Nate reached for her hand, anxious to get her away from Reed and Sparks. There was no telling what she'd say.

Her eyes went wide. "Oh, you're a scrappy bird. You don't smell like death today."

"Alden's mom?" Reed asked in a whisper.

"Grandmother." Nate gave her weathered hand a gentle tug.

Sparks went to her other side and offered her arm, and Fran took it with a happy, dry laugh. She put her head on Sparks's shoulder.

As they reached the door, Nate let go of Fran's hand. Sparks led her inside to the sound of tinkling bells. He leaned into Reed, suddenly very tired of worrying.

The truth tickled in his throat. It would be so easy to tell Reed what he was and let Reed decide his fate. Throw him out for hiding what he was. Sell him to the Breakers. Either way, he wouldn't have to lie anymore.

"Isn't there somewhere else you can get mended?" Reed asked, a gentle rumble at Nate's ear.

Nate pressed his forehead to Reed's chest. The space between them was a snarl of wire—the kind he could usually untangle without snapping a single strand. But he couldn't tinker his way through this knot.

"Why does it matter?"

"He's a chem pusher, Nate." Reed cupped the back of Nate's neck, grip light, like he thought the touch would hurt him.

"That's what matters. I don't care if he gives his credits away to addled old women."

Nate sighed. "It's safe enough here. I like Fran. Alden's not going to hurt me."

"Not this time around?"

Nate couldn't look up. He'd been a starving, sick mess when he'd gone to Reed, begging for a place to stay with nothing but a handful of tools to offer in return. Alden had fed on him for so long he hadn't been sure of the day or even the month. He couldn't let himself think about it, not now.

Even then, Reed must have suspected him a fiend.

"Nate." It was a soft, wistful sound. "There has to be another way."

Alden came out, barefoot and hot as a live wire, his eyes wild and his limbs shaky. "What is this? House calls?" He stumbled into Nate and Reed and blinked like they were the ones who were at fault.

"A train crashed," Nate said.

"Did it land on your face?" Alden pulled his robe tighter around him. "You look a fright."

Reed scowled and drew Nate close. "He needs help."

Alden squinted for a long, silent moment and then laughed. "Of course he does. Come inside, Natey."

Reed's grip tightened.

"I just got a hundred people out of a flaming train car," Nate snapped, shrugging Reed off and pushing Alden away as he passed. He ignored the pained sound of Reed calling his name. "I can manage on my own!"

Nate slammed the door shut behind him, leaving Reed

and Alden out on the sidewalk and the smoke and horror out of sight. He stumbled into the washroom and splashed cold water on his face until the water ran red, pink, clear.

The crank-light over the wash basin sputtered. His hands shook as he filled them with dingy water from the rain barrel on the roof. Charred flesh and strangled screams lingered in his throat, and it wasn't until he sank to the floor and began to cry that he tasted anything else.

CHAPTER
FIVE

Three hours later, Nate's head still pounded. He sat on the floor in Alden's room and massaged the bone around his ears, willing away the throbbing pain.

Alden hunched over his cluttered desk, scrawling out figures in shorthand code so complex that Nate had never figured it out. He frowned at his work, his forehead resting in one hand and lips pressed together in a tense line. His writing took up all the space in the margin of one of Fran's dusty old storybooks.

"Don't you have somewhere else to be?" he asked without looking at Nate. "You shouldn't stay here long."

"I can't go yet." Nate frowned, unsettled by what sounded like a warning. And even stranger, like sincerity. "I don't think I'd make it. I feel like I spent the night in a waste trench."

Alden's gaze snapped up. "Already?"

"No. I mean from this." Nate ran his fingers over the tight, even stitches Alden had given him with surprising expertise after catching Nate trying to manage it himself. The pokey ends of the plasticky thread itched.

"Good." Alden turned his attention back to the paper under his fingers.

"Everyone thinks the Breakers blew up the railway. It had to be them, right?"

"I'm working, Nate." Alden sounded different. Tired in a way Nate couldn't place.

It was probably from being clear-eyed after a chem-fueled morning.

Nate tried to stay quiet, but his thoughts rattled around in his head, dancing to the beat of the throbbing ache there. "Reed and Sparks saw them too. At the wreck."

"Saw who?"

"The Breakers."

Alden's pen stopped moving. "Now *that* sounds like a tall tale."

"Sparks said they wore fine clothes."

"I'm told people from Gathos City wear fine clothes too."

"No, she was sure. They had food with them. And medicine."

"*Medicine.*" Alden hummed. He set his pen down and loosened his braid. "Did anyone follow you here?"

"You mean trappers?"

"I don't." Alden's jaw tightened. "I mean Couriers. *Breakers.* But while we're having this lovely conversation, is there anyone else you may have led to my doorstep?"

Nate ducked his chin. Something twisted in his chest, tight and sore, stung by the bite of Alden's sharp tongue. "No."

"Then it's no bother." Alden waved his hand dismissively. He closed the book and opened the lockbox beside it with a key pulled from a hidden space beneath the desk. "Let's take care of your achy head so I can work in peace."

He held up a small vial.

Nate shrank back. "Alden. No."

Alden rolled his eyes. "I'm not looking to make a customer out of you. You're not good for the money, and you smell like wet ash."

Nate caught the vial Alden tossed with a flick of his wrist. Dark, purplish liquid swirled against the glass. "What is it, then?"

"Gathos City meds. Not the latest concoction from the Breakers, but it will make you sleep and stop your head from hurting." He made a beckoning motion with his pale fingers. "It's also expensive. If you're not drinking it, I will."

That wasn't an idle threat. Nate recalled the jittery, bright-eyed high that Alden had been on earlier and gulped the spicy tincture down. He coughed and gasped at the tingling burn trickling from his throat to his belly.

"I thought Remedy tasted bad." Stinging tears welled up as Nate wiped his mouth. "This tastes like gasolex."

Alden laughed. "That's the spirit." He crossed the room like a dancer and sank down onto the cushions beside Nate to pry the vial out of his hand.

"You promise it wasn't chem?" Nate asked, a thread of guilt running through him. What if he'd done exactly what Reed suspected?

"It really matters to you, doesn't it?" Alden twirled the vial in his fingers. A crease formed between his thin eyebrows. Nate couldn't tell if it was sadness or wonder.

"Yes."

"I promise it isn't chem. Real doctors in Gathos City give

this to people with real headaches. I can't say I obtained it legally, but it's perfectly proper." He touched Nate's nose. "Your reputation remains spotless."

Sheepish relief washed over Nate. Alden had done many things, had whittled Nate's trust down to a bruised remnant, but he'd never tried to push chem on him. He'd even locked it up at night, especially early on, when Nate's grief had made him itch to feel anything else.

Nate wiped his nose where Alden had touched and missed, poking his cheek instead. The pain dampened. And his head started floating away.

He gave Alden an accusing squint.

"I said it was medicine. I didn't say it wasn't strong." Alden watched him, the corner of his mouth twitching. "Did you really do what you said? Save those people from the train?"

"I climbed up and opened doors. It's easy for a Tinkerer."

A soft, odd smile graced Alden's face. He stood without a word, and as the fabric of his robe swirled beside Nate, the tincture kicked in. Nate tilted down into the bed and closed his eyes.

At thirteen, Nate had been fresh on the streets, still soft from his childhood in the city and four years of sheltered life with Bernice. He was smaller than other kids his age—and unprepared. Spooked by the sound of someone picking the lock at Bernice's door, he'd scooped up what he could and climbed out the window and down the fire escape.

When a trapper with a belt full of leashes had chased him

down a narrow alley, he'd hidden on the back stoop of a shop, cramming himself under a rain barrel platform.

Alden had opened the back door, tossed the trapper a credit, and thanked her for finding his "cousin." Still shaking, Nate had let Alden push him over to a rusted fuse box connected to a snarl of taped-up wires running up the brick wall.

"I've heard of you. The little Tinkerer. You set up the alarm system at the herbalist's on 9th."

"How do you know that?" Nate asked, wondering for the first time if the Old Gods were real and this boy was one of them. He only looked a little older, but he spoke in the tired way adults did.

"The streets talk. I listen."

Alden stayed very close to the door and picked at his fingernails while Nate worked. He didn't look like anyone Nate had ever seen. He wore his hair long and his body swathed in an embroidered robe like one of the mothy old nightgowns in Bernice's closet.

"They say you were with an old woman."

"She's dead now." Nate winced as a frayed wire pricked his palm. "I fixed the stove at the herbalist's too."

"Fix my alarm system. If you electrocute yourself and die," Alden said, "you're fired."

"Does that mean you're paying me?"

"No."

Nate rubbed one of the oozing scratches along his ribs. "Then what do I get?"

"We can start with your life, dove. You're clearly incapable of managing on your own."

It took Nate five hours, but eventually he fixed the security system Alden had rigged to go off whenever someone approached the back stoop. Since he was already covered in grease and small cuts, Nate worked on the electricity too. He increased the power intake so Alden could run a few indoor lights—and his cooler box, if he was careful.

"You should put a switchpad on this door back here," he told Alden that evening. "It wouldn't be so hard with the right parts."

"How do you know so much tinkering?" Alden asked from the doorway, slowly smoking an entire package of hand-rolled cigarettes that smelled like rot.

"My aunt taught me. She made the trains go fast."

Alden laughed. "You're adorable. Stay with me."

A current of relief ran through Nate. Alden's shop was well-established and secure. Nate would never find a safer place to stay.

"Fix things," Alden went on. "I always have something that needs fixing."

It only took Nate a few days in the curio shop to see that Alden pushed chem. Fiends came in wild-eyed, clutching credits or trading away jewelry and tech. Representatives from the pleasure houses bought in bulk, collecting huge bottles of pills that looked like chunks of sugar.

"And that, Natey," Alden said, "is why you don't take candy from strangers."

When Nate didn't keep busy enough, he let himself wonder

what Alden would do with him if he knew what Nate was. Sometimes, people lingered in the shop, gossiping over cups of muddy tea. They talked about the city and the riches there. They whispered about people called Breakers who had piles of credits to give anyone who found a GEM and handed them over. Alden always laughed and sent them off forgetting what they'd wished for in the first place.

Alden got chem from all over, accepting deliveries in the back from toothless chemists with patchy hair and sores. He entertained in the basement, taking his guests downstairs and never, ever allowing Nate to follow.

"There are some places you oughtn't go," Alden said, playing with Nate's hair.

Nate had given up on trimming it, and it hung shaggy and soft in his eyes.

Before Nate knew it, a year had gone by. He'd fixed enough things in Alden's shop to develop a reputation for tinkering. Every few days, Alden's clients dropped off broken tech for Nate to repair.

"Keep them," Alden said when Nate showed him the palm full of credits he'd earned fixing things while Alden's visitors spent long hours in the basement. He gave Nate a long look. "They're yours."

———

Nate was fifteen and running the register when an older boy stormed in, fit to take the front door off its hinges. Recognizing the haunted look in his pale-green eyes, Nate said, "Lemme grab Alden for you."

"I'm not looking for chem. I'm looking for a boy—"

"We're not that kind of establishment." Alden pushed through the curtain from his side room. "The boys here aren't for sale."

The boy—broad-shouldered, almost a man—spoke to Nate as if he couldn't hear Alden. "His name is July. He's got short red hair, about this tall," he said, patting his collar. "You see him, you tell him Reed is looking for him. His sister's looking too. We only want to help."

"This is touching." Alden took an antique brush off the counter and ran it through the ends of his hair. "But if you're not buying anything, I won't have you loitering."

"Alden," Nate said, "he's trying to find his friend."

Alden smiled. "It's a cold, ugly world. We're all trying to find a friend."

Reed wrenched the brush out of Alden's hand and threw it across the room. It knocked over a display of beaded necklaces, and they shot across the counter, hissing along the glass. Alden's eyes flashed with rage, but he held very still as Reed pushed him against the wall with a forearm to his throat.

Nate froze. He only had to reach out his fingers, and he'd have the stun gun in his hand, but he didn't know how to use it. And Reed wasn't hurting Alden. He was only holding him still.

"If you push chem on that kid one more time," Reed said, "I will find you where you sleep, and I will cut your heart out."

"I sincerely doubt that, Mr. Reed." Alden's breath whistled. "You're clearly a man of many scruples."

"Stay away from July, and you won't have to wonder one

way or another." He gave Alden another violent push and let him go.

Alden gasped for breath and massaged the reddened skin at this throat.

"Reed," Nate said hesitantly. "If your friend, July . . . if he comes in here, where should I find you?"

Reed turned his troubled gaze to Nate. He was pretty, but muscular. There was something kind about his expression, something gentle about the shape of his mouth.

A jolt of want ran through Nate, so hot and startling he studied the speckled floor so that Reed wouldn't see it on his face.

"Walk along Downing Street in the night," Reed said. "And my gang will find you."

The door closed with an angry thump. Alden turned on Nate, red-faced and shaking, hand raised like he wanted to slap him. After a harsh breath, he lowered his hand. "Go upstairs. I don't want to see you right now."

That night, twisted up with guilt but not sure what he'd done wrong, Nate slipped through the dark into Alden's bed.

Alden reached for him and drew him close, his breath a gentle sigh in Nate's hair. Nate knew what it usually meant to share a bed, but Alden never pushed him for it. Nate was grateful for Alden's disinterest in his skinny frame and narrow face. He cared about Alden, but not that way.

When the weather dried up for a season, Alden's supply of chem dried up too. Once the last of the tiny pills in little white boxes ran out, Alden spent days yelling at Nate and his grandmother, who lived in the bedroom behind the shop. He threw up everything he tried to eat and couldn't think straight long enough to do the bookkeeping. He forgot to turn on the security system and lost a whole shipment to thieves. He got as thin as an insect.

On days when Alden couldn't get out of bed, Nate fed him sips of sugar-water and wet his forehead with cool rags, the way Aunt Bernice had done for Nate when he'd been young and sick with fever.

"I wish it wasn't like this, Alden."

Alden looked away. "Me too, Natey."

———————

Nate's left hand started trembling one winter morning. By nightfall, his whole arm tingled and every breath sliced through his chest. The next day, he passed out in the washroom after scrubbing his teeth. When he came to, shaking and sobbing with pain, Alden was there, pushing Nate's hair out of his face with a desperate, hungry look in his eyes. Beside him, a dusty little machine blinked orange and chirped an alarming noise.

"You cut your lip," Alden said. "You were bleeding, and it happened sudden, like they say it does, so I checked. I know—I know what you are. I know why you're sick and how to help you, and you can help me too."

"Are you going to sell me to the Breakers?" Nate choked on his tears. His body was trying to turn itself inside out, and his heart hurt so much.

Alden's breath rasped out, his gaze clouded with indecision long enough for Nate to let out a frightened sob.

"No," he finally said, still touching Nate's cheek, his fingers icy and shaking. "I'm going to keep you."

For the first time, Nate shrank away from him.

CHAPTER
SIX

On the way back from Alden's the next evening, Nate's head throbbed like it was full of sludge. Alden's medicine had worn off, but fuzziness lingered. He hadn't been in a hurry to leave, and now that he was out on the street, guilt twisted through him like the knots in his bootlaces. He should have left the moment he could stand. There was no reason to linger at Alden's like it was still his home.

Nate's shoulders tightened at the lingering smell of smoke from the wreck. The street was still busy with people congregating on their stoops and in the street in the last of the light.

"The sick-dens are full," a young woman said, holding her pregnant belly with two hands. "Not right, giving these dogs good beds."

Her friend spit in the street, so close that Nate had to dodge it, and asked, "What choice would they have? The Old Gods wouldn't leave them bleeding."

"Then send them back where they came from."

Their conversation faded. Usually, music could be heard from nearly every corner. Buskers with drums or a group singing snatches of songs remade to tell the stories of the

Withers—stories of hunger and hope. But tonight it was only rapid-fire conversations and eyes darting to the smoke rising in the distance.

As he approached the secret entrance to the gang's hideout, Nate heard a scuffle behind him and spun. He raised his hands, as ready for a fight as he'd ever be, but no one was there. A scrawny alley cat sauntered across the dark pavement. His heart jittered in his chest, and his racing blood made his hands go tingly. He waited several minutes, eyeing the shadows for signs of movement. Satisfied he wasn't being watched, and clumsy with lingering fear, Nate climbed into the duct.

Reed made a quiet, surprised sound when he opened the hatch. He pulled Nate in, his attention focused on the stitches at Nate's hairline, as if he didn't want to make eye contact. "Your hands are cold. But that looks well enough."

"Alden's steady every once in a while."

Reed flinched, and Nate immediately regretted saying anything at all. His breath gusted out with a tired sigh, despite having slept for a day. He hung up his coat and dropped all the tech from his pockets into a small bucket by the door so Reed could see that none of it was missing if he cared to look.

Reed climbed up to get his bag from the scaffolding. "We'll head out now that you're here."

The gnaw of guilt in Nate's bones worsened. He'd held them up when they'd been ready to scavenge. He crouched to unlace his boots and jerked, startled, when Sparks put her hand on his shoulder.

"Whoa," she said, laughing. "You look fit to bite my hand off. I just wanted to check your head. Doesn't look too bad."

Brick came up beside her and peered at Nate. "Heard you were a hero out at the train wreck."

He braced himself for teasing, but she wore a crooked grimace—Brick's version of a smile.

"Until I got trampled."

Sparks gave his shoulder a squeeze. "You can't help being small."

"Never had that problem." Brick threw her shoulders back and angled her body through the hatch. "You did a good thing, Nate."

The duct made a hollow ringing sound as they climbed down together, their voices mingling like distant music. Nate envied the companionship of their nighttime scavenging runs. At least he'd have Pixel to keep him company when the hideout got quiet.

Reed hopped down from the scaffolding and lingered at the hatch on his way out. "Do you remember when you found us?"

Nate fought an embarrassed grin and nodded, pushing his hair out of his face. "Don't remind me."

He'd gone to Reed after seeing Brick's brother, July, walking into a public den known for chem use and flesh trade. Reed had asked him for help with a smoking electrical wire outside their hideout.

"You climbed up that pole without a look down. I'd never seen anyone do that before. You weren't scared at all."

"My aunt showed me how to use my belt to shimmy up pipes and poles." Nate shrugged, squirmy under the intensity of Reed's gaze and unable to pinpoint what shone there. "I knew what I was doing."

"You fell."

Nate rubbed one eyebrow. "Well. I looked down."

At you.

Reed stepped closer, one hand motioning like he meant to touch Nate. But he stopped and swallowed. "You landed on me, and we were fine, you know?"

It had been one of the most mortifying moments of Nate's life, but after that he'd met Brick and Sparks, and he'd spotted Pixel hiding behind a trash bin. And he'd felt something—a deeper longing than anything he'd ever known. A desire to belong.

Months later, when he'd left Alden, half-starved and weak, he'd gone straight to Reed, and Reed had let him stay. Everyone had use for a Tinkerer.

Nate didn't know why Reed was bringing it up now, over a year later. He had a feeling Reed had a lesson in mind, something about being careful, but he couldn't figure out what he was supposed to say. "I remember."

Reed watched him for a long moment and offered him a small smile. "Good."

They exchanged the night's code, and Nate locked the hatch behind him, hands aching with emptiness. He lingered there, catching his breath and shaking off the unease of their conversation and his relentless desire to pull Reed close and *hold* him.

Pixel skipped over, ducking under his arm and demanding his attention.

"Did Sparks do that?" Nate asked, gently tugging one of Pixel's ponytails. Stripes of frayed blue fabric wrapped around each puff of curls. Sparks didn't have the heart to tell Pixel she was too old for babyish hairstyles.

Pixel pushed her shoulders back and preened. "Sure did."

Neither did Nate. "You should be sleeping."

She held her rag doll closer, and her smile became a stubborn line. "You should be sleeping too. Your head's all tore up. "

Nate could rewire an entire power intake in less than an hour, but he wasn't any good at being stern with Pixel. Especially when she turned her big, dark eyes on him. Pixel was an uncommonly pretty little girl. Even Reed's strong will couldn't withstand her gap-toothed, sunny smile when she wanted something.

"My head's mended now," he said, showing her the line of fresh stitches.

"Did the Servants fix it?"

"No." Nate touched his cheek, struck by the shadow of a memory that faded into the fuzziness of his lingering headache. "They were busy helping the people at the train wreck."

"Reed said you needed lots of sleep."

"I slept all day. I don't need rest now. You do. That's how you grow."

But Nate didn't stop her when she followed him around instead of burrowing in her bunk. He straightened up the hideout to the sound of distant shouting. Late in the night, it was usually quiet outside. Uneasy, Nate recalled the tension on the street on his walk home. It had felt like the staticky air before a lightning storm. Something was happening.

He shook the dirt out of Reed's tattered blankets. The

patched-up fabric smelled sweet and warm, and he spent more time than he needed dusting the blanket off and folding it up.

Pixel leaned against the scaffolding and watched Nate. The mismatched button-eyes of her rag doll watched him too. He imagined the doll knowing, somehow, that Reed meant more to him than he let on.

Reed laughed too loud and endured the stinking heat of summer and the barren depths of winter without a complaint. He sat down to meager meals with a smile on his face, like he was the luckiest man in the Withers.

And he made Nate feel useful.

But Nate wanted more of the warm feeling he got when Reed was close. It was different than the sensation of a full belly. It was better.

It was more than he should want from Reed.

Reed had grown up in an ugly place where people traded their bodies away to stay alive. "My ma didn't have a choice," Reed had explained once, tripping over the words. "The trappers, they'll take anyone alone. Get back before it's dark." Trappers sold their victims' freedom to the pleasure dealers. And pleasure dealers handed out chem to make the long nights easier to bear.

Now that the Breakers had taken over most of the pleasure houses, the trappers were more relentless than ever. Fired up on good chem and desperate for more.

Nate shivered. Their quiet hideout offered a little bit of peace from the horrors of the streets of the Withers, but it wasn't escape. Everything terrible was still out there, where his gang dodged from shadow to shadow.

A low hum of anxiety weaved through Nate's ribs.

He sat in Reed's bed and pulled Pixel down to sit beside him. "If you're not going to sleep, you have to stop playing." After a brief tug of war with the rag doll, she let go and put her head down in his lap with a huff.

"Sparks said the people on the train caught on fire," she said.

"Not all of them did."

"Why'd you save them?" She rolled onto her back to look up at him, wrinkling her brow.

"Because I could help. I knew how to open the doors."

She bit her lip for a long moment and nodded once.

A bang at the hatch startled them both. Pixel rolled out of his lap as he leapt up. The password sounded in code, each knock louder and more frantic. Nate rushed to unlock the hatch and wrenched it open.

"You just left," he blurted out.

"We're moving." Reed grit the words out like a curse.

"What?" Nate staggered back, clumsy with dread, as Reed climbed out and reached down to offer Sparks a hand. "But we're settled. The shutters . . ."

"You heard me. Start packing everything you can carry. Bring all the food you can." Without another glance at Nate, Reed climbed up the row of bunks and began tearing down the concealed bags and boxes that contained their few belongings.

Brick struggled through the hatch after them, wild-eyed and winded. She took Nate by the arm and spoke in low tones. "Trappers. Reed thinks they followed you back from Alden's. We can't risk it if they saw us. Gotta take cover."

The floor seemed to drop out from under Nate.

This is my fault.

He'd gone up on the trains and gotten hurt. He'd walked home from Alden's in a daze, too lost in his own head and muffled from medicine to make sure he wasn't being tailed.

"Think on it later," Brick said with a hiss, holding him steady when he swayed.

Nate took a gasping breath and nodded. "Where are we going? The basement on 30th?"

"Until we can settle." Brick let go of him. "Sparks knows a decent place in the bank."

"The bank?" So far, they'd avoided relying on squatting in the biggest abandoned building in the Withers. The bank meant more prying eyes—more people who would want to sell him to the Breakers if they found out what he was—and gangs that did far more than scavenge to survive.

The only good thing about the bank was its size. It was big enough to disappear in, and the Breakers hadn't managed to infiltrate it the way they'd taken over other neighborhoods across the Withers.

"You heard me." Brick gave Nate a long look that didn't leave room for argument. Her pale cheeks were flushed a splotchy pink, and sweat matted her hair.

Nate had no right to argue when they'd been out there, running. When he'd caused this.

Nate filled a backpack with every glinting bit of scrap wire and tech he could get his hands on. He ignored the bustle and panic around him and the rush of his own thundering heartbeat. They had to move before the sun came up, or they'd be too exposed. Night, tar-black from electricity rationing, would help them dodge hungry trappers. They weren't a fighting gang. Even with Brick's and Reed's muscle, the group was too small, and no one carried anything deadlier than a hand blade. One or two trappers with stun guns, and they'd be split up and sold off.

Pixel grabbed the hem of his shirt and followed him like a sniffling shadow.

He swatted at her hand. "Hush that crying." Snapping at her sent regret lancing through him, but if she was too scared to pack up, she had to stay quiet.

"I don't mean to," Pixel said. "I don't want to go."

"I know, Pix. You stay close to me now." He forced softness into his voice. "We'll get everybody tucked up safe, okay? Just like home again."

Nate caught Reed glancing at him, his expression stricken. He probably hated lying to Pixel as much as Nate did. Over the past year, they'd never stayed in a hideout long enough to call it home. But it didn't stop them from settling in, from trying.

Pixel wiped her face and nodded, keeping her eyes fixed on Nate as he worked fast, stubbing his fingers and tearing his fingernails. He strapped on his belt and reached for one tool after another, swiftly snipping and tweezing the wires out of the security system he hadn't finished installing.

"Three minutes!" Reed called out. "Move it."

Nate stumbled, caught by Reed's strong grip at his elbow. He flinched, mind racing to figure out what he'd done wrong.

"Here," Reed said. He pressed the pendant he'd saved for Pixel into Nate's hand. "Hang on to this. If something happens, sell it to keep her fed. Do you understand?"

"Nothing's going to happen." Nate's chest went hollow. "Reed—"

But Reed dashed to help Brick pry the stove from its make-shift mooring, leaving Nate clutching the cold silver. He pushed it deep into his pocket and kept packing things up. The emptiness lingered, an ache of fear he couldn't shake.

Over time, they'd managed to collect enough scraps of canvas and cloth for Sparks to sew duffels and backpacks. They stuffed each bag with bedding and spare clothes and bowls and the ticker and a few more odds and ends.

The lumpy pile of bags didn't look like much.

It was everything they had.

Reed and Brick divvied the heaviest items up. "I've got the burner," Brick said, hefting their portable stove under a freckled arm. Reed grabbed the food and utensils, and Sparks strapped a bulky bag of bedding to her back. Nate carried their remaining tech in his backpack and in his pockets and tool belt.

Reed studied their ranks as they lined up, packed and ready to run. Nate fell into line last and nudged Pixel into place. He met Reed's eye and nodded, chest tight with nervous energy. Reed's face gleamed, and every soft line in him had gone hard.

"Nate will run with Sparks and Pix," Reed said. "I'll take Brick. Thirtieth Avenue basement. Does everyone understand?"

Sparks adjusted the bag on her shoulder. "Got it."

"Yes," Brick said loudly. She gave Nate a pointed look.

"I understand," Nate said, directing it to her. He'd nodded—it wasn't a contest.

She was probably sore he'd been followed. And she ought

to be. He ducked his chin, and his breath shuddered, fear and guilt welling up in his chest.

Pixel grabbed on to Nate's hand and sniffled.

"Nate, go first. If you get slowed down, we'll find you on the way. Don't look back. Run." Reed took Pixel's backpack and slung it over his shoulder. "Sparks, drop the bedding and carry Pix if you have to. We'll pick up anything you leave behind."

They crammed down the duct, metal groaning with every bump and slide. Nate landed first and caught Pixel. He held the door open as Sparks squeezed out with her big duffel. Sparks took off through the dark alleys toward 30th, and Nate ran behind, clutching Pixel's small hand.

After three blocks, Pixel stifled a whimper with every step. Nate scooped her up onto his hip. She was tiny, but she still weighed too much for him to carry more than another block. They stopped again, and Nate handed her off to Sparks.

"I don't like leaving our stuff out here," Nate said. "I'll carry it. With the straps, it'll be easier than carrying Pix."

"Those blankets weigh 'bout as much as you do," Sparks said, gruff and out of breath. She positioned Pixel on her back, and they took off again, pace too slow.

Nate hadn't been on the streets at night in months. Chem fiends lurked in the shadows and hunched over acrid bin-fires, stumbling around like walking corpses. Everything sounded darker and uglier at night. Laughter chased them as they ran between tall buildings.

A storm rumbled in the distance, unusual this time of year. Sparks slowed and craned her neck, listening. The sky remained unwaveringly dark.

"That wasn't thunder," she said, hushed.

Nate grabbed her arm and urged her on. Whatever the explosion had been, it was far away. They couldn't worry about it now.

He ran until his throat burned and his shoulders ached from the heavy duffel. His head pounded, raw and hurting where the stitches were still fresh. After four more turns, they reached 30th, a narrow side street lined with stinking trash bins used as waste trenches. Sparks walked along the bins, counting each under her breath. At the seventh, she put Pixel down and climbed up into the bin. Nate took Pixel's hand as Sparks's footsteps thumped along the wooden plank that kept her feet out of the putrid liquid inside.

Metal creaked with a high whine. She'd found the secret entrance to the half-flooded basement below the building.

"Rats?" he asked.

"None yet." Sparks's voice echoed. "Send Pix in first."

Nate hefted her over the metal rim of the bin and pried her hands off the edge when she tried to hang on.

"Nate!"

"It's all right. Sparks is down there."

She clenched her small jaw, took wobbling steps across the plank, and dropped into the basement, landing with a soft yelp and a splash.

He followed and sloshed knee-deep in frigid wastewater. His eyes watered from the putrid smell of sewage. Pixel took his hand. He waded with both girls toward the high ground at the far end. The farther they got from the opening, the darker it got, like they were walking off the end of the world. Their harsh, panting breaths echoed, hushing back at them as the water whispered around their calves.

Sparks lit a small flare from her coat pocket. Rodents squeaked, scattering away from the light.

"Keep everything you can above the water," Nate said. Scum swirled around them on the surface of the black water. "That stink will never wash out."

"Are we gonna stink forever?" Pixel bumped into Nate with gentle splashes, clinging to his thigh.

"You? You'll probably smell better, stinkbug."

Sparks gave a short laugh and trudged up the incline. She tossed their bags onto the dusty concrete that hadn't been touched by the flooding. Nate helped her pile them against the far wall. It didn't take long. When they finished, it was only quiet and cold, and all they could do was wait.

"Stay close," Nate said, sitting flush against Sparks with his back against the pile of bags. The smell of her perfume didn't do much to ward off the stench of their wet shoes and clothes, but she was warm. He pulled Pixel onto his lap. They huddled together, listening for the others.

The basement wasn't much of a secret—but even trappers avoided it because it was so foul. At least Nate couldn't see the color of the dank water now. Last time he'd glanced down into the basement from the waste trench above, a bloated rat had floated by.

Worst piss I've ever taken.

"Stop fidgeting," Sparks said.

Nate rubbed his chilled hands together. "I'm not."

"You are."

"I'm worried about Brick and Reed. They stand out." Even at night. Brick's hair was wild and flame-colored. Reed had the type of face you never forgot. Staring across the dark basement, Nate pictured every detail of it—the cat-like green of his eyes, his full mouth, and the wicked dimples that snuck up when he smiled.

"I told him not to go out looking for you," she said. "And I told you not to help those people. It got us noticed."

He watched her over the top of Pixel's head. "You would have done the same thing if you knew you could get those doors open."

Sparks didn't answer him.

They shivered in silence, time measured in hollow drips and the whisper-scratches of tiny claws. Dawn broke, casting a pale-gray light through the opening near the dank ceiling. It shouldn't have taken this long for Reed and Brick to reach the basement.

Where are they?

Dread crept up Nate's legs like the rancid water around them. He tried to take a deep breath, but the air resisted like his chest was full of rocks.

Brick splashed into the basement with a grunt. Pixel let out a startled cry.

"We're here!" Sparks called, rising to a tense crouch and cracking another flare open.

Nate scrambled to his feet, his pulse buzzing in his ears.

Brick took a few churning steps toward them, her eyes wide and scared in the flickering light. No one followed her.

Fear gripped Nate's throat. "Where is he?"

"Help me carry him," Brick gasped out. She waved her hand wildly at the entrance.

Nate rushed into the water, kicking cold splashes up to his waist. Sparks ran alongside him, her longer stride carrying her ahead. She climbed up and helped Brick ease Reed's limp form down into the basement. They hefted him above the water carefully.

Even in the dim light, Nate could see the dark stain at Reed's middle.

"No." He grasped his wet hands at Reed's throat to find a pulse.

"Easy, Nate, don't get that filth on him." Brick pushed him away. She didn't have to put much effort into it.

Nate staggered back, his knees weak. His blood roared in his ears.

"He's alive," Sparks said, the sound broken by a small sob.

Nate followed, hands balled into fists to keep from reaching for Reed again. "What happened?" He fought to speak, his thoughts going to bad places too quickly to keep up. "Where's he hurt?"

"Reed took the long way so they'd follow us and not all of you. A man came after us," Brick said. "No one I've seen before. He went straight for Reed and tackled him, asking where the Tinkerer was. He had a knife, and it was so quick, we couldn't—"

Sparks swore under her breath and shouldered Reed higher to keep him out of the water. She shot Nate a sharp look. "See?"

Nate recoiled, guilt like ice at the back of his throat. He

choked on it, trying not to cry—he had to stay calm. Had to help. There was no time to drown.

"Whoever he was, I broke his neck." Brick helped Sparks lower Reed to the dry ground. "He won't be following us or hurting Reed again." She wiped her eyes with the back of her hand, her face wild and moon-white in the light of the flare.

Reed didn't stir.

Being a Tinkerer made him second-in-command, and despite his numbing fear, Nate had to take charge now. Until Reed woke up and told them how to fix this mess.

My mess.

"Pix." He steadied his voice. "You need to stay in the corner there, out of the way. Sparks—"

"I got it," she said, already crouching and stripping away Reed's T-shirt to try to find the gash at his belly.

The smell of gut-blood assaulted Nate, gagging him. "Sparks, how bad is it?"

"Bad. Maybe bad enough for the med clinic at the gate."

"They won't take him. Not without workhouse papers."

"Maybe bad enough that he's gonna die, Nate," Sparks said with a snarl. Her breath came out ragged as she composed herself. "He's gut-stabbed. I know a place, a Servant woman . . ."

"The sick-dens are full," Nate realized aloud. "Sparks, they won't be able to help him."

"We wouldn't get that far anyway." Brick's voice was soft and grim. "I can't fight and carry him at the same time."

Nate closed his eyes. No sick-den. No Servants. No time.

He hugged his middle until the basement stopped spinning.

I can't lose him.

There was only one thing he could do. He let out a sharp breath. "I can help."

"How?" Sparks spat.

"Trust me. We've got to get him somewhere warmer, where we can heat up water and clean him off. Brick, can you carry him up the fire escape here?" Nate asked.

"I can carry him as high as you need."

Nate glanced up. The floors above them were full of crowded apartments. "We'll have to break in."

Brick shook her head. "But we don't—"

"We have to! Climb up now and find somewhere dry where we can keep a decent lookout, okay?"

As a rule, they never broke into anyone's home. Each of them knew how important a home was. But the rules didn't matter now. "Can you get him upstairs with Brick's help?" he asked. "Keep him warm? Keep him from bleeding out for now?"

"*For now*?" Sparks asked, broken with the same worry aching down to Nate's bones. Reed was beyond help. Gut wounds festered. If Reed woke up again, he'd be begging for the stillness to take him.

"Alden's got stuff nobody's supposed to have. Stuff that can help him." Nate touched Reed's clammy cheek. "Get him dry and warm and safe. And alone. I'll be back in an hour. Keep him alive for an hour. Please."

"Don't say *please*," Sparks said. "It won't be for you." Her mouth trembled until she clenched her jaw. "But I'll do it."

CHAPTER
SEVEN

"Do you know what time it is?" Alden asked, standing in the doorway to his shop in a lacy nightgown that hugged his lanky body like a bandage.

"Alden, I don't have—"

"It's seven in the morning!" He tapped his bare wrist. "I'm closed. I went to bed two hours ago. You better have a truly profound reason for waking me. Better than a bump on the head."

"Reed's hurt. He's dying." Nate panted on the doorstep, hunched over and winded from running twelve blocks across the Withers. A sob caught in his aching throat, and he slammed his palm into the doorframe.

"Oh, dear," Alden said. "By the smell of you, I'd say he was accosted by a rogue sewer rat."

Hot with a flash of rage, Nate pushed Alden back with both hands and kicked the door shut behind him. His chest heaved, and his breath whistled. He didn't care if he looked sick and crazed. Reed was running out of time.

Alden stared at him, one slender strap of his nightgown slipping off his pale shoulder. He fixed it, sighed, and ran his fingers back through his sleep-snarled hair. "You honestly expect me to do something about this? I might have some strong meds from the city, but I'm no miracle worker. Take him to the med clinic and pray to the Old Gods."

"They won't help him. You know they won't."

"Then what do you want from me?" Alden stepped closer to Nate and dashed his hands out, quick as a snakebite, pushing Nate back against the door. "Sympathy? I told you a long time ago you'd get nothing running with a gang of thieves."

Nate wilted against the door. But anger steadied him. Alden had no right to tell him what to do—not now. Not ever. "I can save him."

Alden's expression went blank before spots of color rose on his cheeks, splotchy and ugly. "No."

"I can feed him. They're patching him up. If I feed him, he'll live. I know it." It didn't matter that Nate might not survive doing it. "I can make him strong."

"We had a deal," Alden said slowly. He bracketed Nate against the door with trembling arms and leaned in, his hair forming a dark curtain around both their faces. "The deal was, you don't share. Not with your whore boyfriend, not with anyone."

"I'll come twice a week. Or more. I'll come whenever you need me." Desperation thinned Nate's voice. He grasped for leverage—bluffed. "I'll let you feed me to your clients."

Alden shuddered and gave a quick shake of his head. "Nate."

They both knew he had nothing to offer. Not really. He couldn't risk feeding Alden again. And Alden would never expose what he was to a stranger.

Reed was going to die.

"Alden, please." Nate's head fell against Alden's arm. He blinked, and the anger sapped out of him. Tears skipped down his cheeks. "I . . . *they* need him. I can save him."

For a long moment, Alden held very still. But his eyes darted, searching Nate's face. "Whenever I need you?" he asked, breath tickling Nate's skin. It was a wish. Nothing more. "You swear on it?"

"I swear. I swear it, Alden."

Alden straightened and tucked his hair behind each ear. "On top of all of this outrage, you expect to take my Diffuser out of my shop?"

"You can come with me if you don't want it out of your sight," Nate said, dizzy with hope. Alden was going along with it.

He was so close now—he could make Reed better.

"Skip along on a dashing rescue to save your boyfriend? I think I'll go back to bed." Alden yawned dismissively, but his eyes glittered. Both of them knew he wouldn't leave the shop. Even for this. "You can borrow my Diffuser. If you crack it, I'll sell you to the Breakers."

Nate didn't believe the threat, but it didn't seem like a good time to say that.

As Alden went to get the Diffuser from its hiding place, Nate slid down the door, trembling. Each passing second wound him tighter. Reed was bleeding and dying.

If I don't get back fast enough . . .

"You're in over your sweet head." Alden handed Nate the small, velvet-lined box that contained the whirring glass

Diffuser. It was genuine biotech from Gathos City. Even Nate, with his affinity for tinkering, had no idea how it worked. It was priceless.

People would give Alden anything for good chem.

"I'll bring it back. First thing tomorrow." Nate clutched the box to his belly.

"Listen to me." Alden grabbed Nate's wrist, his grip strong—painful. "Don't feed him for long. I don't care how bad he's hurt. No more than thirty counts. That's it."

"All right," Nate snapped, impatient with Alden's greed. This was no time to quibble over Reed getting more.

Alden helped Nate to his feet and held him close, his palm splayed against Nate's back. "What's your dear Reed going to say when he finds out what you are?"

"He won't know," Nate said. "He'll sleep through it."

"And his gang? You don't think they'll tell?"

Nate flinched.

"Oh, by the Old Gods' balls. One of them already knows? This is such an exciting morning." Alden released Nate with a gentle shove. "You should bring your special friend by. We can get acquainted."

"She's a little kid. She'll never know you. I'd slit her throat before she sees this," he said, gesturing around the shop. "Or you."

"Don't be ugly, Natey. You know I'd never harm a hair on a child's head." Alden took Nate by the chin and searched his face like he was memorizing every bruise. "Now run along, before you've nothing to run to at all."

―――――――――

The way back took longer. Nate jogged slowly to keep the delicate Diffuser safe. He must have looked unhinged, clutching a box and half-covered in sludge and grime. The observation wouldn't be far off. His mind reeled with thoughts of Reed cold and gone and all of them left alone.

All because he'd drawn attention to the gang and recklessly led trappers to their doorstep.

This morning, no one paid him any mind. People hung in doorways and peeked out windows, expressions wary—as if expecting something to explode. Nate covered the last few blocks as fast as he dared.

Brick met him at the bin. Sweat soaked through her baggy shirt and dampened her hair. The tangled strands stuck to her neck like fresh blood. "What's that box?"

"Medicine," Nate said. "Is he—"

"He's breathing," she snapped, mouth tight. "We broke the lock on a window four flights up. No one's home."

"Nate! Get up here!" Sparks called out from the fire escape high above them. "Your hour's long up."

The fire escape gave a sickening sway as Nate climbed ladder after ladder, following Brick. How had they made it up, carrying Reed? The old metal creaked as he scurried across a rusted landing.

Brick crawled through a narrow window, and Nate froze on the swaying metal outside. Reed was in there—dying.

What if I'm too late?

"Come on!" She snatched him by his coat and dragged him through the window.

He swayed a moment, eyes adjusting to the dim light. It

smelled like rot and mold. Like sickness. Reed rested on a pile of blankets in the corner, Sparks kneeling beside him. Junk surrounded them—piled as high as the ceiling. Pixel cowered between two stacks of boxes. Tears streaked down her face.

"You said an hour," Sparks said. "It's been three."

Nate scowled at her. "I went as fast as I could."

"Tell that to Reed. He's hardly breathing now."

"I have medicine!"

"He doesn't need medicine. Don't you get it? He's dying." Sparks wasn't the type to cry, but her heavy makeup was smeared below her eyes like bruises.

"Let me try," Nate said. "This isn't . . . Alden paid a lot for it. I think it'll work."

"Reed wouldn't want chem, even now." Brick hovered at the window, watching the path they'd climbed.

"Will you both quit prickling at me and let me concentrate? I need to mix this up—it's like tinkering, and I have to pay attention. Start scouting somewhere for us to go."

Brick straddled the windowsill. "You think we're going to leave him here?"

"None of us can stay long." Nate sank to the blankets beside Sparks. "What do you think's gonna happen when whoever owns this place gets back?"

Sparks's jaw went tight. "They won't take kindly to us getting blood and filth all over."

Nate pointed to the window. "Hurry and see if the bank's clear, and come back and get him. We're running out of time."

"I'm not leaving him," Sparks said.

Nate pulled his hair back in a tight ponytail. "I don't care if you stay. But don't blame me if we all end up nailed by A-Vols for squatting in here when we don't have anywhere else to go."

If he was the type to pray to the Old Gods, he'd do it now. He needed them to go.

Sparks's gaze blackened, and she stood. "This isn't on me. You're the one they were after."

"What would trappers want with a Tinkerer?"

"I don't know!" Sparks scrubbed one eye, leaving a wild streak of makeup jutting to her hairline.

Nagging fear hit Nate like a shadow on a cool day. He shook it off. He had enough to fear right here in front of him, bleeding. If this worked, he'd have plenty of time later to worry over who was looking for him. "Stop fussing at me and go find us somewhere safe to take him."

Sparks lifted her hand like she meant to strike him. He flinched but didn't turn away. Her shoulders slumped, and a hoarse sob snagged in her throat. "Do you really think chem from that sludge-rat friend of yours will save him?" she asked.

"I do." Nate swallowed. "But he won't be all the way better. You have to find somewhere he can stay. Maybe for a long time."

Pixel stifled a whimper.

"Pix, I need you to be brave." Nate flashed her a weak smile and turned back to Sparks and Brick. They'd accept his plan or do as they pleased. He'd have to figure out the consequences of that later.

"I'm with you," Brick said. "But when we're settled and safe, I'm not taking orders from a half-grown kid. Tinkerer or not, you haven't run with Reed as long as I have."

Sparks's fingers and shirt were stained with Reed's blood,

and sweat dampened the curls at her temples. Nate took her hand, feeling the stickiness of dried blood there. "Sparks."

She wrenched her hand out of his grip and climbed onto the windowsill beside Brick. "If he's dead when we get back, you better not be here." She climbed away, her breath noisy with swallowed sobs.

Brick followed after a lingering look at Reed, and Nate closed the window behind her. He flipped the latches to seal it.

"Lock the door," he said.

"Do I have to feed him?" Pixel whispered, trembling. She was even better at keeping secrets than she was at getting what she wanted. And the secret she held close weighed more than she could carry.

More than any child should carry.

"No, Pix. I told you. You're not old enough to do that yet." Nate's fingers twitched into fists. He hated hearing her talk about being a GEM out loud. The longer they could keep it a secret, the better. The thought of anyone using her nauseated him.

"*You're* going to feed him?"

Nate opened the box. The Diffuser whirred inside, its moving parts like a moth's wings. "I have to."

"But it hurts you." She twisted the hem of the tunic that hung down over her spindly legs.

"Reed's hurt worse."

The shape of the Diffuser resembled a flower bulb, rounded on one end and tapered to a forked tip edged with shiny metal. "Sometimes, you have to do something scary for the people you . . . for helping someone."

"Will he find out?"

"I don't think so. I can't fix him all the way, but I think it'll fix him enough that he'll get better, if Sparks keeps watching him. She's better with that kind of thing than she lets on."

Nate watched Reed closely for the first time since Brick had dragged him into the basement. The room tilted. Reed's skin, normally so rich and warm, had gone waxy and gray. His lips were dry, parting with labored, uneven breaths. Other than the gentle furrow of his brow, he didn't seem to be in pain. He barely looked alive.

Forcing himself to look closer, Nate peeled away the cloth pressed to Reed's side and gasped at the sight of the open gash there. Deep-red blood oozed from the uneven tear, raw and meaty and terrible. Nate coughed, gagging. "It'll look better when I'm done, but someone has to sew it up."

Pixel shuddered. "Stop touching it."

"You can't get squeamish on me now. I need your help."

She squared her narrow shoulders. "I can help. I'm not scared."

Nate snorted. "*I'm* scared. It's okay to be scared, but you can't let it freeze you up." He smoothed the makeshift, blood-soaked bandage back onto Reed's skin and shifted down onto his side. Reed's whole body was cold. It sapped the heat from Nate's skin.

"Do you love him?" Pixel asked, watching.

"We all love him."

"But you *love him* love him," she said.

"You're not old enough to understand."

"I'm not a baby. You look chem-struck when he talks to you."

"I don't . . ." Nate sighed.

He did.

It didn't matter. It didn't change anything. "Take the Diffuser out of the box and open the top. There, like that. See? It turns into a mask."

"For him to breathe in the magic?"

"It isn't magic, Pix." Though it might as well have been, for as much as Nate understood it.

"What kind of GEM are you, not believing in magic?" Pixel asked, holding the bowl-shaped opening up to Reed's mouth.

Nate wanted to believe that it was magic. Magic was better than the plain truth.

Years ago, he'd gotten bored when Alden had slept clear through two days. He'd found an instruction manual tucked between bookkeeping he wasn't supposed to be rifling through.

The cover had been ripped off, but the second page said, "Genetically Engineered Medi-tissue Frequently Asked Questions." Many of the dusty pages were stained and missing.

The book described ratios of Cellular Regeneration Formula to body weight, which Nate figured was a fancy way of talking about Remedy. One of the margins contained Alden's incomprehensible shorthand—alongside the page that described how much blood could be diffused from a GEM without serious side effects. The units of measurement didn't make sense to Nate, but he got the gist of it. Feeding others made him tired and weak and hastened his increasing need for Remedy.

He knew exactly what feeding Reed might mean.

Maybe it was his destiny. After all, GEMs were made to die.

Only a fraction of the page about organ harvesting remained in Alden's book. Nate had read it with his blood pounding and his hands shaking. *Consider sedating the GEMs well in advance of the procedure to discourage emotional attachment.*

He'd memorized every word before tucking it back into the place Alden had hidden it, and a seed of resentment began to sprout that day. Alden knew more about who Nate was than he did—than Bernice had, maybe. And he hadn't shown Nate the manual.

One water-stained paragraph stuck with him—a shred of hope for Pixel. GEMs didn't begin to degenerate until age fourteen. She had years.

That had to be enough time for her to find a better way to get Remedy.

Pixel watched him, trusting and calm. His heart lurched. He wanted to tell her that she'd be fine, even if he never got better again after this. Even if he never woke up.

"Maybe it really is magic," he said, indulging her. "Wait— don't hold it to his face yet. It has to be attached to me first." The angle was awkward, but Nate couldn't risk sitting up while Reed fed. Pixel was too small to hold him up once he passed out.

Reaching over, he pushed his sleeve back and guided Pixel's small hand to press the sharp fork of the Diffuser against the inside of his arm. "I've never done this by myself, so help me push."

Alden had always inserted the Diffuser for him, expertly locating the strongest veins in Nate's arm or hand. Without

Alden's guidance, Nate improvised, shoving the forked tips into his flesh and hoping they hooked into a blood source.

Nothing happened on the first thrust but a cold flare of pain. His vision went spotty.

"Ew." Pixel stared at the place where the forks dimpled into Nate's flesh.

Nate eased the forks back out and took a woozy breath to clear his head. "I know. And it doesn't feel so great either. Let's try here," he said, pushing again. This time, as soon as the tips sank in, the Diffuser chamber filled with dark-red blood and the gears inside whirred faster, buzzing like a swarm.

"Wow," Pixel breathed. "Look."

The Diffuser began to process his blood. It shimmered and spread, moving through the glass chamber and flowing out the mask in a pale-pink cloud.

"Hurry," Nate said. "Help me move it to his mouth."

Pixel nibbled at her lip and shivered. She maneuvered Nate's arm and the Diffuser along Reed's chest until the mask rested at Reed's chin. Reed breathed in, the pink cloud flowing between his lips in a wisp and vanishing.

"Hey, it's working." Nate tucked his face against Reed's shoulder. Heaviness and warmth spread through him. Feeding wasn't painful once the fork was in. Alden had explained once, in a litany of energetic rambling while bandaging up Nate's bleeding arm, that GEMs had different hormones. That something inside of them triggered a feeling of calm and sedation when they shared their blood.

"Brilliant," Alden had said, manic and fever-eyed. "Oh, Natey, you're brilliant. I love you."

"Hey," Nate whispered now, moving his tongue slowly to try to form words. "Listen up, Pix, before I fall asleep."

"I'm here." She held the Diffuser steady with one hand while the other stroked Nate's hair out of his eyes.

"When we're done, pull the little sharp bit out and wipe it off and put it away and hide it. Keep it safe. It's Alden's."

"*You* keep it safe."

"And look in my pocket. There's a thing for you. From Reed. Hang on to it. He wants you to have it."

"Let him give it to me, then." Her small, fierce voice cut through the fog in Nate's mind. "When he's better."

He abruptly remembered what else he had to tell her.

Alden had told him to feed Reed for thirty counts, but that wouldn't be enough. He wasn't going to let Alden's greed push him around. And if he gave too much and that got him sicker—or got him dead—well, that'd be worth it. All of this was his fault. He had to fix it.

"Count to one hundred. You can do that, right?" Nate asked slowly. That was the longest amount of time the dusty old manual had recommended. Alden's rules could rot. He was going to give as much as he could—and more if he had to.

"I can do that. Should I do something for your arm?"

"Wrap it up and fix my sleeve to hide it. Tell them I passed out."

"Like when you're sick?"

"Like that, except from the bump on my head, yeah?" Nate blinked slowly and couldn't open his eyes again, and that was all right. He was so tired and warm here, sleeping with Reed.

"He looks better, Nate. He's breathing more. I think it's working."

"Count," Nate mumbled. "You gotta, or . . ."

"One," Pixel said, her voice quiet and thin, as if the sound came from a speaker that needed tinkering. "Two. Three."

Nate went to sleep.

CHAPTER
EIGHT

The first time Nate had fed Alden two years before, he'd wondered if he was falling in love.

The next day, when he finally woke up and the grogginess faded, Alden's sallow skin had warmed and the tight lines around his eyes had smoothed out.

"You look happy," Nate said.

Alden took his hand and kissed it. "I am."

The last time Nate had fed Alden nearly a year later, he'd ached distantly. It was like being stuck in a dream and knowing something was wrong—that he *had* to wake up.

He became aware of someone banging on the shop door, and Fran, wrapped in heavy blankets, using a walking stick to poke Alden's still form. He'd thought, for a lurching moment, that Alden was dead. But it was worse. He was flying, too gone to see that Fran was gaunt with hunger and thirst, that Nate looked like a skeleton, that the shop was in disarray. The last thing Nate remembered was summertime, and now the shop was cold. The furnace lay bare.

When his legs would carry him, he'd left without saying goodbye.

Something heavy pounced on Nate's chest, ripping him away from delightful numbness. His hands stirred and found skinny arms.

"You've been asleep for three days," Pixel said. "You toad! I thought you were killed."

Nate didn't want to open his eyes, but even in the fuzzy tilt of waking up, he knew something was wrong about Pixel being close. The smells around him and the softness beneath him were too familiar to be anywhere but his old pile of cushions on Alden's floor.

"You shouldn't be here." Nate strained against sticky dryness in his throat.

"Why is that?" Alden asked, close by. "Are you insinuating that I'd do something untoward to our very *young* friend?"

"Alden's nice," Pixel said. Her small hands gripped Nate's bare ankle. "He has pretty things."

"Water," Nate croaked. He opened his eyes to slits, but the candlelight pierced him like sunbeams.

Alden wound his arm under Nate's head. He tipped a narrow cup to Nate's lips and filled his mouth with small sips until he could swallow. The water burned at first, but the more Nate drank, the more his head cleared.

Alden helped him finish the water the same way he did every time Nate woke up blurry and sick. "What do you think you were doing letting that boy feed on you for so long? Have you lost your mind, or were you actively trying to kill yourself?"

His voice went thin in a way Nate had never heard before. "I *told* you not to do that."

"Alden." Nate stared at the bluish circles under Alden's eyes.

Alden met his searching look with an icy glare, his mouth pinched with hunger.

He wasn't really concerned. He was only worried about losing his fix.

Then Alden's questions sunk in. "Reed! Did it work? Did it fix him?"

Alden's expression tightened. He said nothing as Pixel crowded Nate's vision, fluttering like a moth.

"He woke up!" Pixel said. "Sparks came to tell us yesterday. After you were done, he was so much better. I told Brick you got tired from running, like when you get sick sometimes. Brick said maybe Alden would take you in 'cause you used to live with him, and Alden didn't mind because he wanted the medicine box back anyway. And I wanted to stay, and Brick said it was okay 'cause Miss Fran's real nice to me. Alden gave Sparks medicine and needles to sew Reed up. You were sleeping for a long time. And you wouldn't drink neither. Oh, Nate, I thought you were killed for sure."

Nate smiled, his lips stinging with dryness. "Reed's okay." That was all he really needed to know.

"Aren't you concerned that Reed and his young associates will question how you managed to restore a dying man?" Alden sat at the edge of the pile of cushions, his hair pulled back in a severe bun.

Pixel rested her cheek on Nate's chest and hugged him

gently. "Nate told them it was fancy chem. Like city medicine. It'll be okay, right, Nate?"

"I'll worry on it later." Nate put his arm around Pixel's back and watched Alden. "You'll be safe, Pix."

Alden rolled his eyes. "It's a wonder any of you sentimental fools have lived this long. You must realize Reed will try to find out how you managed to buy medicine. You're not exactly wealthy."

"Pixel, go on and rest now," Nate said. "I know you've been staying awake, looking after me." There was no sense in scaring her.

"You can sleep at the foot of Miss Fran's bed." A brief, fond smile softened Alden's features. "She thinks I've brought her a granddaughter to dote on."

Pixel burrowed closer but didn't resist when Alden helped her up and guided her through the curtained door to his grandmother's room.

Left alone, Nate drifted, dozing lightly, and woke to find Alden beside him again.

"We have trouble." Alden tucked Nate's hair behind his ear. "Bigger trouble than the mess you got yourself into at the railway."

"Is that a bedtime story to scare me or the truth?" Nate asked.

"What would I accomplish by scaring you? You don't listen to reason." Alden's hands fluttered like distressed birds. "You don't listen to me at all."

"I—"

"Your diminutive friend was correct, Nate. You were half

dead when they brought you here. I couldn't help you. All I could do was wait to see if you'd wake up or drift into the stillness."

"I'll try not to damage what belongs to you again." Nate worked his way onto his elbows.

"Is that what . . . is that really what you think of me?" Alden asked, gripping Nate by the arms and forcing him back into the bedding with a stilted, trembling gentleness.

"I know what I am to you," Nate said.

"Do you?"

Nate was being manipulated, but his skin went rough with goose bumps. Even in his wildest hungers, Alden hadn't looked at him the way he watched Nate now, with longing and impossible sadness.

"What do you want?" He tugged Alden's sleeve, wanting to replace Alden's expression with the indifferent smirks he wore so well.

"That's no matter, is it?"

"Stop making no sense. You told me I don't listen, but you don't say anything that's not some game."

"Maybe I'm not sure I can trust you anymore, Natey." Alden pulled his sleeve out of Nate's grip restlessly. He sat cross-legged on the floor beside Nate's bedding and pressed his fingers against his forehead.

"I'm not in a position to sell you out," Nate said.

"But you might say too much, confide in the wrong person. I've told you time and again that I don't come by Remedy cheaply. I'm told they were looking for you, for the Tinkerer."

He exhaled noisily. "If you get caught, guess who they'll be looking for next?"

Nate frowned. Alden never let anyone push him around. He fed A-Vols credits and chem and sent them on their way. Something—someone—else worried him.

"Exactly," Alden said, studying Nate's face. "It will be my lovely neck on the line."

"So you're only looking out for yourself."

Alden stared a moment and then laughed once, sharply. "You're starting to learn, sweetness. That's good."

"You can trust me," Nate said. "Tell me what's going on."

"Other than my dearest friend feeding his very life to a street thief?"

Nate checked a flinch and waited, refusing to respond to the bait. They'd never called each other friends. They'd never called each other anything.

Alden, for once, turned away. "There's a problem with Remedy," he said.

Everything went gray. "What?"

"My supplier hasn't shown up, and I can't track her down. The last batch I've got . . . I don't know." Alden never sounded this unsure—scattered. "I'm trying to stretch it, but it's not lasting long."

"You weren't worried few days ago."

"You weren't *dying* a few days ago. I thought we had more time. I didn't think you'd be at the shop this much. I didn't know you'd throw your life away for your gang—despite being clearly warned not to feed for too long. "

"I'm not dying," Nate said, hollowed out by Alden's words.

"How would you know one way or another?" Alden asked, clipped and too loud. "You've been sleeping the days away. And I *told you* you can't be here so often."

Alden had told him all along, from the very first time Nate had shown back up at the shop, that he needed to be careful. That Alden wasn't made of Remedy. It had always seemed like Alden's way of making him suffer for leaving. For the past year, every one of their interactions had been too thick with shame and anger and fear to untangle the real meaning of a threat.

"I didn't mean for any of this to happen. I couldn't watch Reed die when there was a way to help him."

Alden's black eyes pierced him. "Do you love him?"

"Reed?" Nate blinked, thrown off. "I told you, we're not—"

"Fucking. Yes, you did mention that. Call me a romantic, but I didn't know that was a prerequisite for loving somebody."

"What do you know about love, Alden?"

A huff of breath shook Alden's narrow shoulders. He shot Nate a rueful, ugly smile. "It's a simple question."

The room had darkened as the candles began to sputter and die out around them. "Why do you care?"

"I told you, Natey. I'm a romantic."

Nate rolled onto his side with a groan, his body aching from being still too long. "You're a lunatic, is what you are."

"The little girl says you love him," Alden said.

"Pixel." She wasn't as good at keeping secrets as Nate thought.

"We had a lot of time to chat while you were off in dreamland."

What kinds of things could Alden possibly talk about with

Pixel? He never left the shop. He spent his clear-eyed time working endless figures and counting his inventory. When he was soft and sleepy with chem, he sat in Fran's bed and listened to her stories, never flinching when she called him the wrong name. He didn't know anything about children.

Nate couldn't imagine Alden ever having been a child at all. "She's a little kid. She believes in magic and—"

"Hope?" Alden lips quirked.

Nate nodded, unsettled by the look in Alden's eyes.

"Hope's a fragile thing in this world," Alden said. "Her happy ending is still out there, somewhere. The rest of us, well . . ."

"Very poetic, Alden."

Alden watched him, letting the silence drag. Another candle sputtered out, rattling with its last breath. "You could have said that you don't love him, but you didn't."

"Then I guess you have your answer," Nate said, tired. His stomach rumbled, but his limbs were heavy, and eating sounded like too much work. "It isn't important."

"Who's to say what's really important?"

"Running out of Remedy is important." He didn't want to fight with Alden anymore. He didn't want to fight with anyone. "To both of us."

Alden rolled his eyes, but his fingers were gentle as they combed through Nate's hair. "That's what I've been trying to say. I'll keep my ear to the ground, so to speak, and you . . . well, be careful."

"That's our plan? *Be careful*?"

"*Our plan*?" Alden gave a cold smile. "You'll have to come

up with your own plan. *My* plan is to keep the Breakers off my doorstep. They don't take to competition."

Nate's bones ached. He couldn't shake the sense that he was missing something. *Why won't he tell me the truth?*

Alden collected the burned-out candles, tossing them one at a time into the basket where he kept misshaped stumps to melt them down. With his back to Nate, he murmured, "There's nothing I can do for you."

Brick arrived at Alden's shop the next day. She lingered in the front room, peering into containers full of stinky incense. When Nate walked through the curtain door, he startled her, and she nearly toppled a glass jar off the shelf. Nate squinted in the glaring light. Alden had kept him in a windowless room far in the back, where guests weren't allowed.

"Reed thought maybe you would need help walking," she said. "I told him there was no way I was carting your skinny ass across the Withers again, and he said to come check on you anyway."

Nate could never tell when she was joking and when she wasn't. She had a naturally pleasant face, creased with laugh lines and sunspots, but she always managed to twist it up into a frown.

Brick shot Alden a caustic look. Alden hadn't killed Brick's little brother with his own hands, but he'd been part of the strung-out days and nights that ended with July's body in an alley.

Alden didn't look away.

"I don't need carrying." Nate hurt, but he could walk fine. Alden was worse off, hungering fiercely behind the counter and glaring at Brick.

Nate was far too weak to let Alden feed, even after a small dose of Remedy. Alden's hunger lingered in every darting look, every sharp breath and unsettled step around the shop.

Fran came through the curtain from her room in the back. "My first lover was a ginger," she said. "Fiery thing like you. Orange and pink in his intimate areas, oh, like a sunset."

Brick's skin went about as red as her hair.

Pixel had spent the morning playing with Fran's jewelry box. She darted through the curtain with several strings of glass beads around her neck. "Brick! Alden has the best things."

Brick crossed her arms. "I bet he does."

Nate scurried to get the necklaces off of her. "Let's get moving, Pix. Aren't you excited to see our new hideout?"

"Should you be saying that in front of him?" Brick gestured at Alden.

"Don't trust me? I'm terribly wounded," Alden murmured, ushering his grandmother out of the room.

"It's fine. He doesn't know where it is." Nate dropped one necklace after another on the counter. The beads clicked and rolled against the glass.

"Keep the purple one, little Pixel princess," Alden said as he came back. He grabbed a penknife off the counter and tapped it against the glass rapidly. "It suits you."

"Really?" Pixel asked, snatching it away from Nate as if expecting him to protest. She pulled it on and smiled, weaving her fingers around the shiny beads.

"Stick that thing under your shirt, or you won't make it a block without losing it," Brick said.

Nate helped Pixel get it hidden. Alden's generosity unsettled him. He'd never seen Alden give anything away for free, but there was something oddly genuine about his affection for Pixel. "Thank you, Alden. I'll pay you back for it."

Alden smiled too sweetly. "I'm certain you will."

CHAPTER
NINE

Nate panted as he followed Brick up the dark stairwell to the room Reed and the gang had taken over in the bank. He squeezed Pixel's hand—more for his own comfort than hers. "This building is too tall."

"Better up here than in another basement." Brick lit the way with a crank-light. She stepped around a pile of fallen plaster and dodged a sticky pile of sewage. "Mostly."

It was impossible to get away from the stink of the Withers. In the summer, waste-trenches in the alleys steamed until the air thickened with rot. In the winter, the smoky-sour scent of burning garbage clung to everything.

A handful of kids, street-dirty and thin, passed them on the stairwell. They carried bags full of garbage coated with sludge. Pixel's fingers twitched. That'd be her fate, if she were alone. Dodging trappers every day and twisting trash into makeshift sticks of kindling to sell at the market.

At the next landing, the kids gathered around two Servants in long robes. The Servants handed them rolls of gray bread and jugs of water. Nate and Brick hung back in the shadows as Pixel darted over with the other children and accepted a roll.

"Gods watch you," one of the Servants called to Brick and Nate, her voice as gentle as a lullaby.

Startled by a wave of sadness, Nate took off up the stairs.

"What spooked you?" Brick asked as she caught up to him with Pixel.

Nate shrugged. He couldn't explain the hollowness in his chest. When he reached the bend in the stairs, he looked back, feeling foolish. The Servants were already out of sight.

"How do you get to be a Servant?" Pixel asked with a mouth full of bread.

"Who knows?" Brick huffed. "They pick who they want."

"People who have magic?" Her eyes darted to Nate, and he shook his head tightly.

"People who have a strong stomach. There's no magic here," Brick said, gesturing at the crumbling walls and the sticky garbage on the stairs. She guided them through the hole in the wall that led from the stairwell to Reed's new hideout.

Nate stumbled, surprised by the muggy wind blasting through the room. He caught sight of the dizzying view and sank to an unsteady crouch.

"Why . . . why is there no wall?" he asked, trying not to look. The hole where a wall should have been was ragged and scorch-marked—the scar of an old fire.

"Doesn't matter." Brick helped him to his feet and nudged him toward the solid interior wall.

"No wonder nobody claimed this place." He leaned against the wall and closed his eyes until the dizziness passed.

"Everyone knows to stay well enough away from the edge, and we're safer high up," Brick said. "Trappers aren't welcome here, and the A-Holes aren't stupid enough to come up this high."

"How high are we?" Nate had lost count as they climbed. Brick smirked. "Eighteen flights."

He dared a look at the gaping hole. That explained the distant gleam of Gathos City's silver towers.

"You scared?" Pixel asked, pressed tight against his leg like she needed to hold him up.

"A little." Nate took shuffling steps after Brick. He stayed close to the interior wall. Climbing a pole twenty feet high was one thing. The view sent swooping waves of fear through him. People weren't supposed to be this high up.

It wasn't going to be fun getting a decent alarm system up. But that was the first thing he needed to do. They'd have to construct a door or set up trip wires, and he'd have to get up into the walls to find live wires. Whatever he had to do, it would be worth it to make sure the new hideout was safe.

He was never going to let anyone get hurt because of him again.

Reed ducked his head out from a bunk built with pieces of old desks. His hand rested gingerly over the bandage at his belly. "Nate."

Nate lit up inside, like he'd set a tangle of wires singing with electricity. He'd tried to keep his mind off Reed. Otherwise, he would have obsessed—wondering how he was healing, what he was doing. Now his fears and relief jumbled together senselessly. He stumbled and slapped his palm against the wall for balance, certain he'd float out into the whistling wind.

He wanted to blame this foolishness on having fed Reed,

but it was more than that. Being close to him again made Nate's bones feel like they'd settled back into the right places.

Reed reached a hand out. "Sit down. You look green."

"I missed the move." Nate gestured around the room vaguely before taking Reed's hand to sit on the bed beside him. The thin mattress creaked. His legs trembled.

"I missed most of it too," Reed said, barely audible over the hum of the wind. "Brick, take Pix to Sparks's bunk."

As Brick led Pixel away, Nate's stomach sank faster than it had when he'd seen the sickening view. Reed didn't shoo the others away unless he had something serious to say. In a gang as tight as theirs, it was better to keep everything out in the open.

"Pixel said you got sick and passed out."

"I guess I'm no good with blood." Nate forced a weak grin, gaze caught on the pink stain on Reed's bandage. He dug his trembling fingers into his pocket, heart skipping a beat until his callused fingers found the delicate chain knotted up around the small pendant. "Here," he said. "You found it for her. You give it to her."

Reed's eyes widened. He slipped the pendant under his blanket. "Thank you."

"Thought I sold it?" Nate asked, lips pressed together in a flat smile he didn't feel.

"No. I . . ." Reed shook his head. "They said you saved me with chem—medicine—from Alden."

"I did. Are you mad?"

"Of course I'm not mad you saved my life, Nate." Reed exhaled a sigh. "I'm sorry I put you in that position."

"You didn't get yourself stabbed for fun."

And it was my fault.

Reed's bare shoulders twitched. "How did you pay for the medicine?"

"Alden still owed me," Nate said, sharp and frustrated. He didn't want to talk. He wanted to take Reed's hand and feel the thrum of his pulse.

"You tinkered for him that much? Enough to save a life?"

"You don't believe me?" It was easier to push back than admit he was probably dying, and he'd made it worse by helping Reed. Nate looked around the room, willing the conversation to end. If they wanted the hideout set up, everyone needed to leave him be and let him tinker while he still could.

"But there's more to it than that, isn't there?" Reed watched Nate closely, his pale eyes glittering.

Nate exhaled hard and pushed a strand of hair behind his ear. "It's complicated with me and Alden."

Reed frowned. "How complicated? If you're . . . if you're still with him, Nate, you know I'd pay that no mind."

Nate coughed out a laugh before he could stop himself. "I was never *with him*."

"You can't blame me for thinking it," Reed said. "I've seen how he looks at you, like you're a heap of food. And you're there often enough."

Another hysterical, tired laugh bubbled out of Nate. He was unraveling from the bones out. "I'm sorry," he said, breathless.

I'm scared.

"If you keep secrets from me, I can't keep you on," Reed said.

Nate studied his callused hands. Reed only meant well

for the others. He was being reasonable. Any sane man would take one look at Nate's half-crazed, stifled laughter and send him packing.

But it hurt. He was trying so hard, and nothing was going right, and he was getting dangerously close to giving up—something no one in the Withers could afford to do. That was the path to the stillness.

He would be no good to any of them after that.

Nate's eyes heated, and he closed them tightly, fighting the swell of emotion that threatened to crumble him in front of Reed and the others. "He doesn't give me chem, Reed," he choked out. That, at least, was the truth. "I wish you'd believe me. I'm not—" His voice broke. He wasn't a fiend. But what difference did it make?

"Nate." Reed leaned into him, skin warm and soft. He pulled Nate's face to his shoulder. "It's been a hard few days for all of us."

Nate muffled a sob against Reed's warm shirt. "I'm trying." He was trying harder than Reed would ever know. He shook, struggling not to pour snot and tears all over Reed.

Reed had never held him like this before, arms strong and certain—warm hand stroking his back. Nate didn't want to let go. But he lifted his face, wiped his eyes, and showed Reed that he could smile without any more blubbering. This wasn't about affection. It was necessity. Each one of them had broken down crying at one time or another.

"You need a meal." Reed dragged his thumb across Nate's cheek. "We saved most of the food, and Brick got the stove set up. There's stew on."

"I need—" Nate choked to a halt. His face heated where Reed's thumb skimmed away tears. Vicious loneliness tore at his insides.

Is this what Alden's hunger feels like?

Reed gave him a long look and held very still, as if lashed down by the thread of distrust woven between them.

"Stew, it is, boss," Nate said, forcing a smile. He stood. "You can . . . I'll start going through what we brought over and see if I can't get a few trip wires hooked up to a siren before night falls."

"Pixel's organized your things. Have her help you," Reed said. "There's not much else to keep her busy here."

Nate followed the smell of meat to the little cook pot in the corner. He couldn't stop thinking about the tightness around Reed's eyes—wariness he couldn't blame on Reed's wound.

That night, the wind grew cold, and they huddled around the stove to share a bowl of thin stew. The crank-light cast long shadows.

"I walked around the rest of the floor, made sure everyone knows we're no threat to their spaces," Reed said. "No one's fond of the Breakers up here."

Brick passed the bowl to Pixel. "Surprised anyone said that right out."

"I'm not." Sparks laughed. "Reed might as well be a Servant for the way folks take to him."

Reed ducked his chin, a shy grin dimpling one cheek. He was good at a lot of things, but taking compliments gracefully wasn't one of them.

Nate shivered from more than the chill. Sparks nudged him with the stew bowl, and he took his turn, determined to quit staring at Reed's mouth.

"More kids than I expected 'round here," Sparks said. She caught Pixel's eyes lighting up and smiled. "I'll take you with me down a couple of floors where they're teaching letters tomorrow."

Nate touched his boot against Pixel's. "Only if she helps me finish the ductwork in the morning. We've almost got it, right, Pix?"

They each took only a few bites, saving the most for Pixel, who finished it without complaining about the bitter taste and chewy dried meat. For the first time since Reed had gotten hurt, it felt like family again.

Sparks took the empty bowl from Pixel and wiped it clean. She glanced up at Nate. "I found a bunch of rubble down the hall. If Brick'll haul it for me, we'll build a little wall for you."

"Yeah." Brick snorted. "So you can get from one side of the room to the other without crawling like a bug."

Nate's legs were still weak from getting close enough to the edge to smell the rancid latrines one floor below. He ducked his head, eyes gone hot with a startling rush of relief. "Thank you."

———

Once Sparks and Brick got the wall up, Nate's heart stopped jumping around behind his ribs every time he stood up. He spent days rewiring the electricity in the narrow crawlspace.

"Think you can fit in there?" he asked Pixel, aiming a crank-light at the ragged tear in the ceiling.

"Better than you can!"

He gave her a leg up, and she scrambled into the duct without a look back. "Stay on this side." Nerves gnawed at his bones. He didn't like the thought of her making her way near the edge.

Her small hand darted out from another hole in the duct, two frayed wires tight in her grip. "Found some more torn-up ones."

Nate handed her the pliers, and she twisted them together and crimped the edges without checking with him first.

Reed walked up, bumping his side gently. "She's really learning."

"I didn't teach her that. It comes naturally to her." He tracked her progress by the fall of dust from the ceiling, occasionally calling up to check on her. She was quick and sure, only answering when she needed a bit of wire or sticky rubber remnants. "She'll replace me in no time," he said with a soft laugh.

He glanced aside and caught Reed giving him a strange look.

Just after nightfall, the room's solitary light fixture flickered to life, bathing them in a pale glow. It wasn't much brighter than moonlight, but even Brick burst into quiet applause. Pixel climbed out of the ductwork, jumping down into Sparks's arms. She shook dust of out her hair and grinned like she could power a thousand lights.

As the others celebrated, telling quiet stories in the light, Nate curled up in his bunk. Sleep refused to come. The alarm system wasn't enough. He needed more trip wires and a better lock once they scavenged or traded for a decent door.

It wasn't like Alden would know where he was or send someone after him, but Nate couldn't stop thinking about the promise he'd made. Alden would surely expect to be fed by now—or soon. Even if there was a problem with the Remedy supply.

Nate couldn't bring himself to find an excuse to go. Not until he had to.

He couldn't bear the thought of Reed questioning him.

For now, there was no reason for him to leave the bank. The neighborhood was crammed full of crowded residences. They wouldn't find anything to scavenge without breaking their rule: never lift from people's homes.

———————

Once Reed declared himself well enough for a night out scavenging, Nate sketched crude pictures of the tech he'd need to put together a battery to keep their basic trip-wire security running.

"We have to hoard power for the night," he said, tracing the edges with a charcoal twig.

"Is that a cat?" Brick asked.

Sparks shook her head. "It's a star driving a ship. Right?"

Nate frowned and traced the lines again. "No. Look. The circuits go this way. I can't do the colors right, but they're—"

Reed covered his hand, pinning it to the ground. A silent laugh shook his shoulders. "They're playing with you, Nate. It's clear enough."

Nate jerked his hand away and flung the twig against the wall. It splintered and fell in pieces. "It's serious! You need to find this. You need to find it soon!"

Reed stared at him. "All right. We'll find it tonight."

The girls looked at each other, stifling laughter. He couldn't blame them. Here he was, acting like a prickly batch of explosives.

When they left, Nate went to his bunk and rubbed his forehead with his rough fingers.

"Teach me how a double switch works," Pixel said, crouching in front of him. She held a new rag doll—a scrap of blanket with hair made of wire.

"Not right now."

"Why? You're not resting." Her lips pulled into a scowl, and when he realized she was mimicking him, a tired laugh escaped his chest.

"All right. Get Sparks's tweezers and help me get these stitches out of my head."

Pixel's fingers were gentle and sure, and she babbled softly while she worked. Each thread tugged eerily in his flesh, but it didn't hurt.

He tuned her out, too unsettled to focus.

The stitches made him think about Alden. He should have pressed for answers. *A problem with Remedy.* What did that really mean?

He wouldn't have to wait long to find out.

———

By the end of the week, his head spun every time he stood up. He tried to focus on his tinkering and not the way his body weakened like a fraying wire.

Satisfied with the security system and lights, he set to work on the ticker system. He crammed into a gap in the interior wall, trying to find the old information system cables that transmitted to anyone with a ticker and a live wire.

Transmissions came from all over—official notices and alerts from Gathos City, gossip and serialized stories from locals broadcasting with salvaged equipment. A few dogged broadcasters gave regular reports on incoming food deliveries from Gathos City and pockets of violence within the Withers. And once in a while, the Breakers put out recruitment calls, promising anyone clever and quick a better job than the workhouses could offer.

Nate didn't care about any of that. The gang needed a working ticker so Reed could gauge the relative safety of scavenging on any given night.

It took Nate an hour, but he finally found the cable and gathered enough slack to lower it down the wall to the ticker they'd set up on a rickety shelf. He climbed out of the space and took an uneven step, breathing hard and sneezing from the loose plaster and mildewed insulation in the wall.

He sat cross-legged on the floor and carefully connected the ticker to the wire. It flared to life in his hands. Words scrolled by, almost too fast for him to read.

Reward for GEMs. Safety guaranteed.

"You ought to go rinse off before you finish that up," Reed said at his shoulder.

Startled, Nate dropped the ticker to the ground. He grimaced at the fine dusting of pale pink all over his skin and clothes. "You're right," he said, scratching his itchy neck. "Next time, I'm wearing something over my face. I think I breathed in a decade of dust."

"I'll go with you," Reed said. "Sparks says I'm clear to get this mess clean with water, instead of getting wiped down like a babe." He grabbed a bath sheet from the corner of his bunk and pushed his bare feet into his boots.

They took a slow pace up the stairwell. It smelled like dirt and piss.

Reed walked with a hitch, more careful than pained now that he'd healed up decently. Nate, sneezing and breaking into short fits of coughing, lagged behind.

"There's a family up near the roof growing a few pots of herbs," Reed said when Nate stopped and held the rail to catch his breath. "Sparks saw it. I don't know how they manage it."

"Seeds are hard to come by. But you can grow in water and gravel, if you know what you're doing." Bernice had kept a little herb garden on her windowsill. The leaves had been weak and pale, but they'd tasted better than anything her food vouchers were good for.

"You should see if there's something that could clear that cough up," Reed said.

Nate recalled being ill once as a child, and the rancid taste of bottled cough medicine. With the memory came a brief rush of images—his mother's expansive greenhouse full of dark-green vines, a fountain that gurgled clear water, a window stretching from floor to ceiling, and the silver pillars of Gathos City crowding the view.

"Did you ever live anywhere but here?" he asked, dazed by the sharp memory.

"Are you trying to change the subject?"

"I'd have better tactics if I meant to do that," Nate said with a faint smile, climbing the stairs again. It seemed like ages ago that he'd brought home peaches to make Reed smile.

Reed walked beside him, staying close. "I've always lived on this end of the island. When I left my mother, I didn't go far."

Nate wasn't sure if Reed meant *far* as in distance or *far* as in trade. The idea of Reed prostituting himself as his mother had was too foreign, too impossible to consider. Unsettled by the ugly thought, Nate slipped his hand into Reed's.

Reed stilled for a breath and kept walking, squeezing Nate's hand. "I can tell you've been all over the Withers," he said. "The way you talk, there's something different about you."

The sound of running water and laughter washed down the stairwell as a door opened and slammed shut the floor above them. Reed stopped walking and shifted to face Nate, standing a stair below so that they were almost eye-to-eye.

"Must be from my aunt," Nate said. "She raised me. She came here from Gathos City before they closed the gates."

"I bet she had good stories." Reed let go of Nate's hand to reach past his ear and loosen the tie that held Nate's hair out of his face. It swept forward, sticky against his face.

"Now *you're* trying to distract *me*," Nate said, shaky, caught in the snap of goose bumps along his skin. He leaned into the brush of Reed's fingers.

"I wish I could," Reed said. He closed his eyes and pressed his lips to Nate's.

Nate froze, struck still by the tenderness of it. Reed's knuckles brushed against his ribs with a halting touch that tickled.

It was so chaste and honest and careful.

And Nate was going to sneeze.

"Reed." Nate caught his wrists and stilled him.

Reed drew away, searching Nate's face with a worried gaze. Before Nate could explain, he doubled over and sneezed into his elbow.

"I'm itchy and gross." Nate sidestepped Reed with a thin laugh. He wanted nothing but more kisses. *Wanted*. He shook with it, feverish inside. "Let me get clean."

Reed continued climbing the stairs as if nothing terrifying had happened, but his voice was hoarse when he asked, "Any soap up there?"

"Not that I've seen," Nate said, grateful for another sneeze that hid his stutter.

What would happen after he took a shower? More kissing? He'd have to tell Reed to stop, eventually. That this wasn't right—not when Reed didn't trust him, and he didn't deserve Reed's trust.

But he wanted to try it again. As soon as possible.

When he wasn't stinging all over from insulation dust.

"Why did you do that?" He couldn't stop himself from asking. From needing to know. "You made me stop before."

"Because you didn't know what you were doing. You were bleeding, you were—"

"I know what I want!" Shocked by his own outburst, Nate

lowered his voice. "I knew what I was doing. It wasn't the first time I wanted to kiss you."

Reed went still at the door to the next floor. He leaned back against it, letting it catch his weight, and placed his hand at his side. "I know what I want too," he said very softly.

With Reed close and quiet, Nate was struck by the vivid green of his eyes. And the exhaustion in them. A tender ache formed at the flat of his belly, and he didn't know how to ease it. But he knew he wanted to take Reed's hand and hold it.

"I'm sorry," he whispered, not sure if it was for lying to him or for needing him.

A crease of hurt formed around Reed's pretty eyes. He recovered with a faint, tired smile. "Wishes," he said. "You first."

Hating the small, prickly space between them, Nate brushed his knuckles against Reed's hand. He gasped when Reed clasped their fingers together. "A hot bath. Big enough to dunk my whole body in."

"New boots that don't pinch." Reed's thumb brushed over the back of Nate's hand.

Nate tried to remember how to talk. "Sausages. With city meat—not gull."

"You are always thinking about food," Reed said with a soft grin. They were close enough to kiss again, but it was an easy closeness. "Let's go."

Their hands unclasped. Everyone in the Withers was careful about showing affection in front of others. If people knew who you cared about, they'd have a way to control you.

Reed lingered, close enough for Nate to feel his breath stir Nate's hair. "Come on," he said reluctantly, pushing the door open to reveal the men's showers. The lines between men and women weren't drawn too firmly in the bank—or anywhere else in the Withers—but Nate didn't see any women or children. He wondered briefly if Sparks had any trouble at the women's showers the next room over and figured she must be okay if she hadn't said anything.

"Come on." Nate's heart still beat too fast, thumping against his ribs. "Your turn. More wishes."

They took their places in line for the three showers, boots squelching in the standing water on the concrete floor. The showers were faucets rigged to the rain barrels on the roof, with very little pressure and no heat. Each man hung his clothes on a wire rack and scrubbed down quickly in the frigid water.

"Real soap," Reed said. "The kind my mom used to have. It smelled like flowers."

"That'd be a welcome change," Nate said.

Reed turned, grinning, and punched Nate's shoulder. "I wouldn't call your natural aroma pleasant either."

"What? I'm very pleasant." Nate wiped his nose again and pretended to smell his own armpit. In truth, he smelled pretty bad and looked forward to the shower, cold or not.

"Wishes," Reed reminded him in a whisper, shuffling forward as the line moved. They were at the end of the line. The others waited silently, shoulders tense and elbows out. Nate tried to imagine being there without Reed and shivered. He'd rather stink for days than brave taking his boots off without someone else to guard them.

"Wishes . . ." he repeated, touching his lips absently. What had Reed's kiss meant? What did Reed really want?

It didn't make any sense. Nate was a problem—sick, untrustworthy, and too loyal to a chem pusher. He'd almost gotten all of them killed.

"Fine, I'll wish for you." Reed patted Nate's back, the simple touch jolting heat through Nate. "New tools. A better pair of gloves. Yours have holes in half the fingers."

"That's two, and you're cheating."

"I can go on. A new blanket. Shiny filament tech nonsense that does something interesting and very electrical. I can tell you're trying, Nate."

The words slipped out too fast, like Reed was afraid Nate would hear them.

Nate's mouth went dry. It was his turn to change the subject. "Kiwi."

Reed blinked. "What's kiwi?"

The man in front of them started his shower in a hurry and shot Reed and Nate a sour look.

"Not for me, for you," Nate said, lowering his voice and trying not to grin. He hadn't felt like this in as long as he could remember—electric with hope, lit up by Reed's quiet faith in him, by the touch that still warmed his back. He didn't care if they were talking too loud in a room where people rushed in and out, eager to be safe wherever they spent their time hiding. For this moment, he wasn't afraid to be trusted. "It's a fruit. Another furry one, like peaches, but . . . sharp. It makes it feel like your tongue is going to stick to the inside of your mouth."

"You've had one?"

"When I was little."

It was Reed's turn at the shower. He began to undress and winced as he leaned over.

Nate took his arm and urged him to stand up straight. He glanced over his shoulder. They were alone now. "I'll get it," he said, crouching to help Reed out of his pants and boots. He flushed, his knuckles skimming through the hair at Reed's calves where the muscles were wiry and his skin, warm. "Your turn."

Heat seared up his back and pooled in his belly, dizzying him.

"Am I wishing for you or for me?" Reed held on to Nate's shoulder for balance and stepped out of each leg of his pants. His brow furrowed.

Careful not to let Reed's clothes get into the water on the floor, Nate stood and clutched them to his middle. "For you," he said.

The water splashed down on Reed's head and shoulders. He yelped and started laughing, his body tense and twitching. "Hot tea and a big, fuzzy blanket," he said, teeth chattering.

"That's two again. You're terrible at this."

"I have a lot of wishes," Reed said. The water clumped his eyelashes together as he watched Nate. It made his eyes gleam like he was sad and happy all at once.

Nate handed him the bath sheet and turned away politely—and reluctantly. Reed dried himself off with one end of it, leaving the other draped over his arm and dry for Nate.

"Thanks," Nate said, gesturing at the sheet. He undressed in a hurry, already chilly before hitting the water and grateful for the way the cold settled his eager body down. A cough burst out of him, and he doubled over, willing it not to become the type of cough that went on and on until he saw spots.

Reed grabbed his arm to steady him. The grip tightened painfully.

"Ow!" Nate gasped and looked up at Reed, shocked by the sting and the iciness in Reed's eyes. "What?"

"Your arm," Reed said. His thumb rested at the edge of the marks and bruises where the Diffuser had pierced him.

How could he have forgotten? His insides went hollow, every wish shattering. He placed his other hand over Reed's as if he could will him to unsee it, to believe in him again. "Reed, it's not—"

But Reed was already throwing him off with a disgusted growl. He dressed quickly, shaking with the kind of anger Nate had only seen in him once, when he'd turned a young man away from the gang. The kid's arms had been like Nate's all over, ravaged by crude syringes.

"Let me help you," Nate said, shivering. He hurried to wash the dust out of his hair. "Wait a second, Reed, and I'll help you get dressed. You shouldn't be bending down too much!"

Reed grabbed his boots and walked away without looking back. Only the bath sheet remained, half wet and half dry, hanging on the rack beside Nate's clothes.

Nate followed Reed's wet footprints back down the stairwell, wanting to run but afraid to catch up. He knew what was coming. The hurt of it numbed his cold fingers.

Reed met him at the entrance to the hideout, his hair still

damp and gleaming. "I can't make exceptions. Not even for *you*," he said, putting a strange emphasis on the last word.

"I told you. It's not what it looks like," Nate said, the words barely escaping the tightness in his throat.

"I've heard every excuse. Every single one. You have to know that, Nate."

Reed's eyes shone.

Stopped short, Nate choked on all the things he couldn't say. Unless he explained what he was, Reed would never believe him. Fiends lied and thieved and crossed their friends and lovers. Chem warped the mind, and hunger trumped all else. Nate had seen this, day in and day out, when he'd been with Alden. Anything he said would come across as a desperate attempt to stay with the gang.

He *was* desperate to stay, but not desperate enough to force them to choose between cashing in on the Breakers' offers or hiding him from those who would.

Reed let out a ragged breath, his posture softening. "Shake it off, clean up, and you can come back. You'll always have a place here."

"But you'll never trust me again, will you?" Nate swayed, and Reed steadied him.

"Don't ask me that. You have no right." Reed shook his head. "What you've been doing puts us all in danger."

It was truer than Reed knew, but not in the ways he imagined. Nate would never steal from them or allow anyone to come into the den. He'd never push chem on the others. He'd never give them away.

But what he was put them at risk. If the Breakers found out Nate was a GEM, they'd go after all of them for hiding him.

If he left quietly and they never knew, Pixel would be safe for now, too young to need Remedy. As long as she stayed clear of the Breakers, she had a good six or seven years before she had to keep the sick away. The gates might be open by then. Remedy might flow freely between the city and the Withers.

"Are you listening to me?" Reed asked, propping Nate up against the wall.

"I'm sorry." Nate choked, undone by the gentleness Reed showed him, even now. "I'll get my things. If you give me—give me an hour. I'll draw out how to run the security panel. Maybe Pixel can give it a try until you find a Tinkerer."

"Don't." Reed sighed sharply. "Don't talk like you're not coming back. I know you, Nate. You're not a waste. Clear your head and come back. Don't disappear."

They both knew what that meant. Those who got too deep in chem stopped eating or sleeping. They got mixed up with the wrong pushers and got killed, or took too much and shook apart and died.

"You don't understand," Nate said, rough with frustration. "That's rot, and you know it."

"I—"

"Brick likes you," Reed said, "and she owes you a debt for helping us find July. She'll take you back if you're off that stuff. I can ask Sparks if she'll squat with you, clean you up."

Reed's kindness became too much. His bright hope kindled an ugly fire in Nate. It was too late. They couldn't have this.

They'd never be close. And Nate couldn't stand imagining an impossible life together.

Nate pushed Reed before he knew what he was doing, startling Reed back a few steps with more surprise than force.

He couldn't stand seeing now, when it was too late, that Reed cared.

He'd kissed him.

And he'd never do it again.

"You can't fix everyone!" Nate shouted. "Gods, Reed. Let me go."

He staggered around Reed and headed for his bunk. The room was too quiet in the echo of his outburst, and when his breath broke into a sob, he wanted to fold in on himself until he disappeared.

His bunk contained only the blanket that had softened his sleep space in the old den. He tucked it into the backpack he rarely used and gathered up his tools, careful to leave anything the gang might use. Sparks climbed out of her bed and watched, eyes wide. She might have helped if he hadn't shouted at Reed.

Pixel's shrill, small voice filled the room. "No! You can't toss him out! He can't—Nate! Nate, tell him you can't go."

Reed caught her at the door on her way back from the showers with Brick. She began to cry, hiccupping and struggling as Reed and Brick held on to her, both of them trying to calm her down. After landing an elbow at Reed's groin, she broke free and dashed across the room to launch herself onto Nate's back. He twisted and caught her up in a fierce hug. She made him solid for a moment.

"You know I'll be fine," Nate said, speaking quietly at her ear, his words only for her. "I have somewhere to go, and you know it isn't what Reed thinks. I'll find a way to see you, Pix. Don't tell. It'll be all right."

He met Reed's eye across the room and understood in an instant the pain that made Reed stand rigid and cold. Reed had the same fuel in him, the same desire to shelter those he loved from the pain in the world. Nate had shouted at Reed for trying to save him, yet here he was, ready to promise the moon to Pixel. What right did he have to say things would be all right?

No wonder Alden had laughed at him.

"I don't want you to go," Pixel sobbed out against Nate's shoulder.

"I know, Pix. I know you don't."

She grasped at him like she was drowning, and it took Sparks and Reed both to pry her away. Nate's hand brushed against Reed's as they managed to get Pixel into Brick's arms and under a heavy blanket.

He caught Reed's gaze and said, "I'll try."

It wasn't the kind of hope he should give Reed, but he couldn't leave with Reed thinking he was so far gone that he'd walk away from the gang without a fight.

Reed didn't smile, but relief shone in his eyes. "I would walk you out, but I've got to get Pix settled before she makes herself sick."

"You sure you don't want instructions for the system?"

Sparks rolled her eyes. "You draw like a toddler, Nate. Pixel can handle it."

"Didn't you learn anything from July? I thought you were better than this." Brick rocked Pixel and glared at him.

"I'll have to do right by you, then." Nate wished it were that simple.

But chem fiends were sunk so deep in their hungers that the chem was part of who they were, as unchangeable as the blood in Nate's veins.

Nothing was ever simple.

With his backpack weighing at his shoulders, Nate made his way to the door, his breath uneven with unshed tears. He paused, turning back to Reed to get the code word out of habit. Seeming to know, Reed crossed to him and pulled him into a loose hug.

Nate ducked out of the embrace. "I can't," he said, hoarse.

Reed stared at him. "Walk well, Nate. Please."

CHAPTER
TEN

R ed smog-clouds bled on the horizon at sunset. Flickering bin-fires lit the street, and the warm glow hid the grime of the Withers. Bruises and sickness faded in the firelight.

Pleasure peddlers and chem pushers sold their wares in the shadows. Keeping his chin ducked low, Nate hurried through the crowd. His bloodshot gaze and runny nose made him look like someone who needed a fix or a warm body to bed, and he didn't want to talk to anyone. Not tonight.

A man holding up a pair of shiny blue shoes bumped into Nate.

"Name your price, kid!"

No one had shoes like that in the Withers. Nate's fingers drifted to the angry scar at his hairline.

"You hear me?" The man leaned close, his big grin full of brown teeth. "Straight from Gathos City. Only singed a bit."

"No." Nate stumbled back. "No, thanks."

He turned and ran, pushing through the crowd and dodging around the hot fires. He had to get away from the shoes and clothes and fancy timepieces people had pulled off the commuters.

When Nate reached the railway, long lines stretched behind every ladder and stairway. The noisy crowd writhed like a dying sludge-fish. He'd get trampled before he ever made it onto the walkway. He swallowed back a frustrated sob and tried to remember the quickest way to Alden's without taking the rails.

Nate stayed out of the shadows. If he got himself robbed now, he'd have nothing. Everything he owned thumped against his back. His tools and tool belt. A blanket. Some mismatched socks. His dusty coat in a bundle. No food, no credits, no spare tech. He had no choice but to go straight to Alden.

Alden, who had hidden the GEM manual from him—had kept him from understanding the limitations and the wonder of his own blood and body. He'd known more of Nate's origins than Nate himself and hadn't told him. Hadn't let him see.

Pixel says it's magic.

And Alden had used him. Made him weak and helpless. Twisted his feelings up until he didn't know if they were friends or if he was nothing more than a *thing* Alden wanted to keep.

Nate's hair swung in his face and tickled his nose. He scrubbed tears away, aching. None of that mattered. It didn't even matter that Alden would be angry at him for avoiding the shop.

He wanted to go back. To Fran. To the familiarity of the bed on the floor and the chimes that sang in the doorway. To the comfort of their old routine and the reliability of Alden's unpredictable moods.

Near the shop, shadowy forms gestured wildly. Shouting rang out like bells. The train crash had set off a current of fear and excitement. People who normally avoided the streets at night were out gossiping and admiring what they'd stolen.

Nate shifted his backpack, his thoughts broken and jagged like shards of glass. Going up on the rails to rescue the passengers had been stupid, but he'd do it again today if he had the choice. Reed had gotten hurt, but Nate'd saved him. And he would have kept Reed safe at the bank.

But Reed didn't have faith in him.

Why should he?

Nate was a liar, and he was unreliable. Inconsistent. He'd done so much and tried so hard, and it didn't matter. It didn't even matter that they'd shared a real kiss—that maybe Reed really wanted him.

That maybe Reed had trusted him.

Everything would be easier if he'd never met Reed.

But not really. No matter how bad it hurt, Reed was in his blood.

Nate loved him.

And Reed would never know.

Nate hunched over in front of Alden's shop, taking deep breaths to quell the shudder of swallowed-back tears. The windows glowed weakly from the crank-lights and candles inside.

"Nine!"

Straightening, Nate tried to place the familiar voice and name. It wasn't until a skinny girl ducked into his line of sight that he recognized the name—and Val. She carried a messenger bag crafted out of black rubber and plastic ties.

How did I miss that before?

Val was a Courier. By street standards, she really was an old lady—an old lady Nate didn't want to talk to tonight.

"I'm busy." He tried to step around her.

"I can tell you're busy. Look at you sweating. I didn't figure you for a fiend." Val dodged from side to side, effortlessly blocking his way.

Nate lost his balance. He flailed his arms to keep from toppling over with the momentum of his heavy load. "I'm not a fiend! And if I was, I'd be somewhere better than this—or in oblivion." He rubbed his eyes. "I wouldn't have to think about anything."

"Having a bad day, kid?" She rested her hands on her hips.

"How can you tell?" Nate asked, wiping his eyes with angry scrubs.

"You don't look much better than you did the last time I saw you. You're poorly. What is it?"

"I told you. What I have isn't catching."

Val studied him as others passed, conversations a lively hum all around them. "Is that so?"

Rattled, Nate edged toward Alden's door. His body hurt, and his lungs ached, and he wanted badly to rest. Val let him pass this time. Watching him.

A prickle of worry made his hands go cold.

"How sick are you?" Val asked.

He stared at Alden's door, her gaze burning at his back. Someone had followed him from Alden's back to the old hideout. And that's why Reed had gotten hurt. He wasn't going to get someone else hurt. "I'm not sick." He cleared his throat and stepped away from the door, forcing his gaze to track farther down the street. "I'm tired."

"Are you sure about that?"

Nate whirled to face her. "I'm just trying to get . . ." It wasn't really *home*, but it was all he had. "I need to sleep, that's all."

"You smiled the last time I saw you," Val said. She rubbed her hip absently, wincing. "Something's chased your smile away."

"You are really nosey."

Val grinned. "And quick. I've got deliveries to make. I'll leave you to your frowns and wherever you're trying to get. But, Nine?"

Nate gave up on trying to correct her. "Yes?"

"If you want to get better, you should . . ." She hesitated and flashed him a stilted smile. "Gods watch you!"

Before Nate could ask her what the sludge that meant, Val jogged away, limping like a fleeing child. He didn't remember her limping before. She disappeared into the shadow of a tall building, and Nate shivered.

———————

Alden's shop was still open for business and would be well into the night. Nate didn't bother knocking. He stumbled inside to the sound of the door chimes and went straight to the side room. Alden sat at a small folding table, teaching a young girl how to inject chem.

Nate dropped his backpack in the corner. "I need to talk to you."

He didn't wait for Alden to respond before he went to the

washroom in the hall and wet his face. He'd lost his tie, and his hair hung in his face like knotted rope. Too thin, too tired, and wearing livid circles under his eyes, he looked like the chem fiend Reed had always suspected him to be. He'd fit in here, wasting away with Alden.

"My dear, my darling." Alden slipped into the tiny washroom and squeezed behind Nate to look at him in the mirror. His arms snaked around Nate and held him close. "When you come into my shop, stomping around so fussily, it makes people nervous. If they're nervous, they leave, and if they leave, I can't sell anything, and if I can't sell anything, I can't afford to keep freeloaders sleeping on my spare bed and eating my food and using up the last of my stash of Remedy. It vexes me."

"Reed threw me out." A shudder ran through him. Saying it out loud made it final.

Nate bit his lip and squeezed his stinging eyes shut. He'd lost his family.

"Oh my," Alden said. "How sad." He pulled Nate's hair aside with one hand and kissed his ear. His lips were as cold as rain.

Nate elbowed him away with a raw, quiet sob. "You're flying."

"Very much."

Some chem made Alden focused and quiet, and some made him sleepy. The worst kind made him pushy and hungry like a street cat, his hands unsteady and too busy.

When he opened his eyes, Alden stood behind him, watching him in the mirror. They made a strange pair—Alden's pale skin and Nate's bronze complexion, both marred with bruises and exhaustion.

Nate scrubbed at his tears, hating the pressure in his chest, the rage and grief aching to be released. "I saw a girl I know outside." His voice wavered. If he didn't act like everything was fine, he was going to shatter apart. "The one I told you about from the railway. I think she's a Courier."

"Was she small?" Alden clawed his fingers into Nate's arm and met his gaze in their reflection. "Unusually nosy?"

"You know her?"

"Valerie," Alden said, spitting the name out like a seed.

"Val, yeah."

"Did you talk to her?" Alden grew sharp, loud. "Did she see you come here?"

Chem often made Alden paranoid. Once, he'd screamed at Nate, accusing him of changing all the codes on the security system when he'd been too high to remember them.

Nate searched for that same wild suspicion in Alden's dark eyes now, and when he saw none, a chill came over him. "I don't think so."

Alden released his painful grip. He glanced away and shook his head, his shoulders sharp and tense. His gaze was clear in the reflection, as if something had chased off the haze of chem.

"Go lie down," he said hollowly. "And stay out of the front room. Don't let anyone else see you."

Nate followed him out of the washroom and sank onto the mattress on the floor. As soon as his head reached one of the tufted cushions, exhaustion weighed at his eyes.

Alden locked up the shop early, his skeleton keys clicking

and tingling. He snapped the latches shut at each window. The room grew darker with every candle Alden blew out.

Nate rolled toward Alden when he came to sit beside him. Alden's fingers carded into Nate's hair absently. If anything, they still had their old habits—the comfort of routine.

"How do you know Val?" Nate asked, murmuring. In the dark, they could tell secrets.

"As you clearly noticed, she's a Courier. As you may also have noticed, my business receives quite a few deliveries."

Nate rubbed the spot where his ribs ached with a sinking feeling. Val delivered chem. He had no reason to feel disappointed—it wasn't like he actually knew her. But after what she'd done to help him on the rails, he'd felt an odd sort of kinship. Turns out, she wasn't doing anything any better than Alden was.

"Why are you worried about it?" Nate asked. Alden had always kept Nate away when deliveries came in. He'd always figured the caution was a product of Alden's abiding paranoia.

Alden coughed out a toneless laugh. "I didn't say I was *worried*, little bird. Let me be more explicit. I dislike her. I don't like people I dislike talking to people I do like."

"You don't like me."

Alden let out a deep sigh. "You tire me." Without another word, he folded himself over Nate's middle like a heavy blanket and passed out.

Only Alden could make falling asleep a dramatic exit.

Outside, the street rustled, silence peppered by shouts and laughter and scraps of music. Nate played with Alden's long hair, weaving it between his fingers as he waited for sleep to catch on to the exhaustion he felt. But his mind wouldn't quiet down.

He stared at the boxy shadows on the walls—shelves full of jars and dusty old books from the time when the area around the shop had boomed as a colony of artists and makers. Fran told stories about it on her clear days, holding a scarf and waving it around like an actress on stage. Nate didn't enjoy reading the few books he'd gotten his hands on, preferring to keep his fingers busy instead. But he'd known his letters by the time his parents had sent him away to live with Bernice.

Closing his eyes, Nate stretched his memory back as far as it would go. A trembling kiss from his mother. His father's dark hair and dark eyes and silence. A woman his mother's age with hair shorn close like a pelt. Strong hands on his shoulders, squeezing too hard.

Before that, it was only scraps. Feelings. Never feeling safe for long. Cold metal against his skin and words he didn't understand. Rushing down a dark hallway in his mother's arms. Adults yelling in another room, scaring him.

He'd only cried to Bernice once, asking why his parents had sent him away. She'd taken him to the roof of her building, where the wind whipped her white hair around and cleared the yellow smog away.

"See the towers?" she'd asked.

They shone on the horizon, lights twinkling. *Home.* He'd nodded and scrubbed the snot off his face with his sleeve.

"To the folk in those towers, you are not a person." She'd spoken slowly, raising her voice over the whistle of the wind in their ears. "To them, you're not a boy. You're no one's son. They made you to carve you up or bleed you dry."

"But Mom—"

"Your mother made a mistake! Your father knew that. I knew that. But she wouldn't listen to reason."

Nate's breath had sucked out of his chest, as if the wind had stolen it away. And Bernice had taken him by the chin and forced him to look at her wrinkled, spotty face and her milky eyes.

"She wanted you so badly that she went against the rules, took advantage of her position and made you with her own genes and your father's. But the city was never going to let her keep you, so she got you away. And now you're here. And I won't have you crying about it. Do you understand?" she'd asked, the hard lines around her mouth softening.

Not trusting himself to speak, he'd nodded tightly. And she'd taken him to her tiny, dusty apartment to teach him how to fix things.

———

Nate slept fitfully, dreaming of falling in a motorcar, trapped in the metal as it twisted to scrap and burned. He woke pinned by Alden's thin body. A familiar chemical smell tickled at his nose, and he squinted at the plastic blinds heated by the morning sun. The rogue spring in Alden's bed that always seemed to find its way to Nate's kidneys poked him reliably.

Alden lifted his head and frowned, his face framed by wispy tangles. "Why are you here?"

The warm morning light did nothing to mask the sickly

cast to Alden's skin or the reddish patches that would eventually become sores if he kept up without a break.

Chem wasn't treating him well.

Nate arched a brow. "I find you irresistible?"

Amusement danced across Alden's face for a moment before his eyes went sharp. "No. Wait. You told me." He paused a moment, squinting at Nate's face. "Reed bounced you from the gang. Why?"

"For being a chem fiend."

Alden laughed, the sound close to Fran's dry cackle. He wasn't much older than Nate, but too much of him was so old, wasted. "I'm surprised it took this long. You didn't tell him the truth?"

"How could I?"

"Well, *I* certainly wouldn't, but I'm not a tender little flower like you," Alden said, drawing away. The robe he'd worn to bed stuck to his body in sweaty folds. He wrinkled his nose. "I must make myself respectable before the business day begins."

"It's too early." Nate squirmed toward the warmth of the slotted sunbeams from the window. He closed his eyes as Alden fussed through his morning routine.

Nate had spent months waking like this, listening to Alden gossip about people he didn't know or hum bits of songs he didn't like. Watching Alden comb his hair and fasten on glittery bits of jewelry before opening a bottle and shaking out whatever cocktail of capsules and powders would get him through the day.

This morning was different, though. Alden dressed and

played with his hair and shook a few capsules out of bottles as if playing with a rattle, but he said nothing.

"Why don't you keep someone else around here?" Nate hated where his thoughts took him. *Has Alden been alone since I left?*

"This isn't a house of charity, Nate. Despite what you appear to think."

"That's not what I meant."

Alden spun in the ancient dressing chair he kept in front of his bureau. "Do you mean to insinuate that you are so very, very special that I couldn't bear to replace you with some pale substitute?"

"No, I—"

"Do you think I have no friends? That I can't find someone to warm my bed? That I haven't?"

"Alden—"

"Spare me, Nate. I have a headache—and a new houseguest, it seems. Next thing we know, I'll be running a sick-den."

"I'm not that sick." Nate rose to the bait, despite knowing exactly what it was.

Alden pointed a hairbrush at him. "You are. And that should be *your* problem. But you've made it my problem too."

"Then I'll leave."

"Gods know what you think of me, Nate, but one thing I won't do is send you out to the streets to die. You can die here," he said cheerfully, "in the comfort of my home."

Nate gasped, the wind knocked out of him. "*You're* the one who's sick."

"Honesty is no affliction." Alden's hands dropped to his

lap. He glanced up at Nate, gaze unsteady for a moment too long before he hardened his expression.

Anger swelled in Nate, and he latched on to the comforting flash-burn. If they were going to be honest now, he had plenty to say. "I would have died here last year if I hadn't left."

The pain flashing through Alden's eyes failed to satisfy Nate the way he'd hoped.

"I realize that," Alden said dully.

"How long do I have?" Nate asked, the words sounding like they came from someone else's throat. His hands went cold, and the room lurched as if the whole building was sliding into a sinkhole.

"Not as long as you would have had if you'd listened to me. You wasted your time, your *life*. Saving a thief who threw you out anyway."

Nate's fingers curled into fists. He'd do it again if he had to. "Tell me!"

Alden gestured vaguely with his hairbrush. "I only know what I've heard, and secondhand accounts aren't exactly—"

"How long?" Nate asked, hoarse and loud. Alden made it his business to know *everything*. He had to know.

"I have one dose left, Nate. I've been rationing it." Alden ignored Nate's noisy sound of disbelief. "But I'm going to have to cut it more, and I don't think we're going to like what happens after that."

If Alden was evading this much, the answer couldn't be good.

"Tell me. Please," Nate said, forcing the shaky words past the panic in his throat.

"A month. Maybe two. But you'll be in bad shape in a few weeks. I can keep you alive awhile, but you won't want to be."

Nate ran trembling hands through his hair. "Can't we get Remedy somewhere else?"

"Certainly! Go to the gates of Gathos City and tell them you're a GEM." Alden's jaw tightened, and his nostrils flared. "I'm sure if you ask politely, they'll send you a batch with the next shipment of wilted lettuce."

"This isn't funny!"

"No," Alden said, dark eyes glittering. "It's not."

"Aren't there other dealers? Anyone? I can't be the only GEM who needs it."

"Do you think I haven't exhausted every opportunity to get Remedy?" A haunted look shadowed Alden's face. "Every avenue?"

"Even the Breakers?"

Spots of color appeared at Alden's cheeks. "You don't know what you're asking."

Nate scrubbed his face, troubled by the roughness in Alden's voice—the edge of fear there. It bore no argument. "Your grandmother was right," he whispered. She'd poked him and told him he was dying.

"Every so often. They're tricky, grandmothers." Alden set the brush down and came back to the bed. He held Nate, his breath warm against his hair. "Do you want to know a terrible thing?"

"Like having a few months to live?" Nate asked, his ears ringing with muffled hysteria. He didn't fight the narrow tug of Alden's embrace. He barely felt it.

"I hoped you'd stay away, that your gallant Reed would be the one to watch you die." Alden was cold, but his hands were gentle, and they combed through Nate's hair, over and over, as if it soothed him as much as it soothed Nate.

"You really can't," Nate realized aloud. The manual had been clear about that much. He'd only last a few days if Alden tried it.

"Can't what?"

"Feed. Ever again."

"Well, I *can*, dear," Alden said, sighing. "But I won't."

"This is how much you're supposed to have." Alden indicated a line on the delicate glass vial on his work area in the back room he rarely let Nate see. He dragged his fingernail to a line on the side of the vial much lower than the first. "This is how much I can give you today."

Fine tremors ran through Alden's fingers when he tipped the liquid into Nate's mouth.

Nate's headache faded in minutes, but dull pain pooled under his skin like a bruise. When Alden didn't shoo him out of the room, he lingered, surprised to see vials and equipment he didn't recognize. Alden had never spoken of cooking his own chem, but the scrap paper covered with figures and the intricate tools on his workspace told another story. Was he pushing his own blends?

I don't want to know.

Ignoring Nate, Alden divided pills into piles with a small plastic card. Unsettled, even now, with Alden's practiced ease with chem, he sat on the floor in front of a cabinet full of dusty bottles. He found a rag and wiped down each bottle, arranging them by shape.

He still felt guilty for borrowing Alden's Diffuser without giving him anything in return. He had to make himself useful another way. And he had to keep his hands busy, or he'd curl over himself and scream.

The bottles clinked and shone in his hands. They were old—blue and green and brown, painted with symbols he didn't recognize. He blew on the opening of one to see if it would make music, like an instrument he'd seen a busker near the rails play. But it sounded like wind rattling across a broken pane of glass.

Alden poked him with a long, bare toe. "What are you doing?"

Nate's eyes were sore from squinting. "I'm cleaning these bottles."

"Yes, I see that. But it's been four hours. And you've re-arranged them a dozen times now." Alden crossed his arms. "And it's getting dark. Go ... do something normal." When Nate stared at him, he rolled his eyes and pointed at the curtains to Fran's room. "Talk to Grandmother. Learn to knit. Rewire my alarm system for the fifth time. Relax."

"Relax and wait for the stillness to come?" Nate's fingers tightened around one of the bottles. He set it down carefully when his hand prickled with the urge to throw it to see what sound it would make shattering against the wall.

"We're all waiting for the stillness. I don't see why you can't enjoy it." Alden offered Nate his hand and grunted with the effort of wrenching him up. They stood very close. "I have ways to help you enjoy it," he said softly.

Nate jerked his hand out of Alden's grip. "I'm not going to sleep through the rest of my days. I have things to do."

"Suit yourself." Alden handed him a crank-light. "You won't have to go far when you change your mind."

After twenty minutes in bed, Nate chose to rewire the alarm system.

It's the fourth *time, not the fifth.*

It took two days.

After that, he started putting together the battery packs Reed and the gang needed to keep their system running at night. He paid too much attention to every pang of hurt and exhaustion that meant he was running out of time, but it didn't drown out the sounds of distant explosions and the lingering smell of smoke. The world wasn't going to stop when he was gone. He had to do something to keep them safe, no matter where they hid.

Alden rolled cigarettes on the table next to Nate's mess of wires and circuits. "What is this for?"

"The gang."

"It seems I can't be rid of your Reed, even when he's gotten rid of you."

Nate fumbled and pinched his finger with his pliers. A small bead of blood welled up. "Alden! Do you have to do that right there?"

"I can do this right here as much as I please, because this is my shop. And my home. You are my ungrateful, messy guest," Alden said without venom. "And you should watch your tongue."

There were plenty of other surfaces for Alden to work on, but he lingered near Nate all day long. Probably to keep a running tally of every bit of tech Nate managed to rummage from dusty drawers and cabinets.

Nate sucked on his finger, grimacing at the taste of blood. "Fine."

"Do you plan on dropping that tech on their doorstep like the winter witch leaving presents for little boys and girls?"

"I'll pay a Courier."

Alden slapped his hand down on the table, startling both of them. He stared at the scattered cigarettes and Nate's dropped pliers.

"I told you," Alden said, careful and slow, like he was fighting to make every word sound even. "You can't go talking to strangers. To customers. To Couriers. To anyone. Gods, Nate. You never listen to me."

He stalked away to the basement, leaving Nate with a half-finished battery and heavy knot of hurt in his chest.

Unable to focus on the battery after that, Nate found a ladder and went up in the crawlspace to repair the ticker cables for Fran. She kept a ticker by the bed in the back room where she spent most of her days, and lately, the signal had gone patchy. Her room had the nicest furniture in the house—a real bed on a frame and plush, musty carpeting. The season lingered in the mildness between winter and spring, allowing Fran to keep her back window open instead of boarded up.

The sounds of the alleyway—sex and laughing and

fighting—filled her room that afternoon as Nate sat on the floor beside her bed, fingers as tangled in the wires of the ticker as hers were in her knitting.

"What's that?" he asked, waving his pliers toward the mess in her lap. The yarn was orange and slightly shiny, something synthetic that must have been hand-spun from recycled plastic and old cloth.

"A scarf for Alden," she said, looking over the edge of the bed to study Nate as if watching a cat play with scraps of thread. She wore reading glasses with mismatched lenses. "It will be cold again before it gets warm."

"How do you know?"

"When you come to be my age, your bones remember. Frontward, backward. You'll see," Fran said.

Nate smiled. "You're good to him."

"The Old Gods will take me soon," Fran said with calm certainty. "He'll need to keep warm."

"You can't know that." Nate turned his attention back to the wires under his fingertips. A shiver ran down his arms, making the fine hairs stand on end. "You're as strong as a girl half your age."

Fran chuckled and continued knitting, the needles clicking together with an even, calming rhythm. "Flattering bird, tweeting away at me. Come back to nest, have you?"

"I'm short a few eggs," Nate said, wincing when his sore finger caught on a sharp edge in the guts of the ticker. "Did you know many GEMs?"

"Not many. Alden's mother—Gods keep my dear girl—worked at the gates. She said she saw them now and then in motorcars. They wore gray." Fran paused her knitting and fluttered her knotty fingers at her throat. "And collars, here. Like animals. But she was a fanciful girl, always telling stories."

"They always died before they were grown?"

"The GEMs? They went away, every one, while they were fresh, like you." Fran glanced at him. "You're not so fresh now."

"It's always been that way?"

"When I was a girl, before Winter Heights fell, there were no GEMs. Magic brought them into the world, but the magic doesn't want to stay. Don't be afraid, little bird. You'll fly to a better place."

"Like the Mainland?" Nate asked. He knew what she meant—the room behind death, the unknown sleep—but the Mainland was easier to think about.

Fran hummed. "You like stories too."

"Happy ones," Nate said.

"The clouds aren't gray on the Mainland," Fran said. "The rain tastes sweet, and the ground is a great carpet of soft grass."

"That's a good story."

"When the sludge pulls our flesh from our bones, we'll float away to the Mainland," Fran said.

Unsettled, Nate went silent. But the knot in his chest loosened little by little as he listened to the click-pull of Fran's knitting. He weaved together the wires and circuits that would bring the ticker back to life. Fran liked to hold it and read the Gathos City news, even if her old eyes could barely make out the scrolling text.

"Did Alden know his mother?" Nate asked. Alden would hate him prying, but Nate's new expiration date—and Alden's nasty attitude earlier—made him less inclined to worry about what Alden wanted him to do or not do.

Fran continued her knitting without slowing or missing a stitch, but her lips tightened before she spoke. "He did, for a decade or so. She didn't die well. It was here, in this house. Alden wasn't well after that. He takes his medicine now, so he won't be thinking about her."

It was rare to get such a lucid streak out of Fran, so Nate pressed on. "What about his father?"

"Never a father around here. My Alba was an independent girl. She inherited this shop from my husband after Alden came along. He's never known anything but this place. He was only a boy when he took on Alba's work."

Nate tried to picture a child in the shop with no one but an eccentric old woman to keep him company. He snorted, realizing it wasn't all that different from his childhood with Bernice.

"Grandmother." Alden peered through the doorway. "Are you troubling our young Tinkerer?"

"Are *you* troubling him?" Fran asked.

Nate laughed. "I've just finished up. Here you are."

He scrambled up and tucked the ticker against the folds of quilted fabric that covered her from the waist down where she reclined on the bed like a moth-eaten queen. She placed a warm, leathery hand over his and smiled.

"It's still not working," she said.

Nate leaned over her and squinted at the ticker, frowning. Fixing a ticker was child's play. "It looks all right to me," he said, nodding toward the scrolling words. Then he looked closer.

The Breakers will catch you when you fall.

It repeated in a loop. Nate squinted at it, trying to make sense of the message. Maybe it really was broken.

He reached for the ticker, and a normal broadcast resumed. Food ration delivery times and weather alerts and decades-old lung-rot symptom warnings scrolled by.

"Can you fly, pretty bird?" Fran asked.

"She's off again," Alden said at Nate's ear, making him jump. Fran watched them vacantly, her gnarled fingers continuing to knit the orange scarf for Alden.

They settled Fran's blankets together and cranked the light beside her bed to keep it going while she finished her knitting. She'd sleep soon, her wasted body exhausted even by lounging in bed.

"She told me she's going to die," Nate said.

"She's been saying that for six years. I have a pile of scarves to prove it. Come on," Alden said, taking Nate's hand and leading him out of the room. "You need to eat something."

They sat behind the counter with crunchy bread that tasted more like ash than usual. Alden broke pieces off and ate them delicately, glancing at Nate between bites.

"You're acting strange," Nate said.

"You're acting stranger. Aren't you afraid?"

"When I think about it, I guess." Chewing a gritty, unappealing mouthful of bread, Nate considered what Fran had told him about Alden's mother. If Alden had watched his mother die, no wonder he dreaded keeping Nate around. Maybe that's why he was so short-tempered.

After a long silence, Nate asked, "Do you want me to leave?"

"Don't be stupid. I told you to stay," Alden said in a tone Nate didn't feel like arguing with.

"If I'm going to die anyway, why don't I let the gang turn me in to the Breakers?" Nate asked. "If we planned it right, you could split the bounty with them."

Alden sighed. "I knew that was coming, but Gods behind the stars, you're not even addled yet. Honestly, Nate. How have you lived to see sixteen?"

"I'm serious. If I'm going to die anyway, shouldn't someone profit from it?"

"The difference," Alden said, "is that dying is the end of the road. Giving yourself to them isn't the end of anything."

"No one knows what happens when a GEM goes to the Breakers."

"Have you ever heard a good rumor about it?"

Nate frowned. "No."

"Rumors are rarely born out of thin air. There's truth in some of what they say." Alden cleared the plates—pink ceramic with a rose print and chips along the edges—and walked to the front of the counter. He stood before Nate as if he'd come to purchase one of the dusty bracelets under the glass. "If I had you the way they'd have you, I'd never let you go."

"I know," Nate said, conscious of how close Alden was, even with the counter between them. Alden's hunger simmered, barely suppressed by the chem he put in his body all day to forget how badly he needed Nate's blood.

How hard is it for Alden to be around me?

Feeding Reed once hadn't been a risk. It was the small doses, the little tastes of euphoria, that had driven Alden to a fierce, abiding hunger. It had gotten so bad before Nate had walked away that it wasn't a stretch to imagine what would have happened to him in Gathos City—or how much Alden wanted him now.

Unwilling—or unable—to check his desires, Alden had kept Nate weak. He'd fed on him daily, leaving Nate dazed and euphoric. Nate's memories of those weeks were shadowed and not unpleasant, but he remembered his own horror starkly from the day he'd awakened enough to find the seasons changed entirely. He'd lost months in Alden's arms.

"And they're not burdened with caring about you," Alden said softly. "You'd be nothing more than meat to them."

Nate's gaze snapped up as Alden's words sank in. "All right. Okay." He tried to smile, his heart skipping an uncomfortable beat. "It's a bad idea."

Alden wiped the dishes with a cloth and replaced them on a tilted shelf. His hands shook. "Make your bed on the floor in my grandmother's room."

Nate preferred his bed in Alden's room, and he opened his mouth to protest. But Alden turned and watched him with a plain, anguished sort of hunger that made Nate's breath hitch.

"All right," Nate said. "Fran could use the company."

Nate could have stayed up for hours working on the battery and listening to the street outside, but the look on Alden's face sent him to bed early. And once Fran fell asleep, snoring like a kitten, Nate got up and locked the door.

CHAPTER
ELEVEN

That night, Nate struggled to sleep, aware of every creak in the old building and every distant shout in the night. He tossed and turned in his pile of musty blankets, wishing he could turn a crank-light on and find something to do to settle his restless mind and the itch to move.

Memories nagged at him. Good days at the shop—days spent drinking watered-down tea with Fran and fixing things until his back ached and accomplishment warmed his guts. Bad days—Alden flying on a new strain of chem, too frantic to carry on a conversation and convinced there were snakes in the bathroom sink.

The bad days weren't as bad as the hurt that had lingered after Nate had walked away.

And after he'd walked right back, when staying away had become impossible.

The first time had been a quiet evening, when the shifts at the workhouses changed and long shadows promised a break from the heat. It was then that fiends sought the solace of a chem-soaked night, the hope of a better day. Nate chose a busy time, so it wouldn't be too conspicuous when the clatter of chimes announced his entrance.

Alden stood behind the counter, counting out little glass vials for a tattooed white woman with graying hair who scratched relentlessly at her hip. Nate couldn't make out what Alden was saying, but he saw his shoulders tighten and one hand dart out to push his hair behind his ear in an uncharacteristic gesture.

Normally, Alden wore his hair with the confidence of a brightly feathered bird.

But this wasn't a normal day. It was Nate's first time back at the shop since he'd left for Reed's gang. If Alden felt a fraction of the tension coiling Nate's guts into ugly knots, it was no wonder he fidgeted.

As Alden helped another customer, Nate let his eyes drift to the glass cases that held cut-glass jewelry and trinkets that were decades older than him. Dust covered the shelves and gathered on the polished concrete floor, but in the cases, time had stopped. Blue and black velvet cradled beaded bracelets, incense burners, ceramic mugs, and paperweights etched with the Gathos City skyline. Once or twice a month, someone asked Alden to open the cases, but they never made a purchase. Instead, they'd cradle a relic, fingering an emblem or the tiny paw of a crystal cat, and then they'd hand it back and wistfully ask for the going price of chem.

Nate crouched, studying a shiny cigarette case, when he felt the rustle of Alden's silky robe beside him and realized everyone else had left the shop. Golden light poured in the front windows, making the thin blinds look like flames. The embroidered flowers on Alden's robes glowed.

And his dark eyes glowed too. "Why are you here?" he asked, pulling Nate up by his collar and releasing him like he'd touched sewage.

"You know why."

Alden let out a soft, incredulous huff of breath that carried the sticky-sweet scent of a chem tincture. "You made it clear you didn't need me anymore."

Nate had practiced this conversation for weeks, every rehearsal becoming more frantic as his headaches grew more frequent. He'd whispered to the ghost of their friendship as he'd crossed the Withers from Reed's hideout back to the shop. He'd found the right words. But now, faced with the way Alden gripped his robe with bloodless knuckles, he forgot everything he'd meant to say.

"No one else has Remedy."

"Is that so?"

Frustration rose in Nate like a curling wisp of smoke. "You know that. Tell me what I need to do. I'll find credits."

"You'll *find* credits." Alden rolled his eyes. He swept his hair to the side and began to braid it. This was familiar—a sign that he was doing figures in his head. "Are they finding spare credits in the street these days, then? Along with gilded shit and sugared gull bones?"

A pang of emptiness made itself known in Nate's chest. He'd missed the musical sound of Alden's voice, the way his words filled the space between them.

He ducked his chin and studied Alden's long toes where they peeked out from colorful sandals made with braided plastic. "Tell me what I need to do."

"I thought you were done being told what to do." Alden spoke softly now. The shop was growing dark.

"You stopped giving me a choice." Nate forced himself to look up. Something shifted in Alden's eyes. "I deserved a choice."

"And you made one. You chose to leave, to live with people who can't keep you alive. People who would grind your bones to dust and sell them by the ounce if they knew what you were."

It was Nate's turn to roll his eyes. "My bones are worthless, and if you knew Reed and the girls, you'd like them. They're just trying to survive together. And they appreciate me."

"I appreciated you." Each syllable cut like a blade.

The weight of Alden's arm across his chest and his breath too slow at his ear. The Diffuser, still bloodied, cast carelessly into the cushions beside them.

A shiver of revulsion ran through Nate's body, sudden and strong enough for Alden to plainly see. Nate took a sharp step back, tripped over his own feet, and slammed his hip against the sharp corner of a display case.

Alden had gone utterly still, his fingers frozen at odd angles. He'd lost weight, and his robes hung on his thin shoulders like silk on bone. "Tell me what you're really asking. Tell me you want Remedy for free and want to give me nothing in return. Tell me you're willing to put my shop, my life, and my grandmother's life at risk just by being here. Just by being what you are."

"Alden."

"Tell me you're lying to the people who shelter you. That *your* life is worth more than the rest of us."

All of it was true. But Nate was a coward, and the words bubbled out of him softly, a wretched admission. "I don't want to die." He'd never admitted it before, never let himself name the chasm of the stillness that loomed before him. Closer with every ache.

"We're *all* going to die, Nate!" Alden shouted.

Nate braced himself against the glass counter, rattling a display of plastic beads. They clacked together like mocking laughter, and his voice tripped on the choking promise of tears. "If you don't care, turn me in."

Alden turned and closed the blinds, driving away the last light. He opened a small box of matches and began lighting candles. "Don't you think I would have already?"

Nate watched Alden's hand tremble above the flickering light of a weak flame.

"I don't know what to do," Nate whispered.

His head ached with the stuffy pressure of a building headache, and walking over here had exhausted him. Without Remedy, he'd soon grow too ill to hide it from Reed. And Alden was right: he was putting them all at risk.

Alden opened the curtain to the next room, where the lights Nate had wired cast a warm, familiar light. "Learn to negotiate better, for one."

"What?" Nate asked, scraping tears from his lashes with his dirty hands.

"You're more than a GEM. As it much as it pains me to admit, your tinkering isn't worthless." Alden gestured tightly. "I have things to do. Come get your dose so I can go on with my evening. And next time you come, bring tech and propose a plan to make yourself useful every time you come here."

Nate took an unsteady, disbelieving step. "You're not going to try to feed?"

"Force you?"

"No—I— "

"You try my patience. Get your *fix* and get back to your Reed," Alden said, so acidic that Nate hurried like he'd been pushed. He held the curtain aside, back rigid, as Nate passed through into a room he no longer felt welcome in . . .

A muffled knock at the bedroom door startled Nate from his memory. Legs momentarily weak with a rush of unreasonable fear, he scrambled off the floor and knocked back softly, careful not to wake Fran, who snored in her bed. "Alden?"

Alden let out a muted sigh. "We appear to be under siege."

Nate unlocked the door and peered out, more concerned with his alarm system failing than he was about Alden's veiled warnings the evening before. Shadows flickered at the front window, outside the range of the trip wires and alarm circuits.

Alden handed him a stun gun.

"What am I supposed to do with this?" Nate asked, squinting in the dark. Through the blinds and flimsy curtains, torchlight danced. The streets were full of people.

"If someone breaks the door in, shoot them with the stun gun." Alden leaned against the front counter, his nightgown clinging like a shroud. He held a polished wooden stick the length of his arm. Nate had never seen anything like it, and Alden didn't look like he knew what to do with it.

"What's happening?"

"Who knows. An overabundance of speed-chem. A stampede toward the nearest rain barrel. The Breakers. A parade. I don't pretend to understand the whims of our neighbors."

But he did. Alden had an uncanny way of knowing exactly what people needed when they came to him with wordless hunger. He watched the window warily, his fingers clenched tight around the wood.

"Why won't the A-Vols stop them?" Nate asked.

Alden made a low, displeased sound. "The A-Vols have no reason to stop a riot. It appears others have been incentivizing their loyalty."

"The Breakers?"

"I didn't wake you up for a midnight chat." Tension clipped Alden's words.

If the crowd outside decided to raid Alden's shop, the alarm system and the stun gun and Alden's stick weren't going to save them. But the late hour dulled Nate's senses. It had to be close to dawn, and finally, his body was ready to sleep.

Little by little, the crowd outside thinned. Here and there, Nate made out the shapes of baskets and bags in people's arms. "It's food they're after," he realized, fear and concern mingling in the dark. "They're hungry."

Hunger was nothing new in the Withers, but this was different. A chaotic, desperate need.

Alden didn't move. "Of course they are."

Nate thought of Pixel and knew that Brick, Sparks, and Reed would sooner starve than let her hunger like that. That they *would* starve for her. A pang of grief hollowed him out. He should have been with them, doing something to help. But there was no sense in wishing now. Tomorrow, he'd figure out how to get tech over to them. It was more than nothing.

The night stretched on, the streets slowly quieting, until Nate could only hear the steady tick of a clock on the wall and not the rustle of hurried footsteps outside. In the absence of immediate danger, he swayed with sleepiness, nearly dropping the stun gun he was reasonably certain didn't work.

"Sit down," Alden said.

Nate wobbled across the room and sat at his feet, resting his head against Alden's legs.

He couldn't recall falling asleep, but woke in his bed and wondered if it had all been a dream—until he saw the hollow pinch of exhaustion around Alden's eyes.

Nate stood. "I'm going to go to the market." He pulled his coat off the hook on the wall. The pockets were deep enough to hold the battery packs from the back room. "I'll see if anyone's talking about what happened last night."

Alden caught his wrist. "Not today."

"What?" Nate glared at him. "Why not?"

He let go of Nate's hand, but unfolded to stand in front of the door with his thin arms braced against the jamb. His robe hung like a curtain, and the sun shone through, illuminating the pale swirls in the embroidery. "You don't need to be flitting in and out of here all day long."

"But I haven't left at all. You told me to do things. I'm bored!" he lied, desperate to get the battery packs to Reed and to know exactly what was happening—and how it might affect the gang.

"There are worse things to be."

Nate waited for Alden to fall asleep so he could sneak out, but Alden stayed more alert than usual. Instead of smiling at the sound of the door chime—the herald of a fiend in need—he tensed, like he expected an attack. When Nate fussed around the shop, trying to keep his hands busy, Alden herded him back into Fran's room.

But Alden couldn't stay awake forever. When Nate found him with his head in his arms at his work desk, fingers still gripping a pencil, he made quick work of packing up the battery packs and collecting a few odds and ends from the shop that he could trade for softer bread and some stew meat for Fran.

He disabled the chime on the alarm system long enough to slip out the back door and into the alley where he'd first met Alden. It reminded him so much of leaving to sell tech for the gang that his chest tightened. He'd forced himself to stop thinking about Reed all the time, but now, everything he'd tried so hard to forget flooded back.

How were they? Were they hungry? Safe? Finding a new hideout? Did Reed miss him?

If he brought the battery packs to Reed himself, Reed would see that he was still useful. And he could check up on everyone, even if he couldn't stay.

He could say goodbye.

Surely Alden wouldn't fault him for that.

Nate made his way toward the tall buildings in the distance, the bank nestled in the cluster of them. He walked slowly, wary of the unnaturally empty streets. Three people fighting poured out of a doorway, falling down the stairs and carrying on without missing a beat. He dodged them hurriedly, trying to ignore the way they snarled and clawed like animals.

At his slow pace, it took him an hour to reach the market square. When he got there, he checked the street signs, wondering if he'd gone thoroughly addled from lack of Remedy and gotten himself lost.

The market was empty. A single torn awning fluttered from bent metal where a table lay in crooked shambles. It was as if the shopkeepers had carefully collected every sign that they'd existed and disappeared. A gull perched on a crumbled stone bench, cocking its head and cawing.

Nate could still feel the grit of ash in his mouth from the bread he'd shared with Alden. People were going to starve without the market. Hardly anyone had food vouchers. There wasn't enough work.

Even the bird sounded hungry.

Tightening the straps of his backpack, Nate hurried onto a narrow side street. Two families stood at the entrance to an alley full of tents, forming a loose circle around three toddlers who played in nothing but stained rag diapers. The adults weren't talking or laughing. They were simply watching, standing guard. Nate approached slowly, making sure his footsteps were loud.

"What happened to the market?" he asked.

A woman with sores on her hands spun around and softened once she sized him up. "Where have you been? In a pit?"

"More or less."

She huffed. "Room for more in there?"

A shorter woman put her arm around her and pulled her

close, affectionate and protective at once. "Nothing's coming in from Gathos City. No need for a market. There's nothing to buy, nothing to sell."

"Nothing to eat," the first woman said.

"If you missed the riots, you better share that good chem you're on. We could all use it."

"I'm sorry," Nate said senselessly, backing away. Hunger etched lines on their faces, on the toddlers with skinny arms and distended bellies.

"He's flying too high to know his own name. Sounds nice." They laughed and turned their backs to Nate, blocking the babies from his view. He was glad for it.

With the streets empty and too many small fires to count in the distance, he'd never get to the bank and back in one piece. His backpack felt like it was full of stones. He'd been stupid to think he could do this. Even flagging a Courier would be too risky—with every mouth desperate, nothing he could pay would guarantee the safe delivery of tech.

Nate headed back the way he came, too rattled to walk slowly. He jogged as best he could, getting winded every few blocks and pausing to wheeze until he could move again. He was so busy watching for someone following him that he nearly stumbled onto a person sprawled out on the ground. He sucked in a breath. It was one of the people who'd been fighting viciously.

They were dead.

And not just dead, but carved up in places, as if someone had tried to butcher them and had quit in a hurry. Fresh, bloody footprints and slimy trails of gore surrounded the body.

Retching, Nate began to run and didn't stop until he was back in the alley behind Alden's. Doubling over, he vomited again and again, clinging to a scrap of chain-link fence to keep from collapsing in his own sick.

Alden opened the back door and dragged him inside, silently depositing him in the washroom and leaving him there. All Nate caught was a flash of lips pressed tight with rage before the door slammed shut on him.

Nate pulled his backpack off and clutched it like one of Pixel's rag dolls, sobbing into the dusty canvas until he felt like there was nothing left inside of him.

Alden didn't speak to him for three days.

———————

When the chimes rang out early the next week, Nate snuck back out and peered through a fold in the curtain. An old man with a shock of white hair walked in using a cane.

Alden met him a few steps in and offered his arm, leading him to a stool at the front counter. "Careful now."

The old man swatted at him. "I'm not made of glass, boy."

Nate tensed, expecting Alden to lash out—no one addressed him like that. But Alden laughed quietly and began to rummage beneath the counter. "How is it out there?"

"How do you think?" The old man coughed, thin and wheezy. "They've sealed the delivery gates. No food, no supplies."

Nate's worries simmered under his skin, half-formed like the echoes of a bad dream. The battery packs wouldn't be enough to help the gang. He'd have to try to hack the ticker feeds—learn everything he could. He'd never tried to scavenge for information, but it couldn't be that hard. The gang needed to know where to take shelter. He'd get what he learned to them somehow.

A clattering drew Nate's attention back to the front room. The man had dropped his cane. Alden crouched to retrieve it for him and pressed a small plastic box into his knotted fingers. "This is all I have left. Go slow."

"Low supplies at Alba's? The world really must be ending."

Alden ducked his head, lips pressing into a tight smile. He pushed his hair back behind one ear. "No one calls it that anymore."

"Ah, well. Let an old-timer have his memories. Take care, son." He patted Alden's hand and left the shop with the box clutched to his chest, chimes tinkling in his wake.

"Spy on me again, and I'll chain you to Fran's bed," Alden murmured, his back rigid. They'd had a few stilted conversations, but Alden was still sore with him for sneaking out of the shop.

Nate dashed down the short hallway, boots silent against the ragged old carpet that smelled like mold. Alden's threat was rot, but his heart raced anyway. He ducked into Fran's room.

"Who's chasing you, bird?" Fran asked.

"No one." Breathing hard, Nate offered her a small smile. It took awhile for his body to settle, but even after it did, regret lingered, an ache that ran from his chest to his fingertips. He'd stolen something from Alden—a private moment, when Alden had precious little that belonged only to him.

But he'd learned something too. It wasn't getting better out there. He needed to work harder—do anything in his power to give Reed and the girls an edge. A chance to survive.

Wary of taking apart Fran's precious ticker, he rummaged around until he found an old, cracked one in a pile of junk in her chest of drawers. He broke it down to a meaningless pile of tech-guts.

Shadows spread across the room. Fran snored.

Moving like a ghost, Alden lit candles around him and left a plate of bread without saying a word. Nate worked feverishly, carefully reconstructing the ticker with a modified tuner.

Rogue broadcasts ran on a different wavelength than the official Gathos City notices. If he tweaked the tuner to pick up frequencies the tickers didn't use, maybe he'd come across another signal. The Breakers had to communicate somehow. Couriers were too busy running chem and passing threats from one gang to another to carry secret messages about explosions and chaos.

Late in the night, Alden stumbled into the room and dragged a cushion next to where Nate worked on the floor. He moved like he wasn't quite awake and threw his arms around Nate's waist before falling asleep. His breath was sweet with chem.

Nate tried to keep working, but he hadn't slept much since sneaking out, and the rhythm of Alden's breath lulled him. He curled up alongside Alden on the cushion, and Alden's arms convulsed around him.

What does he dream?

Nate held still and feigned sleep as Alden startled awake. His heart raced against Nate's back. Alden's breath didn't settle back to the gentle rhythm of sleep. He pressed his face into Nate's hair and clenched his fingers in the loose shirt Nate wore to bed.

"Nate," Alden said, mournful and soft. He wept quietly as Nate stared into the darkness and didn't sleep at all.

———

Nate's repaired ticker couldn't make sense of the jumble of information polluting every channel.

"Is it broken?" Alden asked when he glanced over at the frantic messages.

"No. Yes. Sort of," Nate said, resisting the urge to shake it. "There's another channel there, but I can't find the right frequency. It bleeds through in the middle of the others."

He didn't tell Alden that the word "GEMs" had interrupted other broadcasts three times in the past hour. It left him uneasy, as if someone was around the corner, watching him.

Alden wrinkled his nose. "Find the channel that will tell us when Gathos City will deal with our little famine problem. The Courier who brings us bread has been remiss in his duties. I've stockpiled, but it won't last forever."

"If the Breakers hadn't blown up the railway, none of this would have happened."

"If someone hadn't coughed their lung-rot onto their neighbor, none of this would have happened. Such is life. The good news is, the rest of us will likely die alongside you."

Somehow, it hadn't occurred to Nate that Alden and Fran might soon follow him into the stillness. The thought shook him. Alden always seemed to have a way of getting what he needed, hunger for chem more powerful than any other currency. But he wasn't streetwise the way Reed was. He relied on his shop and his trade. And Fran was too old to walk across the street, let alone scavenge for food.

Facing the stillness alone was one thing. Imagining Alden and Fran dying alongside him made his muscles twinge and ache.

The ticker chirped at Nate uselessly. After Alden locked up for the night, Nate climbed up onto the front counter and started tinkering with the crank-light, determined to push back against the sense of helplessness that overwhelmed him. The front room needed more light at night. Maybe people wouldn't be as apt to break the window if it was bright inside.

An icy cramp gripped him without warning. He cried out and dropped his pliers. They landed against the counter with a clatter that sent cracks spidering across the glass.

Alden was picking through a pile of capsules. He traced the jagged crack and glanced up until Nate looked away first.

Nate climbed down—more falling than anything—and banged his side against the counter. He stumbled into the washroom, feeling the weight of Alden's gaze until he pulled the door shut behind him. His knees buckled, and he pressed his cheek against the cold tile floor. Something was different this time. Pain lanced through his head and his gut, cold stabs that grayed his vision.

Tears ran down his face, shivery-cold, and he made chattering hurt-sounds with every breath. He couldn't think. Everything was agony.

Alden found him minutes or hours later.

"Oh, Nate."

By dawn, Nate couldn't move. He curled up at the foot of Fran's bed. Shadows reached for him, the stillness beckoning. Fran wiped his face with a wet towel and crooned a woozy mix of old love songs and lullabies until Alden tucked her in and brought Nate to his bed. Nate grasped at him, tossed on a sea of feverish delirium and spasms of pain.

"If I give you any more, that'll be the last of it," Alden said, hoarse after holding Nate through a long fit. "Can you wait another day?"

"Fran g-g-got my hair all w-w-wet." Nate stammered the words out. "I'm c-c-cold." He didn't think he could wait another day, but he didn't want to beg either.

Alden found a dry bath sheet and rubbed Nate's hair with it, drying it to a tangled poof around his face. He smiled weakly and shook his head. "It's not a good look for you, sweetheart."

An explosion sounded in the distance, rumbling and low.

"I'm s-s-still cold." Nate's teeth chattered.

"I know, love," Alden said, wrapping Nate in another blanket and rubbing his arms and thighs to warm him. "Try to sleep, and I'll stick you in the sun tomorrow, like a plant."

"I'd have to be a weed to grow around here," Nate managed.

"You'd find a way."

Alden talked to him until the pain carried him off.

The door to the shop slammed open, chimes blasting. Only one person had ever come into Alden's shop fit to take the door off its hinges. Nate scrabbled at the bed weakly, pressing his back against the thin wall shared with the front room.

"Where is he?" Reed bellowed.

Alden's tone remained cool. "Your little ginger friend? I'm certain that whole mess was cleared up ages ago."

Something crashed against the wall. Nate tried to push himself up, only to find himself doubled over and moaning on the cushions. He clung to the edge of one, trying to hear what they were saying in the other room.

"Nate!" Reed shouted.

"Ah, of course. Forgive me, Mr. Reed, but didn't you toss him out of your little—" Alden broke off with the sound of what Nate could only assume was choking.

"Pixel told me what he is," Reed said. "So I'll ask you again. Where is he?"

"Reed!" That was Pixel's voice, small and scared. "Don't hurt him!"

Panic flared, stealing Nate's breath. He wasn't afraid of Reed—he could never be afraid of him—but this couldn't be. Nate'd lied for so long. He'd fed Alden and lied and put them all in danger. If Reed knew, he'd be tangled up with all of it too.

Nate's vision fuzzed over as he struggled to sit up, his arms trembling. Each breath caught in a high-pitched wheeze. Gods, he was going to pass out before Reed found him.

The bedroom door opened, startling Nate into losing his balance and landing face-first in the cushions. Panic took over, amplified by the way his breath caught in his throat. By the time Reed and Alden turned him over, Nate was fighting, kicking and clawing for his life.

"Nate! Nate, stop! It's me, Nate. Nate, stop! I'm trying to help you." Reed grasped for Nate's thrashing arms. "What did you give him?" he snarled at Alden.

"This isn't my doing," Alden said acidly. He slipped behind Nate and propped him up into Reed's arms. "You must stop fighting, Natey," he said at Nate's ear. "You need to breathe."

The words sank in distantly, but Nate's instincts told him to fight, to get away from the grip at his throat. He struggled, but his strength gave out long before his will. He gasped and choked against Reed, with Alden pounding on his back, telling him to breathe, please breathe.

Nate sobbed, spent. It hurt to be held, but he was too tired and weak to get away from them.

"Pix." He gasped. "Pixel."

"She's with Alden's grandmother." Reed smoothed Nate's hair away from his teary face. "She's fine."

"You sound bad, honey," Alden said, gentle with him, pulling Nate back against his chest and resting his sharp chin against Nate's shoulder. It forced Nate to look at Reed, who gripped Nate's shirt and crouched in front of him, green eyes wide and unsure.

Nate's thoughts unraveled. He couldn't remember what he'd done wrong, how it had all started. "I'm sorry," he said, choking.

"No, don't say that." Reed reached to wipe a trickling tear from Nate's jawline.

"I couldn't—"

Alden tapped Nate's mouth gently. "No. Stop talking and keep breathing."

"Pixel wasn't right after you left," Reed said. Alden snorted, and Reed's gaze flickered to him briefly. "After I *made you leave.* She wouldn't talk to anyone and started having nightmares again. I took her on a walk this morning, and she cried and told me everything."

"Be more precise, Mr. Reed," Alden said.

Reed glanced at Nate, wary. "Can I?"

"Alden knows me best," Nate said.

A flash of pain crossed Reed's features. "I know that you're . . . that you're a GEM."

Nate tensed. "That's all?"

Reed's brow creased with a confused frown. "Is there more?"

Alden made an exasperated sound at Nate's ear. "The girl is too. Pixel."

"Pixel . . ." Reed blinked.

"I know." Alden shook his head, his chin pivoting against Nate's shoulder. "The percentage of GEMs in your little gang is alarmingly high."

Nate hiccoughed. Everything was changing too quickly. "Reed—you can't—"

"She's safe with me, Nate."

"Until the winter comes and the Breakers' bounty looks a little sweeter?" Alden asked.

"Until someone rips her out of my dead hands," Reed shot back.

"Which they will, as soon as one of your brats sells her out. There's a reason Nate's kept this from you."

"Quit that." Nate elbowed Alden weakly. When Reed

frowned and both of them quieted, Nate went on, careful and slow. "You didn't have to come. Go home. Tell Pix I'm fine."

"You don't look fine."

Nate turned away.

"Is this your doing?" Reed asked Alden. "Pixel told me how you—that you—"

Alden tensed like a cat ready to pounce.

"It's not his fault!" Nate said. "It can't be helped."

"What do you mean?" Reed asked.

"The same thing will happen to Pix when she's older." Nate wheezed. "We get sick. I wasn't lying about getting medicine from Alden." He could feel Alden's satisfied smirk without looking and elbowed him again.

"Can you let us talk? Alone?" Reed asked.

After a long pause, Alden shifted to stand, tucking Nate into Reed's arms. "Ten minutes," he said, oddly quiet, before leaving them in his room.

"I'm sorry," Reed said. "Nate, I'm so sorry."

"No." Nate didn't want to spend the time before the stillness itchy with regret. "I don't want to do this."

Reed stiffened. "I can get Alden."

"No, not . . ." Nate sighed and rubbed his cheek against Reed, trying to show him that he liked being close, that he wanted Reed here. "I don't want to say sorry back and forth. We're both sorry, okay?"

"Why didn't you tell me?"

"Because I didn't want this to happen. You're as trapped as I am now. You have to keep this secret too."

"You know I will," Reed said.

"But the Breakers—"

"Nate, no."

"I didn't want to make you lie to the girls."

"You're not *making* me do anything. Neither is Pix." Reed brushed at Nate's hair slowly, the faint tickle of it pulling Nate away from the pain. "It's all a mess, but it isn't your mess. You didn't start this."

"How bad was it coming over here?"

Reed laughed humorlessly. "Bad."

"Fires?" Nate asked, twisting to look at Reed's face.

"A few."

"Brick and Sparks told me . . . told me how you're . . ."

"Scared of fire?" Reed asked.

"Not *scared*, but . . . yeah."

Reed's pale-green eyes went far away. He scratched his eyebrow and released a quick breath. "After I left the pleasure house, I took up with a gang. Not a gang of scavengers like us. Runners. They weren't bad kids, just rough."

"You ran chem?" Nate asked, as surprised by that as he'd be if Reed told him he'd grown wings.

Reed nodded tightly. "I wasn't much older than Pix. I dropped packages at a public den once in a while. To nice people. They gave me sweet gum and food. I liked them."

Nate clenched his teeth. They must have liked him too.

"When I was there bringing a package upstairs, someone cooking chem dropped a gaslight on a blanket," Reed said. "The whole place went up. I got out. A few others did too, but most of them were so . . . they watched the flames like it was something beautiful. I saw—I saw a girl with her hand on fire, watching it go black."

Nate thought he knew everything about chem and how it could ravage someone, slowly twist them inside out. But Reed's gaze had gone hollow and haunted. He carried things Nate couldn't see and would never know.

"Wishes," Nate said. "You first."

Reed's voice went thick for a moment. "Home."

"What kind?"

"One we don't have to leave. Somewhere Pixel won't have to be scared. Somewhere she can stay."

Nate fought through a wheezing breath. "How about a tree house?"

"I've never seen a tree big enough to hold a house," Reed said.

"I've seen them in drawings."

"Your turn."

Nate hesitated. Pixel didn't know that Alden's supply of Remedy was running out. So Reed wouldn't know either. "I already told you." His vision fuzzed around the edges. "A tree house."

"That's cheating."

"You," Nate said.

"I'm not a cheater."

"No." Nate squirmed, already wishing he hadn't said it. But he had to say it now. "I meant my wish. It's you."

"I sent you away." Reed's voice thickened with anguish. "I made you go when you were sick."

"I told you. I know what I want."

A shudder ran through Reed when he took Nate's hand in both of his and drew it to his lips, his lashes wet, and his eyes closed gently. He kissed Nate's palm, and Nate recognized something in the bend of his neck. The same need for forgiveness that chased Nate like a shadow.

"Reed," he whispered, knowing he'd have to say it again and again for Reed to ever believe him. Knowing he didn't have time to do that. "You're my wish."

Reed dropped Nate's hand and closed the distance between them with a soft kiss. Heat blossomed through Nate, and he tugged at Reed, made it more than soft, undone by the sweetness of Reed's mouth. He made a low sound—a bittersweet wish, pain and longing. They touched as much as Nate could bear to. Reed's palms were warm, gentling him when the shivers of quiet kisses became tremors of pain.

As Nate caught his breath, Reed nosed at him and pressed quick, easy kisses at his jaw. His cheeks were wet. "I'm here."

"Stay." Nate began to cry again. It was nothing more than a dry, anguished sound.

"Shh," Reed whispered. "Nate. Rest. I won't go."

———

Nate heard voices, but they were far away. His breath didn't fill him up all the way. So he held very still, and that helped a little.

"Why isn't he getting better?" Reed's fingers stroked Nate's bare foot with restless twitches.

"I had to start rationing." That was Alden, slow and tired. "If I give him what I have left, he'll feel good for a few hours, maybe more, and then he'll ... At least this way ... Tiny doses. I can keep him comfortable."

"*Comfortable*? That's it?"

"That's it for now. If it gets too bad, we should try to make him sleep. It would be easier that way," Alden said.

Reed's grip tightened at Nate's foot. "What are you saying?"

"I'm saying I can't save him." Alden sighed. "That's what you want to hear, right? I can't save him, Reed. He's going to die."

It grew quiet for a while. Reed's grip eased. He began rubbing small circles at Nate's back. Alden was there in a whisper of long hair against Nate's cheek as he leaned in close, his clammy fingers briefly pressed to the pulse at Nate's throat. Then he was gone again, his voice near and far.

Nate floated, not with the heavy lethargy of Alden's tincture for his head, but on a current of pain and breathlessness. It was hard to tell when he slept or not, or how quickly the time passed.

"You don't look so good yourself." Reed didn't sound angry.

"Fishing for the lurid details?" The sound of Alden drifted about the room. "It'll pass. I have other means of distraction. I can't—he can't let someone feed when he's like this. He'd sleep, and he'd never wake up."

"Is that what you meant?" Reed breathed in noisily. "That you'd take his blood to make him sleep?"

"Don't look so scandalized. I'm not a monster."

"I didn't say—"

"It's a bit more complicated than that," Alden said. "But I didn't make him like this, and I haven't touched him since he came back here. As a matter of fact, I believe *you* were the last one to feed on him, dear Reed. And I'm certain you hastened this . . . situation."

"I didn't ask for it." Reed's voice went coarse. "I wouldn't have let him!"

"Are you so sure? You would have died without it. According to him, at any rate. He was distraught. Do you want to know what he promised me to save your life?"

"Stop," Nate said, the sound little more than a wheeze. He reached toward the sound of Alden. "Stop it."

"He said he'd feed me as often as I wanted. So generous, our boy," Alden said, out of reach. "You do realize that's what he was doing all along? Paying me back. I've never owed Nate a thing. I've been keeping him alive."

"You're not doing a very good job of it now." Reed caught Nate's wrist and stilled him.

"Ah, well. As Nate said, that can't be helped. I'm afraid I don't have my fingers in every pot in the Withers."

"Then we have to go somewhere else," Reed said.

"To Gathos City? Yes, ship him off. They have loads of Remedy up in the towers."

"No. There has to be somewhere else. Some*one* else. How much do you know?"

"The Breakers will catch you when you fall," Nate whispered.

"Go back to sleep," Alden snapped. "You're supposed to be resting."

"Is his mind slipping?" Reed asked, looking pained.

"It's some rot from the tickers. I don't know what it means."

Alden's words snapped out—clipped with the sharp edges of a lie.

Reed rubbed Nate's shoulder. "We'll find someone who can help you."

Alden didn't let go of Nate's hand. "And maybe we'll all go down with you."

Worry fluttered through Nate. He shifted, trying to roll onto his back to look at them. When he tried to speak, a low moan rumbled in his chest.

The smoke. Can't you smell it?

"Don't listen to him. The gang is okay," Reed said. "We left the bank before it burned. It'll be okay."

"Pix," Nate whispered.

"She's safe. I promise. They're all safe."

"I don't see the need to lie to him," Alden said. "The shop is dead today. When the fiends don't come out, it's bad."

"Tell me," Nate said hoarsely.

"Sparks and Brick are hiding down the street. They're safe. Pixel's asleep with Fran. I promise." Reed sighed. "But it's getting rough out there. There's not enough food. People are building barges and trying to sail across the sludge-channel to the city."

"They'll find a rude welcome," Alden said.

"This can't last forever," Reed said. "Gathos City needs the trains back in service."

Swept away by pain, unable to keep his focus steady on what they were saying, Nate closed his eyes. His breath caught in his chest with a bubbly hiss.

"Aren't there other things that can help him?" Reed asked, whispering now.

"Anything strong enough to help him would kill him. You could try herbs, but I don't have anything like that here."

"There were a few growers at the bank, but it's nothing but steel and ash now. They already looted the herbalist's place. I doubt I could find anything quickly."

Alden sighed. "I'll boil water. The steam might help him breathe. If the riots get any rougher, we've only got a few days left here. I've got to find shelter for my grandmother."

"The Servants might take her," Reed said.

"I'm not in the market for a caregiver, Reed. We're both invested in this mess—I recognize that. But you keep your cute little nose to yourself and let me mind my own business."

"You should keep your *thoughts* to yourself if you're not trying to have a conversation."

Alden snorted. "Any more advice?"

"No," Reed said.

Nate tried to open his eyes, but his lids were gummy and heavy. He tried to hear Alden over the sound of his own labored breaths.

"I can't hide him from them much longer. They're getting too bold."

"The A-Vols?" Reed asked.

Nate pictured the furrow at his brow and the way it made him look younger.

Alden's answer came a beat too late. "Yes, who else?"

It was quiet for a while. Nate woke with a soft whimper as Alden placed a steaming, wet cloth on his chest.

"Easy." Alden rubbed Nate's chest slowly. "Go back to sleep."

Time passed, but Nate couldn't measure it no matter how hard he grasped for the end of the wire. It was easier to stop. To sleep.

Someone was speaking to him.

He fought to open his eyes, but it was too hard to coax his lids up. He'd never known exhaustion like this. The stillness beckoned, and it was warm and gentle. Heavy.

Reed's fingers were fire against Nate's throat.

Alden was quiet, raw. "There may be a way to get him Remedy," he said. "But you're not going to like it."

Their voices drifted away, heated—too far above the surface of Nate's awareness for him to understand. The ground was opening up below him, pulling him deep into the dirt and the sludge. It was like Fran said. He'd be bones soon, drifting to the Mainland.

Liquid spilled between his lips, and he swallowed involuntarily, throat cooling. It burned into his chest, hot and cold at once. The heaviness lifted like smog before a storm front.

He opened his eyes.

"Nate." Reed's hand brushed his face, pushed his hair back.

The room swam into focus. Alden hung back, fingers twisted in his robe. He watched Nate, his eyes darker than Nate had ever seen, and his hair was tangled. Alden sucked in a deep breath when their eyes met. Pain crossed his face, and he looked away.

Something's wrong.

Reed held him up and helped him drink. He struggled to swallow the warm water, and he lost sight of Alden.

The Remedy cleared Nate's head enough to string his thoughts together. "What are you fighting about?"

"We aren't fighting." Reed glanced aside. "But I don't trust him. And I definitely don't trust his friends."

"What friends?" Nate asked.

Alden doesn't have any friends.

"Associates. Contacts. Call them what you will." Alden returned to Nate's line of sight, his arms crossed, his mouth an unhappy twist. He plucked at his sleeve, shifting from foot to foot, looking everywhere but directly at Nate. "I can't help you. I tried." His chest heaved. "*They* can."

"No." Reed's words growled out. "I don't—"

"Then watch him die!" Alden shouted. He took a ragged breath and quieted. "But I won't. Not when there's a way."

Reed was squeezing Nate too hard. "Why haven't you mentioned your *friends* before?"

Something changed in Alden's eyes, desperation hardening to an icy sheen that made Nate want to look away. "You had a taste, Reed. You tell me." He bent over them, fingers twisted into white knots, his voice deadly soft. "Would you share?"

Nate thudded into the cushions as Reed sprang up, growling and pushing Alden into his desk. Papers scattered, and a glass jar fell with an ugly crack—and Alden was laughing, Reed's hands twisted into his robe. "Not all of us are as altruistic as you are. What did you think I wanted with him?"

He's lying.

It still cut, pain blossoming behind Nate's ribs. He caught his breath, wheezing through the hurt.

Isn't he?

Whatever had driven Alden to fear and poison didn't matter. Nate didn't want to die, not like this—helpless and listening to the two of them bicker like gulls.

"Take me," he said.

Reed released Alden with a shove and turned, stricken. "Nate. No."

"It's not up to you." The stillness hung over Nate, cold and so close. He struggled onto his elbows. "I need your help. Alden won't do it." He hadn't traveled more than twenty paces from his shop in all the years Nate had known him.

Alden flinched. "It's not—"

"You saved my life," Reed said to Nate. "I owe you the same. But I don't trust him."

The Remedy wasn't sticking. Nate could already feel the brief wave of strength leaving him, and there was nothing left, no more respite from the pain closing in on him. His voice wavered. "Reed, promise me."

"All right." Reed sank to a crouch and pushed Nate's hair out of his eyes. "Let's get Pixel and go."

"You can't take Pixel there." Alden rushed forward, reaching for Nate. "She can't go!"

Reed drew his shoulders back. "I'm not leaving Pixel with you!" he shouted.

Alden went rigid, and a flush lit his cheeks, splotchy, as if Reed had slapped him. "I didn't ask you to. She can't stay here."

Frowning, Nate tried to catch Alden's eye. He was missing

something in the strange quiet of Alden's words, in the way he seemed to be shrinking, all the anger drained from him.

Reed's voice softened as if he could see it too. "Brick and Sparks will keep her safe. We've always kept her safe."

Turning away, Alden steadied himself with a hand against his desk. "Of course."

The room swooped, and Nate cried out at the sense of suddenly falling—only to realize he was being lifted up into Reed's arms. Carried like a child.

Alden was always so dramatic, wrapping his words in finery. This time, his voice didn't bite. "You can't come back here," he said, weary. "Do you understand?"

Reed carried Nate past Alden through the front room, where Pixel launched at them, crying and questioning Reed too quickly for Nate to understand. The chimes at the door rang out. It happened so fast that Nate couldn't ask after Fran, ask where they were going—what he'd made Reed promise to do. His vision went spotty, and his grip loosened.

The last thing Nate saw, before he didn't see anything at all, was Alden bracing himself in the doorway of his shop, black hair curtaining his face like a veil.

CHAPTER
TWELVE

"Nate! Stay awake, okay? Stay awake!"

Nate bobbed like trash floating in the sludge-channel, up and down on unseen waves. He struggled to get away from whatever moved him with sickening lurches.

Reed rumbled against his skin, comforting. "Hold still, Nate."

Nate forced his eyes open. Reed was carrying him along a quiet side street he didn't recognize.

He tried to ask where they were going, but the words came out as a low groan. It was nearly sundown, and garbage and patches of blood cluttered the empty street.

"What happened?" Nate managed to croak.

"More fighting. More fires." Reed shuddered and squeezed Nate.

Upon closer look, some of the garbage wasn't garbage at all. Bodies, crumpled and bloodied, lay in the street.

Pixel skipped alongside them, hopping over the worst piles of trash. Nate watched with horror as she skipped over the splayed legs of a corpse. The glass bead necklace Alden had given her clicked against the silver pendant from Reed, and she hummed to herself absently.

"Alden said . . . not Pixel. Not supposed to come."

"It's too rough out here," Brick said, winded. "Have to stay together."

"We couldn't move until the riot cleared," Reed said. "There's no more time to find her a safe place to hide."

Every wheezing breath felt like drowning. Nate coughed out a weak sound of frustration and pain, hating being carried. His head spun. Fear skittered through his veins with each sluggish beat of his heart. He let out a low whimper.

What would the stillness feel like?

"Reed." *I'm scared.*

Reed shifted Nate's weight. "Just a little longer."

"Where's Sparks?"

"She's tailing us to make sure no one else is," Brick said.

"We're going to see Alden's friends," Pixel said, staying close to Nate and Reed while Brick forged ahead, kicking refuse out of the way.

"No." The word was a moan. "Pixel. Not safe."

"Nothing is safe. I'm not letting her out of my sight." Reed dodged around smoldering trash and coughed as the smoke washed over them. When he cleared his throat, he was steady again. Deep and sure. "Be still, Nate. Don't waste your breath."

Too tired to be stung by Reed's admonishing tone, Nate tucked his face against Reed's neck. They wouldn't be out here on the street if it weren't for him. They'd be holed up safe somewhere. Reed always knew where to hide—knew hiding was the safest, smartest thing to do.

Nate's eyes closed on their own. "I'm sorry," he mumbled.

"Hey, now," Brick said, louder. "Stay awake."

Reed gave Nate a light shake and walked faster. "Nate. Don't go to sleep."

"How long?" Nate meant to ask, "How long was I out?" But his voice wouldn't work. He floated, losing track of the steady beat of Reed's footsteps.

"Only a little while." Reed sounded pained. "We gave you the last of that stuff Alden had, remember? It doesn't seem like it's helping very much."

A nearby explosion shook the ground, and Reed stumbled, dropping Nate to his feet beside him as he caught his balance. Pixel and Brick crowded close, and Brick slung her strong arms around Nate to keep him on his feet. For a long second, Nate wondered if this was it—if they'd die huddled together.

Because of me.

"We're okay," Reed said raggedly. He hefted Nate back up. "Run!"

Brick and Pixel dashed across the street, away from the direction of the explosion. Reed's pulse beat hard against Nate.

"What if Alden's friends are all blasted up?" Pixel asked, sniffling.

Nate's heart sank at the undercurrent of hope. He wanted to fight, to struggle out of Reed's arms and explain that no one Alden knew would do anything kind without wanting something in return. It was a risk he was willing to take—but not something he'd gamble Pixel's safety on.

His voice caught in his throat, a broken moan.

"You want to know a secret?" Reed asked.

Pixel sniffled. "I can keep them. Ask Nate."

Reed laughed, winded. "Alden gave us directions to a basement. It'll be safe down there."

"I don't like basements." Pixel grimaced. "They're full of rats and pee."

"Hopefully not this one. Come on." Brick tugged Pixel along and cast Reed a worried look over her head. She caught Nate watching her and gave him a grim smile.

They ducked into a shadowed alcove. A group ran by with torches that reeked of gasolex. Nate couldn't tell if they were running *from* something or not, but their yells echoed with merriment—a distorted sound like a party gone sour.

The last sprint was the shortest—or Nate passed out. The next thing he knew, Reed was carrying him down stairs lit by bright lights fastened to the walls. Squinting at the glow, he admired the tinkering he saw. Clean installations with no wires hanging down. Someone knew what they were doing.

"We need help!" Brick called out, knocking on a steel door on thick hinges. It reminded Nate of something, but he couldn't place where he'd seen the gleaming metal before.

A ticker affixed to the wall chirped at them: *Identify yourself.*

"I told you we needed a name," Pixel mumbled. "Tell them it's the Alley Cats."

Brick's cheeks went scarlet. For a moment, Nate thought she was going to laugh.

"We were sent by Alden!" Reed tripped over the name, as if it pained him to speak it. "He said you would be able to help a GEM." He went hoarse. "He's sick."

When the door opened, Nate moaned quietly, overcome

by the sweet, comforting scent of honey. If this was dying, he'd go to sleep unafraid.

A woman stood in the doorway, filling the frame with her tall, strong form. She looked the way Nate imagined the Old Gods, beautiful and frightening—pale skin smooth, and hair shaved down to brown stubble. There was something familiar about her eyes, like he'd seen them before. "My name is Agatha."

Pixel pushed between Brick and Reed, brushing by Nate's leg. She squirmed out of Reed's grip and stepped up to Agatha. "You're a GEM."

Agatha laughed a deep, lovely sound. "I believe you are too, little one. Bring your sick friend inside. It looks like you'd better hurry."

The air inside the basement tasted stuffy, but it didn't smell like gasolex and violence. Scent memories threaded through Nate's awareness—flashes of polished metal and fear.

On one wall, dark-green plants grew under glaring lights. Even from the middle of the room, Nate could feel the heat they generated. It was more green than he'd ever seen in the Withers. If he hadn't been vomiting into a pail, he would have gone to touch them and smell them and taste them. Instead, he retched, no longer able to control the sounds that sobbed out of him.

As Nate coughed and tried to breathe, Agatha hunched over a polished metal workbench, decanting pale liquid like a chem fiend, but clear-eyed and steady-handed.

Nate slipped in and out of consciousness. It was like trying to see at night with a faulty crank-light. He reached his hand out, afraid of falling.

Reed.

"Please hurry," someone said. "Please."

Nate's awareness strobed. Pixel in the corner on a red couch, crying with a piece of bread in her hands. Brick at Nate's shoulder, pinning him down on a tabletop as his body moved on its own, lost in convulsions. Reed's face in front of Nate's, saying things Nate couldn't understand over the sound of his own senseless cries. His boots thumped at the table with every violent jerk.

Where are my tools?

They couldn't move again without his tools.

Reed cupped Nate's jaw fiercely as Agatha hurried over with a liquid that splashed into Nate's mouth with a familiar, sharp taste. He swallowed, coughed, and swallowed more as she continued to pour it down his throat.

The sounds in the room slowly cleared. Nate heard Pixel's muffled sobs and Reed at his ear, wet and hoarse. "Gods, Nate."

"I'm okay," Nate exhaled.

Agatha peered over him, her eyes pale-brown. He knew them. "You were nearly too far gone," she said, faintly accusing.

Brick hung back, red tangles matted against her skin and sweat running down her pale face like tears. "No more screaming." Without another word, she walked to the couch and sat heavily beside Pixel.

Nate tried to twist his thoughts back together. Alden had warned them not to bring Pixel here, but he didn't know why it mattered so much. And he didn't know why Agatha was cross with him for being sick. He wanted her to be fond of him, but it felt like the memory of a longing. Nothing made sense, so he focused on what he knew. "You make Remedy," he said to her.

She grasped Nate's wrist, fingers gentle at his pulse point. "Yes."

Nate watched her face and saw fine lines around her eyes he'd missed before. "Is that how you're so old?"

GEMs didn't get old. He'd known that since he was a child, when Bernice had told him he'd never become like her, frail and weathered, with a lifetime of memories and knowledge.

"Yes," Agatha said with a rueful, severe laugh. She helped him sit up, her grip strong and sure. "That is how I've survived for this long."

Nate ached like one of his gutted tickers, broken apart and spread across a clean worktable. But it was a sore kind of hurt, not the mind-numbing agony from before.

Reed stood beside the table, close to Nate, his hand warm and heavy on Nate's thigh. Tremors ran through him, his nerves as hot as electricity. Nate wanted to touch him, to reassure him, but his mind raced. He had to put the pieces together, light up the fog in his mind.

A realization struck him with a sting of betrayal. Another thing he should have known all along.

"You sold Remedy to Alden," he said.

"You're a clever one." Agatha flashed her teeth. "Any Remedy in the Withers comes through me. I like to think of it as a service. It served you well until now, I imagine."

Brick held Pixel on her lap and watched them closely, her

blue eyes clouded with worry. Her gaze darted to a door like the one at the stairway, heavy and locked with a massive hinge. Once again, a distant familiarity struck Nate.

Reed's fingers twisted into the loose fabric of Nate's pants. "Why did you stop giving it to Alden? Nate almost died."

"To flush him out, of course. So we could help him," Agatha said. "Not Nathan specifically, but any GEM Alden was hiding. Though it turned out to only be you. We had a deal that he would send any GEMs he acquired to us, and he did not keep that end of his bargain. We had to remove the middleman."

"Alden said we wouldn't like what you had to say," Reed said.

Agatha placed her hand over her heart and shook her head. "A chem dealer with his own personal GEM? Of course he did," she said, gentle. Pained.

Alden *had* been shifty—always hiding something. The scrawled notes in his books. Telling Nate not to leave, not to be seen. It was too much to untangle, too much to consider. Had Alden selfishly kept him from his best chance at staying well? Of surviving?

If Nate hadn't left Alden for the gang a year ago, he may have never left the shop again, may have wasted away long before now.

So of course Alden wouldn't share him with Agatha.

"What do you want from us?" Nate asked. Nothing was ever free. He couldn't keep up. He was missing something, and when he missed things, that's when the wires sparked up and bit him.

"Let's start at the beginning." Agatha sat at the edge of the table by Nate's boots. "You know what your blood can do. The magic of it. Correct?"

"It's not really magic." Pixel wiped her nose. "Nate said so."

Agatha turned kind eyes on Pixel. "But it *feels* like magic, doesn't it?"

"He didn't ask for a story." Reed pulled Nate to the edge of the table and wrapped an arm around his chest too tightly.

"Then let me skip to the story's end. You came here because you're dying."

"They brought me here." Nate's voice strained in his sore throat. "Alden sent us."

"Alden is an abuser. I shudder to think of how you must have suffered at his hands. But you'll be safe now, with us."

Nate's head spun. Agatha was so warm and concerned. Somehow nurturing, despite the predatory glint in her eyes. "Alden didn't . . ." He rubbed the little sore spot on his finger where he'd pinched himself with his pliers. Alden had never hurt him.

Had he?

Reed made a bristly sound. "Don't make it sound like you invited him over for gull pies. You tried to kill him!"

"I did not try to kill him. We had no choice but to make him come to us." Agatha studied Reed. "We didn't make him ill. He was dying because Gathos City built a failsafe into the genetic code of GEMs so we couldn't survive outside of their control."

Reed's grip tightened at Nate's shirt.

"Gathos City never saw us as people," Agatha went on. "So they never truly understood how dangerous we could be."

She wore baggy pants and a plain T-shirt like Reed's, but

there was something elegant about her—and something strong. Whatever she wanted, he had no doubt she'd find the means to get it. And her smile did nothing to soften the threat.

Nate held on to Reed's arm, trying to reassure him. He needed to know: "Do they really do terrible things to GEMs in Gathos City?"

The answer was already in his bones, in the heart-pounding moments between waking and forgetting his nightmares.

He needed to hear it, though, even if he had no reason to trust this woman.

Agatha's smile pressed into a tight line. "Yes. It's worse than you can imagine. Worse than what people say. They take our bodies and do with them what they wish. What you would never wish for."

Alden's words echoed in Nate's head: *They'll take everything, Natey. Don't you know that?*

But Alden hadn't been talking about Gathos City. He'd been talking about the Breakers.

"Tell us what you want him to do," Reed said.

"We've developed new purposes for GEM blood. New opportunities." She turned her gaze from Reed to Nate. "I can offer you safety, food, and shelter in return for sharing your blood. And I will supply you with Remedy, of course."

Nate rubbed his eyes until he saw stars. The cold, clean table was familiar, like a fading scar, and he couldn't place why. "I don't understand. You want me to feed someone?"

"Of course not. That's barbaric. Our methods transcend the butchery our makers intended us for."

"You're not taking his blood!" Reed grip stretched Nate's shirt.

"Reed," Nate said sharply. His head was clear now. He could speak for himself. Agatha's promise of shelter and food had gotten his attention. This could be his chance to keep the gang safe. Always. All he had to do was feed people—maybe heal them. She clearly cared about him. How bad could it be? "What kind of methods?"

"Perhaps I should show you," Agatha said. She offered Nate her hand and helped him off the table. He stared at where her skin touched his, struck by a memory of her touching him before this place, before any of this. But how could that be?

Reed held Nate's other arm, tugging him closer the moment Agatha let go.

"It's okay," Nate said to Reed quietly, trying to reassure him. Reed's fingers dug in to his arm. "Is it?"

He shrugged Reed away, trying to think straight without worrying about Reed worrying about him. "I said it's fine."

But as soon as Reed let go, emptiness followed.

Agatha led them to a metal door opposite the one they'd entered. Brick helped Pixel off the couch, and Nate stared at the hinges. Shiny and thick, they didn't look like any tinkering he'd seen in the Withers. She turned a small wheel, and the door unsealed with a sticky pop.

"I don't think we'll wake her, but we should keep quiet," Agatha murmured. She pushed the door open and let Brick and Pixel inside first.

Agatha yanked a heavy switch on the wall, and Nate lost his footing. Reed caught him as he sagged, struck by the warped familiarity of the room. Rows of lights hummed from the low ceiling. Thin pipes lined the wall, towering over him and fanning out like veins. He spun, fighting the arms around him, looking for the blinking red lights that would mean the machine was about to turn on.

Mom, do I have to?

It hurt so much when the needles went in, even when he held very still, did just what he was told. They'd learn so much about the magic in him, his mother would say, because he was such a brave little boy.

"Nate?" Reed grabbed his wrists. "Nate."

Coppery fingers reached to devour Nate. He blinked and sucked in a breath, shaking off the memory. The one he tried, always, to forget. "It's fine," he said, straightening with a cough.

Reed stared at him, brow creased. He let go of Nate's wrists and pulled him closer, brushing his lips at Nate's hair. "I'm right here."

His solid warmth pulled Nate back into the basement, into the present.

Nate took his hand, squeezed it tight. He'd been wrong to push Reed away. Nate needed him close. Maybe they needed each other.

The pipes and barrels and panels didn't have any blinking lights on them. They were old—made of warped, hammered copper. The metal shone unevenly, patchwork pieces welded together. A gauge on the largest cylinder displayed numbers in units he wasn't familiar with. The iron furnace glowed, its stovepipe reaching like a crooked finger and poking up through the low ceiling.

The more Nate saw, the more he wanted to take it apart, coax secrets from the greasy gears.

"What is this?" Reed studied the ceiling where thin pipes fanned out like a spider's web. "What does it do?"

"It's a still."

"It's beautiful," Nate said, unable to disguise his admiration for the patchwork tinkering.

"I wish I could agree, but it pales in comparison to what I could achieve with the proper materials." Agatha rested her long fingers against a shiny metal panel. "It gets the job done."

"How does it work?" Nate forced his arms to hang at his sides. As much as he yearned to explore the machine, he didn't want her to know that he was a Tinkerer. Not until he understood her plans.

"The same as any still. With some modifications, of course." She opened the panel with a delicate touch. Behind the metal door, glass tubes knotted together like clasped fingers, each full of tiny whirring gears.

"That's a Diffuser," Nate said, drawn closer by the marvel of it. Where did they get such miniscule gear-work and fine glass?

"On a grander scale, and not exactly." She closed the panel, obscuring the buzzing tubes. "The still doesn't produce as well as I'd hoped, but I'll be able to make repairs and vast improvements with the new parts from the city."

Nate pushed a stray tickle of hair behind his ear.

Produce what?

Pixel put her arms around Brick's waist. "I don't like it in here."

"It's because we're underground." Reed patted her shoulder. "We'll go back up soon."

"How did you get new parts from the city?" Nate asked. He rubbed his cold hands together.

Agatha gave a low chuckle. "They delivered them to us."

Brick let out a soft sound of alarm. "Is she sick?"

Nate whirled to look for Pixel, expecting to see her swooning with fear, but she stood shivering and stubborn-jawed next to Brick. He followed Brick's gaze to a stack of shallow bunks tucked behind the machine. The dim light cast heavy shadows, and he squinted to make out a lumpy form on the lowest bunk.

It was a young woman. She slept on her back, one arm hanging limp over the side of the bunk.

"Ah, that's Juniper. She's resting," Agatha said. "I was about to get her started on intravenous fluids when you all came by to visit."

"She's a GEM too," Pixel said.

The gentle scent of honey and warmth clung to the bunk where the woman slept. But she didn't smell strong and healthy like Pixel and Agatha did, and the sweetness had an aftertaste to it—sour and sad. Juniper breathed very slowly, her mouth slack and pale.

A dizzying mix of shame and dread churned through Nate. He must have looked like this every time he'd fed Alden.

"Yes, little one. She is a GEM. She arrived a year ago from Gathos City." Agatha drew the bunk's curtain closed. The girl's pale fingers peeked out, twitching. "We invested in her escape. She was a being kept by a family who not only fed upon her but used her in ways . . . well, in ways I wouldn't discuss with a girl your age."

Nate wondered how many GEMs were still there—locked high in Gathos City's towers. Alone. Beyond the reach of anyone willing to free them.

Reed examined a shelf full of stacks of white plastic boxes. He stumbled back as if bitten and turned to Agatha, gaze hot. "This is chem. All of this is chem! I've seen it on the street."

"The very finest," Agatha said. Her pale eyes gleamed. "Did you know that the majority of street-chem is laced with gasolex and cooked-down sludge? It's utterly toxic. It's killing people. This? This is safe."

Nate's ears rang. He stared down at the floor where his boot rested against a drain shaped like a flower and flecked with dark-red stains. He'd seen those little boxes before too—tucked away in Alden's private stash. And never sold to any of Alden's customers.

Every time Alden had shaken tiny pills out of the white boxes, he'd gone boneless and uncaring, too blissed-out to bother with the shop or Nate. The only other thing Alden had gone quite as empty-eyed for was Nate.

Nate's breath tripped, punched out of him by the realization. "You're making chem with our blood," he said, hoarse.

"Chem. Medicine. It's all in the eyes of the beholder. The people of the Withers are sick, Nathan. You know that better than most, don't you?"

"The last thing the Withers needs is more chem." Reed was trembling, rage hot in his eyes. "This is the worst kind I ever saw—people did all sorts of shit for it, *on* it."

"But they felt so much better when they got it, didn't they?" Agatha asked.

A ropey cable hung from the machine at Nate's eye level. At the end, a delicate silver prong swayed—identical to the tip of Alden's Diffuser.

He glanced at Brick. She stared at the curtain hiding Juniper and shuffled from one foot to the next, restless and caged.

Pixel whimpered. "I want to go. This is a bad place. They're going to hurt us."

"You're perfectly safe here." Agatha's teeth were very straight. "The Breakers will protect you at any cost."

CHAPTER
THIRTEEN

"The Breakers?" Nate recoiled, stumbling back into the sharp edge of one the bunks. There were so many along the wall. They were all empty. "You're with them?"

"Why do you sound so distressed, Nathan? Are you afraid of them?"

Reed grabbed Nate by the sleeve and put his body between them. "Don't play games! Are you?"

Agatha gave him a long look. "This is a serious matter. I would never make a game of it."

"I'm not afraid of the Breakers," Nate said, stepping out from behind Reed. It was a simple lie. He was used to lying.

"Of course not." Agatha's mouth quirked. "I'm not threatening you, am I?"

"Then you admit you're with them." Reed spat the words out.

Squeezing his eyes shut, Nate willed down a sour wave of nausea. The chance to stay safe had been too easy, too good to be true. The Breakers weren't just well-organized chem dealers. They were dealing chem made with GEM blood. Now Reed and Brick and Pixel were stuck in a basement with them, and it was his fault.

I made Reed promise to take me here.

"Admit I'm with them?" Agatha's mouth quirked. "They're with *me*."

Brick let out a low whistle and hauled Pixel onto her hip. "Stars. She's the boss."

"She's mean," Pixel spat.

Hysteria buzzed in Nate's ears. He waved his arm at the stacks of chem and the giant still. The machine wasn't made for healing people. It was made for creating chem that made people hunger so hard they'd do anything for it. Kill for it. Die for it. "You got away from Gathos City, and *this* is what you're doing with your freedom? Pushing chem?"

"And flesh," Reed said with a snarl.

"I'm cultivating power. There's no such thing as freedom without it." Agatha's gaze bore into Nate's, and everything else in the room went away. He saw his fears reflected there. The icy grip of machines, doors that were always locked—hunger on every face. "They can't hurt us anymore if we have power. That's what you want, isn't it?"

Nate's voice stuck in his throat.

Yes.

Her lips curled into a satisfied smile. "That's the world I'm building for us. I run eighty percent of the chem trade now. I expect that to be ninety-five percent by the time Gathos City opens the gates. When they come crawling in, desperate for a taste of the GEMs they can't afford, we'll own them. They'll be fiending for my chem within days. They'll never control us again."

Nate shrank back, dizzy. He bumped into Reed and shivered. Her vision sounded perfect—safety, security. Freedom for GEMs. But not like this. Not if it meant hurting people.

"I take it you don't approve of our methods." Agatha sounded disappointed, as if Nate was the one being unreasonable.

Reed's breath hissed. "Your *methods*? You're blowing things up! You're starting riots."

"*We* didn't start riots. People did," Agatha said with a light shrug. "We were simply trying to import better tech. Honestly, it was a bit of an overreaction for Gathos City to stop food deliveries over one little train wreck. But they did, and here we are, far more poised to succeed than I could have hoped."

"*Succeed*?" Reed asked, voice thick with disgust.

"The trauma of starvation will linger even when bellies are full, and the Withers will need me more than ever. Chem makes people forget the chaos and tragedy of our world," she said, as cold as Alden when he calculated the need of his clients. "It's a gift. The train wreck helped me give that gift to more people."

"The train . . ." Nate's hands went cold. The heavy door to the distillation room. That's where he'd seen it before. He'd opened the same kind of door once—on the burning train car. He could still smell the sour ruin of burning hair and charred flesh. "You blew up the railway so you could scavenge tech from the trains!"

"Gathos City puts the very finest technology into their

transit system." Agatha gestured to the door. "Let's talk in the other room. I don't want to disturb sweet Juniper."

"She isn't moving," Pixel said. She pointed with an angry wave and glared up at Agatha. "You hurt her."

Brick made a soft, hushing sound and carried Pixel out of the distillation room, back to where they'd started—where Nate's sweat still shone on the polished table. The muscles at her arms twitched like she was fighting the instinct to run.

Nate wanted to run too.

The phantom sound of the train whistle haunted him. He'd been inside the cars. He'd seen it himself. Radiant lights. Polished metal. The guts of the train would have been the same—smooth and new and powerful. How could he have been so stupid?

They'd fooled everyone.

The Breakers hadn't blown up the train to make a statement. They'd only wanted the tech on board—to use it to make more chem.

"You killed all those people," Reed was saying as he pulled Nate toward Brick and Pixel. "You're killing people now!"

"That's how times change. The way things changed for our kind, what they made us become, what they wanted from us." Agatha advanced on them, as tall as Reed and sure-footed. She filled the doorway, terrible and perfect. "I'll make them beg for our chem. They'll crawl for it. It's *our* time now."

The plants had been so lush and green that Nate hadn't noticed all the narrow cabinets lining the opposite wall. Each was sealed with a padlock.

"It's all chem," Nate said, sick to his stomach. What he'd

done for Alden—that had been his choice. They'd hurt each other willingly, their choices locked in Alden's back room. This was so much worse. Chem wasn't a miracle, and GEMs weren't magic, and in that moment, Nate hated himself fiercely. Hated Agatha. Hated Pixel. Hated his mother for making him, and his father for not stopping her.

He stood as tall as he could so that Agatha could see that he was unafraid. He wasn't going to get any closer to the stillness than he'd already been. "I won't help you hurt people."

"That's a shame." Agatha pressed her palms against the table that stood between them. "We've already helped you. Remedy comes with a price. You of all people know that."

Nate's breath caught in this throat. He'd be dead now if it weren't for her.

And if it weren't for Alden.

"I know," he exhaled, taking quick stock of the small room.

The table remained between him and Agatha. Pixel cried quietly against Brick's side at the end of the table. Reed held on to him from behind, his fingers tangled stubbornly in Nate's shirt.

Think.

Another table against the far wall was covered in glass containers and tubes of strange shapes and sizes. He didn't see any alarms or weapons. They could fight their way out if they had to—and Nate knew well enough to get out of the way if it came to that.

"If you won't help us, I won't force you to stay," Agatha said, studying Nate.

"Good." Nate frowned, uneasy. After all of this, he didn't expect her to let him go without a fight.

"Of course, if you leave, you will die. Soon."

"I'll take my chances," Nate said. "I don't want to hurt people."

Agatha gestured toward the door elegantly. "Like I said, you're free to go. Gods watch you."

"Pixel." Nate held out his hand. "Come on."

When Pixel moved, Agatha chuckled. "I didn't say you could take the girl."

Pixel's eyes went wide. "Reed! Nate!"

Her sharp, frightened cry was like gasolex splashed on a bin-fire. Nate lunged for Pixel, and Reed and Brick launched toward Agatha in an explosion of movement. Reed slid over the table and tackled Agatha to the ground. Nate slipped on the polished floor and crashed to his knees.

Agatha was taller than Reed—and wickedly strong. They fell together in a heap and rolled across the concrete. She kicked him away, and he barreled into the lowest shelf of plants. Plastic pots tumbled down around him, spilling mud and sand.

Brick took her time, circling the scuffle, light on her feet. She watched them roll for a moment before swiftly dropping her knee onto Agatha's middle and pinning her to the floor. She hunched over and jammed her forearm against Agatha's throat, ignoring the volley of blows as Agatha tried to fight her off. Agatha was tall and strong, but she didn't have a chance— not with two against one and Pixel at stake.

Nate scrambled to his feet to get Pixel and stopped short, frozen by what he saw.

Juniper, the frail young woman from the distillation room, held the gleaming tip of a sharp tool against the life vein at Pixel's slender throat.

Pixel let out a muffled sob.

Pix.

He raised his hands slowly, numb with a new kind of fear. It stole the air out of the room, out of his body.

"Make them stop hurting her," Juniper said, tears running down her pale cheeks. Her fingers dug into Pixel's arm. "Make them stop!"

By the look of it, Reed wasn't doing much of the hurting. Despite Brick's strong arm against her throat, Agatha landed a punch to his gut that left him doubled over and retching. His wound still wasn't fully healed.

"All right," Nate told the girl, careful and soft.

Juniper's wide eyes darted around the room, wild and scared as a caged gull's.

"Brick." Nate spoke around a knot of dread in his throat. He reached his hands out blindly, as if he could will them to quit fighting. "Reed. Stop."

Juniper let out a piercing shriek. "I'll kill her! Don't care if she's a GEM. Let Agatha go!"

That caught Reed's and Brick's attention. They froze and stared at her. Brick had dirt and hair on her face. She sagged and released the coil of tension in her arm enough to let Agatha speak.

"Juniper," Agatha said, strained but utterly calm. "Good girl."

Reed scooted away from Brick and Agatha, his eyes on

Pixel. It hurt, a deep pang in Nate's chest, to see his fear echoed on Reed's face. They'd both failed to protect Pixel.

It had been too plain how much they cared.

"What do I do? Reed. What do I do?" Brick asked. She trembled. Dirt from the plants shook out of her hair, falling like soot.

"Let her go," Nate said. "Let Agatha go."

Brick shook her head. "Nate—"

"Look, she's going to kill her!" Nate shouted.

"They'll keep her," Brick said, wretched and soft.

Pixel held completely still, rigid with fear. Tears ran down her face, and she shuddered with swallowed-back sobs. Juniper's sharp tool dimpled her skin when she shook her head. "Nate. I don't wanna stay."

Alden had warned them. And they hadn't listened.

Nate had to fix this. He had to help her.

There was only one way to do it.

"I know, Pix." Nate watched her so he wouldn't have to see the look on Reed's face. "But you don't have to stay alone." At the first sound of growling protest from Reed, he kept talking. Raised his voice. "Agatha's right, and we can help her. We can help our *own* kind."

Reed fell silent.

Tinkering had always come easily to Nate, but he'd never done it like this. Severed a thin wire, a warm thread between his heart and another. It hurt far more than being bitten by the jagged edge of a live wire.

Agatha met his gaze, and he lifted his chin, daring her to question him.

"There's a reason our blood heals," he said. "A reason they fiend for us. We're better, Pixel. And *this* is where we belong, not hiding." His voice broke, and he hoped Agatha would attribute it to relief and not the pain of his ribs curling in on his heart and crushing it. "Not with thieves."

Brick lifted her knee from Agatha and fell toward Reed, reaching for him as if blinded. At the edge of Nate's vision, Reed caught her close, and they pulled each other to stand. Clumsy. Shaken.

Betrayed.

Go. Run.

Nate held Agatha's appraising gaze. He swallowed against the tightness in his throat as she stood, elegant even with her mouth bleeding and her clothes stained with wet dirt.

"I'm sorry things had to come this far for you to choose the path of wisdom," she said, tone faintly dubious.

She doesn't believe me. Not yet.

Reed said nothing, and Nate tried to breathe evenly. It was almost as bad as the squeeze of sickness around his lungs. He'd expected an argument or a plea, but Reed had already given up on him. Believed in his betrayal that quickly.

"You don't get to decide for her." Brick spat each word out. "She's with us."

"She never belonged to *you*," Agatha said. "*We* arranged for her to be smuggled out of Gathos City."

"That's a lie." Brick sucked in a breath. "We found her on the street."

"Of course you did. The shipment they hid her in never

arrived where it was supposed to. She's fortunate you found her, but that doesn't make her yours."

Pixel hiccoughed and hugged her arms tightly at her middle. "They're my family! I'll run away! I'll find them. I won't stay with you. It's scary down here." She dissolved into tight, mournful cries.

"Brick, you can't keep her safe." This time, Nate's words were true. None of them could save her once she came of age and the sickness rose up. Not Reed. Not Brick.

This is the only way.

"This is safe? Hooked up to a machine?" Brick asked.

"Safer than running for her life from trappers and begging chem dealers for Remedy." Nate's gaze flickered to Reed long enough to see him flinch. He tore his attention away.

Pixel cried softly, as if trying to silence her own tears with each short, shivery breath.

Agatha opened a cabinet and drew out a Gathos City stun gun. It was shinier than the ones A-Vols carried. She hefted it with a graceful twist and leveled it at Brick and Reed.

Brick showed Agatha her hands, and Reed followed in turn slowly. Sweat ran down their faces, and they breathed raggedly.

Guilt and fear tripped through Nate's blood. They'd come down here to save him, and he was going to get them killed.

Without lowering the stun gun, Agatha crossed the room to Juniper and Pixel. She pried the tool out of Juniper's hand. Wide-eyed, with tears still streaming down her face, Juniper nodded. She reached absently and touched Pixel's shoulder.

"Sorry," she mumbled.

"There now, go rest," Agatha said. "You've done so well."

She made a clucking sound of dismissal, and Juniper stumbled back to the distillation room without a glance back. The door scavenged from the train closed behind her with a sound like a sigh.

Pixel dashed to Nate and pressed her face against his middle. He put his arms around her, everything else momentarily drowned out by a siren of relief buzzing in his ears. She wouldn't be alone. He'd stay with her, no matter what.

"Got you, Pix," he murmured.

"If you need the blood, keep Nate and leave Pixel with us." Reed spoke like he had sludge in his throat. "Alden told me she's not any good as a GEM until she's older. And she wishes to stay with us."

Reed's words hit Nate like a blow, but his heart tripped over what Reed had said.

Wishes.

It was meant for him. An understanding. Nate exhaled heavily, shaking off the pain of Reed's words, knowing they were only meant for Agatha—to make her believe Reed had lost trust in him. Reed knew that Pixel would be safest by Nate's side. He squeezed Pixel tighter, his body shaking with her muffled cries.

"You're in no position to negotiate," Agatha said. "And besides, I'd be a fool to let her remain with you until she's older. You have no means to shelter her or feed her, and no reason to bring her back when the time comes. I shudder to think of the living conditions she's been subjected to in your *care.*"

Reed's jaw clenched. Brick ducked her head, somehow looking very small.

"The question at hand is this: why should I let either of you go after you attacked me so ungraciously?" Agatha asked, waving the tip of the stun gun as if sizing each up.

Reed shrugged. "You shouldn't."

"Reed," Brick said, eyes angry and sad at all once. She watched Pixel like she wanted to lunge for her—like it twisted her all up to do nothing but clench her raised hands into fists.

Agatha laughed. "Is that so?"

"It's like you said. If you let us go, we'll go back out on the street and probably get burned up in the mess out there." Reed shrugged again. "We won't have anywhere to stay or anything to eat."

"That isn't my problem," Agatha said.

Nate willed Reed to shut up and leave. Nate'd traded his freedom to stay alive by Pixel's side, doing whatever he could to atone for dragging her here. The best thing Brick and Reed could do was survive. Far from the Breakers.

"You need experienced chem runners," Reed said.

"I *have* experienced chem runners."

"Not like us. We've run the Withers straight across and 'round. Day and night." Reed spoke in the confident tone Nate could never say no to. "We were born in a pleasure house. Nobody knows this place like we do."

"And I'm to believe you've changed your mind this quickly?" Agatha asked.

Brick said nothing, but her eyes shone like murder when she glanced aside at Reed.

"We have nothing left if we leave," Reed said.

Nate's heart stuttered. Whatever Reed was playing at, it pained him to hear defeat spoken so plainly.

"We had bargaining power with GEMs in our gang, and now we have nothing. I didn't live this long without adapting, and it's not like you're going to give Pixel back to us."

Nate's scrap of a plan was falling apart. Brick and Reed were supposed to escape to the chaos of the Withers, where they could survive with Sparks. Instead, Reed was recklessly lying. Pretending to lose faith in Nate. Pretending he'd be willing to run chem. Which only meant one thing: he wasn't going to give up.

It was going to get them all killed.

"Agatha," Nate said, voice sticky.

She glanced at him questioningly, and he couldn't think of anything to say that wouldn't sound like he cared about Brick and Reed. Loved them. Desperately wanted them to be safe. Wished he'd died before they'd ever come down to this cold, terrible place.

If he listened to another word of this, he'd shout at them to go and find Sparks on the surface and hide until the smoke cleared and they could make new lives for themselves.

"Can I take Pixel away from here? She's scared." It hurt so much he could barely talk.

He had to get away from Reed before he forgot how to breathe.

"Of course. Follow Juniper. Claim a bunk. Encourage Pixel to rest. Don't wait up," Agatha said. She turned back to Reed and Brick and smiled. "It sounds like we have quite a bit to discuss."

Nate didn't trust himself to look at Reed and Brick. He took Pixel by the hand and led her away, every step harder—like the air around them thickened and grasped at his limbs.

When the door closed behind them with its sad sigh, the heavy snap of a lock followed. He could see the divots and rusted rebar spikes in the concrete where the former door had been, before they'd burned a train car full of people alive to get a new one.

Agatha's machine towered over him, every pipe a clawing finger, beckoning. It was the only thing he'd be good for from now on.

He stumbled to his knees and choked on a broken cry. Pixel's voice hummed in his ear, her face a blur of worry. She touched him and shook him, but he couldn't tell her it was going to be all right. Nothing was ever going to be all right again.

Reed and Brick were going to end up chem runners—doing the one thing they hated most of all because of him. Unless Agatha killed them before they ever got back to the surface.

Either way, he'd never see Reed again. Never touch him again.

Nate wasn't going to die for lack of Remedy. He was going to live in Agatha's basement for the rest of his life, bleeding to make more fiends. And he'd dragged Pixel down here and doomed her to the same fate.

Juniper sat in her bunk, staring at them, her slippered feet dangling over the edge. She swung them slowly, like the ticking hands of a clock, and played with her hair.

"Nate," Pixel was crying. Scared. Helpless. "What's gonna happen to us?"

Nate doubled over, belly cramping up with choked-back sobs. He didn't know what to say.

CHAPTER
FOURTEEN

Juniper kicked Nate's shin.

"Why are you here?" She wore a drab blue dress over baggy pants and swayed her arms back and forth. The gesture was so childish Nate wondered if he'd misjudged her as any older than he was.

He sat with his back against the wall, Pixel cradled in his arms. His body ached, and his breath sucked in involuntarily, shaky in the aftermath of unraveling on the floor until he couldn't cry anymore. "I'm going to stay and help you."

"You didn't want to help us before." She narrowed her blue eyes to slits. "You wanted to leave."

"I panicked," Nate said, which was more or less true. "But I get it now. And Pixel's family. You have to stick by family."

Juniper gave him an odd look, as if she didn't understand the word. "You don't look strong enough to help. The last one who didn't look strong died."

Glued to Nate's side, Pixel trembled. "I don't want them to kill me."

"No one's going to touch you." He hated himself for making a promise he couldn't keep.

Juniper shrugged.

Her words lingered in the quiet.

A GEM died in this room.

Grief hollowed him out, his heartbeat like an echo in his chest. But as long as they were stuck here, he might as well start learning about the basement and how Agatha's operation worked.

He directed Pixel to one of the bunks on the wall, as far from Juniper as he could get. She climbed into the bottom one, and he sat beside her, shielding her with his body. He fidgeted, finding the folds in the sheets. The fabric shone, well-made. The mattress dipped gently under their weight, as inviting as an embrace. Pixel wrapped a soft blanket around her shoulders.

Everything was nicer than anything they'd ever known in Reed's hideouts.

"Why does she trust you around all this glass and tech?" he asked Juniper.

She let out a high, sharp laugh. "Without all this 'glass and tech,' we wouldn't have Remedy, and we'd die. Are you addled?"

"Well, how did *they* die?" he asked, gesturing at the bloodstain on the floor.

"They stayed hooked up too long. It's not Agatha's fault. She's busy all the time, doing important things before the gates open up," Juniper said, her words laced with pride.

Nate inhaled slowly, steadying himself. Juniper spoke of the gates so casually, so matter-of-fact, that it had to be true. His pulse quickened at the thought of the huge gates lifting and what that might mean for all of them. "What happens when the gates open?"

"More people." She rolled her eyes and sounded each word out slowly, as if Nate was a little child. "More credits. They'll all want our chem, because it's better than anyone else's. The city will build nicer places here, and we'll have somewhere fancy to stay."

"What about the people who already live here?" Nate asked, trying to mask his concern. It's not like Gathos City would welcome them to their towers. It's not like they could grow wings and fly to the Mainland.

"They'll have to make room, won't they?"

People were already living ten to a room and sleeping outside in ragged tents. Nate swallowed against the dryness in his throat. He craned his neck to study the tangle of pipes and cables along the ceiling, wondering how far belowground they were. It didn't feel right to be so cut off from the suffering above. "I guess so."

"We'll have fresh meat again too. Not gull or sludge-rats. Goats. Chickens."

"I remember goat." Even in Gathos City, fresh meat had been rare, but his mother had made a stew with it once a month. He tried to recall the way the spiced meat tasted so his mind wouldn't drift back to the front room—to wondering what was happening to Brick and Reed. "I'm from the city too," he added.

"I know you're from the city. Agatha said your mother worked there in the labs," Juniper said, suddenly all venom.

"She did." Nate rubbed his arms, chilled. Agatha had known his mother? He'd never known anyone but Bernice who'd ever seen her alive. The connection made him ache, as if being here with Agatha made him closer to his mother somehow. "Did she say anything else about my mom?"

"No. Nothing else to say. She was one of *them*. One of the people who made us to hurt us."

"We weren't . . . that's not what we were made for."

Juniper's teeth clicked together. She massaged the hinge of her jaw.

"She got me out," Nate offered. His mother hadn't been like the rest of them. She couldn't have been.

"She got *you* out. That's why you don't know." Juniper's nostrils flared. "You don't know a thing. Don't think you're special just because you got to have a mother."

Guilt rose in Nate like sludge at high tide. It had never occurred to him that his parents had left others behind when they'd smuggled him out of the city or that other GEMs had grown up without a parent at all. His hand drifted to find Pixel's—and he squeezed her small fingers gently, wishing he could make up for all the ways she'd been wronged.

The relentless stress of the day hummed in his bones.

Juniper blew her hair away from her face and put her hands on her hips, all the stormy anger already gone. "Do you have a real life here? Do you do things?"

"I'm a Tinkerer. I fix things when they're broken. It's a calling."

"A calling." Juniper's expression grew wistful. She plucked at the hem of her dress. "I don't know how to do anything. I can mend, some. And I know my letters." Her gaze darted away, and her cheeks flushed. "I stayed in one room, mostly."

Despite what she'd done to them, Nate felt a raw tug of

kinship. She'd known horrors in Gathos City, only because of what she was. What they'd made her to be. And no one had spirited her away before she came of age. He didn't want to picture the mistreatment she'd faced from the people who had owned her. "I'm sorry," he said, surprised to find that he meant it.

"You should be." Juniper pulled a greasy lock of hair between her lips. "Your friends hurt Agatha."

It's not like they did it for fun.

Nate bit the inside of his cheek until the urge to argue became manageable.

"They weren't my friends—we were in a gang. It's different." He elbowed Pixel gently when she started to sit up, indignation on her breath. It wouldn't do them any good for Agatha and Juniper to think they still cared about Brick and Reed. "They didn't want to give us up, because they could've used our blood. And I stopped them from hurting her, didn't I?"

"*I* stopped them," Juniper said, lifting her chin. "I might not have a *calling*, but I saved Agatha."

"You did." Nate offered her an indulgent smile. "And you showed me what's really important. Our kind, sticking together."

"You're not *my kind*," Juniper spat out. "And you don't know what's important."

The door swung open, and Nate wrapped his arm around Pixel instinctively. Agatha walked in with a girl trailing after her. As the door swung shut, he spotted two tall, broad-shouldered people carrying pipes. A guard.

A sound of surprise died on Nate's lips. The girl was Val.

"You're sure he's still there?" Agatha was asking.

"Pretty sure. I mean, nobody's seen him leave." Val caught sight of him. "Nine! You made it."

"I made it," he echoed, unable to return her crooked smile. Goose bumps peppered his forearms. He couldn't shake the eerie feeling he was missing something.

Agatha walked to the dangling prong in the middle of the room and pulled it down, eyeing the height from the floor to the gleaming tips. She drew a rag from her pocket and polished the tip. Val dragged a heavy chair on rollers from the corner of the room. It was like the one on the dentist's front stoop—high-backed with a built-in footrest. Except this one had fraying straps attached to the armrests.

Both of them watched Nate expectantly, and a cold tendril of dread wrapped around him.

"Right to work, huh?" he asked with a breathy, nervous laugh. His fingers wrapped around the rail of the bed involuntarily.

"If it makes you feel better, I'm next." Val rolled down the waist of her loose pants and showed Nate a bandage at her hip.

"But you're not . . ." He would have known—would have smelled the honey scent that lingered on other GEMs. The unmistakable sense of comfort, home.

"A GEM?" Val barked a laugh. "No."

"Valerie gives us her serum," Agatha said. "In exchange for letting her live."

The wry amusement faded from Val's face. She scratched the back of her neck and met Nate's eye before looking away.

"Couriers aren't supposed to pick sides, but Agatha's folks don't take kindly to that."

"Quaint, but true. We'll control all of the chem trade before the season turns. I can't have clever Couriers like Valerie slowing our progress down, running chem for the last holdouts in a dying business."

Alden.

"You're loyal now, aren't you, dear?" Agatha asked.

Val ducked her head, shoulders slumping. She offered a faint nod and wiped her nose.

Nate struggled to keep his expression blank. His thoughts buzzed like a dust storm. Val had called him by his full name up on the rails when she'd saved him from getting smeared by the train. She'd asked too many questions after he'd left the bank.

She must have guessed that he was a GEM by then.

Why hadn't she turned him in to Agatha if she'd known where to find him? She'd watched him walk into Alden's shop. He longed to ask her, but Agatha was too close.

Couriers only answered to the highest bidder. But Nate couldn't imagine anyone able to pay more than the Breakers. Or why they would.

"Loyalty is critical right now," Agatha was saying, murmuring to herself as she adjusted wires on the still. "When the gates open, we have to hold the power. The chem. The flesh. I can't have outliers undercutting me."

"But the people here didn't do anything to us," Nate said, ignoring the furtive shake of Val's head. "Why make *them* pay?"

"Do not underestimate the depravity of your fellow Withersons. Surely you've seen firsthand how they'd use you."

She turned to him, and he saw it again—the flash of hollow fear.

"Not to cure lung-rot," Juniper muttered.

Confusion ached behind Nate's eyes. Alden hadn't hurt him—not terribly, not like that. But when Agatha said it, he wondered at his own memory, if he'd made himself believe they'd been friends.

The grief he'd pushed down swelled once more, spreading like an ink stain. But he had to focus. He couldn't let her get to him.

"All right." Agatha patted the chair. "Come here, Nathan."

Pixel burrowed against Nate, and he wished he could take her fear away. Not that he was unafraid. The more he studied the huge prongs in Agatha's hand, the more he wanted to crawl under the blankets with Pixel.

Val fidgeted with the straps on the chair.

He dragged himself off the bed, haunted by how submissive Val's behavior was when he'd seen her so confident and carefree up on the rails. "What does that mean? Serum?" he asked, wishing she'd at least look at him.

"It's an element of blood." Juniper shot him a smug grimace. "Agatha makes Remedy with it."

"With the same machine?" Nate failed to hide his surprise. The still had to have interchangeable parts somewhere—some way to convert for different outputs. His fingers itched with the desire to find tools and pry open the gauges and cylinders to understand how it worked.

"Do you see *two* of them?" Juniper asked.

Nate exhaled a laugh. He'd never played dumb in his life,

and the wrongness of it prickled up his backbone. Legs shaking, he approached the big chair, feigning childlike curiosity. "Guess it's magic."

"I'm sure it seems like that." Agatha twisted a valve on the thin tube attached to the prongs. "In Gathos City, we used a synthetic serum. No mess, no need for volunteers. But I make do."

"*We?*"

Agatha made a sound like a rusted hinge. "There was a time I had freedom to work alongside the Lands. I'm surprised you don't remember."

"You worked with my parents?" Nate blurted.

"If you could call them that. Enough reminiscing. Pull up your shirt. Let's see if you have any flesh on those bones."

Nate swallowed hard against a knot of emotion. She wasn't going to tell him anything. And even if she did, she'd mete it out like tastes of her GEM-laced chem until he craved more and more. He inched his shirt up, exposing his belly and shivering.

"Not much to work with. Hope you're feeling strong today." Agatha batted at his hand. "That's enough. I don't need to count your ribs."

"What's the story with the new runners?" Val asked, awkward and loud, like she wanted to change the subject. She turned a rusted metal crank, and the chair lifted with the squeaking cry of dry gears.

"They're former associates of Nathan and Pixel. Carlos took them to the port. We'll give it a week, see if they can keep up. The girl is strong. The boy is quick." Agatha frowned. "And sharp. They're both clear-eyed, and we need more reliable runners."

Nate wavered, his knees shaky with relief. Brick and Reed were alive. They hadn't mentioned Sparks, which hopefully meant she was tailing them—keeping an eye out. He had to stop wallowing in thoughts of his parents and focus on that.

"Nine must be something special," Val said. "You'd think that door was secure enough without a couple of trappers waiting to brain somebody for knocking."

"There's no harm in being extra cautious these days." Agatha met Nate's eye, daring him to say anything.

He pressed his lips together.

"That's no joke. Wouldn't mind my own personal guard." Val let out a snort and stoked the furnace beneath the big copper tank with a long poker. Coals glowed white-hot inside and cast a flickering red light, boiling water inside of the tank, as far as Nate could figure. He'd seen systems rigged for distilling fermented fruit, but didn't know exactly how they worked. Something about boiling water and steam. He'd always preferred the instant gratification of electricity over the slow game of alchemy.

A wide chimney rose from the furnace and up through the roof.

Nate looked away from it quickly, startled by a thread of hope he knew better than to tug on.

What if . . .

"Is this the room we'll always stay in?" Nate asked.

Agatha's hand snapped out and caught Nate by the hair, twisting it hard enough to drive him to his knees. He gasped and grabbed her wrist, but he couldn't shake her off. She yanked his head back and forced him to look up.

His pulse thundered, and his head spun. She was so fast. She wasn't even breathing hard.

"I don't know what you're playing at, but I'm not as ignorant as you take me for," she said, a growl beneath her soft words. "You're here, and you're here to stay. Keep the girl company. Keep your mouth shut. Learn your place. Stop asking questions. Do you understand?"

Juniper laughed, hoarse and quiet.

"Yes." His eyes pricked up with tears as she twisted her hand, tugging every hair on his head at once. It stung like spitting embers. "Got it."

"If you give me cause to question your motives, I will feed your friends to the sludge." She let him go, and he caught himself against the rust-speckled floor.

Not rust—blood.

"I understand."

Val helped him up with a cold and clammy grip, nothing like the assured strength she'd used to save him on the rails. She patted the ripped cushion on the seat and didn't meet his eye when she gave him a little push. "You're first."

In her bunk, Pixel crammed her body against the wall. Only her eyes were visible, the rest of her wrapped in sheets. Nate climbed into the chair and shook his head, willing her not to watch.

She didn't look away. Her eyes widened, and she trembled, but he recognized a gleam of fierce wonder too. Pixel looked at tech like that, especially when she wanted to know how it worked. How she could make it work better.

Out of habit, he began to roll his sleeve up to expose the

place where Alden's Diffuser had left silvery scars and the recent, fresh scabs. Agatha pushed his hands away and reached for the waist of his pants instead. He squirmed away, making a senseless sound of protest.

"Hold still," Val said—more a plea than a warning.

Shaken by the undercurrent of fear, he froze, his hands balled into fists at his sides. Agatha pulled up his filthy shirt and exposed the skin at his hip. She prodded him delicately, finding the fleshy place above the bone. The muscles at his belly fluttered from the tickle.

Nate began to tremble. The Diffuser tip had always hurt, but it had always felt good afterward, when the lethargy took over and he wanted nothing more than to sleep, warm and safe with Alden.

This was different. He didn't want to keep still. He didn't want to do this. He didn't want to be here.

Reed.

"Do I need to restrain you?" she asked.

"No," he said. His teeth snapped together, and he clenched his jaw to stop the chattering. "It's fine."

She wasted no time. The prongs slid into his flesh like a bite. He cried out and scrabbled at the chair, more panicked than in pain.

"Nate!" Pixel cried out.

The tube in Agatha's hand went dark with his blood. Nausea flushed through him. It didn't hurt any more than it ever had at Alden's. His fear was getting the best of him.

He had to learn to let go of it, to accept this—or it would

be torture every time. And Pixel would spend every second fearing the time when her blood ripened.

"It's okay," he said, head lolling to the side. His arms went weak. Agatha bent over his hip and adjusted the prongs. It didn't hurt anymore.

A new, different pain came instead. He exhaled a silent, rueful laugh.

I miss Alden.

He needed to find Alden, to tell him that the Breakers didn't want anyone else pushing chem. Maybe Alden already knew. He always had a plan. He'd have a plan now, something clever.

Val crowded his line of sight, watching his face. She pushed his hair out of his eyes. "You'll pass out real soon."

The huge Diffuser began to whir, buzzing like flies on a body.

She was right.

―――――――

Nate was drowning. Cold water filled his mouth with every breath. He tried to turn his head, angle toward the surface, toward air.

"Stars," Juniper swore. "Quit that squirming."

The water shifted to Nate's middle and became more of an annoying splash than a torrent. He forced his eyes open and saw her standing over him with a hose attached to the ceiling. The water tasted like metal and smog.

He was naked except for the thin shorts he wore under his pants and the bandage taped to his hip. "Hey," he said, shoving his hands between his legs where the fabric wasn't thick enough to give him any privacy.

"I don't see why I have to wash you," Juniper said, waving the hose indiscriminately.

They were in the corner of the distillation room, where another drain below Nate whisked the water away. He pushed up onto his elbow and reached for the hose, his arm shaking and leaden.

He could barely remember where he was or why, but he knew, to the core of his being, that he did *not* like Juniper. "Give me the rotted hose then."

She sniffed and shoved it into his hand. When she turned to look away, he resisted the urge to direct the frigid stream toward the back of her head.

It didn't take long to rinse the grime off his skin. He craned to see Pixel still in her bed watching him, and decided against offering her the opportunity to bathe. She didn't need to feel this—the ache of being treated no better than a stain on the floor.

Nate managed to rinse his hair, but after a few more moments, he dropped the hose, his fingers numbing and trembling. "I . . ." He didn't want to ask for help. "I'm done."

Juniper took a bath sheet off one of the pipes and dropped it on top of him. "Your clothes are drying. Agatha said you did well. I guess you're stronger than you look. Stronger than she is," she said, jerking her thumb toward the chair.

Val was there, slumped over and pale. Unmoving.

Nate stared. "Did Agatha kill her?"

"Why would Agatha leave a *dead body* in here? She passed

out quick, that's all. Won't get much Remedy out of her. I think your mean friends should have done it instead. They looked strong enough."

"Why Val? Why not other people?"

Juniper watched Nate struggle with the bath towel and sighed sharply. She crouched and took over drying his hair for him, rubbing his head and shoulders with the soft sheet. "One at a time. Because they might tell where we are. Even with the new doors, we have to be safe and keep our secrets. When they're not strong enough anymore, Agatha has them chucked into the sludge. Won't tell down there," she said, laughing.

Nate imagined Reed and Brick in the sludge and shuddered.

"How much Remedy can Agatha get each time?"

Juniper snapped the towel at his ear. "Quit that. I heard her tell you stop asking questions. You're not to be trusted."

"Then why are you drying me off?"

"Because Agatha told me to. And because you smelled like a dead sludge-rat. *Long* dead."

He wanted to snatch the towel back and finish on his own, but his legs and arms wouldn't work. It didn't hurt the way he'd hurt earlier, edging toward the stillness. But he was empty and weak, and that scared him more. He imagined being trapped in his own body, too tired to move or speak or fight—and realized that must be exactly what the GEMs in Gathos City experienced: a lifetime lifeless and bleeding out to make others feel good.

Juniper hauled him up with both hands under his armpits and managed to drag him to Pixel's bunk, where she deposited him in a heap. Pixel wrapped around him, giving Juniper a wary look. She tucked her sheet around Nate. He was too weak to protest being treated like an infant.

"How long has it been?" he asked.

"Not long," Pixel said. "My belly's growling, though."

Nate caught his breath, exhausted from helping Juniper drag him as best he could. "Do they feed you?"

Juniper stood there with her arms crossed and the bath sheet still draped over her shoulder. She breathed hard too, and Nate recalled that she wasn't much better off. She'd been hooked up to that machine too. "Of course they feed me. I'm not a prisoner. You wouldn't be, either, if Agatha didn't think you'd run off and make trouble. They're helping us. We're helping each other. We'll be kings and queens when the gates open and everyone wants our chem."

"This isn't a storybook," Nate said, cross. He didn't sound properly angry with his mouth numb and his throat sore.

She walked off in a huff, and Pixel leaned close to whisper, "Can I really be a princess?"

"Not down here, Pix." He tugged one of her ponytails. "But when we get back out in the sun, you'll be a queen."

"Queen of the Tinkerers."

"That's right."

Juniper returned from behind a curtain in the corner, dragging a basket across the floor. The handles sagged with the weight of the contents. Despite himself, Nate leaned forward, mouth watering.

"Told you they feed us. Didn't know you were hungry. You have to say, is all," she said, talking to Pixel. She crouched, her skirt pooling at the floor like dingy water, and began picking through the basket.

Pixel climbed out of the bed to perch beside Juniper. "All right. I'm hungry."

"We've got . . . apples, bread. Dried something . . . green. Jar of preserves. No label, though, so don't know if it's any good or not." Juniper lifted each item as she spoke in a quiet, singsong voice. "It's healthy to eat. It keeps us strong."

"I want an apple," Pixel said, reaching for it cautiously. She scooted away from the basket and took small, quick bites.

"You don't have to be scared." Juniper huffed and grabbed the bread and a canteen. Without another word, she started wetting the bread and feeding Nate bites. His pride hurt, but he hadn't eaten in days, and he slowly chewed and swallowed each bland bite.

Nate pictured a lifetime of this routine, and the bread in his stomach went sour and cold.

"I'm resting now. It's healthy to rest," Juniper said. "It keeps us strong." She wandered away, taking a roundabout path across the room, as if lost. The curtain at her bed fluttered shut, and she didn't make another sound.

Nate fought his way to sit and spent several minutes getting back into his clothes, with Pixel's help. His ash-covered boots remained on the floor beside his bunk.

A rumble sounded, vibrating the cold concrete alongside the bunk. A small plume of plaster fell like ash from the ceiling. Nate had almost forgotten that the rest of Gathos still existed.

He didn't want to forget.

Or resign himself to a lifetime of being hand-fed and hosed

down and resting and resting and resting to stay fit for Agatha's machine. His gaze lifted to the chimney—and the wide ventilation grating beside it.

Pixel put her hand against the wall. "Are Reed and Sparks and Brick gonna be okay?" she whispered.

He pulled her close to whisper back, "Maybe we should see for ourselves."

CHAPTER
FIFTEEN

I t wasn't a plan, but it was better than nothing. Better than reconciling Pixel to a childhood spent waiting for her turn to be used up.

"She'll trust you more than she trusts me, Pix," Nate whispered. "You have a strong mind for tinkering. Ask her questions. Get her to talk."

"What if she gets mad at me?" Pixel shivered.

He kissed her cheek. "No one could get mad at you."

He should have warned her to be careful, but he couldn't bear to scare her anymore.

Nate tried to stay awake, but the room was so quiet. Juniper snored in her bunk, and Pixel drifted off in his arms, each breath a rhythmic pull that dragged him off to sleep. When he woke up later, Val was gone.

He had no idea how much time had passed.

They settled into a routine. Meals on the floor around a basket of food. Agatha with them more often than not and never following a predictable routine. She worked on the machine, and Juniper hummed songs to herself in her bunk or followed a winding, repetitive path around the room.

Wary of Agatha's warnings, Nate only explored as far as the waste trench behind a curtain. He didn't go near the still.

But Pixel did. And he was pretty sure he wouldn't have had to tell her to. She couldn't keep her eyes off the working parts of the still. The tubes and wires and intricate glass pipes and nozzles.

Agatha wore a pair of shiny glasses while she worked. The two lenses were mismatched and fastened together at the middle. Distorted by the lens, one eye bulged garishly. She climbed up onto the still, nimble in soft shoes, twisting valves and adjusting gauges. Nate watched her as best he could without hovering over her shoulder like he wanted to. Whenever she glanced at him, he closed his eyes.

Pixel followed Agatha like a shadow.

"What does that part do?" she asked, walking her fingertips along a black tube hanging from a hook.

"These carry the blood. So they're changed out between sessions. I boil them. Do you know why?"

"Because 'boiling water makes it clean so it won't make you shit yourself,'" Pixel said, quoting Brick so uncannily Nate had to press his face into the blankets to muffle a laugh.

"It's a little like that." Agatha chuckled.

Even in all her terrible glory, Agatha couldn't resist Pixel's charm or the persistence of her curiosity. Agatha had no way of knowing how well Pixel absorbed information—what a natural-born Tinkerer she was turning out to be.

As he drifted in and out of a light, restless sleep, Nate listened to every quiet word Agatha spoke to Pixel. "The steam catches here," Agatha was saying. "And condensation forms here."

"And it comes out at the bottom there?" Pixel pointed to a tiny spigot at the bottom of the massive still.

"A small, highly concentrated amount. Yes."

"The magic," Pixel said solemnly.

"It only takes a little of our blood to make chem," Juniper said, butting in again. She'd interrupted every few moments, as if eager to show Pixel how much she knew about Agatha and the Breakers.

Pixel stood out of the way, keeping her hands behind her back as Agatha coaxed a few drops of dark liquid into a clear beaker from the spigot. Unlike Alden's Diffuser, Agatha's machine didn't work with a mask. Nate didn't understand the specifics, but it made sense. Feeding another was one thing—this was feeding on a mass scale. Even the concentrated byproduct couldn't be as powerful as what the Diffuser was capable of when used for more than a few counts.

With a small Diffuser, Nate had saved Reed's life, brought him back from a wound that would have dragged him into the stillness. Agatha's chem was stronger than typical street-chem, but it probably couldn't heal. It just made helpless fiends out of anyone who got a taste of what GEM blood was capable of.

"Your machine makes the stuff that makes us better too?" Pixel asked, hopping from one foot to the other.

"It does. The method is quite similar. It's one of Gathos City's best-kept secrets," Agatha murmured. "Remedy isn't that complicated once you know it contains the serum of anyone who wasn't developed from modified cells."

Pixel had always argued when Nate explained that they weren't magical. She asked now with a small, unhappy sound, "From what?"

"Let me think how to explain it to you. Do you know how a plant grows from a seed?"

"It starts out really little and gets bigger," Pixel said.

"Precisely. You and I were grown from different seeds than other people. And we were planted in a different kind of soil than other people."

"Not in somebody's belly?" Pixel asked.

Agatha laughed. "No, not in somebody's belly."

Nate's thoughts drifted to his mother. It had never occurred to him that she hadn't carried him in her womb. It didn't matter. She'd been his mother all the same. Inarguably and wholly. He remembered her like a song, always talking. Unless she was lost in thought. Then she'd looked so sad. He couldn't recall the exact shade of her eyes or her hair, but his heart recalled the feeling of her. Safety in her arms. Wanting to make her smile.

Now, in the dank, stale room, he'd give anything to see her again. He wondered what she'd think about him getting himself into a mess as bad as the one she'd given her life to free him from.

Agatha was still talking about the distillation machine. Every few minutes, Juniper chirped about how brilliant and wonderful Agatha was. Nate rolled to face away from them and listened.

"How can enough come out of us for all those people out there?" Pixel asked.

"Oh, I don't need much to cook chem. That's how special we are. Don't ever forget how special you are, little one."

"I want to know how to do the things you do when I'm bigger," Pixel said.

Nate frowned at the wall. Someone had etched small lines into the concrete. Pixel was clever, and she'd done exactly as he'd said by asking Agatha all about her machines. But her wonder sounded sincere.

Of course she'd want to be like Agatha, building great things.

Better than fixing broken tickers.

He drifted off again and yelped when Agatha rolled him over and placed a cold metal circle against his chest. Tubes ran from the metal to her ears. Nate braced himself for pain, but nothing happened.

"I'm listening to your heart and your lungs." Agatha pulled the tubes from her ears. "And I don't like what I'm hearing. Juniper! Dear, it's your turn."

"Again?"

Nate wondered if he misheard her reluctance. She'd been so eager—willing to kill. Why not willing to submit to the machine as well?

"Once the runners have this last shipment on hand, you'll have plenty of time to rest and get your strength back. And Valerie will return to us in two days. I'll build up our stock of Remedy."

Unable to look away from what he knew would happen next, Nate sat up, holding on to the bunk for balance.

"Are we going to use up Remedy faster because of him?" Juniper asked, casting Nate a hateful look.

"We only need a fraction more. And you'll have plenty of time off now that Nate's here." Agatha reached for the tube and the pronged tip.

Juniper turned her head and closed her eyes.

Nate wondered how the hierarchy worked—why Juniper was so submissive. It sickened him to consider that even among GEMs, some sought power at any cost. They should have been helping each other live. And thrive.

"If the violence moves closer to the shore," Agatha said, "I'll take you up for a walk. Wouldn't you like that?"

"Yes," Juniper whispered.

Pixel scampered down from the bunk above and hid behind him. At some point, she'd taken a stained towel and rolled it into the lumpy shape of a rag doll. "I don't like the hurting," she said.

Nate couldn't help wondering aloud, despite Agatha's threats. "I thought there'd be more of us down here. More GEMs."

"There are more, but they're in hiding. I cycle them in and out of use for their safety." Agatha stroked Juniper's forehead once before she pierced her hip with the prongs, her expression cool and steady as Juniper shoved her hand over her mouth to stifle a cry. "Were something to happen here, or to me, it would be too much of a risk to have all of our brothers and sisters in one place."

"Why would people want to hurt us?" Pixel asked.

"These people are unpredictable. They'll hurt us. Hurt each other. The Withers won't settle until the gates open."

There it was again.

The gates.

He wondered what Alden would say—what Fran would think about the gates opening again after decades spent locked away from the friends she'd known in the towers. He wondered if Sparks would find beautiful things and if Brick would look for honest work.

It pained him too much to think of Reed. The space where he'd held Reed in his heart was a ragged bruise of guilt, fear, and love.

Agatha held her metal tool to Juniper's chest and listened, but she had her eyes on Nate. He resisted the strong urge to look away. "I can see your gears working, Nathan. What do the gates mean to you? Would you return to Gathos City if you could?"

"Everyone I knew is gone," Nate said. "And I know better than to go back there."

"Good," she said.

"How do you know the gates will open?" Nate watched the diffuser in the still become a whizzing blur, pink with Juniper's blood. He'd seen something like it once—sugar spun into a cloud. Sticky and good, the memory at odds with this dark place.

"The date's been set for years. Since the beginning, really. Did you think they'd leave all this land to ruin forever?"

"We didn't know. No one really knows."

"Of course not." Agatha's breath huffed. "Knowledge is a

powerful thing. There's a reason the Withers has been left in the dark, cut off from the information grid."

"Information grid?" Nate straightened, delighted by the notion of forbidden tech. "Like tickers?"

"Stop thinking on it. It's no matter to you."

"He can't help it," Juniper said, faint and woozy. "He's a Tinkerer. It's his *calling*."

"A Tinkerer?" Agatha's voice sharpened. "Funny, it seems like you would have mentioned that by now. What, with all this lovely tech at your disposal."

A traitorous flush heated Nate's cheeks. "It's nothing compared to what you do. I don't understand Gathos City tech."

"But you'd like to, wouldn't you? You think you can know what I know? What I've spent a lifetime learning?" Her breath whistled like the steam in the still.

"No, I'd never—"

She slapped him once. The sound of it struck him before the sting and the heat. "You'll never know a fraction of what I know. What I've seen."

Nate touched his sore cheek, shocked at how quickly her anger had risen and how quickly she composed herself. He couldn't remember her from his childhood in the city, but there was still something familiar about the way she watched him, as if she'd always been there, hovering over him in his sleep.

He shivered. "I understand."

He didn't understand anything.

Agatha's lips curled into a faint, thoughtful smile. "Were you one of the Tinkerers at the train wreck?"

Wary of her flaring anger, Nate lowered his gaze. "Yes."

MARIA INGRANDE MORA

"I sent trappers after you. After all three of you."

"Why would you do that?" He thought about Dresden and his daughter—wondered if they were dead—or worse, separated and sold off by trappers.

She came closer again, satisfaction gleaming in her eyes. "Because it's up to me who looks like a hero and who looks like a villain. I couldn't have unknown players out there rescuing the enemies of the Withers." Her laugh was quick and unamused. "I nearly had you killed, but lucky for both of us, I ended up with a trapper with his neck snapped instead. Where have you found so many vicious associates?"

Nate's mouth went dry. Brick had done that. She'd protected Reed—protected all of them. "I don't know."

Calm again, as if nothing had happened, Agatha patted Juniper's sweaty face. "If I catch you hiding something from me again, I'll bleed your friends dry and make Remedy with every last drop. You can survive another week knowing they died because of you."

Juniper's mouth hung open, slack and silent.

A hairline crack formed in Agatha's calm exterior, and her eyes went dark. "Look what you've done, distracting me with your lies."

Nate's pulse hammered, a relentless flutter below his ribs. All he could see was Reed in the chair instead of Juniper— Reed gray and still like he'd been with his gut torn open. He swallowed, throat sticky. "I'm sorry. I don't have anything left to hide."

Agatha's mouth became a distorted twist of amusement. "I believe that. It's freeing, isn't it? Stripping down bare. Nothing left but the hard truths of your life. I hope the path is clearer to you now, Nathan. You can't run from what you are, but you can fight with it."

Nate gave a faint nod, staring at his knees. His pants had holes in them. His skin, usually filthy, was clean from being hosed off. His feet were bare—long-toed and thin. Big for his size.

Fight. We can fight.

He could get Pixel out of here. She'd spent hours getting familiar with Agatha's machine. Familiar enough to show him how to climb it safely without releasing steam or toppling it. He'd climb up with her and lift her to the grating on the ceiling. Sparks would be close by. She'd never go far knowing Pixel was trapped underground. They'd find each other.

The prongs made a soft sucking sound as Agatha pulled them from Juniper's limp body. She bandaged Juniper and left her in the chair, her arms splayed out to each side.

"You're not the first GEM to resist us, Nathan." Agatha wiped the prongs clean and unscrewed the tube. She dropped it into a metal bin and tucked the prongs into a cabinet attached to the machine. "You'd be the first I'd have to kill, but I'd do it in an instant if it meant protecting the rest of my flock. I don't care who your mother is."

Is?

Before Nate could ask what Agatha meant, she left the room. The door slammed shut behind her.

Pixel leaned over the edge of the top bunk. "Now?"

"Not yet." Nate's heartbeat kicked up. His thoughts scattered. Too much to consider at once. "Maybe."

This is our chance.

The door opened, heavy hinges creaking, and Agatha came back in with a handful of plastic ties. Dread washed over Nate, and he scrambled to his feet. "You don't have to—"

She took him by the wrist with an iron grip, yanked his hands to the edge of the bunk, and fastened him to the metal.

"Agatha—"

There was no use protesting. She was too strong. She caught his flailing hand and fastened it as quickly as the first. The sharp edge of the plastic pinched the thin skin at his wrist. He tugged without thinking, testing the hold. His wrist didn't budge. Trapped, Nate struggled harder. His arms stretched out painfully, one to the side of the bunk and the other to the bunk above. He was exposed.

Helpless.

He couldn't get Pixel out like this.

Agatha's hands slipped into his hair, and this time he knew what to expect and froze. She clenched her fingers very slowly, not quite tugging.

"Good. You're wise to settle down. I have errands to run. And sadly, I can't trust a *Tinkerer* roaming free around my precious things," she said. "Pixel, there's clean water in the bucket here. Give some to Juniper if she wakes, and feel free to give some to Nathan if he asks for it. I trust you'll be a good girl?"

"Yes." Pixel climbed down and perched behind Nate, her pointy chin on his shoulder. He could feel the coiled tension in her body, but she kept her voice light and made herself small. "What if Nate has to go to the bathroom?"

Agatha laughed. "I won't be gone that long. I'm sure he

can hold it. This is to keep you safe too, little one. Nothing bad will happen to you if you stay here. With me."

She left without another word. The lock clicked behind her.

Pixel jutted her chin. "I wish she'd fall in the sludge and die."

Nate couldn't help laughing, the sound wet and short. "Me too."

His tired smile quickly faded, and panic that began as a tickle expanded until it pinched his lungs as hard as the ties at his wrists.

He started tugging.

He needed his hands.

He couldn't do anything without his hands.

They were useless, already swelling up, trapped against the bed. The ties were too tight. There wasn't enough air down here, no windows, no wind.

Nothing but blood and the musty smell of death.

Horror gripped him, snagging his breath, graying his vision. It smothered his thoughts and left room for nothing but terror and the thunderous beating of his heart.

This was no place for Pixel. He had to get her out. He was supposed to get her out. He couldn't get her out.

"Nate!" Pixel climbed around him and stood with her hands at her hips. Her eyes glittered. Hard. Determined.

She took a deep breath and dumped the bucket of water over his head.

Breath catching on a ragged gasp, Nate stared at her. Cold

water soaked his shirt, dripped down his face and sputtered at his lips.

The panic didn't go away, but it became something he could give a name to. And then he could breathe again. Tears and water ran trickled down his cheeks.

"I'm stuck," he finally managed, unable to find more words to explain.

Pixel narrowed her eyes. "I saw." She nodded toward one of his wrists, where blood ran down his forearm. The thin, hard plastic had cut through his skin. "Stop flopping and hurting yourself and tell me what to do."

Her courage startled him into a breathless smile. "Pix. You should be the one in charge."

She grinned, brilliant white baby teeth and the crooked adult ones crowded together. Her small, warm hands wiped the water out of his eyes. "When I'm in charge, I'm not gonna hurt anybody."

Nate's chest ached. "I believe that," he said, voice thick. He bowed his head and shuddered, trying to gain control of the lingering impulse to fight the ties at his wrists.

Pixel still had a chance.

She coaxed him to look up. When he blinked, more tears fell, and she kissed him on the tip of his nose.

"Pixel. You have to go without me."

"Go where?"

"Up." He nodded toward the grating. "All the way up."

He'd send her to the stars if he could.

"I can't leave you here."

"It'll only be for a little while. You have to go first. And even if I weren't stuck, I might not be able to climb into the places you can."

She sucked in a loud, deep breath, squared her shoulders, and blew it out. "I'm ready."

Nate exhaled hard. No more crying. They had work to do. "Do you have the tool?"

Pixel produced a small wrench from her boot—swiped as she'd tailed Agatha. It wasn't much to work with, but it was better than nothing. Nate fought the urge to tug his wrists again and tilted his head, directing her attention to the still.

"It'll slow her down if she gets distracted by the still being messed up. We don't want to break it permanently—just make it hard to fix. If the bolts are too tight, skip them."

"I'm strong."

"You have to be strong enough to keep moving, Pix. Go!"

She darted for the still and climbed the rounded edge of a tank, gripping her boots against the thick bolts that circled it, connecting it to the tubes that ran toward the ceiling. There was one playground in all of the Withers, the only one that hadn't been made of wood and scrapped in the winter. Kids still played on it. He'd taken Pixel to it a few times.

"Watch out for the hot pipes!"

"I know," Pixel said. "I listened. This is the c-c-condenstated part."

Climbing toward the ceiling, she wore the same look of determined joy she'd had on the decaying playground. Children in the Withers had to fight for this. Climbing. Falling. Swinging. Laughing. Every unfettered moment hard-won.

"Wait," he said.

Juniper groaned where she sprawled across the chair, and he quieted.

"That part there. Can you get the bolts?"

"I think so." Pixel crouched, straddling a wide pipe, and twisted the wrench. She stuck her tongue out and grimaced. "But this isn't the right spot. If I do it over here, instead, it'll make that part there fall, see? It'll take her ages to fix it."

He hadn't considered it that way before, and she was right. "Yes! Keep going."

"Almost. Got it!"

A bolt fell to the ground and rolled into the drain. She started on the next.

He'd planned on guiding her through dismantling the key elements of the still, but she was working too quickly for him to keep up. It was like watching a flame grow. She understood the machine without needing a word of instruction.

Agatha had tech and tools from Gathos City, but there was no way she could quickly repair the Diffuser. It would give Pixel time to run and give the gang time to get away, to hide themselves away from the Breakers.

Pixel's foot slipped and kicked a glass tube that rang out like a low bell but didn't crack. Fear knotted Nate's shoulders.

If they broke it, that was something else entirely. Not an escape, but an end.

He didn't know if he could do it—if he could kill that beautiful machine and his only chance to survive on the Remedy it distilled.

"Nate!" Pixel called out, shooting him an impatient glare.

She'd already made her way higher, and another bolt fell and rolled. "Is it enough?"

"It's perfect. You need to hurry now. Can you reach the grating?"

He held his breath as she squeezed between a grid of pipes and balanced on a thin beam over the core of the still where the Diffuser rested behind its thin metal panel. Everything shone around her in the gleam of the lights hanging from the ceiling. She reached the grating, made herself as tall as she could, and pushed her fingers through the holes.

Nate slumped with relief. She was tall enough to reach without a boost.

"Don't worry about it. Get up and see if you can climb out."

Pride warmed Nate's chest as Pixel unfastened the grating without asking for his help and carefully turned it to balance it across the opening without dropping it. She shoved the wrench back into her shoe, crouched, and leaped up to grab the edge of the grating.

Her fingers slipped, and she fell.

"Pix!" he shouted.

Juniper stirred.

Gasping, Pixel held still a long moment, draped over the pipe she'd landed on belly-first. "Wind. Knocked. Outta me."

Nate didn't breathe either, not until she rose back to a crouch and wiped the sweat off her forehead. "Go slow."

"I know how to do it."

The next time she jumped, she caught the edge of the grating and didn't let go. She swung her body back and forth, gaining momentum, and curled her legs up to hook her heels into the hole. It only took her a few more counts to squirm her small body up into the ductwork.

"Nate. What now?"

"Fix the hole. Keep going, Pix."

The metal made a tinny, grinding sound as she replaced the grating.

It was like she'd never been there at all.

CHAPTER
SIXTEEN

"Can you move?" Nate asked. Talking to an empty room and a sleeping girl made his skin prickle up.

"Not much." Pixel's muffled voice wavered in and out. Dust rained down from the grating, and she sneezed. "Where do I go?"

"Out and up. Don't stop or turn back." Without Pixel there to chide him, he tested the ties at his wrists compulsively. The plastic dug deeper, stinging. "Try to find an opening in the pipe that goes up, but don't get in it if you can't get out. Go, Pixel. Get going."

"Nate."

"You have to go."

The sound of her quiet crying slowly faded. He closed his eyes and hung his head, sick with relief and hope. The windowless room had to have good ventilation, or they'd die from the fumes of the furnace. Pixel was small. She'd fit. She'd get out.

A rustling sound caught Nate's attention. He looked up and frowned. Something was different.

Juniper wasn't in the chair anymore.

He twisted in a panic, searching the room. She couldn't have gone far.

She came at him from the corner of his vision. Her dress and loose pants fluttered like beating wings. There wasn't any time to brace himself against her fury.

"What did you do?" she yelled, tackling into his middle, angular and stronger than she seemed.

Pain blinded him as his shoulder made a sickening wrenching sound and popped. The ties sliced into his tender flesh. For a horrible moment, he thought his arm had ripped clean off. Pain enveloped him, hot as flames.

Juniper was screaming, draped across his lap like a sack of rocks—as if she'd used every last bit of her strength to come at him. "Where is she?" Rage distorted her voice. "Where did she go?"

Nate drew his legs up and drove his heel into her gut, sending her sprawling back. Blood spread from the bandage at her hip. She tried to push herself up, and her arms gave out.

"Nate?" Pixel shouted, the sound dampened.

He yelled, "Keep going!"

Juniper's eyes widened. "You're letting her get away! She'll die out there. She'll burn."

"You'd rather keep her here? Look at you!" Nate tripped on a sob. His shoulder was on fire, wrenched from its socket. He twisted, trying to relieve the pain, but every movement made it worse. He choked, stomach heaving.

He was going to get Pixel out, no matter what it took. All he had to do now was buy her time. She was smart and quick. Once she got to the surface, she'd find a way to reach the gang.

The more he got Juniper to think and talk, the farther Pixel would get before Agatha got back, caught on, and made him pay.

"Look at us," he said. "Is this any better?"

Juniper rolled over and struggled onto her hands and knees. Her arms shook violently. Sweat matted her hair to her face. When she turned a feral gaze on him, he shrank back and hissed at the pull at his shoulder. "Agatha won't have to kill you for this, because I will," she said. "And she'll be so proud of me."

"Go ahead." Nate choked on every word. The fiery pain at his shoulder radiated down his back. He was drowning in it. "I'd rather be dead than live like this. You're no better off than you were in Gathos City."

"You don't know that!" Juniper's voice became an eerie shriek, guttural and high-pitched at once.

He imagined her tearing him apart with her delicate fingernails. His head swam. He wondered if he'd pass out before she made it to him. If Agatha would find nothing but his hands dangling from the bed frame like ornaments.

Keep going, Pixel. Keep going.

Deep booming sounded at the door.

Juniper straightened, stiff as a scared cat. She sat back on her heels slowly.

Nate gasped, pain squeezing his lungs. "What is that?"

"Not Agatha. And the Breakers she keeps up front to guard us don't knock." Her breath whistled. "They never come in. They're not allowed in."

The bone at the top of Nate's arm made a wrenching,

scratching sound. "If it isn't Agatha or her guards, who is it?" he asked, the words slurring as his ears buzzed.

Juniper lost her balance. She drew her knees up and hugged them. Nate was struck again by her childish nature. She wasn't a kid, but she'd never grown up either.

"I don't know," she said. The fury in her eyes was gone, replaced by wide-eyed, tearful fear.

Nate blinked sweat from his eyes. "Whoever it is, they won't be able to get that door unlocked without tools. Trust me, I tried when it was on the train."

Metallic clanging rang out.

Juniper whimpered. "That sounds like tools."

"Then they'll get in here pretty soon!" Nate shouted.

If she gave up now, she'd spoil any chance they had to survive.

"Juniper! You have to do something."

She looked at the ceiling grating. "I can't climb. I'm too tired."

"Get me free." Nate coiled his good arm. The tie didn't give. Blood ran down his forearm from his wrist. "I can help you up."

"You can't help me. You're as small as I am." Her gaze darted to the ties and the blood, indecision plain on her features. "And Agatha would be mad."

"She won't be mad if you're safe because you let me help you."

"You're trying to trick me!" The shriek returned, weaker now, but still as eerie—like wind down an alley. "I'm not stupid. This is all a trick."

The clanging rang out, louder and echoing. Nate strained

to listen—struck by the memory of early morning knocks at the hatch door of their old hideout. A flicker of hope snuffed away. No pattern sounded. No message from Reed in his secret code. Only violent banging and groaning hinges. It sounded like a beast behind the door—something angry. Something hungry.

"Let me go!" Nate yelled over the sound of Juniper's terrified moans. He jerked his hand senselessly, ignoring the searing pain at his wrist, caught up in the momentum of her fear. "Cut these rotting ties, Juniper!"

The door fell inward, slamming down with a sound that vibrated through Nate's bones. He drew his knees up to shield himself and watched—stretched out and helpless—as a crowd poured into the room like ants erupting from a stirred mound. They surged over the mangled bodies of the guards Nate had seen at the door before. Juniper slithered across the floor and crawled into his bunk, shaking so hard it rattled his bones.

A box of chem broke open and spilled across the floor. Snarling, stumbling people fell to their knees, palming the little white pills. Shoving them into their mouths and pockets.

Fiends.

Nate's blood went cold. They were all chem fiends.

And they'd found Agatha's stash.

A burly man grabbed Juniper and wrenched her out of the bed like she weighed nothing. She screamed, reaching for Nate, but there was nothing he could do but kick his legs out at the man. Unable to move, Nate watched the man bury his teeth in the soft skin at Juniper's bare arm. Juniper screamed and sagged in his grip, her eyes going blank, as if someone had snipped a wire inside of her.

"Nothing's happening," the man snarled, spitting her blood down his chin. He dropped her, and she crashed against the floor, her head snapping onto the hard concrete. She didn't move.

The fiend turned to him.

Terror washed over Nate like icy rain. He coiled his legs up, prepared to kick and fight, but he already knew it was hopeless. The man was huge, and Nate couldn't use his hands—let alone a weapon that might make it a fair fight.

The man staggered at Nate and pitched forward as another fiend tackled him from behind. They rolled around on the floor, trading punches, blind to the others ransacking the room.

No one noticed the grating on the ceiling, high above.

The wild-eyed fiends tore open cabinets and pulled down shelves, grabbing every box and jar of chem in Agatha's distillation room. They jostled and dented the cylinders on the still, but even crazed with want, they seemed to realize it wasn't going to dispense what they needed, no matter how much they shook it.

"I heard if you eat a GEM's heart, you'll live forever," a woman with no teeth said.

The man beside her turned red-rimmed eyes on Nate. "And never get sick."

"Think he's one of them?"

"Only one way to find out," he said.

Nate stared at the man's nose hair. It stuck out like a thorny bush from each nostril. The last thing he was ever going to see was an ugly nose.

He squeezed his eyes shut and tucked his chin to his chest.

Now he understood the blank look in Juniper's eyes. His mind could only hold so much fear and pain. He was starting to float, detached from the chaos in the room, as if he'd taken one of Alden's sweet tinctures.

A grunt sounded, and nothing else happened. No one touched him.

He opened one eye and then the next. And then he stared. Red hair. A mess of glaring orange freckles. Strong, bloody arms.

"Brick!"

"Sorry we took so long." Brick stepped on one fiend's throat while she fought the other off.

"*We?*" Nate scanned the crowd. The fiends were fighting each other. They'd ripped down one of the stacks of bunks and were tearing apart the thick mattresses, as if expecting to find more chem in the scraps of rubber inside. Most of the crowd had already left, gone back into the front room where the sounds of shattering glass and metal against concrete made ugly music.

A few more bodies were scattered around the room, one with its head smashed in, purple-gray mush mingling with white bone and glistening blood. The poker from the furnace rested alongside the ruined flesh, iron stained with flecks of their insides.

Nate wondered if any of this was real, if he'd died in his sleep. Maybe the stillness was a nightmare—vivid and rank with the smell of sweat and hurt.

"Is Pixel . . .?" He couldn't finish the question. Couldn't

bear to think that she hadn't made it to the surface, away from this ruin.

Brick shook the fiend off and threw her to the floor beside the man she'd choked until he'd stopped moving. The woman rolled away and curled up, groaning and clutching her head.

"Pixel climbed right out of a drain on the street. You shoulda seen Reed's face. He looked like he saw one of the Old Gods naked and singing about springtime."

Nate blinked. "But she's okay?"

Brick huffed a sound that must have been a laugh. Nate couldn't tell. Her hands were bloody, but she didn't favor anything or limp, so he doubted the blood was hers. "Sparks has her. They went up high on a roof to get away from these sludge-eating fiends."

Shaking and numb, Nate nodded. Every time he blinked, it was harder to keep his eyes open. "Can you get me free?"

Warm hands touched Nate's face. His throat. His hair.

Nate's ears rang.

He forced himself to focus when his mind wanted so badly to switch off for a while.

Kind green eyes studied him from beneath a furrowed brow.

"Reed." It wasn't until that moment that Nate let himself consider how badly he'd wanted Reed to come back and how much it had hurt to walk away from him. From all of them. From what they were.

His family.

He choked on a low sob. "My hands hurt."

"Gods, what did she do to you? Hold on."

"Nate, I wish you'd seen it. Reed made like a fiend and got these fools to listen to him. He knows the way they talk." Brick pulled her knife out of the sheath she wore under her shirt and started scraping at the thick plastic binding Nate to the bed. "He told them the Breakers were hiding enough chem to fly to the moon and back with. Mountains of it for the taking. Crowd got bigger than we wanted, though."

"Don't worry him," Reed said, working on Nate's other wrist. Sweat dripped into his eyes as he glanced up at Nate as if he expected him to disappear at any moment. Brick nudged him to the side to use her knife. Reed's breath caught, and he cupped Nate's face. "Hang on."

Nate watched them, dazed. "My shoulder," he said, his tongue thick in his mouth.

"The trick's getting it back in quick as you can, before you get swelled up," Brick said. She paused, close. "Reed, he looks bad."

Nate couldn't get his arms to move at all once they were free. Reed and Brick eased him onto the floor, and he watched the ceiling spin slowly. Brick lifted his arm, Reed shoved something soft into his mouth, and the world exploded. He waited for darkness to take him away from the pain, but for once, his awareness lingered. Wave after wave of hurt crashed into him. Someone rolled him over. He vomited up water and soft bread.

"You look as bad as you did before," Brick said. "I thought they were going to help you down here."

"I'm not sick." Nate grimaced at the mess on the floor that indicated otherwise. "You about pulled my arm off my body."

"I didn't pull it off; I put it back where it goes."

Reed eased him up, and he moved his arm gingerly, surprised to find that while it throbbed, he could move it without blacking out. Or throwing up again.

Nate started to tell them, decisively, that this day could die in whirlpool of sludge, when he smelled smoke.

Reed stiffened beside him. "Let's go."

Flames caught the pant leg and boots of the body by the furnace, licking along the filthy fabric. Smoke curled, thick and smelly where flesh began to char and bubble.

Nate shrugged away from Reed. He pushed up with his good arm and approached the burning body.

"Nate!" Reed's voice was raw. "What are you doing?"

The heat from the flames warmed Nate's clammy skin. He held his sore arm against his belly so it wouldn't dangle and make the relentless throb worse.

"Think he's gone addled?" Brick asked.

Nate ignored them. The whole room narrowed down to one thing: the poker. Long and heavy. Strong. He plucked it off the body, gaze momentarily snagging on the wreck of the man's skull. Someone had done this—torn this man apart. For chem. For a few days—maybe a few hours—of flying.

He lifted the poker, dodging the growing flames, and approached the still. The metal flickered with firelight. He caught his warped reflection.

"Nate." Reed was behind him, skirting the heat of the flames. "Nate, come on. We need to get out of here."

Nate opened the delicate latch and exposed the fine glass inside. His arm protested, the pain lancing down his side. He stroked the smooth surface with trembling, bloody fingers. So many intricate pieces. Priceless Gathos City tech. Tinkering beyond his comprehension.

He thought of the young mother dragging her terrified child down the alley.

And the body in the street, butchered.

He thought of Reed huddled under a bed.

And Alden crying out in his sleep.

So many lives had already been ravaged by Agatha's chem, by the horrors she could create with his blood, with Juniper's, with her own. With the blood of nameless GEMs he'd never know.

He had to fix this.

It was his calling.

I'm sorry, Pixel.

He raised the heavy iron as high as he could, his shoulder screaming, blood pounding. He drove it down, shattering the glass and scattering the miniscule gears. They pinged against the metal still, cascaded across the floor, rolled into the drains. The still hulked above him, shiny and powerful. Useless now—gutted without the Diffuser at its heart.

Nate laughed until his throat ached, kept laughing when Brick caught him around the waist and dragged him away from the machine.

Nate fought Brick's tight hold. "Wait!"

Brick ignored him.

Reed marched behind them, eyes dark as a stormy sky. "We can talk outside," he said.

Nate tried to elbow Brick, but his arm wouldn't work. And his good arm still held the heavy iron poker. It dangled from his grip, the tip making an awful screech as it dragged against the concrete.

"Brick!" Nate dropped the heavy poker so he could wave his hand at where Juniper was lying, smoke thickening in the air around her body. "Reed! You can't leave her."

They both stopped in the doorway, turning to survey the hazy room where toppled bunks and crumpled bodies littered the floor. The dangling tube swung faintly, as if pushed by a gentle breeze.

"The girl who tried to kill Pixel?" Reed asked.

"She's horrid, but Agatha was pretty bad to her. And Gathos City was worse. We can't leave her down here to get burned up," Nate said. He wasn't sure if he really wanted to save her or ever see her again. In fact, he was certain he never wanted to hear her shattered voice again. But he couldn't walk away knowing she'd burn alive either. "She's still breathing, Reed. What if she wakes up and she can't get out?"

"Okay." Reed sighed sharply. "No more talking about burning up." He jogged back to Juniper and hauled her up with a wince.

Reed's belly wasn't healed all the way. Nate avoided his gaze, guilt like grime on his skin.

The body by the furnace burned. With nothing but metal and concrete around it, the fire stayed contained. The smell of cooking meat chased them through the open door.

In the front room, every light but one was broken. Glass covered the floor, and the table Nate had rested on was turned over, one leg broken. The plants were gone. Two more bodies were in the corner, one stabbed and the other with her neck broken. They wore A-Vol patches on their sleeves.

Brick followed his gaze. "She was buying them off. Hiring them as her muscle."

Grunting under Juniper's weight, Reed started sifting through the cabinets, tearing one after another open and feeling around inside.

"What are you doing?" Nate asked.

"That stuff. The stuff she had to keep you alive." Reed's chest heaved with harsh panting. "The fiends didn't need it. Why would they take it?"

The realization tightened Nate's chest. "They didn't take it."

Broken jars littered the shadowed floor.

Remedy.

It pooled at their feet, swirling around shards and grime. "Brick, put me down."

"Sure about that?" she asked, easing him to his feet.

His legs wobbled, but he managed to sink into an unsteady crouch. Grimacing, he swiped his palm through the liquid on the floor and darted his tongue at it. The taste was unmistakable, even cut with filth. Humiliation curdled in his belly as he dropped to his knees and scooped more up as best he could, cupping the liquid to his mouth and sucking it off his fingers.

"Nate," Reed said softly.

Nate didn't know how much time he was buying. Days? Weeks? The units of measurement in Alden's manual hadn't covered drinking spilled Remedy off of polished concrete. He choked on a quiet sob and used his sleeve to soak more up and wring it out onto his tongue.

"Will you quit watching me?" he snarled out, hating Brick and Reed seeing him like this, scrabbling for a little more time. He'd known what he was doing when he shattered the Diffuser, but he wasn't in a hurry to go to the stillness.

Reed handed Juniper to Brick and crouched beside Nate. He picked up pieces of glass and set them aside, clearing another pool of spilled Remedy. "There's a lot here."

Nate hunched over himself, overcome. His shoulders shook from weeping. Reed rubbed careful circles at his spine.

"You did the right thing."

"When Pixel's older . . ."

"We'll figure it out." Reed took Nate's hand and guided it back to the Remedy on the floor.

With Reed beside him, Nate didn't feel as wretched. The last of his pride eroded, and he pressed his lips to the floor, drawing as much as he could into his mouth.

It spread through him, cool and soothing. Despite the pain, despite his tears, his body grew stronger. The fog in his mind faded. His legs stopped trembling.

"We need to go, Nate. She could be back anytime." Reed helped Nate sop up as much as he could. It was more than he'd ever had at a time—more than Alden had ever given him.

Nate shivered at a sudden hollow feeling. The thought of Agatha returning frightened him, but there was something else. Something he was missing. He reached for Reed's hand, and they stood together.

"I can feel it working," Nate said, shocked to find that he could stand easily. "I wish Juniper would wake up so she could have some too."

Brick tapped Juniper's pale cheek. "She's not waking up anytime soon. Shouldn't I leave her here?"

"One of the fiends tried to *eat* her." Nate struggled to form the words. He wiped his eyes with his good arm. "We can't leave her. They might come back before Agatha does."

He knew he shouldn't feel protective of Juniper, but the need snagged at him anyway. The way her face had gone blank, as if she'd reached the limit of what she could endure.

What happened to her in Gathos City?

Reed sighed. "All right."

They made their way up the stairs, stepping over another body. Nate couldn't tell if the person was dead or knocked out.

Light rain bled down brick walls and darkened the streets. Low clouds glowed like lamps in the dying yellow light.

Nate breathed in the scent of wet char and tangy water, clearing away the tickle of smoke in his throat. "They're opening the gates," he murmured.

"For sure?" Brick's hands twitched. "How do you know?"

"Agatha knows. She said so. I don't think she was lying. Everything she's doing is to get set up here before folks from Gathos City start coming over."

"Won't make a difference," Brick said. "They'll come *here*, but they won't want us *there*."

Nate nodded, pretending not to hear the hope laced through her words. He walked like he was in a dream, staring down at his wet boots and the pockmarked pavement below them.

He couldn't get his head around everything that had happened—the fiends, Juniper bleeding, the bodies, and the

Diffuser smashed up. It felt like minutes since he'd been carried away from Alden's, but years and years too. A lifetime. He wondered if this was what it was like to get old, full to the brim with memories like Fran and Bernice.

They approached a gnarled fire escape. Reed set Juniper down gently between two plastic bins. She didn't move. A thick knot bruised her forehead, and blood soaked her clothes from the bite on her arm.

Nate startled at the sound of creaking and looked up, expecting one of the Breakers to be crawling down at them. Relief chased away the dizzying spike of fear. Sparks picked her way down the fire escape, with Pixel trailing behind her. Pixel's skin and clothes were covered with a fine layer of plaster dust. She'd wiped her fingers through the chalky residue to draw whiskers on her face.

"Nate!" She hopped down the last few steps and bounded into Nate, squeezing him tightly. "You got free."

"Wasn't sure you'd come back out of there the way the fiends were running," Sparks said. She wore a bandana in her hair, her curls wild and tangled, and stubble lined her jaw. Her dark eyes shone with relief as she wrapped her arms around Reed and clasped Nate on the shoulder.

"Ow." Nate ducked away, pain reverberating from her touch.

Reed took her by the arm. "He's hurt."

She shook Reed off and clasped Nate's hand in a careful grip instead. "I told Reed you didn't mean that garbage you said to the Breakers. 'Bout hating the rest of us."

"I didn't think he meant it," Reed mumbled.

Sparks huffed a breath. "Sure."

They'd forgive him more readily than he deserved. Reed, so stubbornly good, would absorb the hurt Nate had caused him with the things he'd said.

But Reed's forgiveness didn't matter. Now that it was clear to everyone how much danger Nate had put them in, there was no hope left for a future with the gang. He had no right to call them his family after he'd put them all in Agatha's sights.

He had no right to love Reed.

But the soft, private smile on Reed's lips when their eyes met still sent a current of affection through him.

He was going to miss Reed so much.

"Agatha could be anywhere." Reed steeled his expression, his shoulders tensing. "We need to hide."

"She won't be alone either. When I was up on the roof waiting *forever*, she went that way with five or six people," Sparks said, pointing.

Nate guided Pixel to take Sparks's hand and hung back, breathless with guilt. All four of them had narrowly escaped death to give him a chance to live. And he'd shattered his only chance by destroying the Diffuser. They'd be right to hate him. Even with the gates opening, there was no telling that enough Remedy would make its way into the Withers—if any made it out of Gathos City at all.

It won't in my lifetime.

"I can help you get settled somewhere before I go," Nate said. "If you let me rest up for a few days, get my arm working again. I'll tinker as best I can for you. Lights, locks. I know it won't make up for this. Nothing will."

Reed blinked at him like he'd grown another arm out of the side of his head. "What?"

Nate scratched his neck, embarrassment blistering. He should have known it was too much to ask. He'd never been anything but trouble to them, and the sooner he made his own way, the better. "You're right. I'm sorry. I can go to Alden's. Or maybe the Servants."

Sparks came closer, squinted at him. "What happened to him in there? They hit his head?"

"No," Brick said. "But *I'm* about to hit his head. Stop feeling sore, Nate. We didn't round up half the fiends in the Withers to send you off to get snatched up by trappers or whatever trouble you'd manage to find next."

"Besides." Sparks's expression shifted like she'd stepped into a shadow. She glanced at Pixel and back at Nate. "Alden's place burned up this morning. Heard some fiends griping about it. No one knows where to go for cheap chem."

"What?" High-pitched ringing sounded in Nate's ears. He staggered back. "Where's Alden?"

"Figured he ran off."

Agatha and a bunch of her Breakers. Sparks had pointed in the direction of Alden's shop.

Nate's memories snapped together. It stung like a jolt of electricity.

You can't come back here, Alden had said.

He'd known. He'd known they'd come for him once they had Nate.

"No." Nate's feet began to carry him in the direction of the shop with dragging, dizzy steps. "He doesn't go anywhere. He doesn't leave. He won't leave. He's never left."

"Whoa." Reed grabbed his good arm. "Nate. Stop. What are you doing?"

"I have to see!" He had to know it was true, because he could already picture the shop gone—obliterated by fire. Nothing left inside. Nate's hands ached, gone cold in the rain that spat down at them listlessly.

"Then I'll go with you. Sparks, Brick—keep Pixel safe," he said. "Keep moving. We'll meet up at sunset. In that alley behind the gull-catcher's place."

Pixel wrestled Brick's grip, reaching for Nate. "No! We have to stay together."

"Pix, you gotta stay with the girls." Nate let her scrabble her small hands at him. "Let us go check on Alden, and we'll find you when we're done." He caught one of her frantic hands and lowered his voice. "Look how scared Brick is. You have to keep her safe."

Brick glared, and Sparks snorted.

"She needs you to take care of her," Nate said.

Pixel laughed softly, until the laugh became a dry sob. "What if the Breakers catch you?" Tears welled up and spilled down her face.

A shiver ran through Nate. The Breakers *would* catch them if they didn't hole up soon.

"They can't catch us." Reed crouched at Pixel's side, rubbing her back. He looked up at Nate. "We're alley cats, remember? We're quick and smart, and we stick together, no matter what."

Nate swallowed, wondering if he was imagining something pointed about Reed's gaze.

"What do we do with this one if she wakes up?" Brick asked, hefting Juniper up.

Pixel scowled. "Don't let her poke me with anything."

"Tie her up if you have to," Reed said.

"Gently," Nate added. He shuffled one step, then another, as if blown by a strong wind.

None of them fussed with goodbyes. The girls dodged into an alley, finding the shadowed places beneath dripping fire escapes.

"Can you run?" Reed asked.

"I think so."

They took off. The cool air whipped at Nate's face, tickled where the rain wet his hair. He was sore inside and out. Raw. He breathed raggedly. Every footfall sent aftershocks of pain through his shoulder.

None of it bothered him. Even with Reed beside him, all he could think about was what they were running toward and how much his mind screamed at him to run away from it.

He didn't want to see Alden's bones. Fran's. Both of them cooked to nothing in the only home they'd ever known.

CHAPTER
SEVENTEEN

Thick clouds grazed the tallest buildings in the Withers. Smog-tainted rain fell in heavy torrents, bitter on Nate's lips. It seared the cuts on his wrists. His footsteps splashed, and his clothes stuck to his body, weighing him down as he ran toward an anemic column of smoke and steam where Alden's shop was.

Reed raced beside him, his blood-soaked shirt slowly going pink as the rain washed it. He reached for Nate's hand, and Nate shook it off. He had to concentrate. One foot after the other. If anything distracted him, he'd fall, and that would be it. He'd be done. Empty. He wouldn't be able to take another step. He wouldn't be able to look.

They turned the corner, and he stumbled to a stop. He'd known for a few blocks what he'd see. That much smoke didn't come from a bin-fire. But the wreck of Alden's shop stole his breath, chilled him to the bone.

The windows were gone, and the inside of the shop gaped at them like a toothless maw. Charred. Wisps of smoke rising from the ashes of Alden's things.

A single wind chime hung from the door, which had been torn off its hinges.

"Nate," Reed said.

A low growl escaped from Nate's chest. A warning.

Don't say anything. This is my fault.

They'd never have set their sights on Alden if it weren't for him.

He made himself keep walking, every step revealing more ruin. The glass counter was gone, reduced to rubble and gleaming shards. The curtains that shielded Fran's bedroom from the rest of the shop were burned away. Smoke poured from inside her room.

Nate choked on the smell of it and stepped through the doorway, his shoes crunching on broken jars. He wiped the rain out of his eyes and yelped when Reed grabbed him and yanked him back.

"Nate!"

"What—"

A wooden staff crashed against the broken plaster in front of Nate. In the dim light and the smoke, Nate struggled to identify his attacker.

"Alden." His throat tightened.

Alden stood in the charred room in a torn, bloodied robe, swaying like a ghost in the blackened shell of his shop. His hair was singed at the tips, curled to wisps of ashy-white. A split lip and cut eyebrow bled like a red curtain down his cheek. He pushed his tangled hair out of his face.

"Oh." He dropped the wooden staff, and it clattered to the floor. His bare feet left a trail of blood. "It's raining."

"Alden." Nate approached slowly, the way hungry kids stalked sludge-rats. Alden tensed up when his darting gaze found Reed. "It's me."

"They took everything." Alden shivered. "I couldn't stop them."

"Alden, where is your grandmother?" Nate asked. He didn't want to hear the answer. "Where's Fran?"

"She went to sleep." As Alden spoke, tears ran down his face. "They were at the door. I made her tea. She didn't know, Natey. I didn't hurt her. I swear I didn't hurt her."

Nate reached Alden and took his hand, grasping it tightly. Alden's fingers were thinner than he remembered. His knuckles bled, bruise and ragged.

Nate tried not to imagine him fighting—or what he'd had to fight off. "I know."

Alden's wavering gaze shifted from Nate's hand to his face. He blinked as if he'd only now seen him. "Hello, little dove," he said. "Did they fix you up?"

"Yeah." Nate's voice broke. "I'm better now."

"Everything's gone." Alden held one arm across his middle, and his hand trembled violently. "It hurts. And I don't have anything left to make it stop."

Nate touched Alden's face carefully, wiping blood away with his sleeve. "What happened?"

"They came for my things." Alden glanced at Reed, wary in a way Nate had never seen him, not in the worst of his throes of want, not ever. "But Grandmother didn't see," he whispered to Nate. "She didn't see any of that."

"Good," Nate said helplessly, fixing Alden's robe where it had slipped from his shoulder. "That's good, Alden."

"She wanted her bones to go to sea, Natey, but I couldn't get her out fast enough. The fire wouldn't stop."

Nate didn't know what to say.

"No matter. Everything's gone now." Alden pulled his hand out of Nate's and fidgeted with the ruined ends of his hair. "Why are you here? I don't have anything. The Diffuser's gone too. They took it."

Nate's throat went sour. The Breakers might not be able to mass-produce chem, but they still had a way to abuse GEMs. "How did they get into the safe?" he asked, sharp with anger.

Reed nudged him with his shoe. Nate realized too late that Reed didn't want him to ask—didn't want to know.

"I was persuaded to open it," Alden said, shoulders moving in a shrug that became a shudder and ran down the length of him. "I asked why you're here," he said, recovering with an agitated breath.

"I thought you were dead." Nate cringed, not sure if this was any better. "They told me your shop burned."

"The rumors are true." Alden's breath huffed. "It must be the talk of the Withers. Wherever will the lost find salvation now?"

Nate's chest ached. Alden's broken empire only mattered to those who couldn't afford the Breakers' superior chem. He'd been losing his grip on the fiends of the Withers all along.

"Come with us," Reed said. "Pixel's with the girls. She'll want to see you. We'll take you to the Servants to get mended."

"I am not one of your charity cases." Alden glanced at the

open door and the rainy street beyond, fear flickering in his gaze before it hardened. "You shouldn't have brought Nate here. If he got away from her once, he won't get away again. They'll make him sleep like they do in Gathos City." His voice went ragged. "They'll cut him apart. What were you thinking coming here?"

Nate was frozen in place, struck numb by the way Alden unraveled before him. It was like watching the train crumple apart.

"Alden," Reed said in the gentle tone he used with Pixel whenever she woke screaming in the night. He took Alden's elbow carefully.

Alden shook him off and pushed him hard, losing his balance. His body folded forward, and a strangled cry tore from his throat. Reed caught him, and Alden fought briefly before he slumped in Reed's arms, hair falling over his face. The rage appeared to drain out of him, and he let out a hoarse, sobbed breath.

Reed's eyes widened, and he turned a questioning gaze to Nate. He stroked Alden's back, maybe without meaning to or maybe because he was Reed.

Nate wanted to reach for Alden, but resisted, struck with the awful thought that Alden would crumble to dust if he touched him.

"Nate," Reed started to say, shaking his head. His pale-green eyes held a mix of apology and pity.

It made Nate want to lash out at him like Alden had. They couldn't give up—not on wishes, not on anything.

Before Reed could say more, Alden straightened, flipping

his hair out of his face and wiping his nose with a delicate sweep of his hand. "You'll have to forgive me for that outburst. It's been a long day."

Silence stretched between them until Alden sighed and crossed his skinny, bruised arms. "So. You don't look especially better-off. How did you get away from Agatha?"

"She was out." Nate edged toward the door—hoping Alden would follow him. "Reed tricked fiends into killing her guards and breaking the door down."

"She's nothing without the fools who fight for her—for her chem," Alden said, quietly bitter.

"I, uh, broke her still. So now she can't make chem anymore. Or Remedy."

Alden took a step toward him, one hand outstretched like a gull's claw. "Tell me how she made Remedy," he said, frantic. "In a still? How?"

Startled by the feverish questioning, Nate stumbled on his words. It didn't matter anymore. He'd wrecked it all. "Serum, she said. It's part of blood. Not GEM blood. But she mixed it with other things. Plant stuff. Chemical stuff. I couldn't tell."

"Blood. That . . ." Alden clenched his jaw. "Of course."

Reed cleared his throat. "Agatha's still out here somewhere."

"Yes, I noticed when she brought her friends here and they *set my home on fire.*"

"Nate isn't going to leave you here."

Alden shot an icy look at Nate, and he shrugged. Reed was correct.

"If you won't come willingly, I'm going to carry you," Reed said, meeting Nate's surprised look with a resigned shrug.

"And it won't be pleasant for either of us. Come as far as the gull-catcher's shop. We're meeting the girls there. Find some-where dry. Sleep."

"I'll have plenty of time to sleep," Alden said, monotone. He turned to the wall where the shelves were cracked down the middle, forming triangles and angular shadows.

Nate held his hand out for Alden. His sleeve was stained with blood and greenish Remedy.

Alden traced a trembling finger along the swollen wound that circled Nate's wrist like a bracelet. "Did you get enough?" he asked in a whisper that sounded like an apology.

Enough for now.

"I'm fine, Alden. Let's go."

Alden took his hand.

———

Alden's haunted gaze drifted up to the tops of the tall build-ings and the crumbling, ornate carvings around the higher windows. He stared like a child, frightened and curious at once. Cradling his arm over his middle, he winced with every footstep.

"You've really never been out here?" Reed asked, voice soft with unmasked concern.

Alden didn't answer.

Nate exchanged a quick look with Reed, pained at the thought of Alden's entire life spent indoors, surrounded by his mother's things and the sound of his grandmother's paper-rustle voice.

They stopped to drink acidic water from a broken gutter

and made their way to the rails—the shortest path to the spot Reed had picked to meet up with the girls. The rain had stopped, and the evening sun shone through breaks in the thick cloud cover. People came out of their homes, clearing broken concrete out of doorways and sweeping glass off the street.

There was something beautiful about every small effort to return the Withers back to the way it had been before the train wreck and the fires and the mobs of angry people. Wretched or not, this was their home. For most people, the Withers would be the only home they'd ever have. Even if the gates opened, the city wasn't going to welcome every Witherson to its gleaming towers.

They traveled slowly, silent except for Alden's coarse breaths. Every few minutes, he swallowed back a sound of pain. He was hurt more than he was letting on. Reed threaded Alden's arm over his shoulder.

He's never quiet. Not like this.

The sickly sweet tang of decay hung in the air as they passed a building reduced to rubble. A lumpy pile of bodies rotted in the street below them. No one ever left bodies out in the Withers. They brought them to the shoreline and pushed them into the sludge or burned them in the street. But someone had left those bodies there. Someone had run away from them and never looked back.

The rails were crowded, but no one spared a glance at Alden's barefoot, hobbling form. He fit in with the other dusty, bleeding travelers. Everyone walked with the clumsy momentum of fear. A family passed, carrying bloodied children who clung tightly, wide-eyed and silent.

Alden's pale skin gleamed with sweat. He scanned the faces of everyone who passed as if afraid he'd recognize someone. With his shop gone and a surplus of Breaker chem on the streets from the fiends' raid on Agatha's basement, Alden had no power. There were no more bargains to be made.

Reed kept silent, his jaw tense and twitching as he matched Alden's sluggish pace and carried the brunt of his weight. They'd already be at the meeting place if they could run.

And it wouldn't take skill to track them.

Nate longed for a ticker and his tools, something to keep his hands busy and his mind quiet. Walking wasn't enough.

Sadness pressed at him, sudden and heavy. "Fran knew she would die."

"I'm sure it was a lucky guess." Alden shivered, beyond the help of anything Fran could have knitted to warm him up. "Everyone knows they're going to die."

"She told me about the Mainland," Nate said. "She believed in it."

"While I appreciate your conviction," Alden said, measuring his words out like each one taxed him, "I feel the need to remind you that my grandmother also believed that the cockroaches in her bedroom were trying to get a look at her knickers."

Reed's tense expression softened to a twitch of a smile.

"How will she get her happy ending now?" Alden asked.

"Your grandmother?" Reed adjusted his grip on Alden and cast Nate a concerned look.

Alden's voice went icy. "My grandmother is dead."

"Pixel," Nate explained, remembering a day that felt like

a year ago, though it couldn't have been much longer than a few weeks. Alden had told him that hope was a fragile thing, but here they were with nothing left but hope.

"I never would have fed from her." Alden stumbled and caught himself with a low, breathless curse.

Nate wanted to believe him, but the memory of the fiends in Agatha's basement was too fresh. They'd all been regular people once. People who'd made choices—good and bad. Chem had wrenched those choices out of their hands.

"This is our stop," Reed said.

Nate went down the stairs first, watching Alden closely as he shuffled down the steps, swaying and nearly stumbling to his knees. Reed caught him and met Nate's gaze in silent assurance that he wasn't going to let him fall.

Whether Alden liked it or not, Reed had made him part of the gang when he'd led him out of the shop.

But even with the help, Alden wasn't going to make it much farther.

They pressed on silently. If Nate gave his fears a name, grief would swallow him up.

Down on the street level, bin-fires cast a warm glow. On this block, every street ran slightly downhill, affording a view of Gathos City in the distance across the channel. It glittered, each tower radiant with more lights than the Withers had altogether.

The gull-catcher was an old man, blind in one eye and hard of hearing. He sold the fresh carcasses from his shop on the street level and spent every morning up on the roof, setting traps and coaxing gulls with gruel made of bug guts and water from the waste trenches. Nate had never been able to bring himself to buy the fresh meat, to shake the thought of the man's bare hands stirring piss and plucking gulls in the same morning.

But he sold him wire to set his traps every once in a while, and the old man had taken kindly to Nate and listened to stories about his gang. Kindly enough to ignore the girls on his back stoop, tucked behind rows and rows of bones drying on twine.

Pixel dashed out from where they were hidden and threw her arms out to hug Alden. Nate caught her at the last minute with his good arm and swung her away before she could hurt him. Alden favored his middle more and more with every step.

Sparks followed her, gesturing to the shadowed form of Brick and what appeared to be a struggling Juniper. Her bandana was gone but to Nate's relief, she appeared unhurt. "She woke up and wouldn't stop fussing. Brick gagged her. Didn't have to tie her up. She's weak as a babe." She saw Alden, and her mouth thinned to a frown.

Nate held Pixel close. She peered up at Alden, her small eyebrows furrowed. "Alden. Are you sick?"

He stared at her for a long moment, as if he didn't recognize her. A faint, hazy smile tugged at his lips. "A touch, princess. I need to sleep."

"I know a sick-den near here," Sparks said. "Ivy House. I went there when I was kicking chem. It's like a med clinic, but the Servants don't care if you're registered. And they take the dying." She looked away from Alden quickly. "I mean . . . people hurt real bad."

Alden didn't answer. His eyes had fluttered closed, and he listed against Reed.

"They're not full anymore?" Brick asked.

Nate's breath sucked in, afraid to hope for a way to get Alden help. "After the wreck, all the sick-dens were turning people away."

Sparks scratched at her neck. "I don't know. Only one way to find out."

"All right." Reed crouched and hefted Alden into his arms.

Alden went limp. The blood on his feet was black in the dim light. Nate wanted to cover him in blankets, hide him so no one could see the bruises and the angles of his bones.

"Why are you doing this?" Nate asked softly, the question only for Reed.

Reed turned his green eyes on Nate. Soft, inscrutable pain flashed there before he blinked it away and grimaced with the strain of carrying Alden. "Because he's your friend."

Nate's fidgeting fingers ran over each raw circle at his wrists. The rain had washed the worst of the blood away, but the flesh was wet and ruined to his touch. His shoulder throbbed with hot, determined pain, and it pulled him away from the tangled rush of confusion and warmth Reed made him feel.

He turned to Sparks. "Show us the way."

CHAPTER
EIGHTEEN

Sparks led them to a narrow street lined with brownstones in the neighborhood Nate had lived in with Bernice. Bin-fires in front of every house cast a faint glow. The group climbed stairs to a burned-wood sign on the door that read "Ivy House." Nate smiled with a twinge of affection. His mother would have liked that name. But there were no creeping vines here, only a crumbling brick stoop.

It was the kind of quiet street the gang had avoided when scavenging. These were homes crammed full of families relying on subsidies from the workhouses. It was a relatively safe area, but Nate glanced over his shoulder. He couldn't shake the sense that someone was following them, despite Sparks's careful watch.

Children played on the street a few doors down, pushing a ball around with plastic sticks. Pixel watched them longingly.

"Sorry, Pix. You have to come in with us," Nate said. He didn't want to frighten her, so he left it at that.

"Sickness in there," a woman said from the stoop next door. She sat barefoot, nursing a sleeping toddler wrapped in a yellow sheet. Her gaze settled on Alden, who sagged between Sparks and Reed. "The stillness calling?"

"I don't know. They'll take him?" Reed asked.

She shrugged. "That's what they say. Long as they stay in there, I don't much care." She frowned at Juniper, who still wore Sparks's bandana—across her mouth. "What's that all about?"

"Addled," Sparks said. "Took a handful of chem."

"More than a handful, I'd wager," Brick added.

After a moment of silence, the woman laughed, startling the toddler—who squawked at her breast until she coaxed it to latch on again. "That'll scramble somebody up." She sobered. "Hope it ends quickly for that one. Gods watch him."

"Thank you," Reed said. They hung back as Nate went to the door and knocked, nerves sharp. The last time they'd gone looking for help, they'd ended up in the Breakers' hands.

A small peephole slid open.

"Why have you come here?" a soft voice asked.

"Our friend needs help," Nate said.

"Do you vow to enter peacefully?"

It didn't seem like much of a safeguard. Nate exchanged looks with Reed, who shrugged, fit to fall over where he stood, shouldering most of Alden's weight.

"Yes, we do. And I'm a Tinkerer. I'd be happy to be of service."

The door opened slightly, and a tall, thin figure peered out at them. He wore glasses with a thin crack down one lens, and his young, pale face was mottled with scars. Dingy, long robes marked him as a Servant.

"Is everyone else healthy?" he asked, his voice softer than Nate expected. He couldn't have been any older than Reed.

The question hit Nate like a rush of icy cold water. It seemed like a lifetime ago that he'd worried about hiding his sickness from Reed. "Yes."

The boy gave them a wry smile. "Are you sure? You all look a bit worse for wear."

"We could use shelter if you have any," Reed said. "But no one is sick but him."

"I would imagine not. All of you look very young," he said, as if unaware of his own age. He held the door open. "I'm James, a Servant of the Old Gods. And this is Ivy House. Bring him in."

As Sparks passed through the door, they exchanged a look that left Sparks ducking her head and smiling. Nate wondered if he imagined that James's hand brushed against hers ever so briefly.

Reed gave James a quick handshake and introduced himself. "It's quiet here. You didn't have any violence?"

"There was a fire down the street last night, but fortunately none of the damage on this block was serious," James said.

"We're not bringing trouble," Reed said. "You have my word."

Juniper made a muffled sound and elbowed Brick, who held her wrists together easily with one hand. Blood oozed from the bite at her shoulder, and the stain of it ran down the front of her dress like a spill.

James arched his brow delicately. "Is she here of her own volition?"

Brick rolled her eyes and tugged the bandana out of

Juniper's mouth. "You want to run off, go ahead," she said. "Plenty of nice people out here would welcome you right into their homes, I'm sure."

Juniper opened her mouth, glared, and shut it again. "I'll stay," she mumbled.

James gave them a long look and clasped his hands together. "Well! Please shut the door behind you, and let's take a look at your friend."

Nate walked inside in a daze and pulled the door closed. He blinked to adjust to the dim light.

The dusty, wet smell of the apartment reminded Nate of Bernice's. This had been one of the wealthier neighborhoods in Winter Heights half a century ago. Faded floral wallpaper clung to the walls in patches. A chipped chair rail ran the length of the long hallway. The floors were made of real wood, and they were scarred with deep gouges and scuffmarks.

Nate caught up to the others as they passed several closed doors. Someone coughed wretchedly behind one, and Sparks murmured, "Gods watch us."

"You're in charge here?" Brick asked, dubious.

"Tonight, I am." He seemed to realize what she'd meant and let out a soft, awkward laugh. "I've been here for two years, if you're worried about that."

At the end of the hall, their quietly shuffling group reached an open living room. Nate hadn't seen so much furniture since he'd left Bernice's. The chairs and couches were decades old and drooping and frayed, but they looked impossibly comfortable. A single candle in a glass cylinder lit the room. The soft light made everything pretty. It was paradise.

Only Juniper looked unimpressed.

"We don't have electricity at the moment," James said. He noticed Nate's quick glance and shook his head. "No one on the block does."

"Is there somewhere we can put him down?" Sparks asked.

"Yes, of course." James smiled, pushing up his glasses, and dragged a thin pallet bed from under the couch to the middle of the room. "We don't have any other rooms free, but you may rest here for now."

Reed and Sparks eased Alden onto the low bed. He didn't stir. Nate sank beside him as James covered him with a dingy sheet.

Pixel climbed onto one of the couches, curling up, and closed her eyes. Nate couldn't recall the last time he'd seen her sleep. Brick led Juniper to a chair in the corner. Juniper's legs gave out, and Brick scooped her up and sat her down, more careful than Nate had ever seen her be with anyone but Pixel.

James handed Juniper a small cloth. "For your shoulder. Staunch the wound until it stops bleeding."

She pressed the cloth to her shoulder and squinted at him, her brow knit with a little frown.

"Nate's hurt too." Sparks gave him a gentle push toward James and spoke to him with an easy familiarity. "Not that he'd tell you."

James glanced at him. "May I?"

Nate extended his arms and studied Alden while James shone a crank-light on the throbbing wounds at his wrists. Alden's lips were pale, and his skin had gone ashen. He'd always been thin, but it was worse now—his cheekbones too sharp and the skin around his eyes papery. Even gut-stabbed and bleeding out, Reed hadn't looked this bad.

"You and the girl need salve and bandages. If you'll wait a moment, I'll retrieve them," James said.

Nate squinted in the dark, finding Brick already snoring with her mouth wide open. He wondered how long they'd been running since they left the bank, never sure where they'd find a place to stop and close their eyes. Sparks had disappeared to somewhere else in the house. Juniper curled up on the chair, very still but awake. She clutched her shoulder, and her pale eyes watched him from beneath a fall of hair. She wasn't restrained in any way, but by the way she'd stumbled and dragged her feet, she wasn't getting far if she tried. They'd have to figure out what to do with her later.

Legs trembling, Nate sank to a crouch beside Alden's bed. He touched Alden's hair. The rain and wind had blown it to a snarled mess.

Reed sat on the floor on the other side of the bed. "Maybe the Servants will have something to help him," he offered.

It was a wish, and nothing more. The truth buzzed like an insect in Nate's ear. He rearranged the sheet over Alden, his knuckles brushing against Alden's chest where his robe hung open. "He's cold. He feels like stone."

Alden's labored breath made a low, unsettling sound.

Nate's fingers trembled until he curled them into fists. "He needs his hairbrush." Alden couldn't die like this, not with his hair a mess. Not when he'd treasured it, worn it like finery around his shoulders.

Reed said nothing.

James came over with a small jug of water and a basket. "I'm afraid this is all I can spare. You'll have to share it."

Reed took the jug and woke the girls up to distribute water quietly, leaving James and Nate at Alden's bed beneath a broken pendant light that cast a jagged shadow in the candlelight.

James crouched beside Alden and gave Nate a knowing look. "He isn't simply sick, is he?"

Nate shook his head.

"Was he beaten?"

Nate's throat clenched as he tried not to picture that. "Yes."

James lowered the sheet and carefully opened Alden's robe. Nate gasped. Deep-purple bruises mottled Alden's belly. The skin had gone hard and shiny in places.

"Gods," Nate whispered. He pressed his hand to his middle absently, struck by how much pain Alden must have been in as he'd staggered around his shop, feral and feverish.

"He's bleeding inside," James said. He raised the sheet and tucked it around Alden's thin shoulders. "The stillness will come in a day or so. I'm sorry."

Nate felt like James had punched him in the chest. He'd expected a long examination, like his careful dissection of broken tickers. "Is he going to wake up?"

"He may or may not. There's no telling the state he'll be in." James took Nate's hands, one after the other, quickly coating the worst of the cuts on his wrists with a sticky salve. He wrapped them with soft, clean cloth. "Speak to him calmly and tell him that you're close by. That's the most any of us can hope for in the end."

"You're not staying?" Nate asked, panic rising in his throat.

James gave him a gentle smile and adjusted his glasses. "The last few days have been unkind to the Withers. We nearly have a full house tonight and less help than usual. Another den nearby was lost in a fire, and we've been helping them set up a temporary shelter."

Nate nodded, trying to follow along. It didn't make sense. And it didn't matter. Not anymore.

"If I get more help, I'll send them by to check on him," James said, approaching Juniper carefully—as if he expected her to take off running. He held his hands out and waited for her to nod before he coated the bite on her shoulder with the same salve. "My advice is to sleep while you can in case he wakes up in a state."

"Wait—there's one more thing." Nate rubbed his palms at his face, willing his thoughts to unsnarl. His body screamed with exhaustion. He wanted so badly to close his eyes with Alden and forget about this nightmare. "Does anyone here have a hairbrush?"

James gathered his salves. "Yes. I believe so. I'll bring it in after I finish my rounds," he said, soft and kind.

Nate willed back tears, relieved that James didn't question his odd request. He couldn't bear to explain why it meant so much to him. All he could see was Alden with that brush in his hand, holding it like a lifeline, punctuating his words with quick waves and tugs of gray bristles down his inky hair.

Reed returned as James walked away. "The rest is for you," he said, pushing the jug into Nate's hands. As Nate swallowed down gritty, warm water, Reed asked, "Any news?"

Nate set the jug down. "He's beyond help," he said, toneless. "Could be tonight. Tomorrow."

It couldn't be real. He was telling a story.

Reed settled down beside him, close but not touching. His body radiated warmth, and Nate wanted to lean in and find comfort in it, but he held very still.

"I was so jealous of him." Reed spoke softly, apologetically.

Nate stifled an incredulous laugh. "Of Alden?"

"Yes. You were always going to him. I thought you were lovers. And I thought he . . ."

"You thought he was giving me chem."

"Yes. And I hated him for it. But I think I hated him for loving you even more."

It was something Nate would have given his hand to hear a month ago, but tonight the words rolled off him like beads of oil. He was so tired.

"Alden said once . . . he said he hoped it would be you watching me die, and not him. I didn't understand." Nate let out a dry sob. "Reed, I want him to wake up. So I can tell him . . ."

"Tell him what?" Reed asked, pained.

"That I shouldn't have gone to the Breakers. I should have stayed and died there. And then he'd be okay. That I'm s-s-sorry." Nate tripped over his words. "I'm so sorry."

"He wanted you to go." Reed went breathy with exasperation. "Nate. He didn't want you to stay and die."

Nate pressed his lips together, but he couldn't hold back the low choke of a sob. They'd hurt each other, scraped the space between them raw—but Alden had never stopped feeling like home in his own jagged way. "He's my best friend."

Reed put his arm around Nate's good shoulder hesitantly and pulled him close. "I know."

Resting his head against Reed, Nate felt a bruised kind of relief that Reed left it at that. He didn't want to talk about it anymore. Didn't want to know what Reed saw from the outside looking in.

Reed's breath warmed Nate's hair, steadily evening toward the sleep none of them had been able to afford. Not for days. He slumped against Nate, heavy with exhaustion, and Nate shifted to carefully brace him where they sat with their backs against the sofa that smelled like dust and mildew. His palm rested against Nate's knee, and Nate took it carefully, as if cradling glass. His thumb idly stroked the warm skin at the back of Reed's hand, seeking comfort when sleep refused to come. Not with every rattling, terrible sound Alden made.

He closed his eyes, cocooned in the dark room with everyone he loved.

"Nate. Nate."

Nate startled at the dim glow of a crank-light.

Sparks tried to pry him from Reed's sleeping form. "James brought you a hairbrush," she said. "Well, not for you. Though you could stand to use it."

Nate wiggled out from beside Reed and eased him onto the floor, careful not to wake him. He tucked a cushion under Reed's head. "Thank you."

Sparks's face was freshly shaven, her hair clean and damp. When her appearance matched who she was, the tightness around her eyes went away. She gave him a sad, encouraging nod as she handed him the brush. It was metal with glossy purple bristles—nothing like Alden's carved bone brush with soft bristles that felt like they had come from an animal. Nate stared at it, unsettled by the sense that he'd seen it before. But nothing in the Withers looked like this.

Shaking off the prickle of a memory, Nate ran the brush through one of the worst tangles. Alden's hair got caught in the bristles immediately.

"Here," Sparks said, prying the brush out of his hands. "Stick to tinkering."

"Show me how," Nate whispered. *He* had to do this. No one else.

Sparks's eyes flickered in the early dawn light glowing through the window. She took a careful handful of Alden's hair and gripped it tight. "This way, it won't hurt him."

Starting at the tips, she brushed short, firm strokes. Little by little, the strand she held in her palm began to straighten out, gleaming despite the singed-gray tips.

"Want to try?" she asked.

Nate reached for the brush and weaved his fingers into Alden's hair, gripping as Sparks'd done. He brushed from the tips and worked his way toward his hand stroke after stroke.

"There you go," Sparks said. "Perfect."

Their eyes met. "Thank you."

She touched his head with a tired smile. "I'll do yours when you're done."

By the time Nate finished with Alden's hair, the early morning sun lit the whole room in soft blues and greens. He set the brush aside, took Alden's wrists, and massaged them gently, trying to work blood back into his hands.

Alden's fingers were rubbery and cold, as if all the life was already gone from them.

Reed rolled over in his sleep and threw one arm over Alden.

"Well. I never thought I'd see that." Nate smiled. He couldn't recall much from the haze of being sick in Alden's shop, but he remembered the sound of their voices mingling— Reed's deep and warm, and Alden's brittle. He wondered what they would have thought of each other if they'd met outside of the shadow of all the things they'd done. All the things that had been done *to* them.

Sparks covered her mouth and yawned.

"You should keep sleeping," Nate said. "We have to leave tomorrow."

She frowned, disappointed. "Already?"

"We won't need to be here after tomorrow."

She glanced down at Alden, her shoulders sagging. "Oh," she murmured, touching the part of his hair she'd untangled. "Sorry, Nate."

He didn't say it was all right, because it wasn't. Instead, he gave an absent nod.

Sparks scuffled to tuck herself against Brick. Pixel slept curled up so small she was barely visible among the cushions on the couch. Juniper was still too, some of her hair woven between her fingers, as if she'd clutched it as she'd fallen asleep.

Nate listened to Alden breathing and the softer, gentler sound of Reed's snores.

Bernice had gone in her sleep. Nate didn't know what to look or listen for. Every few minutes, Alden made a quiet, whimpering sound. But he didn't stir or struggle. And his noisy breathing stayed the same—steady in its own unnatural rhythm.

A shadow crossed Nate. He turned to see a plump silhouette in the door. It wasn't James. It was a woman in a tunic and heavy boots. A long Servant's robe draped over her arm.

"Hello?" she called out very softly. "Jamie sent me to check on you. Is anyone awake?"

Nate picked himself up, careful not to trip over Sparks and Brick. It was dark in the hallway. His hair hung in his face like a curtain. He wanted to go back to sleep. "I'm awake. Mostly."

"The young man who's ill . . ." Her voice trailed off unsteadily. "Will you tell me his name?"

"It's Alden," Nate said. "He owned a curio shop on the other side of the Withers. It burned in the fires."

"Alden," she echoed.

"You sound relieved . . ."

And sad.

"I was looking for someone. But that's not his name," she said.

"Will you pray for him?" Nate didn't know much about how Servants worshipped the Old Gods, but it seemed like a prayer or two couldn't hurt.

"No." She made a quiet, embarrassed sound. "Oh! That must sound terrible. Jamie will. He's very devoted. I'm a bit of an odd duck as far as Servants go."

He smiled at her nervous awkwardness. "You don't believe?"

"I'm afraid faith in the Old Gods didn't quite mesh with my previous line of work. But I believe in service. And there's no better place to serve than here."

"James said you were helping another sick-den."

"I was. I just got in. I'm sorry I wasn't here earlier to help. There aren't enough of us to go around."

Nate wiped his eyes and nose. "Alden's dying."

"Jamie told me. I'm so sorry." She reached for him, but drew her hand away before it touched his shoulder. "It's never easy to lose someone you love to the stillness. Is there anything you need? I'd be happy to check him over, but if he's sleeping peacefully now, it's probably best to leave him be."

"I already borrowed a hairbrush. I think it was yours." Nate craned to look at her, but he couldn't make out her features in the weak glow of a crank-light in the hallway behind her. Heavy with the sound of Alden struggling to breathe, he sank down the wall.

"You don't look like you got much brushing done," she said, so fondly he didn't mind being teased.

Something about what she'd said snagged at him. He abruptly realized what it was. "I hope you find your friend."

She sat beside him, groaning on the way down. "What do you mean?"

Nate bit his lip. "The person you're looking for."

"Oh." She made a quiet, strangled sort of noise. "Thank you." Her sorrow sent a pang of hurt through Nate. Were there other people like this woman looking for Pixel or Sparks?

What about Brick and Reed? He pictured their mothers toiling endlessly in the pleasure houses, always wondering what had become of the children who had grown up as brother and sister under the weight of so much hurt.

She tilted her head back against the wall and sighed. "I don't normally babble to our guests like this. It must be the hour. It's easier to tell secrets when you've been up all night, isn't it?"

Nate nodded, but he was out of secrets to tell. All of them were raw and open wide, and they hurt so much. Something about her voice unraveled him, and he began to cry, too exhausted to be embarrassed by the tears that shook him.

"Oh dear." She patted his knee awkwardly. "Should I get your friends?"

"No." Nate hiccoughed. "They should sleep."

"James said they were all a little worse for wear. The nice young lady with the curly hair—Sparks?" she asked. "She was here for a bit of time, but we hardly ever see young people. And never children."

"We'll leave soon."

"Oh dear—I didn't mean that it's bad. I'm glad for the company. Much better than the usual. Does that sound terrible? Jamie says I shouldn't talk to our guests. Ever, really."

"We have to leave." Nate's mouth tasted like gravel. His stomach turned. "The Breakers . . . We crossed them. And they'll be looking for Pixel. And—" A sob caught in his throat. Now it all seemed so impossible. "I don't know what to do."

"The Breakers are not welcome here." Her words lost their

warmth. "This is a place of peace. Servants are beholden to the Old Gods and no other power. We have made that very clear."

A rueful smile tugged at Nate's lips as he wiped his nose. "Even if you don't believe in the Old Gods?"

"Even then."

"You're not afraid of them?" Now that he understood the foundation of the Breakers—that they were nothing more than an organized, powerful gang—he feared them more. Power and chem drove people to do terrible things, and Agatha was smart enough to use that drive as a weapon. She was out there somewhere with Alden's Diffuser. It was only a matter of time before she found a way to use it to her advantage.

"I . . ." The woman hummed. She held her robe over her lap. It smelled like sweat. "I respect the fact that they're dangerous. And vengeful. But I will not let fear rule me."

Nate sniffled. "Vengeful" was an oddly specific way to describe them, but it suited Agatha. "You know a lot about the Breakers."

"The people who come here are sick. Oftentimes, they simply want someone to listen. There's release in that, I suppose. I hear a lot of things others don't hear." She gasped. "I'm so sorry. You're worried about your friend, and I'm telling you stories. I've never been any good at bedside manner."

"Have you known anybody who died?" He sniffled. "People you *know*, I mean. I guess a lot of people die here."

"You're right. Lots of people die here. Every day." She hummed a sad sound. "My husband died. He became very ill, and I couldn't find anyone in the Withers who could help him."

"I'm sorry," Nate said, struck by the way she said "the Withers" like it was someplace strange and not her home.

She stood, her back sliding up the wall with a sleepy whisper sound. A beam of sunlight cut through the hall from the living room behind her, lighting a swarm of dust motes like a sky full of stars. Sunrise was so strange. Glowing, soft, and then dazzling all at once. The hallway wasn't dark anymore. Nate looked up at her, squinting into the light, and pushed his hair behind his ears.

She froze.

Her skin went pale like she saw something terrible.

Do I look that bad?

She sank back down into an unsteady crouch and brushed her trembling fingers into his hair, pulling it into a loose tail. Slowly and very gently, she guided him to turn his head to one side and then the other.

When she closed her eyes, tears scattered down her cheeks.

His breath quickened with fear he couldn't place. "What?"

"Oh, Nate." She gasped. "Love, I've been looking for you for so long."

CHAPTER
NINETEEN

Nate shuddered and scrambled away from her, his back against the wall. He had nowhere to go and nothing to do but stare at her kind, familiar face.

She couldn't be his mother. His mother was dead.

But she pulled him into her arms, and she smelled the same—warm and safe, like the soft edge of a lingering dream.

Fear and hope mingled sickeningly in his gut.

This isn't real.

She was dead. Pulled into the depths of the sludge in a flaming car.

Her embrace tightened.

"Ow."

She drew back, brow knit. "Are you hurt?"

"My shoulder." The room spun. He didn't know how to begin to explain what had happened. Or what *was* happening. "I . . . it popped out."

She adjusted her hold on him, gentle and trembling.

Sometimes, people saw things that weren't there. Sometimes, his dreams were so real they left him hollow all day as they faded to nothing. He'd gone so close to the stillness, maybe it had bruised his mind.

"What's happening?" he asked, hoarse and frightened.

"When James said he heard talk of GEMs on the tickers... I didn't think I'd really find you. I couldn't bear to hope." She wept, tripping on every word. "Oh, Nate. I can't believe it's you. You're okay. Are you okay? You're so thin. Where have you been?"

She was asking too many questions, and all he could think about was her nickname. His father had spoken it fondly, always with a smile.

Ivy. *Ivy.* The sick-den was named after her. After his mother.

He shrugged away to look at her. Her small, strong hand cupped his good shoulder, and she stared at him with tears running down her face.

"You're dead. You crashed." His voice was flat, numb. "You didn't come back for me."

If his mother was *really* alive, she wouldn't have left him.

"We faked the crash and went into hiding." Her chin trembled. "When your father got sick, we couldn't come for you like we'd planned. And then Bernice was gone, and you were gone. I couldn't find a trace of you."

The longer he studied her face, the more he knew her. His ears rang. It was too much—so much at once. She was alive, solid. Touching him. His father was dead. She'd been alone all this time.

Looking for him.

Memories brushed against him, as flimsy as gauze. A

Servant paying close attention. A familiar voice. She'd been here in the Withers, all along.

"You wanted me?" Nate asked, his buzzing thoughts settling there. It was such a stupid, childish thing to ask. But he couldn't breathe until she told him the truth. He had to know.

"Of course I did." She touched his hair and cheek, patting him like he'd disappear if she stopped. "You're my son."

"I'm a GEM," he said, stubborn hurt twisting the words.

"You were always our son."

Nate bit his lip hard and gave in to her tugging hold. Her arms were stronger than he expected. He was nearly a man, but with her arms around him—with his mother's arms around him—he felt like a little kid.

The questions he'd never been able to ask were sludge in his throat. He had to get them out. "Why did you make me broken?" he asked between hiccoughed breaths.

"Because I was impatient and selfish, and we lost the fertility drawing year after year. I was always around babies in the lab. Tiny little GEMs. And I wanted a child. I wanted you so much, Nate."

Nate recalled something Bernice had told him. "My father thought I was a mistake?"

He could barely remember him—only that he had been terribly quiet and had never held him.

Ivy's nostrils flared as she sucked in a tight breath. "He didn't agree with what I did."

"Because you couldn't keep me." A flash of resentment ran through him. "Didn't you care about that?"

"I didn't think about what it would mean for you or for us.

I didn't think—" Her voice cut off, and she stiffened, squeezing Nate's arms protectively.

Nate lifted his head, heart pounding.

Reed stood in the doorway to the living room, staring at them. Pixel pressed against his side, and Brick and Sparks crowded behind him.

"Hey." Nate's throat tightened. "It's okay. This is Vivian. She's one of the Servants here. She's . . . she's my mother."

It didn't sound real. The word tasted strange.

Pixel's eyes went wide.

"Please call me Ivy. I prefer it."

Nate swallowed. "Ivy, this is . . . this is my family."

Reed stalked toward Nate and Ivy, careful as a cat. Brick picked Pixel up and watched them with a hunted look. But Sparks's frown softened to something sweet. She met Nate's gaze, and it grew to an encouraging little smile.

"Hello," Ivy said. She held her ground when Reed came close, wound tight as a spring.

Nate could only stare. He'd taken after his father, with his dark, thick hair. Ivy was different and familiar all at once. Dingy brown hair like Bernice's fell in wisps from her braid. Her gray eyes mirrored Nate's, framed by fine lines that gave her pale skin the texture of soft paper. Her teeth were brilliantly white and straight, nothing like the weathered teeth of everyone else her age in the Withers.

Reed waved the girls off, and they ducked back into the living room, tugging Pixel along with them. He stood tall, as if he planned on acting as a wall between Ivy and Nate if he had to. "Is she with Agatha?" he asked, ragged.

Ivy's breath hissed, and her grip on Nate's arms tightened. "Agatha? You've seen her? Has she gotten near you?"

"Wait. This is Reed. He's . . ." A blush spread across Nate's face. The last thing he'd ever expected to do was introduce a boy to his mother. Not that they were together that way. But that didn't stop a traitorous flutter around his heart. "We're . . ."

Reed's eyes widened. He cleared his throat. "Nate's with me. With my gang. I mean . . ."

Sparks made a strangled sound from the other room.

"Yes," Ivy said, as if she wasn't listening. "But Agatha. She's incredibly dangerous. You've met her? Did she follow you here?"

"She tried to take me and—" Nate cut himself off, unsure if he should tell her that Pixel was a GEM. "I don't think she followed us."

"Jamie will keep an eye out and alert the neighbors. I'll feel better when our security system is running again." Ivy let go of Nate, but her gaze stayed close, like she was scared to look away.

"I can check your system. I'm really good at alarms. I'm a Tinkerer," he said, surprised to find himself nervous to tell her. She was more a stranger than not, but he hoped she would appreciate the things he'd learned and done.

"Nana taught you engineering!" Ivy smiled. She wiped the tears off her face. "I'd hoped she would, but there was never any sense trying to tell her what to do. There was a time she could have left Winter Heights, but she stayed. Stubborn woman."

Nate blinked. "No, Bernice taught me. She was a Tinkerer."

"Bernice was your great-grandmother, Nate. My mother's mother. She was a brilliant electrical engineer in her day."

He stared, drowning in the flood of information. His mother. His great-grandmother.

Engineering. Science.

Suddenly, hope and fear twisted together, and Nate asked before he could stop himself, "Do you have a Diffuser?"

Ivy's expression darkened. "No. I don't believe in using GEMs that way. Not after the way things got in the city. Our research was never meant to be twisted into something so ugly. I cannot fathom how Agatha of all people came to disagree with me on that."

As quickly as hope had swelled in Nate, it crumbled away. He exhaled a shaky breath. Nothing could save Alden now.

"Is it safe to speak about this here?" Reed asked, gesturing at the doors that lined the narrow hallway.

"Each of those rooms contains a handful of frail, elderly people. Most of them have weeks to live. A few have days." She smoothed her braid with her fingers, nails bit ragged. "None of them can hear us. How about your people? Your gang?"

"They're safe," Nate said before Reed could answer. He pressed his fingers against his eyes, against the frustrated tears threatening to spill. His thoughts buzzed like the hum of a Diffuser. He could have helped Alden. What good was his blood if he couldn't save the people who mattered to him? Couldn't choose who he'd die for.

"What is it?" Ivy asked, taking his hand.

"Agatha had a huge machine . . . a still. She was using it to make chem. It had a Diffuser in it, and I broke it. I shattered it." And now Alden had no chance to survive, and none of the GEMs in the Withers could get Remedy.

"Don't feel bad about that," Ivy said. "I'll never do enough to atone for my part in the GEM program. It was wrong to harvest GEM blood—for any cause, let alone what things evolved to."

"It's more than that." Nate thought of Pixel and Juniper in the other room. Of the others—he had no idea how many—Agatha had hidden away across the Withers. "She can't make Remedy now that I wrecked her machine."

Ivy took a step back as if Nate had pushed her. She braced herself against the wall. "She was making it? Here? Not bringing it in from Gathos City?"

"Um." Nate glanced at Reed. He wore a stern, concerned expression—but the tension had settled. He wasn't about to grab Nate and run. He was listening. "She was using her still to draw blood from regular people. Not GEMs. And she did some stuff with it, mixed it up. And that made Remedy."

"Blood." Ivy pressed her hand to her mouth and frowned, gaze gone distant. Thoughtful.

"Blood . . . um, serum. I think. It's not the kind of tinkering I understand."

"No, no. Of course not. Trust me, I helped make GEMs, and I couldn't crack the Remedy formula. I tried." She leaned against the wall opposite Nate and Reed and fidgeted with her braid. "She was making it here. She must have other GEMs then. That's fantastic. The more liberated from Gathos City, the better—as long as they can stay safe. Oh. Oh! But you're . . . you're almost seventeen. Where were *you* getting Remedy?"

"Alden." Nate's heart went sore. He glanced at the entrance to the living room. "I should check on him."

"I'll come with you," Ivy said. "I'd like to ask him about it."

Reed bristled and placed himself between Ivy and the door. "He's ill."

The force of his words made Nate's breath stumble. The last thing he'd ever imagined was Reed sticking up for Alden in any way. "We won't wake him up," Nate said, brushing his knuckles against Reed's hand—knowing if he grasped it properly, he'd never let go.

Reed's fingers twitched against his. He gave Nate a slow nod and shifted to allow Ivy to pass.

In the living room, Brick and Pixel shared the couch, pressed together and clearly having been straining to listen to every word spoken in the hallway. Pixel squirmed like she could barely stand to sit still.

Nate snorted an amused breath and sought the others. All the air sucked out of him.

Alden kneaded his blanket as if he was trying to get away from his own body. Sparks knelt beside him, trying to catch his hands and still them. Juniper crouched behind her, watching wide-eyed like she'd never seen somebody in pain before.

"Get James," Sparks said. "Please."

Nate dropped to his knees at Alden's other side. "Alden. Hey." He didn't know what to say—what he could possibly say. "Shhh."

"He's in the kitchen." Ivy touched Sparks's shoulder.

Sparks gave a quick nod. Her curious gaze darted between Nate and Ivy. She rushed out of the room, sure-footed. It was strange to think that Sparks had spent so much time with his mother while kicking chem, and neither of them had ever known.

Nate moved over to let Ivy close. He tried to show Alden that he was there, but Alden was dazed, each labored breath a low, hurt sound.

She touched Alden's neck and forearm. "His fever's high. Jamie said it was likely sepsis. It's never easy."

James's Servant's robes fluttered as he came in quickly, holding a metal box with a lid. "I thought we might..."

"Yes," Ivy said. She saw Nate's curious look. "We don't use the medicine we have for everyone. It's in such shortage. But hopefully we can ease his suffering."

"You mean kill him?" Reed stood by the couch with his arms crossed. Pixel peeked around his hip, trying to see over the huddle around Alden.

"No, no." James began opening small glass vials. "Unfortunately, his body will handle that well enough on its own. I can reduce the fever and his pain. He may have some lucidity after it kicks in. At least for a little while."

Nate stopped listening, because they were talking about Alden like he wasn't in the room. He caught Alden's hand and squeezed it. James took Alden's other arm and prepared injections.

It was too familiar.

Alden's wavering gaze caught his. "Natey."

"I'm right here."

"Pix... Where's... They can't have her."

A prickle of worry chilled Nate's back. James and Ivy didn't know what Pixel or Juniper were. Ivy's expression sharpened as she helped James.

"She's here. She's got your beads still. They're so pretty."

"I'm not—an infant," Alden managed. "Where are we?"

"Safe. A sick-den, with Servants. This is Ivy. She wants to know about the Remedy you had."

"It's gone. I couldn't get it right. I tried."

"What did you try?" Ivy asked, rubbing her thumb gently at the spot where James had injected Alden's arm.

He turned his head slowly, furrowing with a fraction of the icy glare Nate expected. "Who are you?"

"We can trust her, I promise." Nate squeezed Alden's hand.

"You're a tremendously bad judge of character." Alden squinted, looking around the room. "Where is your Reed?"

"I'm here," Reed said, sounding surprised. He shuffled to stand behind James where Alden could see him.

"Do *you* trust this woman?"

Reed's lips parted for a long moment before he gave a small, firm nod. "Yes."

Alden's breath made a sound like water gurgling through a rusted pipe. He closed his eyes as if it had exhausted him to speak so much. When he opened them again, his gaze was a little clearer. Not sharp, but aware. "I tried different formulations. Half the sludge-chem that comes out of Gathos City was made in labs. Same ingredients. Different results."

Nate pressed his hands to his eyes. His wrists throbbed under the bandages. He recalled Alden staying up late, hunched over his desk, over his books. The days he'd gone into his storage room for hours, never letting Nate follow. "You were trying to make Remedy?" he blurted, reeling.

A shadow of mischief crossed Alden's face, as if it delighted him to have kept a secret from Nate. "I got what I had to last longer." He sobered. "Not long enough."

"Are you a scientist?" Ivy asked, her disbelief plain.

What did she think of all of them—a gang of scavengers and lost children? That they were ignorant? Uneducated? *Worthless?*

Alden's chest bubbled with what must have been a quick laugh. "No. You could say I'm a chemistry enthusiast." His expression faltered, and his fingers flicked weakly. "Take her out of here."

It took Nate a moment to realize he meant Pixel, who watched Alden with frightened eyes.

Brick gathered Pixel up. "We'll go."

Sparks held her hand out to Juniper. "Come on. You look like you need fresh air too."

Juniper had tucked her small body between two chairs. She wobbled to stand and stared at the place where their fingers met when Sparks took her hand. Nate wondered if she was like Reed—unused to being loved on in any way.

"Take them to the rooftop," James said.

Sparks nodded and leaned in to tell Juniper, "It has a garden."

James spread his long, skinny arms and herded them out of the room. "I'll bring you something to eat shortly."

Reed lingered. "I should keep an eye on Pixel," he said, reluctant. Like it pained him to leave Nate alone.

Warmth fluttered in Nate's chest, a little beacon when the rest of him was ice and ache. "We'll be okay."

He looked back at Alden in time to see him rolling his eyes.

James tucked blankets and pillows behind Alden's back. He didn't flinch when Alden stifled a cry, but Nate's fingers curled into twitching fists. He didn't know how James and Ivy managed to appear so unaffected by suffering. It had to be practice. Days and nights at the bedsides of the wounded and sick.

"Let me grab something," Ivy said, scrambling out of the room in a rush. She bumped into a chair and swore softly under her breath, the skittering awkwardness only making Nate fonder of her. She was so much more than he'd ever imagined—warm, clever, and a little bit broken. Not a glassy memory or a fading nightmare.

She rushed back in with a hardbound book. "I lost most of my notes. Fires, moves," she said, flipping it open. "But I've always kept this one with me. Can you read this?"

"We can all read! Pixel's even learning," he added, trying to soften his exasperated tone.

"Of course." Ivy ducked her head, apologetic, and held a page open for Alden. "This is as far as I've gotten. The figures aren't exact."

"Let me see." Alden's hands shook. He fumbled with the book, his breath whistling with impatience.

Nate hung back, itching to help, but afraid that if he stepped in, it would disrupt the odd balance they'd struck.

"Nate thinks the formula includes blood serum. It makes sense. It could carry the other enzymes." Ivy spoke with an urgency that shook Nate.

They don't have enough time.

When he'd faced down his own path to the stillness, dread had lingered like grime under his fingernails. Always there. Gritty. Familiar. But now, watching Alden struggle to catch his breath, the dread overwhelmed Nate. He felt like he was falling.

"Blood, for stars' sake." Alden pursed his lips. "Available in abundance, and I never tried it."

"I'd isolated two components in the lab," Ivy said. "It was always the other two I couldn't manage to replicate. Tariq warned me to stop trying, that they'd discover our motives if I wasn't careful. The lab was a shared space. Agatha was one of the first GEMs and my assistant. She must have taken my research further."

"What does this mean?" Alden traced a line of narrow handwriting on the page. "I don't know that word."

James returned and touched Nate's shoulder, distracting him from Ivy's quiet response. "Eat while they're working. I can hear your stomach folding up." He handed Nate sun-dried fruit and guided him to a nearby chair. It was soft, cradling Nate's back and easing the soreness in his shoulder. He hadn't realized until then how clenched-up he was, every muscle in his body wound tight.

"Do you think they'll work it out?" he asked softly—only for James.

"I think they're the best two people for the task," James said.

Nate thought of Reed and the girls upstairs on the roof, keeping Pixel distracted from the rooms of sick people—and Alden. He wasn't the only one who would benefit if Ivy and Alden succeeded. Pixel and Juniper would have a future too.

The fruit was sweet and salty at once, more flavorful than what Nate was used to eating. He didn't like it, but forced it down—not wanting to appear ungrateful. He strained to listen as Alden wrote in the book, his elegant writing taking up more space than Ivy's tight lines.

"It's the same thing," Alden was saying. He drew a symbol. "I know the man who cooks this. It'll always have this stamp. There's a . . ." He wheezed, closing his eyes. When he blinked them open again, his gaze wavered around the room as if he'd forgotten where they were.

"That's the chem for pain kicking in," James whispered to Nate.

"Chem." Nate's hands went cold. "But—"

"He's in more pain than you can comprehend. I gave him something to ease it." James's voice was very soft, but the force of his words silenced Nate. "This is a mercy, not a vice."

Nate wondered how long Alden had been in pain. If chem had been a mercy all along.

Alden glanced up from the book. "My grandmother, Fran. She's sleeping in the next room over."

Nate choked on the last of the dried fruit. He'd seen Alden on every flavor of chem, from gasolex fumes to Agatha's wicked pills. But he'd never been like this—scattered and soft, in a childlike daze.

"She bartered for an old GEMs manual." A smile creased the tired lines around Alden's mouth. "Said she traded a kiss for it. Didn't help a bit, but . . . This part always stuck out to me. What if . . .?" He squinted and wrote again, his bruised lip caught between his teeth.

"Yes!" Ivy kissed his hair, and he gave her an owlish look. "You know where we can find it?"

"By the south port," Alden said. He drew in the margin, tracing a portion of the sludge-coast. "Don't know where he gets it, but he always has it."

"Of course. I was overthinking it." Ivy shook her head. "And all the while, everything I needed was being squirreled into the Withers to make chem."

"Ah, well. We're a resourceful lot." The pen dropped from Alden's hand. He frowned at it until Ivy helped him grasp it again.

"You have Natey's eyes." He squinted until he found Nate. "Did she make you?"

Nate nodded, unsure why he'd hesitated to tell Alden that he'd found his mother—that they didn't share being orphaned. Guilt gnawed on his bones.

The pen rolled away again, and this time Ivy didn't bother slipping it between Alden's clumsy fingers. She patted his hand instead. "That's enough for tonight. I think we've got it. All we need is a Diffuser. I can build a still easily with a good Tinkerer on hand."

"My Diffuser is in the safe," Alden said. "Nate says he doesn't know how to get in it, but he does. He always knows. He's . . ." He twisted and pushed at the cushions weakly, agitated. "I'm tired. I don't—I don't want to sit up."

A pang of quiet horror twisted Nate up inside. Even in his worst chem-fueled rambling, Alden had never been this confused. At least he'd forgotten that the Diffuser had been stolen—and how.

James's hand was warm at Nate's shoulder—the only thing that wasn't icy. Even the air was thick, as if the depths of winter had blasted into the dusty room. "You'll have time to grieve later," he said. "Go be with him now."

"We'll wait in the hallway. Call out if you need us," Ivy said, leading James away.

Nate shuddered, took a deep breath, and pushed himself out of the chair.

I don't know how to do this.

He pressed his fingers to his eyes until the tears stopped coming. Wiping his face, he took a quick, steadying breath.

Early morning sunlight from the window lit Alden's skin. He gleamed like a statue carved of polished bone.

"Is Grandmother all right?" Alden whispered.

Nate sat at his hip and tucked a stray hair behind his ear. "Yes," he said, lying easily—happy to pretend she was fine and not gone, her body ash. "I fixed your hair, by the way."

"A young man of many skills." Alden took a slow breath, like he was building himself up to say something ridiculous. He was boyish in that moment, trying to hide a smile. Then he exhaled a tired sound and reached to carefully trace one of Nate's bandaged wrists. "Thank you."

"The tangles didn't suit you." Nate laughed like a creaking hinge.

Alden gave a soft hum of acknowledgment and closed his eyes. His fingertips fluttered against Nate's arm at the edge of the bandage. Nate studied the deep circles under his eyes and the blueish pale tinge of his fingertips and lips.

"How old are you really?" Every time Nate had ever asked, Alden had given him a different age.

"Would be twenty this summer." He opened his eyes again and struggled to focus on Nate. "Began misbehaving at a tender age. Don't tell."

"I won't," Nate said, heart shattering. Alden must have been a child when he'd taken over the curio shop. When he'd started pushing chem and losing himself in it to forget.

Alden hissed and tensed up, his eyes squeezing shut.

"I'm right here," Nate said. That's all he could say. That's what James had told him to do. "You—you can let go."

"Rushing me out the door, Natey?" Alden asked, peering one eye open.

"Shut up." Nate sniffled and scrubbed at his eyes with his forearms. He took Alden's hand and kissed his dry knuckles.

Muffled shouting sounded outside. Alden's expression gentled to a true smile. He closed his eyes, and the tight furrow at his brow smoothed out. "Take care of that little alley cat."

"Pixel? She'll take care of all of us."

"I like her. Give her shiny things always."

"Does it hurt?" Nate asked.

Alden nodded faintly.

"I'm sorry."

"Mmm. Can't be helped. Please burn me up. None of that pageantry at the sludge-shore." Alden panted, drained by every word. "I'm simply not dressed for it."

Nate choked. "I'm going to miss you."

"Of course you will." Alden sighed. "You're going to be terribly bored."

They fell into silence.

Sunlight shimmered through the dusty window, catching Nate's eye.

When he looked down, Alden was gone.

The stillness had come so quickly, settling in between one labored breath and eternity.

Nate pressed his hand over his mouth to stifle a sob. Tears ran down his cheeks, over his fingers. Grief blanketed him, as heavy as sickness, squeezing his chest until it burned. He wanted to keep talking to Alden, to always hear his voice. To always be his friend.

"Alden," he whispered. "You rat. You weren't supposed to go."

Alden's eyes were closed, but he didn't look like he was sleeping. He looked dead. And the ugliness of it was all wrong.

The window shimmered again. This time, Nate squinted at it and wiped his nose. The hair stood up on his arms.

As Nate drew himself up to look through the dusty glass, the pane shattered with a crack, and the rancid smell of gasolex filled the room. Before he could shout, the fluttering curtains burst into flames.

CHAPTER
TWENTY

Nate didn't spare a moment to think. He jumped across the chairs, launching himself from one cushion to the next, and leapt into the flaming curtains. Pain flashed through his hands. He held on and used his weight to pull.

He had to get them down before the whole room went up in flames.

Come on.

The curtain rod whined, buckled, and finally gave. Nate crashed to the floor with the curtains twisting around him. Burning. His initial burst of excited fear became panic as he got tangled in the curtains and his sleeve caught on fire. He twisted, trying to roll and dampen the flames.

James appeared beside him, slapping and stomping the curtains and Nate's clothes. "Get everyone away from the windows. They're outside!" he yelled.

It was too late.

Another glass bottle shattered on the wall behind him, tossed through the open window. It didn't light like the first had, but the noxious smell of gasolex got worse. Angry shouting erupted outside.

"The Breakers. Jamie! The girls," Ivy was trying to lift Alden. "The little ones. They're GEMs too."

Nate inched back from the window, shaking. He darted a look at Ivy, surprised that she knew.

Alden's head lolled to the side.

"Ivy—he's gone. Help the others."

She gave him a long look and nodded, setting Alden down with painful gentleness before dashing out of the room.

Nate stared at his hands. One was red and angry, and the other—the other was blistering up and throbbing with agony.

He retched, unable to move. James tugged him toward the hallway. "I need to hide your friends."

"But everyone else . . ."

"I know," James said grimly. "We'll figure something out."

No.

No one else was going to get hurt because of Nate. He gripped James and stood, ignoring the searing throb of his hands.

Two men climbed through the window, one holding a pipe and the other, a stun gun. The man with the pipe had a wild shock of white hair and tattoos all over his neck. He charged at James, and Nate dropped his shoulder and launched himself at him, realizing too late that he'd aimed with his sore shoulder.

His vision erupted with black fire as he rolled with the man, sending them both to the floor in a heap. Nate couldn't move. Couldn't help. All he'd done was delay the attack.

He was useless.

"Stay there," the man growled. He kicked Nate's ribs and continued in the direction Ivy had gone.

James grappled with the other man in the hallway. Nate rolled onto his side in time to see a flash of red hair and Brick tackling the man with the pipe. Reed followed, coming behind the man with the stun gun and jumping onto his back to put him in a choke hold. The stun gun sang, blue-white light zipping through the air, narrowly missing Brick.

The fight moved down the hall, out of Nate's line of sight. He wrestled his way to his hands and knees and cried out when his skin stuck to the floor. His arms buckled, and he crashed back down, sobbing with frustration. Clutching his hands against his middle, he tried to roll again, using his shoulder for leverage.

"Oh dear." A gentle hand took him by his good shoulder and eased him to sit up. "You're in a bad way."

Nate blinked through his tears and went very still.

Agatha propped him against the couch and crouched in front of him. She jerked her head toward where Alden's body lay. "So you've seen what happens when someone crosses me."

A snarl tore from his throat.

She laughed. "He took the beating well. Didn't beg. Not at first. But you—you're already crying." Her skin gleamed with sweat, and she breathed hard, like she'd been running. "If I'd known you'd have been this much trouble, I would never have opened my doors to you. There are really no words for the damage you've caused. No possible way you could repay me."

This time, there was no getting away. She held a knife as long as Nate's forearm.

Nate grit his teeth. "I'm not sorry."

Her eyes flashed with rage that didn't touch the smooth

contours of her face. "Know this, boy. You didn't *save* anyone. You delayed me. I'll have another still up and running before your friends have sunk to the bottom of the sludge."

"Remedy," Nate croaked.

"I'm not as stupid as you think I am. I've got more than enough to keep me alive until I can make more. If the others die . . . well, there are always more to come. Pixel isn't the only unripe GEM in the Withers."

Pain made Agatha waver in front of Nate. He squeezed his eyes shut. Whatever she was going to do, it couldn't hurt much worse than the agony searing through his hands.

"I didn't want to do this," Agatha muttered. "I wanted to protect you. All of you." Her knife skated along Nate's side, and she whispered to herself, counting. Counting his ribs. Finding the right place, he realized. The surest way to kill him.

He heard the sounds of bodies hitting the thin wall in the hallway. Grunts and shouts.

I don't want to die.

Nate opened his eyes.

"Agatha!" Ivy stood in the entrance to the living room, her hands stretched out. "Gods, don't do this."

"Vivian." Agatha's breath was hot against Nate's skin. "You should have stayed in the towers. How dare you show your face after you left all of us behind. After you left *me*."

"Let him go." Ivy's words became a moan. "Agatha."

"You knew what they would do. What they would make of me without your protection." Agatha's fingers dug into Nate's tender shoulder. He stifled a cry, sickened by the blank horror on Ivy's face.

"He's my son. I never thought . . ."

"You did not think. Not at all."

"I know." Tears wet Ivy's face, her pale eyes big, hurt. And remorseful. "Please don't take him."

Agatha rasped a toneless chuckle. "You won't have to mourn him for long."

A current of fury ran through Nate, hotter than the fire. No one was going to touch his mother.

He grasped the knife, sliding his hand along the blade until it met Agatha's. Slack-jawed, she looked down at the smear of his blood, and he used that moment to pivot and yank the knife forward, using her strength. The edge sliced along the tender skin at his ribs and landed exactly how he wanted it—in the wooden edge of the couch, trapped under his arm.

Nate had never been strong. But as a Tinkerer, he'd learned how to find the perfect angles. The weak spots. Where to press. How to bend things so they snapped.

Agatha snarled. He twisted her arm, and she lost her balance—and her grip on the knife.

You've gotta mean it, Brick had told him.

If he was going to die, he was taking Agatha into the stillness with him. Where she'd never touch his mother. Or Pixel. Or Reed. Or anyone.

She clawed at him, and he reached back and found the handle of the knife. His hand slipped, slick with blood and burned ruin. Agatha elbowed him in the throat, and he doubled over, gasping.

Ivy swung James's metal medicine box at Agatha's head,

catching the sharp edge near her ear. The glass inside shattered, tinkling like chimes. Agatha shrieked out a guttural sound and sprang up at Ivy. They crashed into the wall by the window.

Nate moaned, trying to breathe. He reached back for the knife again, and his hand slipped once more, fingers refusing to curl into a grip. He crawled forward, bearing his weight on his elbows, wrecked palms facing up. It was slow going. Too slow. Agatha had her hands on Ivy's throat, overpowering her, too much taller, too much stronger.

Ivy went still, her arms dropping at her sides. Limp.

"No!" Nate levered his elbow against a chair and pulled himself up. He staggered to the side, the room tilting beneath him. He couldn't lose her too.

Agatha turned slowly, blood glaring down the side of her face, dripping down her shirt and pants. She gritted her teeth.

Her hands were shaking.

Nate dodged to the side, getting in the sightline of the eye slicked with blood. His only chance. His last chance. He dove for her feet, hoping to get her off-balance—to grapple with her somehow. His pulse thundered in his ears, and his throat vibrated with a broken growl.

He lost his balance and came up short, crashing down to his knees. It knocked the wind out of him. He'd failed. He couldn't fight, wasn't strong enough.

Agatha's breath made a gurgling sound. She stared at Nate—and slowly lowered her gaze.

The gleaming tip of the huge knife protruded from her gut.

"I thought you were better than them." Juniper stood

behind Agatha, chest heaving. "But you're not." She wrenched the knife out of Agatha's middle. It clattered to the ground as Agatha crumpled. The sun shone through the window behind her, lighting her hair up like fire.

Juniper sniffled in a breath and wiped her nose with the back of her hand. Then she sat in one of the chairs and ducked her head.

Agatha made wet, horrible sounds. She pressed her hands to her belly as if she could stop her lifeblood from pumping out, but it was too much. So much. Foul and dark. Nate shuffled past her, dragging himself by his elbows, and went to where Ivy was on her side against the wall.

His wrecked hands smeared blood all over Ivy's neck and her clothes as he felt for her heartbeat—for any sign of life. He couldn't feel anything. Only pain.

It hurt so much.

He pressed his face against her middle and choked on a raw cry. She didn't move. Alden sprawled out on the floor where Ivy had left him, utterly still. They were gone. A great big hole opened up in Nate, as if Juniper had stabbed him too, and carved out everything he needed to breathe.

Ivy coughed.

Nate lifted his head weakly, sure he'd misheard.

Her eyes fluttered open, gray mirrors to his own. Confused, scared—and then wet with relief. "Nate."

All the strength left in him snuffed out. "Mom!" he cried. His arms trembled violently as he reached for her like a child.

She gathered him up in a fierce hold, and he sobbed, no

longer aware of anything but pain and the steady rush of her breath.

"I've got you, Nate." She rocked him, again and again. "I've got you."

CHAPTER
TWENTY-ONE

James took Nate outside in the clear light to work on his hands. Ivy held him on the steps, brushing a wet cloth against his face over and over. The chill of it drew Nate from the haze of the chem James had given him.

Nate drifted, wondering if it would feel better if they simply chopped his hands off.

"I've never done sutures on burned flesh," James muttered, hunched over Nate's hand where it lay on a towel in his lap. He'd put a thick salve along the deep cuts from Agatha's knife, so that all Nate felt from the mending was the long, slow pull of the thread. The burns were the worst of it, relentless. Screaming.

His hazy attention turned to the street, where Reed was still talking to the neighbors. The woman who'd been nursing her toddler stood with the little one strapped to her back with a colorful blanket. She held a wooden staff with a knife strapped to the tip. An older boy stood beside her with a pipe Nate recognized as the one the man with the neck tattoo had held. A dozen more gathered around Reed, who stood with his shoulders back and proud. Reed's eyes were bright as he spoke, too far for Nate to hear. A soft flutter of affection made Nate smile. People listened to Reed. Trusted him. Followed him.

The bodies of the Breakers were two doors down in the middle of the street. Burning.

Sparks jogged over. She'd kept Pixel hidden on the roof—only the two of them had been left unscathed. "Good thing we never scavenged around here. These folks would have beaten our heads clean off and roasted us in the morning."

Ivy's arms tightened around Nate. She hadn't let go of him once since she'd woken up from Agatha's attack. "Hard-won peace is the most difficult to shake."

"The Breakers won't come this way again," Sparks said.

If there were even Breakers anymore. Reed and Brick had taken Agatha's body to the nearest main intersection and left it there. It was cruel, but it was their only chance to make sure the message got to the right people as quickly as possible.

Those who ran for the Breakers had no one left to pay them. No one to supply them with chem. As soon as Nate could get his hands on a ticker, he'd rig it to send the same message as often as he could.

He wasn't stupid enough to think someone wouldn't try to rise in her place, but they wouldn't have GEMs or good chem to bargain with.

"Are you almost done?" Nate asked, hoarse—his throat swollen from Agatha's sharp blow.

"Trust me, you want this done correctly," James said, pushing his glasses up his nose. "Especially in your trade. Even with my best work, it'll be weeks before you can work. And you'll have to stretch your hands and oil them every day if you expect to keep your grip."

"It can't be weeks," Nate whispered.

They didn't understand. Alden was dead, and Nate was outside in the sun like a sleeping gull. As soon as his head was clear, he'd get to work setting up better security for Ivy House.

And figuring out how to save Pixel from wanting for Remedy.

James finished with the needle and wiry thread. He coated Nate's palms and fingers with another greasy layer of salve before wrapping them with so much soft cloth that Nate looked like he was wearing steamed buns for hands.

Maybe James was right about needing time.

"I need to look at your side," James said.

"No." Nate squirmed. "Later. Let me go."

James and Ivy exchanged a look.

"I'll keep an eye on him," Reed said from the bottom of the stairs. "I'll bring him back to you when . . . when he's done."

Nate reached out, and Reed shook his head ruefully, surveying the mess of Nate's bandaged hands. He and Brick had come out of the fight with scrapes and bruises, but neither had been hurt badly—because James had opened the front door to a mob of neighbors who'd dragged Agatha's men into the street and beaten them to death.

"It appears people still respect Servants of the Old Gods," Ivy had said with a tired smile.

Reed took him by the elbows and helped him up. "Looks like you'll be teaching Pixel more tinkering real quick."

They made their way to the room where Alden's body had

been taken. He was the only one there. Proper windowpanes muffled the sounds of excitement in the street.

Reed lingered, resting his warm hand on Nate's shoulder. "Call out if you need me."

Ivy and James had said the same thing, but this time Nate wouldn't need anything at all. He only wanted to say goodbye to his friend.

Nate eased into the chair beside the bed.

No words came.

He expected to cry, but numbness took over instead. Even the pain beneath his bandages was far away—a distant beat. He struggled to look at Alden, his gaze drawn to Alden's bloodied feet, instead of the emptiness of his face.

James came in the room, footsteps ghostlike. "Will you let me prepare him for burning?" he asked. "I'm no stranger to the stillness."

Nate's legs wobbled when he stood, and James caught him by the elbow to steady him.

"I'm all right," Nate said. But he wasn't. Alden's jaw had gone slack, and his mouth sagged. Alden would have hated seeing himself like that, devoid of all his energy and sharp beauty.

Nate didn't want to look anymore. He never wanted to see anything like it again. But once he turned away and left, that would be it. Forever.

James crouched in front of Alden's bare, bloodied feet. "In Gathos City, they remake the bodies of the dead until they look like living dolls. And they put them on display for days."

Nate grimaced. "That's awful."

"It brings the living peace." James shrugged. "But I'd rather remember what someone looked like before all that."

Nate remembered Alden carefully choosing several sparkling glass necklaces to wear on a rainy day, saying that *he'd* glitter if the sun wasn't up for the job. Alden hadn't been a good person. He'd hurt a lot of people. But he'd lived without apology. And that's what Nate would remember: Alden with cut glass sparkling against his pale skin, and his eyes shining with wicked joy.

"Thank you," Nate said to James. He wanted to sink into the bed—to wrap his arms around Alden one more time. But he knew Alden would feel cold and wrong. "Gods watch you," he whispered.

And even though he didn't believe in the Old Gods, he imagined Alden in a different place, listening to Fran's birdsong stories of a time no one else could remember.

───────

Nate only made it as far as the hallway before his legs gave out from beneath him. He slid down the wall and dropped his head to his knees and cried. Low sobs wrenched out of him, a current of hurt piercing through his chest.

Reed crouched and opened his arms, offering an embrace without coming too close. The gesture was so tender and gentle that Nate didn't hesitate—didn't give himself a reason not to fall into Reed's careful hold.

"I'm sorry," Reed whispered.

Nate turned and hid his face against Reed's shoulder. Reed held him fiercely, making soft sounds against his hair like he was gentling a crying child. And Nate didn't mind. He was safe and free to cry, each breath a mournful, awful sound. His head was full—stuffed with too much, more than he wanted to know in one day. Terrible things and wonderful things all at once. He cried for all of them, lost in crushing grief.

CHAPTER
TWENTY-TWO

"You're heavier than you look," Juniper complained, shoving Nate out of a deep, dreamless sleep.

He opened bleary eyes and bit back a cry as he tried to push up with his hands.

Everything rushed back to him. Agatha. His wrecked hands.

Alden.

Pixel sat up in the bed and took him by the forearms, stilling him. "You can't touch things! Jamie said so."

He smiled blearily at her use of Ivy's nickname for the thin, strange Servant boy. Juniper watched him, a pillow clutched against her middle. The knot on her head was now a deep, purpling bruise. She wore a clean green shirt over her baggy pants, and there was something different about her face.

When her mouth twitched, he realized what it was. She didn't look so sad.

"Are you staying with us?" he asked, surprised.

"I can sleep on the floor instead." Her fingers dug into the pillow.

"*With* us. With Reed. With the gang." Nate's hands felt

like they'd grown three times in size. Pinkish clear fluid leaked through the bandages, and he tore his eyes away from them quickly. He didn't want to picture what was underneath.

"If she wants to, she can." Reed stood in the doorway to the small room. He gave Juniper an encouraging nod. "I trust you on account of what you did to Agatha. But we don't solve problems with violence if we can help it. You can't go about gutting anyone else."

"Unless they hurt us?" Juniper asked.

"Even then, there might be better ways. Promise you're not bloodthirsty?" he asked with a faint hint of a smile.

"I'm not." Juniper shuddered. "I didn't like doing that."

Ivy poked her head through the doorway beside Reed. "Anyone awake in there?"

"All of them," Reed said.

"Nate, I need to change your bandages. Think you can walk?"

He started to assure her that he didn't need his hands to walk, but the moment he crawled off the bed his knees trembled, and he stumbled. A flutter of panic rose—was he getting sick already?

"James said you'll be wobbly for a few days." Reed caught Nate with a gentle grip. "Be careful."

It felt natural to have Reed close. Touching him.

Dazed, Nate gave himself a moment to lean in to Reed's side. He wanted to reach for his hand and squeeze it. But he wasn't even certain he had fingers anymore.

"I'll be right here," Reed whispered, knowing exactly what Nate needed hear better than Nate did himself.

Nate followed Ivy in a daze. He didn't remember taking his boots off, but his feet were bare and quiet against the worn wood floor. He realized he was wearing clean clothes too. They were baggy and smelled old in a way he couldn't place.

She helped him up a flight of stairs. "This is my room," she said.

It was full of mismatched furniture from decades ago—all of it faded but very soft. A small unmade bed crowded a corner, and the rest was a jumble of chairs and dressers and cracked mirrors and plastic bins full of bandages and vials. It smelled lived-in and comfortable, like bedding dried out on a line on a clear day.

"You look tired," she said.

"I get that a lot." Nate tried, and failed, to brush his hair behind his ears, awkward under her scrutiny. He sat down and drew his heels up to the chair and hugged his knees.

She pulled a chair up beside him and rifled through a plastic bin full of medical supplies. "Do you think you're growing weak already? I don't know how much Remedy you were able to get at Agatha's . . . I don't know what to expect."

Nate furrowed his brow, taking stock of how he felt. It was difficult to tell with so much hurting, but he was pretty sure it was the kind of pain to be expected. Not the aching, deep weakness of the stillness coming over him. "I don't feel bad that way."

She began unraveling the bandages on his hands. "It'll still be a race against time."

"It's not a race." Nate's jaw clenched. "Not if you can't win."

"Well, that's the thing." Ivy grimaced as she peeled back

the final layer, revealing bright-pink skin and the dark lines of the stitches across Nate's palm and fingers. "Between what Alden figured out and my calculations, I think I can replicate Remedy. And with your tinkering and Pixel's, we can build a still."

Nate's heart sank as he eyed his oozing skin. He tried to flex his hand. His fingers wouldn't move at all. "It won't work. Not without a Diffuser."

"I have credits saved up, some tech from Gathos City I can barter with. We'll put the word out that we need a Diffuser—that we'll pay handsomely for it."

"But that'll draw too much attention. You'd be in danger. Everyone would."

"What's the alternative, Nate?" Ivy asked gently.

He clenched his teeth. While he was willing to accept the alternative for himself, he wasn't willing to give up on Pixel's chance to survive.

"We'll be careful. We'll be smart. And you'll help keep us safe. I'll talk to the Courier I was paying to try to find you, so she can start working on finding a Diffuser instead."

"You paid a Courier to find me?"

"One of the best, I'm told. By Val, anyway."

Where do you live, Nathan?

Nate's stomach rolled over. "The Courier's name is Val?"

Ivy blinked up at him from her work, gray eyes wide. "Yes. Do you know her? Because if you do, she's not very good at her job."

"No, not really. I met her three times. She must have

suspected the first two times, though." He sighed out a breath. "Why didn't she tell me where you were?"

"The way the Breakers have been scrambling for GEMs, she was probably weighing her options." Ivy echoed Nate's sigh. "That's the trouble with Couriers. They're good at what they do, but they're not loyal."

"Agatha was hurting her," Nate said. "She didn't trust her, I think. It seemed like Val was being punished. Like she was scared."

"Well, she doesn't have to be scared anymore. Agatha can't hurt her." Ivy spoke fiercely, but her tone had a haunted edge. "Not ever again."

A current of hope buzzed through Nate's tired limbs. It kindled a longing that threatened to burn him up. "Reed can get the parts we need. He can find anything."

"Hopefully, most of the parts will still be in Agatha's basement."

Nate fought to keep his mind calm. Gamble or not, it was better than no chance at all. His heart rattled at the thought of having more days. "You really think it'll work?"

"I do. And it won't take much. The Remedy Alden was giving you was cut with his own weak formula. When we make it correctly, you won't have to come back to me for it as often as you likely did before."

Relief washed over Nate—not because Ivy thought she could keep him alive, but because she said he'd have to come back for it.

"Is that a mother thing?" he asked.

She dabbed fresh salve onto Nate's skin and arched her brow. "What?"

"I didn't tell you I wasn't going to stay here."

"Well. You were seven years old when I said goodbye to you. You're not a child anymore. You have a life in the Withers." She brushed a loose fall of hair out of her eyes with the back of her hand. "I wish it was a better life, but I would never expect you to stay with me in a sick-den."

"It's not a bad life. They're good people," Nate said, bristling.

"I know. A *safer* life is what I meant, I suppose." Ivy glanced up at him, her fingers gentle. "You're very fortunate you found them. Even Alden. Well . . . he kept you alive."

Nate gave her an indulgent nod. He didn't need her approval to know that Reed and the girls were good. They were the best. And no one knew as well as he did that Alden had kept him away from the Breakers as long as he could.

Ivy's fingers strayed to the cut at his forehead and the rough texture of the scar where Alden had mended him up. "What happened here?" she asked.

"The train wreck."

Ivy's eyes widened. "You were there?"

He ducked, wondering if this was what being in trouble with a parent felt like. "Um. I climbed up and opened some doors, that's all." Now that he was pretty sure he wasn't going to die soon, it sounded a lot crazier.

"I was there too. Collecting a few former acquaintances. It turns out that sheltering Gathos City legislators goes a long way toward getting your smuggling habits forgiven," Ivy said with a sly grin.

"Well, I forgive you for being a smuggler," Nate said, trying to make a joke and finding that he wanted to mean it.

Ivy's eyes brightened. "I can never ask for your forgiveness, Nate. It's too much to ask."

The knotted-up part of him that had always resented her for making him and leaving him eased just a little, but it would always be there. A bruise between them. He gave her a solemn nod.

She let out a shaky, wet laugh and brushed her fingers at her eyes in a flutter. "Now that I've connected with old acquaintances, maybe my smuggling days aren't over."

Scavenging tech. Smuggling GEMs out of Gathos City. It wasn't such a leap. Nate found himself grinning. "Maybe we can help."

She exhaled a happy sound, her hand rising to her throat, where bruises formed a ruddy collar. "I know I didn't have a hand in raising you, but I'm so proud you've turned out absolutely perfect."

Nate wrinkled his nose. "I smell like a waste-trench."

She laughed. "I mean your *heart* is perfect." Her expression sobered. She took clean cloth and rewrapped Nate's swollen hands. "You're good. And brave. It's true that I don't believe in the Old Gods, but I want to shout my gratitude to the stars." When Nate made a face like he tasted something bad, she swatted at him playfully. "Listen, I'm making up for a lot of lost time. Give me a chance to have my mother feelings."

The space between was already staticky and strange, too

thick for him to reach through and embrace her. She was a stranger, and he was too grown up to cling to his mother.

"Did you really leave Agatha behind?" he asked, daring to give a name to the hurt that gnawed at him like a stitch in his side.

Ivy wrung her hands slowly, watching the pale skin twist. She took a small, hitched breath. "Yes. I could only orchestrate the escape of one GEM. It was never a question who that would be."

"But you knew she'd be in danger if you left?" he pressed. He needed to know the hatred and fear that had driven her, made her cruel.

"I suppose I did, Nate." Her words scraped out, hollow and soft. "I have much to make up for. I'm trying. I'll keep trying."

He touched her hand. It was smaller than he expected, smaller than his own. "Maybe getting more GEMs out won't be that hard. We can help them. Agatha said they're opening the gates."

"Of course they are." Ivy squeezed his hand and met his gaze with a watery smile. "But you have to understand . . . Government moves slowly when it comes to reversing mistakes. It should be this year. This season, even, if Agatha didn't put them behind schedule with her assault on the railway."

"Why would they want to let people from here back into Gathos City?"

"It's not about letting people *in*. Gathos City is dangerously overcrowded. There's not enough land, and you can only build towers so high. The Withers is a ghost town in comparison. It's ripe for development. They'll let some people in—the workers they need. But mostly, they'll let people *out*."

Worry rippled through Nate. He couldn't wrap his head around well-dressed strangers and more A-Vols and people who didn't want to save them but take away their homes. If the gates were opening, they needed to know when. They needed to be prepared. "Do you have a ticker?"

"Believe it or not, I'm hopeless with those old things." Ivy tied a small knot with the bandages. "None of my tech works here. Gathos City jams the wireless signal on the entire island."

Nate had no idea what a wireless signal was, but his arms went tingly anyway. The prospect of new tech to tinker with went a long way toward soothing his fear of strangers in the Withers. "You have Gathos City tickers?"

"Not exactly. But I have a box full of marvelous things up in the attic. You're welcome to take the tech apart. It's all useless here." She laughed softly.

"What's funny?"

"I never imagined being able to give you something to play with."

"To *tinker* with," he corrected. Mothers were wonderful and embarrassing all at once.

"Will you teach me what you know?" she asked.

"If you do the same." He reached his hand out to shake on it, seal it as a promise.

They both looked at the lumpy shape of his bandaged hand and laughed. Ivy leaned forward and kissed his forehead. "I will."

"I'm glad I know you now," Nate said.

She wiped tears from her lashes. "I'm glad I know you too."

———————

Sparks was the only one who thought the plan was terrible. "No," she said, shaking her head fiercely. "No!"

They stood in the Ivy House kitchen, scrubbed clean from head to toe and freshly combed and shaven. Even their clothes were clean—or as clean as they could be, thanks to a good washing in hot water and an afternoon hanging on a line on the rooftop. Nate was grateful to have his own clothes back, but still embarrassed from needing Reed's help to get them on.

Juniper and Pixel were with Ivy on the roof, out of earshot.

Nate's hair tickled his nose. It got fluffy when it was clean. "Sparks, it's not like we'll never see her again. We'll be working on the still for weeks. And I'll have to come back here all the time, even when it's done."

"Ivy's from Gathos City. Can you *really* trust her?" Sparks asked.

"You trust her fine, and you know it," Nate said. The way he figured, Sparks knew Ivy House better than the rest of them. She'd been the one to lead them here, after all. And the more he paid attention, the more he saw James and Sparks watching each other and finding excuses to work on chores together. "You like it here."

Brick leaned against a counter, her fingers running along the uneven edge where water damage made the wood buckle and split. "It's safer than running day and night." She eyed Sparks. "Safer than what somebody might want from Pixel come a few years."

"She's ours," Sparks said. She crossed her arms and then uncrossed them to wipe at her nose. Without heavy makeup, her brown eyes were young and gentle. And scared.

"She isn't ours. And I say we let her decide," Reed said. "She's old enough to choose."

"She's a kid!" Sparks swallowed a sob. "She doesn't know better. Of course she's going to want to stay here."

"Aw, girl." Brick walked up to Sparks and pulled her into a smothering hug that hid Sparks's shaking shoulders from the rest of the room. "That's just it."

Nate turned away out of respect. He understood. It wouldn't really be goodbye, but it would hurt all the same. Reed caught his eye across the kitchen table. He offered Nate a small, encouraging smile.

Reed had been the one to suggest leaving Pixel with Ivy. It was Pixel's best chance. If they managed to replicate Agatha's still and the Remedy formula, she'd have everything she needed when the time came. She'd have a roof over her head until then.

Ivy would have someone to care for. And Pixel would be able to work on her tinkering every day.

Letting Pixel stay with Ivy was the only thing Nate was certain about. His chest hurt with the bubbling pressure of all his fears, so he tried to focus on that. And not what was waiting for him on the roof.

"Are you ready?" Reed asked.

No.

Nate nodded. They walked out the back door from the kitchen and climbed the rickety fire escape single file. It creaked and swayed but held fast as they ascended one more story to the rooftop. Unable to hang on to the rails with his bandaged hands, Nate walked slowly, holding up the line—and grateful for the reason to drag his feet.

The sun set at the far side of the Withers, casting long shadows. Vivid orange streaked across the smokeless sky, and the clouds were green. Warm air tickled Nate's clean skin. He watched the smog-clouds move longer than he needed to, because it was easier than turning to look.

Ivy and Pixel stood beside a bin-fire, eyes gleaming and warm from its glow. Juniper sat on the cracked concrete beside them, playing with her hair.

Nate leaned into Reed to steady himself. Then he saw a concrete platform covered in scorch marks—the signature of a sick-den.

Alden's body rested on top of it, swaddled in faded flower-print sheets soaked in gasolex. The sheets covered his whole body, masking all of his sharp angles. Nate had only watched sludge-funerals from a distance. He'd never seen someone burned. He hesitated, his legs humming with the urge to turn and dash back down the wobbly stairs.

Reed squeezed his hand. "It'll go up quickly. You don't have to watch if you don't want to."

"I don't want to do this," Nate said. He'd faked calm until now. Seeing Alden's body there, cold fear stabbed through him. This was too final.

"Here." Brick took the torch from Ivy and lit it in the bin-fire. She offered it to Nate. The flames warmed his face and made a quiet, rustling sound. "I lit July. It's terrible, and then it isn't."

"No. I can't." A sob burst from Nate's chest like crackling wood. There'd be nothing left after this. Nothing but his grief. He couldn't stand to think of a world without Alden in it and didn't want to be a part of sending him away. "I don't want to."

He held out his swollen hands, a desperate attempt to make all of this go away. Even if he had the strength to do it, he couldn't clutch the torch in his bandaged fingers.

Reed took the torch from Brick and guided Nate's hand in a loose grip, holding it steady for him. "Yes, you can."

A quiet, heavy calm took over Nate.

Please burn me up.

It was Alden's last wish.

Confronted with the platform and Alden's body and the fire-streaked sunset, Nate lost sight of everyone else. He felt like the ticking insides of a clock as he took one small step after another, until Alden was right there and the smell of gasolex stung at his nostrils.

The flames rose in a flash, hot the way the train wreck had been. He cringed back, crying out with shock before recovering with a low swear under his breath. Somewhere, Alden was probably watching him botch a funeral by scorching his own eyelashes off.

Reed backed away, taking the torch and leaving Nate with the heat.

Alden had tried to save him all along. He hadn't failed. He'd unknowingly led him to his mother, and he'd led Pixel to a safe place. A real home.

Did he know?

"What should I say?" Nate asked over the crackling sounds of the flames. He didn't watch. He couldn't.

"Walk well!" Reed called out.

Nate began to laugh, but the sound became something else and his eyes went hot. "Alden hated walking."

"I only enjoy one form of exertion, butterfly," Alden had said with a wink.

Shaking his head, Nate lifted his face and watched embers and smoke curl toward the sky. A quick, certain smile tugged at his dry lips. As long as he lived, there'd be something left of Alden.

He didn't say a thing.

TWENTY-THREE

U p on the roof of Ivy House, Nate groped his way along a twisted wire for the gap causing the alarm system to fail. Three weeks had gone by, and the electricity was still off, but a wind-crank on the roof generated enough power to test the system. As he worked, standing on a stack of cinder blocks to reach the ceiling of the rooftop shed, he listened to the quiet hum of Ivy having a picnic with the girls near the fire escape.

They were celebrating the gates opening, for better or for worse. Not that it really mattered to anyone at Ivy House. Not yet. Word had quickly spread that Gathos City was requiring applications to pass through the gates, and no one without proof of workhouse attendance would be permitted to visit the city.

It was another insult. But hope weaved its way through anger. Papers could be forged. Regulations would change.

Everything would change.

Nate wasn't sure he wanted it to.

Pixel's small voice carried like a song. "What will you do?"

"Stay here," Brick said. "What use are those towers if you don't have credits to buy anything? Or anywhere to live?"

"I'll stay with you," Pixel said firmly.

"Will they come after us with the gates open?" Juniper asked. She'd developed a habit of following Ivy everywhere. Needing a break from her questions and quiet, constant chatter, Ivy had given her the "very important" task of sitting with the sick and keeping them company. She'd taken to it immediately, so natural and calm with the old ones that James was already sitting with her every evening to teach her the vows of Servants of the Old Gods.

"You'll be difficult to find if they do. But I wouldn't worry about that," Ivy said. "They have no reason to think you're still alive."

"Good." Juniper made a small, snarling sound. "I'm not going back. Ever."

"I'll go into the city for work when they sort the mess at the gates out," Sparks said with an undercurrent of apology. "Find a tailor to apprentice under and make fine clothes."

Nate found the end of the wire. Every day, a little more feeling came back in his hands. He pinched the narrow red strand, finding the place where rats had gnawed clean through. The thought of going back to Gathos City repulsed him, but a knife edge of curiosity worked its way to the surface of his thoughts. He'd destroyed Agatha's still. Maybe, some day, he'd go back to where he was made and destroy the labs too.

"The clothes are beautiful, Sparks," Ivy gushed, as if able to utterly forget what the city had done to the Withers, to Nate. "You'll love them. I was never one for finery. But I have a sweet tooth, and I miss the food more than anything."

Ivy launched into a description of Gathos City sweets that

would have given Nate hunger pangs any other day. But he couldn't bear the thought of eating. For the first few days, the medicine James had given him for pain had stolen his appetite away. But now that his hands were healing and he didn't need it, his stomach was still like the rest of him—raw and cold.

Grief tightened around his ribs. He took a breath that trembled out and lost his balance when Reed barged into the shed.

"Whoa!" Reed grabbed him by the pant leg. "Careful."

"*Careful*? You almost knocked me over. *You* be careful." Anger rose out of habit, before Nate could remind himself that he didn't have to use it like a shield to keep Reed's tenderness away.

Reed remained silent, patiently giving him a moment to untangle his feelings. His eyes were big and kind—as green as a leaf in the sun.

Nate held on to the wall with his left hand, his right still bandaged and unwieldy. His anger drained, and he ducked his head, ashamed to have snapped. "Sorry. Were you watching me?"

"Maybe." Reed crammed himself into the corner of the shed, dodging around the scrap metal and copper panels and pipes they'd manage to scavenge so far. They didn't have a Diffuser yet, but Val had a lead on one.

Val had come to Ivy House and explained to them, tripping over her words, that Agatha had threatened to find the family she supported as a Courier. She'd been too scared to tell Nate to go to Ivy—and she'd been unwilling to tell Nate to go to the Breakers.

Nate didn't trust her, but the only other person he knew who could find a Diffuser in the Withers was gone.

He worked on the still every daylight hour, sleeping in the shed beside the growing machine and only stopping when his hands cramped up too much to use them. Even then, he read over Ivy's notes and scrawled out his own plans. Pixel helped him, acting as his hands when he couldn't manage delicate work that had come so easily to him before. She never complained, even when he kept her tinkering through meals and Sparks and Brick had to come up looking for her.

Lately, he'd been finding her own notes beside his. Little additions to his figures. Suggestions that spoke to a gift for tinkering that would soon surpass his own.

Peeling paint flecked from the wall onto Reed's shirt and forearms. He brushed it away with his long fingers. "What are you working on today?"

"The alarm. Ivy said it's been broken for ages." He couldn't call her anything else. It didn't feel right on his tongue. "She needs it working with the still up here."

"It's good to see you tinkering again." Reed studied him with a halting smile, like he wasn't sure he was allowed to.

"Trying to," Nate said, frustrated with how slow it was working with one hand. Something else slowed him too—the nagging worry that if he built another still, someone else might take Agatha's place. He pushed the worry aside. For Juniper. For Pixel.

And when he let himself want a future, for himself too.

Reed pushed through the silence. "Did you see all the

mending Sparks has been doing? She's happy as a star about it. Ivy's got some fancy, shiny sewing needles."

"I know the feeling. These are good tools." A new belt hung heavy on Nate's hips, a familiar weight that made him useful. Even at a one-handed pace, tinkering was easier than carrying on a conversation when he didn't know what to say, wasn't sure what they were. What they meant to each other now.

"You were his wish, you know," Reed said abruptly, blurting the words out like a cough.

Nate's fingers went clumsy, and he gave up on trying to get anything done. He hopped down from the cinder blocks, landing heavily and mostly on Reed. "What?"

Reed rubbed his elbow. "He was in love with you."

"It wasn't like that." Nate blanched. He'd said the same thing to Alden when Alden had prodded and pushed him about Reed.

It's not like that.

Was it?

"Nate." Reed touched his shoulder carefully, like he was reaching for a sharp edge. His warm fingers drifted, absently tracing the skin at Nate's collar.

"He thought I was with you," Nate said, struggling to talk through the shivery sensation of Reed's touch. "I think . . . Pixel told on me."

Reed's hand went still. "Told on you?"

It was a betrayal to talk like this when Alden was gone. But Alden had relished gossip, drinking up neighborhood news and stories of woe and betrayal from every chem fiend who sat in his shop long enough to be interrogated. He'd probably love this.

Nate's voice came out choppy and upset. "She told him what I felt about you."

"What do you . . .?" Reed's fingers clenched up in Nate's shirt. "What did you say to her?"

"Nothing. She could tell." Nate's skin lit up like a fever. "Everyone could."

Reed let go of Nate and stepped back as if Nate had struck him. But he didn't have anywhere to go. Another shower of peeling paint fell into his hair like falling ash when his back hit the wall.

"I couldn't tell." The words rasped out of Reed. "I didn't know."

Nate stared at him, recognizing the hurt and longing in Reed's eyes like he'd only just learned how to see. Their past was a fog of lies and pain, but he knew one thing clearly: he'd pushed Reed away again and again.

And Reed had never given up. Even when he'd made Nate leave the gang, he'd begged him to get clean, to come home.

He hadn't known how Nate felt, and he'd fought for him anyway, with the stubborn hope that lit Reed up from the inside out, brighter than any of the lights in Gathos City.

Hope blossomed in Nate now, big and frightening—so much scarier than facing down the stillness. Looking down at his feet, he said, "I don't know how to fix this."

But he wanted to. He wanted it so badly.

Reed took his free hand carefully, rubbing his thumb over the knotted scars on Nate's palm. The sensations were different now. Numb in places and too sensitive in others. Nate shivered, scared to look up at Reed's face.

"I don't believe that. You can fix anything." Reed drew Nate's hand up slowly, turned it and kissed his knuckles.

All Nate had ever known was how to run and hide. He was painfully exposed now, his eyes wet with tears, his fingers trembling in Reed's. There was only one secret left. "I told Pixel I loved you." His breath shuddered. "I always have."

Reed's gaze snapped up. He dropped Nate's hand, and Nate started to stumble back, worried he'd said too much, that it was too much, too ridiculous. And then Reed's mouth was on his, urgent and careful all at once. He pulled Nate against him, leveraging the wall, getting his fingers knotted up in the tangles in Nate's hair. He cursed softly under his breath as Nate laughed and winced at the same time.

"I've never done this before," Reed whispered.

"I can tell."

"Is that bad?" Reed asked. "I know Alden—"

"No," Nate said quickly. "Reed, no."

Reed's chest rose and fell with a quick sigh.

Nate nudged his nose against Reed. "I haven't either. We never did anything. We weren't together."

"Are we together?" Reed tripped all over the words.

"Do you want to be?" Nate asked, knowing he sounded painfully eager.

"Yes. I want to be with you." Reed's exasperated breath puffed against Nate's skin. "I've always wanted to be with you. I thought it was plain."

"I never should have—"

"Stop. No more being sorry. No more."

Reed dragged his mouth across Nate's cheek and found his lips. It wasn't like the broken, urgent kisses they'd shared before. This was sweet and unsure. Nate smoothed his hand up Reed's strong arm in a way he'd never let himself before. Reed was familiar and warm and solid beneath his palm. A startling urge to touch more of him took Nate's breath away.

"I like the way you chew on your lip when you're working," Reed said. "And how I can see you making plans, even when you're quiet. I like that you're brave. Even when you're scared, you're the bravest person I know."

Brick had told Nate once that Reed didn't have enough practice being loved on, and now Nate was sure *he* didn't have enough practice having somebody say nice things. He squirmed against Reed, trying to make the kissing happen again.

"Are you trying to distract me?" Reed said against his mouth.

"I am."

It worked.

Feverish heat unsteadied Nate from his head to his toes. He held on to Reed tighter and laughed a nervous sound into their kisses, certain his legs were going to stop working entirely.

"What?" Reed pulled away a little, like it pained him to stop. "Am I doing it wrong?"

"How am I supposed to know?" Nate's shoulders shook with silent laughter. "I like it. I like it so much."

"You," Reed said, soft and amused. A dimple formed at his cheek, and Nate closed the distance between them with a kiss that left no room for secrets. A noisy thing, hands reaching, needing. They moved together in a dizzying connection brighter than everything else, Reed whispering his name like a wish.

Then someone punched Nate's shoulder. And by the sound of Reed's hissing intake of breath, they punched Reed's arm too.

"Ow," Nate said.

"Are you kidding me?" Brick batted at them both. "You should come out and listen. Miss Ivy's telling the best stories."

Nate spun to face her and grinned like a fool when Reed wrapped his arms around his chest and kept him close. His chin stung from Reed's stubble, and he felt like he might float away to the stars if Reed didn't hold him tight. "What kind of stories?"

Brick gave them a look and pushed a wild lock of red hair out of her eyes. "You'd know yourself if you stopped necking and got something to eat with us."

Reed snorted softly into his hair. It tickled. He gave Nate a little push.

"Hold on." Nate pretended to dust his filthy clothes off as he waited for his body to stop burning up. His tool belt wasn't doing much to hide the extent of his interest in all the kissing.

Reed left the shed first, climbing over a pile of metal, and Nate allowed himself a long look at Reed's limber form. Brick shook her head and grinned.

"Never seen him like that before," Brick said.

Nate rubbed his face, willing the blush away. "Like what?"

Brick waved her hand at him. "All of that. The hugging and smiling and kissing and nonsense."

Nate gave himself another moment to breathe, wiping his

mouth and dusting his clothes off, every bit of his skin feeling brand-new and electric. Then he followed her out to the picnic of flatbread and dried fish.

Pixel sat at Ivy's feet on a blanket. Reed's scavenged pendant hung at her throat, shiny colors swirling, and Alden's beaded necklace circled her small wrist three times. Nate's breath hitched and shook out of him like the shudder at the end of a long cry. Pixel's smile shone, easy and unburdened.

Sparks leaned against the low wall at the roof's edge, eyes closed to the sun. The windy season kept the smog at bay, and the air smelled faintly salty—as if it had carried here all the way from the distant sea beyond the sludge.

Ivy caught his eye. "How does the alarm system look?"

"Still down. You need some wires replaced, but they shouldn't be any trouble to find."

Reed found a place on the blanket and gestured for Nate to sit beside him. As Nate sank, Reed pulled him close, bracketing Nate with his arms and legs. Nothing had ever felt so right or so comfortable.

Ivy shot Nate a quick, knowing look. She clasped her hands together. "What's the mission tonight?"

Brick, Sparks, and Reed started talking at once, describing their plans to widen the ducts from the street level to Agatha's old basement. They'd need another month to get the rest of the old still out. They had to be careful about running into the desperate chem fiends who raided the basement and slept on the stairs—hoping Agatha would return. They were too chem-struck to hear the news that buzzed on the streets and crossed the ticker screens every day: the Breakers were gone.

"Jamie will wait up for you," Ivy was saying.

"I bet he'll wait up for Sparks," Brick said, laughing. She winced when Sparks leaned over and punched her thigh.

Despite the talk of leaving, none of them had made any efforts to find a new hideout. Every room in the big house was full, but somehow they'd made space, sharing mattresses and couches and warm corners to sleep, without fearing what might come once they closed their eyes.

Maybe tonight, Nate would invite Reed to his corner of blankets in the shed—the shadowed place where the night-songs of the Withers carried on the wind.

"What about me?" Juniper asked.

"I can't have you scavenging when I need you here." Ivy tugged Juniper's sleeve until Juniper smiled back at her, half her mouth crooked, like she was still learning how to do it.

Pixel giggled at something Brick whispered in her ear, and Sparks scowled at them both, not quite managing to keep a stern look on her face.

You're going to be terribly bored.

Nate sucked in a deep breath, and the sun-warm air chased the chill from his ribs. He rested his head back against Reed and smiled at the sound of his family.

Acknowledgments

I began to write this book a few months before an unexpected trauma. During that time, one day stands out clearly: grieving beyond reason, I wept on my living room floor, face against the cold tile, for hours. Eventually, I made my way to my desk. Writing, as reading always had been, became a healing escape. Night after night, I worked on this book. And night after night, I grew stronger and more whole. And so did the story—through rewrites and revisions and reimaginings. Eight years later, I am not the same person who began to write this book. And it is not the same book I started with.

I had a lot of help.

Thank you to my first readers, many of whom received zero draft updates in their inboxes at unholy hours of the night and still bolstered me with squee and photos of cats. You were doggedly encouraging when I was looking for reasons to give up.

Thank you to my brilliant agent, Erica Bauman, who favorited a tweet, pushed me to work harder than I've ever worked in my life, and kept me company while I got two piercings in NYC. Thank you for your wisdom, your advice, your endless encouragement, and the hard work that went into finding this book a home. Thank you for reminding me to celebrate.

Thank you to my fabulous editor, Kelsy Thompson, who loves Reed and Nate like I do and championed this book beautifully. You found opportunities within the text I never would have uncovered on my own and found emotional threads to tug on that enriched the story and its relationships. Your enthusiasm was rocket fuel.

Thank you to the entire team at Flux who made this book a reality. To Mari Kesselring for believing in this book and in Nate's gentle courage; to Angela Wade for her careful copy editing; to Jake Nordby for his beautiful cover design; and to Megan Naidl and her team for their marketing magic.

Linsey Miller, you are more than a mentor. Thank you for picking me, believing in me, and sending me brownies that showed up at my front door like magic. Your wisdom, GIFs, DMs, books, and support carried me through this wild ride. You will always be the Patron Saint of Foreshadowing and Also Goats.

Thank you to my early readers and critique partners JD, Sylvie, Sarah, Adam, Kerbie, Tatiana, Julie, Anna, Max, Tracy, Mairi, Caitlin, Raffi, Adriana, Violet, and Melissa for the comments, the edits, the gut checks, and the motivation I needed to keep going when this draft was in its (long) infancy. Likewise, thank you to the Roaring Twenties and the Pitch Wars class of '15, particularly Michael Mammay, who helped me break down and rebuild a third of this book. Thank you to Ryan Douglass for the thoughtful, helpful sensitivity read. Thank you to the entire YA community, the authors and bloggers and readers and artists and bookstagrammers and creators. I have learned so much from you all, and I learn more every day.

A special thank you to Diane Ashoff, who has endured multiple years of texts, who forgave me for killing her favorite character, and who has read and reread this book nearly as many times as I have. Thank you for being a voice of reason and for unreasonably insisting that the real ending of this book consist of Alden and Pixel opening a detective agency and solving mysteries.

Self-care comes in a lot of forms, and for me it often comes in the company of strong women. To that end, thank you to Meagn Goose and Kristen Quinley for countless brunches, Avett Brothers shows, plant-shopping dates, and indulgence in my publishing-related ramblings. I love you.

Thank you to my family for supporting me emotionally (and often tactically) as I performed a balancing act between raising kids, pursuing a fulfilling career, and following my heart on a journey to publication. My grandmother introduced me to fantasy novels. My mother drove me to the bookstore every time I had my braces tightened and let me read at the dinner table—and now she's the best Grammy and friend ever. My father has always expected bravery and capability from me, even when I wasn't sure of myself. My brother and sister have always encouraged exactly the kinds of shenanigans an author needs to indulge in when deeply stressed-out by an inadvisable obsession with writing books. I love you too.

I must acknowledge my good dogs, who have been there for me this whole time, and my cats, who showed up at the eleventh hour and likely wish to take all the credit.

Thank you to my boys. My alley cats. My wishes. You are my greatest joy.

About the Author

Maria Ingrande Mora is a marketing executive and a brunch enthusiast. Her love languages are snacks, queer joy, and live music. A graduate of the University of Florida, Maria lives near a wetlands preserve with two dogs, two cats, two children, and two billion mosquitoes. She can often be found writing at her stand-up desk, surrounded by house plants. Unless the cats have already destroyed them.